Christmas
—— *in* ——
APPLE RIDGE

Three-in-One Collection
The Sound of Sleigh Bells
The Christmas Singing
NEW! *The Dawn of Christmas*

Christmas
—— *in* ——
APPLE RIDGE

CINDY
WOODSMALL

WATERBROOK
PRESS

CHRISTMAS IN APPLE RIDGE
PUBLISHED BY WATERBROOK PRESS
12265 Oracle Boulevard, Suite 200
Colorado Springs, Colorado 80921

The scripture quoted on page 85 is taken from the Holy Bible, New International Version®, NIV®. Copyright © 1973, 1978, 1984 by Biblica Inc.™ Used by permission of Zondervan. All rights reserved worldwide. www.zondervan.com. The scripture quoted on page 40 is taken from the King James Version.

The characters and events in this book are fictional, and any resemblance to actual persons or events is coincidental.

ISBN 978-0-307-73099-2
ISBN 978-0-307-73101-2 (electronic)

Cover design by Mark D. Ford; cover photos by Jim Celuch and Dale Yoder

Published in the United States by WaterBrook Multnomah, an imprint of the Crown Publishing Group, a division of Random House Inc., New York.

WATERBROOK and its deer colophon are registered trademarks of Random House Inc.

Library of Congress Cataloging-in-Publication Data
Woodsmall, Cindy.
    The sound of sleigh bells / Cindy Woodsmall. — 1st ed.
        p. cm.
    ISBN 978-0-307-44653-4 — ISBN 978-0-307-45835-3 (electronic)
    1. Amish women—Fiction. I. Title.
    PS3623.O678S68 2009
    813'.6—dc22

                                                    2009018239

Woodsmall, Cindy.
    The Christmas singing / Cindy Woodsmall. — 1st ed.
        p. cm.
    ISBN 978-0-307-44654-1 (alk. paper) — ISBN 978-0-307-45921-3 (electronic)
    1. Amish—Fiction. I. Title.
    PS3623.O678C57 2011
    813'.6—dc23

                                                    2011035015

Printed in the United States of America
2012—First Edition

10 9 8 7 6 5 4 3 2 1

Book 1

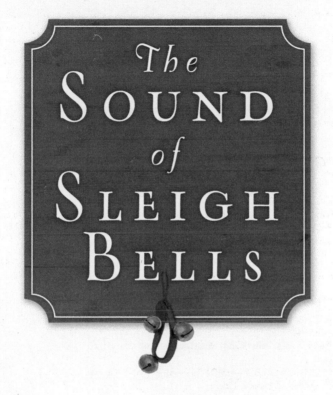

The
SOUND
of
SLEIGH
BELLS

CINDY
WOODSMALL

To one of the most splendid blessings in my life,
Miriam Flaud

One

*T*he aroma of fresh-baked bread, shepherd's pie, and steamed vegetables filled Lizzy's house, mingling with the sweet smell of baked desserts. In the hearth a bank of embers kept a small fire burning, removing the nip that clung to the early-April air.

The noise of conversations rose and fell around Lizzy's kitchen table as her brother and his large family talked easily throughout the meal. His grown and almost-grown children filled the sides of her fourteen-foot table, and his grandchildren either sat in their mothers' laps or in highchairs.

Nearly four decades ago her oldest brother had put effort into finding an Amish bride. When Stephen found the right girl, he married her. He'd handled life well, and the fruit of it fed her soul. Lizzy had focused on her business and never married. She didn't regret her choices, not for herself, but she'd crawl on her hands and knees the rest of her days to keep her niece from the same fate.

Beth was like a daughter to Lizzy. Not long after the family's dry goods store passed to Lizzy, Beth graduated from the eighth grade and started working beside her. Soon she moved in with Lizzy, and they shared the one-bedroom apartment above the shop. When Lizzy had this house built a few years ago, her niece had stayed above Hertzlers' Dry Goods.

Lizzy studied the young beauty as she answered her family's endless questions about her decisions in the middleman role between the Amish who made goods and the various Englischer stores who wanted those goods.

That was her Beth. Answer what was asked. Do what was right. Always be polite. Offer to help before it was needed. And never let anyone see the grief that hadn't yet let go of her. Beth had banned even Lizzy from looking into the heartache that held her hostage.

The one-year anniversary of Henry's death had come and gone without any sign from Beth that she might lay aside her mourning, so Lizzy had taken action. She'd prepared this huge meal and planned a social for the afternoon. Maybe all Beth needed was a loving, gentle nudge. If not, Lizzy had a backup plan—one Beth would not appreciate.

Over the din of conversations, the sounds of horses and buggies arriving and the voices of young people drifted through the kitchen window, causing Beth to look at her.

Lizzy placed her forearms on the table. "I've invited the young singles of the community for an evening of outdoor games, desserts, and a bonfire when the sun goes down."

Two of Beth's single younger sisters, Fannie and Susie, glowed at the idea. With grace and gentleness, Beth turned to her *Mamm* and asked if she would need help planting this year's garden.

It didn't seem to bother Beth that five of her sisters had married before her, and three of them were younger than she was. All but the most recently wed had children. Lizzy knew what awaited Beth if she didn't find someone—awkward and never-ending loneliness. Maybe she didn't recognize that. It wasn't until Henry came into Beth's life that she even seemed to notice that single men existed. Within a year of meeting, they were making plans to marry.

Now, in an Amish community of dresses in rich, solid hues, Beth wore black.

Through a window Lizzy saw the young men bring their rigs to a halt. The drivers as well as the passengers got out of the carriages. The girls soon huddled in groups, talking feverishly, while the guys went into the barn, pulled two wagons with plenty of hay into the field, and tied their horses to them. It was far easier to leave the animals harnessed and grazing on hay than to have to hitch a horse to its buggy in the dark. The young people knew the routine. They would remain outside playing volleyball, horseshoes, or whatever else suited them until after the sun went down. Then they'd come inside for desserts and hot chocolate or coffee before riding in wagons to the field where they'd start a bonfire.

Fannie and Susie rose and began clearing the table. Beth went to the dessert counter and picked out a pie. She set it on the table beside her *Daed,* cut a slice, and placed it on his plate. Then she slid a piece onto her Mamm's plate before passing the pie to her brother Emmanuel. She took her seat next to her mother, still chatting about the upcoming spring planting. Lizzy hoped her brother saw what she did—a daughter who continued to shun all possibility of finding new love. Beth clung to the past as if she might wake one day to find her burning desires had changed it.

Fannie began gathering glasses that still held trace amounts of lemonade. "You've got to join us this time, Bethie. It's been too long."

Flatware stopped clinking against the plates as all eyes turned to Beth.

Susie tugged on her sleeve. "Please. Everyone misses you."

Beth poked at the meal she'd barely touched as if she might scoop a forkful of the cold food and eat it. "Not this time. *Denki.*"

"See, Beth," Lizzy said. "Every person here knows you should be out socializing again. Everyone except you."

Beth's face grew taut, and she stood and removed the small stack of plates from Fannie's hands. "Go on. I'll do these."

Fannie glanced to her Daed.

He nodded. "Why don't you all finish up and go on out? Emmanuel and Ira, do you mind helping set up the volleyball nets?"

Emmanuel wiped his mouth on a cloth napkin. "We can do that."

Chairs screeched against the wood floor as most of the brood stood. Fannie and Susie bolted for the door. Two more of Beth's sisters and two sisters-in-law went to the sink, taking turns rinsing the hands and faces of their little ones before they all went outside.

Lizzy longed to see Beth in colored dresses, wearing a smile that radiated from her soul. Instead Beth pasted on smiles, fooling most of those around her into thinking her heart continued to mend. But her quieter, more stoic behavior said things no one else seemed to hear. Lizzy heard, and she'd shared her concerns with Beth's Daed, Stephen.

Beth took a stack of dishes to the sink and flicked on the water.

"You can leave that for now," Stephen said.

She turned off the water and remained with her back to them.

Beth's Mamm glanced at Lizzy as she ran her finger down a tall glass of lemonade. "Beth, honey—"

Beth turned. "I'm fine, Mamm."

Stephen got up and piled more plates together. "Of course you are. And I'll throw my favorite pie at anyone who says otherwise." He stuck his finger into his half-eaten piece of chocolate pie, placed it in his mouth, and winked at Beth.

She smiled, an expression that probably looked real to her Daed but reminded Lizzy of fine silk flowers—only beautiful to those who aren't gardeners.

"Beth, sweetheart," Stephen said, "you know how me and your Mamm feel. We love you. It's no secret that you're different from our other girls. You've always had more of a head for business than a heart to find a beau, but now…well, we just want to make sure you're doing okay. Since you don't live with us, that's a bit hard to know sometimes." He set the dirty dishes beside the already full sink before he rinsed his hands and dried them. "Officially, your period of mourning was over nearly six months ago, but you haven't joined the young people for a single event. You've not left the store for your usual buying trips. You eat half of what you should. You continue to wear black. And those are things a stranger would notice."

"I…I could plan a buying-and-selling trip. It'll take me most of the summer to get completely organized for it, but I can be ready by August. I know I should have sooner, but…"

Lizzy hoped Stephen didn't fall for the diversion tactic Beth had just thrown his way, but since Beth was listening to him without getting defensive, Lizzy wouldn't interfere.

"Good. If that's where you feel like beginning, I'm glad to hear it. I know the community will be too, because without you they can't sell near as many of their goods." He walked to the table, took a seat, and motioned for Beth.

She moved to the chair beside him.

"But other people's financial needs are not what this is about. Tell me something good and hopeful about you—something I'll know in my gut is true—and I'll end this conversation right now."

The four of them remained silent as shouts and roars of laughter echoed from outside. If anyone could touch Beth's heart and cause her to change, her Daed could. But the silence continued, and Beth's inability to think of anything hopeful to say made Lizzy sick with worry.

The grandfather clock chimed the half hour, startling Lizzy, but no one spoke. Long shadows filled the room, and she lit a kerosene lamp and set it in the middle of the table.

Whatever happened the night Henry died consumed Beth. When Lizzy arrived on the scene, her niece didn't even acknowledge her. The only words Beth spoke were the ones she whispered for days—*God, forgive me.* Lizzy had tried to talk to her about it, but Beth never broke her polite silence on the topic.

Beth's Daed cleared his throat. "I'll wait all night for an answer if I need to, Beth."

Her eyes filled with tears, but it was another five minutes before she uttered a word. "I don't trust my feelings about…certain things anymore, Daed."

"Then can you trust mine?" her Daed asked.

"Always, but I don't want to be one of the single girls looking for a husband. Not ever again. Is that such a horrible thing?"

"It's not what we'd figured on, but we can adjust."

Lizzy repositioned her glass of lemonade. During church the singles sat separately from the married couples. Lizzy's memory of growing too old for the singles and removing herself from them still stung. From that day on she'd carried the title of *alt Maedel*—old maid. She'd been older than Beth's twenty-six years, and her prospects of finding someone had faded into nothingness. If Beth thought navigating life after Henry was difficult, Lizzy dreaded the pain that lay ahead for Beth when she openly admitted to the Amish world that she didn't fit—not with the single folk and not with the married ones.

Stephen had yet to mention anything about the color of mourning Beth still wore. If she would wear something besides black, young men would gravitate to her, and she stood a chance of finding someone.

He covered Beth's hand with his and bowed his head, silently praying for her. He lifted his head. "There's somewhere you'd like to be tonight other than washing dishes or working in that stuffy office in the store. Am I right?"

"*Ya.*"

"Then go."

Beth kissed her Daed's cheek, told her Mamm and Lizzy she'd see them later, and left.

Lizzy moved to the window and watched as her niece walked past small groups of young people. She overheard both women and men asking Beth to stay. Beth shook her head, smiled, and waved before making her way across the road and into the pasture near their store.

"You said nothing that will nudge her to change how she's handling life," Lizzy said.

Stephen placed his hands on her shoulders. "Henry's death is the hardest thing this family has faced. Pressuring Beth isn't the answer. Trusting God is."

Lizzy stood in silence as Beth harnessed her mare to a carriage. She knew where Beth was going.

The cemetery.

Again. And again. And again.

"Please, dear God, move a mountain for her."

Stephen squeezed her shoulders. "Amen."

Two

*S*itting inside her small office, Beth could hear the bell above the door softly jingle each time a customer came in or went out of the store. But the stack of paperwork spread out in front of her was a clear reminder that helping to run Hertzlers' Dry Goods was only a small part of her work.

When dozens of wall clocks chimed the noon hour, Beth jolted. Her day was getting away from her. She grabbed a utility knife and opened the box beside her desk. It'd been delivered that morning and contained stacks of her catalogs from the printer. After pulling one out, she moved the kerosene lamp closer. The heat from the small flame added to late summer's soaring temperature, but she needed the extra light to view all the details of the ordering magazine. The photos were of almost every item she carried, and they looked fantastic.

Lizzy will love it.

Beth's practice in creating a periodical had paid off. A few years back she had gotten special permission from the church leaders to use a camera for the purpose of developing a sales publication. Her first few tries were very clumsy compared to this.

She organized the papers on her desk and shoved some into her satchel. With her itinerary, a catalog, and stacks of order forms in hand, she blew out the kerosene lamp and left her office. As she stepped into the dry goods store, she noticed customers in every aisle, Amish and Englischers. She'd been focused on her trip plans for months, and she finally took a moment to actually see the place. Lizzy ran the day-to-day operation of the store, and by the looks of it, she was having a particularly good season.

Beth went to the door that led to her living quarters. As she climbed the darkened stairwell, the well-worn steps moaned, and the aroma of old wood filled her senses. It made her wish for time to sit on the steps and just breathe it in. Even after she rounded the first landing of the stairway, she could hear the buzz of customers in the shop below. Some days she didn't feel Amish at all. She only felt busy and overwhelmed. It took a lot of Englischer-type work to provide middleman services for a multitude of Amish districts, but she loved it.

"Beth?" one of the Petersheim girls called from the foot of the steps.

She stopped climbing and went back down the winding staircase. "Yes, Lillian?"

"Mr. Jenkins is here. He wants to place an order for his store."

"His appointment was last week, and he missed it. Does he think it's for today?"

Lillian moved to the first step and closed the door behind her. "No. He apologized for not being here when he should've. A family illness kept him away, but he's in the area today and hoping you'll let him place an order before you leave on your buying trip. I told him you're leaving in a couple of hours, but that only made him more determined."

"Okay, I'll take his order, but I need to finish packing first. Help him look through the catalog and the display room while he waits, and take really good notes. It'll speed things along. And please tell him I have to be gone by two o'clock."

Lillian nodded and left.

Beth turned and headed up the stairway. In spite of her best efforts, which began four months ago, she still had too much to do before leaving. Half a dozen calls had to be made, and she needed to sort through her mail before the driver arrived. Right now she intended to finish packing. It wouldn't do to leave without plenty of clean clothing. It was hard enough to earn respect among the Englischers as a businesswoman when wearing Amish clothing, let alone dirty Amish attire.

When she stepped into her attic bedroom, she expected a few minutes of solitude. Instead, she found her aunt going through her closet. Lizzy's youthful face and bustling energy kept her from looking twelve years older than Beth. Her aunt carried a couple more pounds of weight than she had a decade ago, and her dark hair had a few strands of gray, but Beth thought she looked much younger than her actual age of thirty-eight.

Lizzy motioned at the closet and then faced Beth. "Have you discarded every dress you own that isn't black?"

Beth lowered her eyes and studied the pages in her hand. Black hid things—much like ever-darkening shadows in a deep forest. And as odd as it seemed, black helped her carry things too.

Secret things.

She tapped the itinerary. "If I'm careful to stick to the schedule, before my three weeks are up, I'll be able to visit every Amish and Englischer store that we do business with—furniture, quilt, dolls, crafts—you name it. I have an appointment to see each owner, buyer, or manager we're connected to in Pennsylvania and Ohio." She held out the updated catalog.

"It arrived!" Lizzy stepped away from the closet and took the publication.

"I told you it was scheduled to get here this morning."

Her aunt's dark brown eyes reflected awe as she looked at each page. "Wow, Beth, this is the best one yet."

"The community has waited a long time for me to resume traveling, and I intend for this trip to be very successful." After setting the rest of the papers on her nightstand, Beth stepped around her aunt. She grabbed several dresses from her closet and tossed them onto the bed.

Lizzy removed the hangers and folded each dress. "Beth, honey…"

Beth swallowed, her mind racing with ideas of how to avoid the impending conversation—the one her aunt had started trying to have a few days ago. "Mr. Jenkins is waiting for me downstairs, and I have phone calls to make before Gloria arrives. Can you finish packing for me?"

Her aunt's frame slumped so slightly Beth doubted if Lizzy even knew it'd happened. After emptying a drawer of her dresser, Beth shoved the stockings and underwear into the traveling bag.

"Ya." Lizzy's brown eyes met Beth's, and her aunt smiled. "I know you wish you could change the past, but you have to let it go, Bethie."

Beth had no doubt her aunt thought she knew what dark cloud hung over her. But she was wrong.

Beth grabbed the papers from the nightstand and gave Lizzy a quick hug. "Don't start trying to mollycoddle me again. I think we can all agree that at twenty-six I'm a big girl now."

"And I'm thirty-eight, but that doesn't keep me from needing to hear what other people have to say."

"I've heard you, Lizzy. You're concerned, but you're not hearing me. I'm fine." She kissed her aunt. "Now help me with my list so I can get out the door on time."

Her aunt nodded. "I'll finish packing for you."

"Denki." Beth scurried downstairs.

Hoping to stay hidden so Lizzy couldn't start another difficult conversation, Beth gratefully donated the next hour of her life to helping Mr. Jenkins place an order, then made the necessary phone calls. After sorting her business mail, she was down to her last task—finding where she'd laid her personal mail. She'd seen it sometime last week, although she wasn't sure what day.

She stepped out of her office. "Hey, Lillian?"

Lillian looked up from the cash register, where she was checking out a customer.

"Have you seen a stack of six or seven letters with a rubber band around it?"

Lizzy came out of the storage room, reached under a nearby

counter, and smiled as she waved the envelopes in the air. "I wondered when you'd miss them."

Beth moved toward her aunt. "I realized they were missing this morning. I hope to answer them while traveling."

Lizzy pressed the letters against her chest, clearly not ready to give them up. "Gloria arrived. She's loading your luggage and the box of magazines now and needed a few minutes to reorganize her van. Did you verify your reservations for tonight?"

"Yes, my dear aunt. You trained me well."

Lizzy held out the small bundle of letters. "If these were business related, you'd have kept up with them."

Beth loved her aunt like a sister and usually got along with her, but clearly they needed a break from each other. For the last six months, it had felt like they were two old maids bickering back and forth. Lizzy was sure she knew how to direct Beth's life, and Beth was sure she didn't.

Beth simply nodded as she took the letters. Some were from relatives who lived outside Apple Ridge, and some were from friends she'd met over the years during her annual or semiannual buying-selling trips.

With the rest of her paperwork inside her black canvas satchel, she looped her arm through Lizzy's and led her through the aisles, around customers, and to the door of the shop.

When they stepped onto the porch, Lizzy wrapped one arm around Beth's waist. "You'll be careful, right?"

Beth pulled her into a hug, holding her for a long spell. "You drive me nuts, but I do believe I love you more than any niece has ever loved an aunt."

Lizzy took a deep breath that spoke of tears. "Are you sure you're up to this trip?" She put a bit of space between them. "It's hard to be away from family that long, and you'll spend more time with Englischers than with Amish."

"Months of planning and you ask me this now?"

In spite of August's heat, Lizzy's hands felt cool against her cheeks. "It's your first time to go since Henry…"

Why did her aunt insist on stating the obvious? "I know that. I'm fine. I'll always be fine, if for no other reason than to keep you from taking over my life and trying to run it for me. Do we need to tattoo the words 'Beth's fine' on the back of your hand?"

"A tattoo?" The male voice behind Beth was clearly that of Omar, their bishop.

She turned to see his smiling face. His gruff-sounding question didn't hide the amusement reflected in his eyes. Lizzy's face flushed a bit as she straightened her apron. Beth swallowed, never quite sure if he was teasing or nicely sharing his opinion.

His eyes stayed on her aunt for several long seconds, giving Beth a few moments to find her voice. "Uh…well…"

The bishop laughed. "It isn't a completely bad idea if it would get *somebody* we know to stop worrying so much." His eyes and smile moved to Beth. "But I think it will take more than the ink in a tattoo to do that." He gestured toward the van. "It looks like you're about ready to leave."

His sincere smile should warm her. It used to. But now whenever she was around Omar, her guilt pressed in heaviest of all—maybe because as bishop he might see into her, or maybe because he was Henry's uncle. Sometimes she was sure he knew her secret.

The bishop leaned against the porch column. "Your Daed says you'll be gone for three weeks, give or take a few days."

Wishing she knew what to do with her hands, she folded her arms and nodded. At least today if he shook her hand, the sweltering heat provided a good excuse for her sweaty palms. "Yes. It'll be a tight schedule, but I hope to get it all done."

The bishop studied her. "I'm sure you will. You always have."

She forced a smile, sickened at how she hid behind a facial expression. "Denki."

Gloria shut the doors to the back of the van. "I meant to get ice for the drinks Beth asked me to pack. Lizzy, can I get some from your house?"

"Sure, I'll give you a hand."

Gloria grabbed the cooler out of the backseat, and the two women hurried across the road to Lizzy's place. The bishop lifted the weight of Beth's satchel off her shoulder, and she released it. He went down the steps, and she had no choice but to follow him.

Her insides trembled, but she reminded herself that no Amish knew her truth. Not even the bishop. And unless Henry returned from the grave to tell, none ever would.

Omar stopped under the shade of the walnut tree. "Those of us who knew Henry miss him, but we're doing better."

No one really knew Henry.

Hoping to keep the conversation as light and breezy as possible, she kept her response brief and hoped he took the hint. "I know. I am too."

"Lizzy tells me otherwise."

She shifted, wishing Lizzy would believe her and stop talking to Omar about it. Her throat tightened. "You know, if you keep this up, we'll need a tattoo for you as well. It'll say, 'Beth's fine!' "

The man chuckled. "Okay, you're fine." He straightened. "Just don't bring back any forbidden items this trip. We've gone that route twice already, and I'd rather not repeat it, okay?"

"Ya, I know."

That was eight years ago. Did he still see her as a teenager? At the time it'd seemed harmless to purchase enlarged photos and canvas paintings Englischers had made of the Amish. Beth had defended her decision by telling Omar she'd hired Amish to make the frames for the items, no Amish person's face could be seen in any of the settings, they hadn't posed for any of the pictures, and the items were a sought-after commodity by their Englischer customers. Omar felt that snapping photos as the Amish went about their quiet lives was an unwelcome intrusion and that her allowing such photographs to become a part of her business only encouraged Englischers to be bolder with their cameras. He said if she'd told the frame builders what she planned to do with their work, they wouldn't have participated. She hadn't agreed, but he had final say, and she ended up keeping the frames and burning the artwork. She still bought frames regularly and filled them with nature scenes an Amish woman painted for her. Omar was a bit uncomfortable with nature scenes being sold for Englischers to hang on their walls and admire—as if they might fawn over them to the point of worship—but he allowed her to carry the items in the store. The man's heart was in the right place—she believed that completely—but his ways were more conservative than a lot of bishops'. At times she wondered what life in Apple Ridge would be like if he hadn't been chosen to be the bishop.

Lizzy and Gloria came out of her aunt's house and crossed the street. With the cooler in hand, Gloria headed for the van. "You ready?"

"Ya."

Hoping she'd return home with stacks of orders for Amish goods, she looked forward to what this time could accomplish. It'd been a while since she and Gloria had been gone overnight on business, but through the years, traveling with Gloria made for relaxed and enjoyable trips. Her shoulder-length gray hair always stayed pulled back in a loose bun, and her jean skirts with knit tops never changed with the Englischer styles. She seemed as comfortable wearing the same look year in and year out as the Amish were.

Beth hugged Lizzy. "I'll call you in a few days." As she walked toward the vehicle, the bishop walked beside her.

"Oh, wait. I almost forgot." Lizzy ran into the store, and Omar and Beth stopped.

Omar smiled. "Maybe you should just take her with you."

"Uh, maybe not."

A look of amusement and understanding flickered through his eyes. Fresh longing to confide her secret rippled through her, but hoping for that kind of friend was as childish as young Englischers wanting a fairy to bring money for a useless tooth.

The silence stretched between them, and Beth wrestled with her guilt. The store's screen door banged against its frame, ending the fight.

"I made your favorite spice cake." Lizzy placed the tin carrier in Beth's hands, gave her a quick hug, and opened the van door for her.

Three

The edges of papers fluttered wildly as wind whipped through the open windows of the van. Securing the order forms on her traveling desk, Beth continued working between stops. Nearly two weeks of traveling were behind them, and despite her weariness she had more orders than she'd hoped for.

"I'm not sure where that detour was supposed to reconnect us to the highway, but we're in the backwoods now." Gloria's voice barely registered over Beth's thoughts.

She finished jotting down the information that danced in her head and then glanced up. The view of the Ohio River had disappeared, and hills with thick trees rose on each side of them. "Are we north of Steubenville?"

"That much I'm sure of."

"How far back did you begin following a detour sign?"

"Ten miles."

"How far since you saw the last detour arrow?"

"Eight miles."

Beth laughed. "I think you definitely missed something. Let's just backtrack until we pick up that detour sign."

Gloria pressed the brake and steered the vehicle completely off the road and onto the shoulder. "I'll make a U-turn after the cars behind me pass. Sorry about this."

"No apologizing, Gloria. You do a great job." Studying the road ahead, Beth suppressed a yawn. Before a bend in the road, there stood a post with eight wooden signs hanging from it, each one bearing a different store's name. "I think there's a small town ahead."

Watching the rearview mirror, Gloria frowned. "You actually *want* to venture off the planned route?"

"Well, since we already have, and I really could stand to stretch my legs, we might as well look around a bit. We have almost an hour before we need to be at All That's Amish. Besides, maybe someone can tell us a better way to get there from here. We should only be ten or fifteen miles away."

"Okay." Gloria turned on the blinker and merged back onto the road.

Once they were closer to the town, they passed a sign that read Welcome to Tracing.

As soon as they rounded the bend, Beth's heart rate increased. "Gloria," she whispered, "look at this place."

The town had character, like something out of the eighteenth century—two-story clapboard stores side by side, a narrow main road separating the two rows of buildings. There was a hitching post with a horse and buggy tied to it. Wherever Tracing was in relation to Steubenville, Amish lived nearby.

They pulled into a gravel parking lot beside one of the stores.

As they got out of the vehicle, Beth spotted a hand-painted sign that read "Pete's Antiques two blocks ahead." An arrow pointed up a side street. For the first time in more than a year, intrigue ran through her.

Gloria stepped onto the sidewalk. "There's a café. How about a hot lunch? I'm sure we can get good directions there."

Searching for Pete's store, Beth walked several feet one way and then the other. Up a side street and on a small hill stood a cedar-sided building. A feeling she thought had died with Henry stirred within her. "There." Beth pointed. "I'll be in that store when you're finished. We can't take much time, or we'll be late for the next appointment."

"I'll bring the van around to get you. Can I bring you a sandwich?"

"Sure. You know I'm not picky."

"Well, not about food or getting lost, but you're tough on what's worthy to carry in the shops. Otherwise the van would be filled with samples for the display room by now."

"Ya, but I've taken a lot of orders, and Pete may be another one willing to buy."

Gloria laughed and headed for the café. Beth opened the van's door, stuffed the order forms into her satchel, and tucked it under her arm. She hurried across the street. The hill seemed to grow longer and steeper as she went.

Out of breath, she pushed herself to keep her speed as she mounted the wooden steps. The screen door swung open, and a man came out.

"Whoa." He chuckled and pressed his back against the door, holding it open for her. "A woman on a mission."

Embarrassed she hadn't seen him in time to slow down and use her manners, she dipped her head. "Denki." She intended to be polite and keep moving, but when she glanced at his face, his golden brown eyes stopped her cold. Intrigue collided with unease, and she told herself to go into the store. Yet she simply stood. He was in his mid to late twenties, Amish, and clean-shaven, like all single Amish men.

And something about him had her mesmerized. Did she know him?

His pursed lips did not hide his smile or his amusement at her gaping.

Stop gawking and go inside, Beth!

She cleared her throat, lowered her eyes, and slipped past him. Disobeying the wisdom she'd gained about single men, she turned to see him again. His smile was gone, but his eyes lingered, taking her in as much as she took him in.

Had they met somewhere? Maybe on one of her trips through the Ohio Amish community? He seemed oddly familiar.

Moreover, he felt...

An image of Henry moved into her mind, and she came to herself.

He remained at the doorway. "Can I help you?"

"No, I...I'm just here to look around."

"There's the main room, which you're in, and a few rooms off to the sides. There's also more upstairs, including seasonal items. Pete's in the back with a customer, but he'll be out in a bit."

"Denki." Horrified at how brazen she must appear, she made a beeline to the stairs.

Once out of his sight, she found her breath and her good sense again. She'd simply remain upstairs for a bit and hope he'd been in the process of leaving when she nearly ran him over. Rattled, she closed her eyes and tried to even out her breathing. She'd felt a spark of interest for a man once before. He'd been a stranger to her too, and nothing would ever cause her to let down her guard like that again. Ready to forget and focus on her job, she began looking around the shop.

Searching through each room, she spotted nothing outstanding. Pete carried mostly antique pieces, all ordinary, but she couldn't stop walking the aisles of the rooms again and again. Old and new mattresses were propped against the walls, along with bedsprings and slats. Arrays of floor lamps with Tiffany-style stained-glass lampshades were scattered throughout, some old and some quite new. An Amish-made twin bed sat in one room with the dresser and matching hope chest in a separate room. The store carried a variety of items, but if this was how the management organized things, the sales weren't what they could be.

While all the rooms were much the same, she kept returning to one specific room. What continued to draw her back to this area? There had to be something. Threading her way through the packed aisles, she looked behind the bulky furniture. Under a draped quilt between a bed and a hope chest, she spotted the edge of a striking piece of wood, maybe part of a buffet.

She eased the quilt up. Surprised at her find, she sank to her knees.

A carving. More intricate in detail than anything she'd ever seen.

Unlike ordinary artwork, it was made from a log and sat on the ground like a small upturned stump. It stood about a foot high and was a foot in diameter. On it the artisan had created an entire scene of

Amish children playing in the snow on a hillside. The artist hadn't used paint, but she could easily see the carefully fashioned snow. A man stood off to the side, leaning against an intricately carved tree. She ran her fingers over the work, the details of which she couldn't believe or even have imagined possible.

"You like it?" A man's voice echoed through the room, but she didn't look up and was barely able to make herself respond.

"It's amazing."

"The Old Man himself made that. He's been carving since he was five. I think he might just have the hang of it."

"I'd say so, yes. Why are you hiding it up here?"

"It's a Christmas scene. Nobody buys winter stuff in August."

"I think people would purchase this any time of the year."

"You gonna buy it?"

Beth looked up to see a man in his sixties standing in the doorway. "Do you have more than this one piece?"

"Not right now. He probably has more in his shop. Most of what he makes is smaller. He's really good at making canes and walking sticks. We sell a lot of those."

"And this 'old man' is a friend of yours?"

"Yep. Probably the best one I've ever had."

"Does he live around here?"

"Not close, not far. And I can't see how that should make a difference on whether you want to buy it."

She pulled a business card out of her satchel and rose. "I'm Elizabeth Hertzler. Call me Beth. I'd be interested in talking with him."

He scratched his head. "You own a store in Pennsylvania?"

"Yes, but I also supply Amish and Englischer stores with Amish products—from indoor and outdoor furniture to swing sets to picture frames." She passed him a catalog. "If you need it, I have a skilled Amish person who can make it."

"I doubt he'd agree to sell like that. He handpicks his pieces of wood and takes months to create them. He went down a gorge last winter to get this one. He and his brother used a rope, a draft horse, and a lot of determination to drag it out."

"And then you hide it under a blanket."

The man laughed. "I guess so. He hasn't ever complained. Still, I'm not sure how it got shifted to this spot. Since most of his work depicts winter scenes, they catch more attention in cold weather. I put them near the entry of the store at Christmastime, and they sell pretty well then."

"I'm not interested in selling this one, but I'm sure I can find stores that would carry his work and display it in good view year round."

"I thought you owned a store."

"I'm not sure my bishop would allow us to carry this type of work."

"His bishop lets him make it."

"Your friend is Amish?"

"Yeah."

"Maybe that'll help my position if I try to convince my bishop. Regardless, I want this one. How much?"

"Seeing how you like it so much, how about a hundred dollars?"

"A hundred dollars?"

"Too much?"

"Too little. Why would you undervalue his work?"

"It's art by a man no one knows. I get the best price I can." The man smiled. "But if you think you can do better, I'll give you his address."

"I'll take the info with me. Unless it's on my way, I won't have time to talk with him this trip. Does he have a phone?"

"Nope. His bishop is strict about phones. Why'd you ask where he lived if you're not planning to go see him?"

"It's just a natural question. If I'm hoping to do business with someone, it helps to have an idea of their vicinity. Just like before I leave, I'll get your store's phone number and street address."

"I'll jot down all the info you need." He grabbed the carving off the floor. "And I'll get my nephew to carry this out for you. I'm guessing you have a driver."

"She'll be here in a few minutes. In the meantime would you care to look through our catalog?"

"Don't waste any time, do ya?" Pete took the catalog and flipped through the pages.

No, she didn't like wasting time, but her heart and body had demanded she spend over a year grieving. Still, it seemed Lizzy had been right; she should have gotten out among people long before now. Who knows what detours she might have missed while on her road of isolation?

Four

*A*fter removing the entire window unit, Jonah straddled the sill. With one leg inside the schoolhouse and one outside it, he looked up from his work. A row of horseless carriages filled the front lawn of the school. Inside the pasture fence stood a dozen grazing horses, patiently waiting for their owners. Half a dozen workers on the roof hammered away. Under the massive oaks, women filled the picnic tables with breads, cheeses, and vegetables fresh from the gardens, and children played games, enjoying the last weeks of summer break.

The community worked on this old one-room schoolhouse each year before classes began. Sometimes Jonah wondered if it would be easier to build a new one, but anytime the subject came up, the Amish school board voted against it.

The nonstop hammering overhead drowned out the voices of the women and children. With a small claw bar in hand, Jonah removed each nail from the window and checked the soundness of the framing. His mind still lingered on the woman he'd seen at Pete's a few days ago.

Those deep blue eyes against black lashes had almost knocked him over, even with his cane to steady him. Her soft yet deep and confident voice still filled his head. It was embarrassing to give her a second thought, let alone *every* thought. She wore black, the color of a brokenhearted widow. She could have been grieving for a family member, but something about her said the pain she carried was different from that of losing a relative. He guessed she'd lost a large piece of herself. But the rest of her stirred him—as if she needed someone, a friend or relative, to help her sand away the pain etched into her life and dig deeper to carve a new scene.

He'd never considered sanding off someone's old life, not even when they'd lost a loved one. It seemed to him the past carvings should be preserved and a new spot found for fresh carvings. Or perhaps new carvings should include the old carvings. But to remove what had been and start fresh? He was mistaken about that. Had to be.

"Jonah." His grandmother spoke over the loud banging. She held out a cup of water.

He hadn't realized she'd come into the schoolroom. He wiped his brow. "Denki, *Mammi.*" He took a long drink. "Even sitting in a window doesn't provide enough of a breeze in this heat."

"Only bad shepherds use entrances other than the door. Didn't your mother teach you anything?"

"Yes, she did. That you're a troublemaker." He tried to keep a straight face but wasn't able to hold back his laughter.

"How many window units will you need to replace?"

"All of them. The sashes are too rotten to make it through another school year, but so far all the casings have been completely sound."

"So you've been at this for a couple of days?"

"Ya."

"You met the new teacher and had help, then?"

He wasn't fooled. She knew he had plenty of help from the men in the community. Her curiosity centered on the new teacher.

"Yes to both, Mammi. Every man in our community has come to help as time allowed. Right now they're either helping the women with other things or on the roof repairing bad shingles."

"Your presence here has caused a fresh buzz among the young women." Mammi motioned out the window. "You need to find one who suits you before you're too old."

He finished drinking the water she'd brought him and passed her the cup. "If only one of them was half as amazing as you…"

Mammi moved closer. "Stop teasing your poor grandmother and find someone. I've seen you carve life out of deadwood. Can't you try to do that in a relationship?"

"A worthwhile relationship is like finding the right wood. When it's the right one, I'll know it."

"And by the time your idealism blends with realism, you may have missed your chance."

Using the claw bar, he pulled another nail out of the casing. "So, Mammi, why is there a bee in your prayer *Kapp* about this all of a sudden?"

"The new schoolteacher, Martha." She tapped him on the arm, and with her eyes she directed him to look outside near the picnic tables.

Martha passed half a sandwich to one of the children.

"While I was talking with her about the upcoming school year, she kept looking your way." His grandmother held out her hand for the claw bar. He didn't give it to her.

"Maybe she's never seen a carpenter with a bum leg and two missing fingers."

"Nonsense. She was drawn to you. I saw it in her eyes. Now go speak to her. At least give her a chance."

He removed another nail. "She's too young."

"Too young? She's probably twenty-two, and you're only twenty-eight."

"No." He placed several bent nails in his grandmother's open hand. "She's about seventeen, and I'm about forty, figuratively speaking."

"Well, sometimes older men connect well with younger women." She wrapped her frail hand around his wrist and pulled.

Giving in to her, he climbed out of the windowsill. If it'd make her feel better for him to speak to the woman, he could do that much. And while pleasing his grandmother, he'd get a bite to eat from the picnic tables.

She brushed bits of wood off his shirt. "At least talk with her a little before deciding she's not right for you. Tell her you have a question about how she wants something done in her classroom or you want to show her how the window works."

"I have no questions, and if she needs to be shown how a window works, we need a new teacher."

"Jonah Kinsinger, you're as stubborn as your grandfather."

"You know this, and yet you insist on shoving me into some poor woman's life."

She passed him his cane, turned him around, and nudged him forward. "Go. And find the beauty in whatever wood is in front of you."

As innocent as her words were meant to be, they carried a mild dishonor to him. Aside from a few pangs of loneliness once in a while, he was content being single. As the thought rumbled through him, the memory of the stranger in black stood before him again. She'd captivated some part of him, but it wasn't her beauty that had piqued his interest. Like an ancient oak, she carried hidden years, and as an artist, he was drawn to it.

He walked outside, and cold liquid splattered over his head and down his neck. "Whoa."

"Jonah." Mark's surprised voice came from above him.

Jonah looked up to see his friend on the roof with an upturned cup in his hand. A couple of men moved to Mark's side to see what had happened.

Jonah licked his lips. "Mmm. Lemonade."

Laughing, the men returned to work.

Martha brought him a dishtowel, looking more concerned than amused.

"Thanks." Jonah wiped his face. "You're standing in dangerous territory unless you prefer to wear your lemonade rather than drink it."

She motioned toward the picnic table. "Maybe you'd prefer trying on some food instead."

Her sense of humor amused him, which would make the chore his grandmother had laid before him easier.

Why was it so hard for married men and women to accept that he liked being single? Only one thought came to his mind—*they* needed to find a better hobby.

Five

*C*hildren's laughter echoed across the snow-covered hills. Beth shivered, watching from a distance. Her feet ached from the cold, and her fingers were numb. A little Amish boy got off his sled and faced her. A younger girl took him by the hand. They stood motionless, watching Beth.

She opened her mouth to speak, but no words came out. A man moved among the trees, calling to them. When they didn't come, he walked closer and called again. The children motioned for Beth to join them, but her legs worked no better than her mouth. As the man drew closer, he smiled and gestured toward the field where half a dozen other children played. Too cold to move, Beth began to recognize the children. She knew their names, didn't she? But from where?

The frigid air around her seemed too much to bear, but the man and the children appeared as warm as if they sat in front of a wood stove. As if reading her thoughts, the man tilted his head and opened his jacket, revealing heaps of embers glowing in his chest. The children followed suit, showing a bonfire inside their tiny upper bodies.

With stiff fingers Beth unhooked her black cape and looked at her heart. Anxiety spread through her body. Where they had embers and fire, she had frozen tundra.

The man touched his chest and then held out an ember for her. Embarrassed at her frozen soul, she wanted to hold out her hand, but she couldn't. Even if she could lift her arm, he stood too far away. She tried to walk toward him but couldn't move. He held out his hand again.

Her jaws fought against the wires that kept them clasped. "I…I can't."

He looked straight through her, and she understood that he couldn't come any closer. She had to be the one who moved. Snow began to fall, and the sky grew dark, but she couldn't budge an inch. The sadness in the children's eyes ran deeper than Beth could comprehend. They clasped hands and ran back to the others. The man stood, watching her. A tear slid down his face, and one by one the children faded into nothingness.

His eyes pleaded with her to find the strength to move forward and take the ember, but even as she willed herself to take a step, he too faded away.

Beth sat up in bed, trying to steady her pounding heart.

That dream—and a dozen others like it over the last two weeks—was as bad as the ones that had plagued her since Henry died. Nightmares of him clinging to her as rain poured from the skies and formed rivers that swept him away while she remained on solid ground, her clothing soaked as the temperatures dropped and freezing winds began to blow. The images were too close to reality, and she couldn't find freedom whether Henry was alive or dead, whether she was awake or asleep. Thoughts of Henry always brought confusion, but lately the dreams weren't about him.

Sliding into her housecoat, she moved to the wooden steps that led to the store below. The darkness inside the stairwell felt familiar and welcoming, and she sat down. As the reassurance of the place wrapped around her, she began to shake free of the dream.

She folded her arms and propped them on her knees, making a place to rest her head. While trying not to think about anything, sleep drifted over her again. A few moments later the sound of a horse neighing made her jerk awake. It took only a moment to realize the animal had been in her dream.

It was useless trying to sleep, whether on the stairway or in bed. Rising to her feet, she grabbed the handrail, feeling a bit dizzy. She might as well get a little work done.

Making her way down the stairs, through the store, and into her office, she couldn't help wondering when dreams started mixing with a sense of reality. After entering her office, she slid her hands across the paper-strewn desk top, searching for a set of matches. Her fingertips brushed against the carving she'd bought nearly two weeks ago. It took up a good bit of her desk, but she'd made room for it.

Forget the matches. Her mind was too cloudy to think anyway. She walked around her desk and sat in the chair. Gliding her fingertips over the intricate detail of the carving, she wished her aunt would at least go meet with the artist.

She'd lost the argument with the bishop that it wasn't an idol. He quoted the second commandment—"thou shalt not make unto thee any graven image." Because the wood had human images carved into it, Omar felt it was too close to what the Old Testament warned against. Since faceless dolls were commonplace among her people for the same reasoning, Beth had little grounds for appeal. His decision was final, but she held on to the hope that she could convince Englischer stores to carry the carvings. That wasn't working either since Lizzy refused to let her try. She said it would disrespect their bishop. Beth's Daed and uncles sided with Lizzy, so for now Beth could do nothing.

If her aunt was willing to talk with the artist and his bishop, she might feel differently. Then Beth could at least sell the man's work to Englischer stores. But Lizzy seemed more interested in pleasing Bishop Omar than in making a difference in an artist's life.

Beth sighed, wishing they could see the carvings like she did, as no more of an idol than an Amish-sewn wall hanging. Maybe then the strange dreams where the children and the man from the carving beckoned her to enter their snowy Amish world would disappear.

<hr />

Standing on the porch of the store, Lizzy slid her key into the lock and turned it. Inside, she noticed the door to the steps that led to Beth's bedroom stood open. Lizzy moved to the foot of the stairwell. "Beth?"

She heard no movement upstairs. Turning slowly in a circle, she expected her niece's head to pop up from between the aisles. Usually by this time each morning, the two of them had shared a breakfast, talked business, and begun preparing to open the place at nine. "Beth?"

Her heart ran wild, and panic over her niece sliced through her. The young woman hadn't been herself in so long. She handled herself well, but Lizzy knew something ate at her. Suddenly Lizzy admitted to herself that images of Beth taking her own life slipped into her mind at times.

"Beth!"

When she didn't respond, Lizzy rushed to the office and pushed against the slightly open door. Her niece was slouched over the desk, her fingers resting on that carving she'd bought.

Her legs shaking, Lizzy touched her niece's face. "Honey?"

Beth moaned and drew a sleepy breath. Unable to remain standing, Lizzy eased into a chair next to the desk.

Blinking, Beth frowned and lifted her head. "Good morning." Her voice sounded hoarse and groggy.

"Did you sleep here all night?"

Beth took a deep breath and rubbed her eyes. "No." Stretching her neck, she yawned. "I didn't sleep much anywhere. What time is it?"

"A little after eight."

Beth looked straight at her and narrowed her eyes. "Is something wrong?"

Unable to share her fears, Lizzy shook her head. Beth came around to the front of the desk. She didn't look depressed, so why did Lizzy's imagination get the best of her? As soon as the question ran through her mind, she knew the answer. Her niece had changed, and Lizzy feared she might be getting worse rather than better.

Beth brushed her fingertips across Lizzy's forehead. "Then why is there fear in your eyes?"

"I…I couldn't find you."

Beth sat on the edge of the desk. "So you thought mountain lions came out of the hills, into the shop, and ate me?"

"My imagination got away with me, and I…" Lizzy swallowed hard, willing herself to say what was on her heart. "You worry me. It's like you're not the same person anymore."

Beth patted her hand. "I know."

Does she really know how much she's changed? And how completely scared and out of control Lizzy felt concerning her?

"Why are you sleeping in the office?"

Her niece's delicate hands caressed the carving. "It calls to me. Dreams that make little sense fade in and out as if they're trying to tell me something." She raised one eyebrow and mockingly pointed a finger at Lizzy. "And you know how I feel about people talking to me when I'm trying to sleep."

In spite of her humor about it, her niece's blue eyes held absolute rawness, as if Henry had died yesterday rather than sixteen months ago. And Beth had asked only one thing of Lizzy since Henry had died. Just one.

"I've decided to go see this artist of yours."

Beth's eyes grew large, and a beautiful smile seemed to remove some of her paleness. "Really?"

"Ya."

A spark of delight stole through the usual sadness in Beth's eyes, and Lizzy's heart expanded with hope. Maybe her niece would find her way back to herself yet.

"I'll call Gloria and set up a trip," Lizzy said. "I'm not making any promises, though. I'm checking it out. That's it."

"Then you'll meet the carver. And I bet you'll be glad you did."

"Maybe."

Or maybe Beth was hunting for fulfillment outside the Old Ways and Lizzy was helping her.

A s Gloria drove down the back roads to Jonah Kinsinger's place, Lizzy prayed. Her niece had no idea how awkward this upcoming cold call might be. She didn't want to build up the artist's hopes, yet she needed to talk to him about Beth's possibly selling his work to Englischer tourist shops.

Beth was so much better with this kind of stuff, but if she were here, she might pursue the work without regard to the bishop's opinion.

Gloria slowed the vehicle and turned into a gravel driveway. "According to our directions and the mailboxes, this should be it."

From the looks of it, two homes, maybe three, used this triple-wide driveway and turnaround. According to the mailboxes, two of the places belonged to men named Jonah Kinsinger.

"Which one?" Gloria asked.

"Let's stop at this first one. It looks like the original homestead, and the Jonah Kinsinger we're looking for is an older man, according to Beth."

Gloria put the van in Park. Lizzy opened the door, viewing the house. "I shouldn't be more than twenty minutes if this is the right house."

Gloria held up a paperback. "I'll pull under a shade tree and enjoy my time."

Lizzy went up the porch steps, knocked, and waited. Through the screen she could see a woman, about seventy years old, hurrying to the door. Beyond her, two young girls tried to catch sunshine in their aprons. She remembered playing that game as a little girl. It had never held much interest for Beth. If it couldn't be scrubbed or organized, her niece never cared about it, even as a toddler.

The woman smiled as she opened the door. "Can I help you?"

"Hi, I'm Elizabeth Hertzler. I own an Amish dry goods store in Pennsylvania, and I'm looking for Jonah Kinsinger, the carver."

"He and his brother are working at the lumberyard." She glanced at the clock. "But they should be in for lunch within the hour if you care to wait."

"He lives here, then?"

"No, but he'll eat lunch here today."

"I came to talk about his carvings and hopefully see more of his work."

"You're welcome to go into his shop and look around." She stepped onto the porch and pointed several hundred feet away. "The door is at the far end."

"Thank you."

Lizzy went to the van and spoke through the open window. "He's supposed to be back within the hour. If I leave, I could miss him."

"Then wait," Gloria said.

"Do you want to come with me?"

"I'd rather read, if you don't mind."

"Okay."

With sweat running down her back, Lizzy walked to the shop. September had arrived, but summer's heat remained strong. She knocked on the solid door and then tried the knob. The door opened, and she walked in. The room glowed with a golden hue. Unfinished, honey-colored paneling covered the four walls, and sunlight poured in through several windows. A blue tarp hung in a doorway, blocking her view into the next room. What appeared to be a handmade box sat on the table.

Thinking she heard children whispering, Lizzy moved to the window and raised the shade. She expected to see the girls who had been inside the main house, but she saw no one. The voices grew clearer, as if they'd come into the shop with her.

She walked to the hanging blue tarp and pulled it to the side. The adjoining room looked like an old outbuilding—dirt floors, stalls where calves might have once been kept, and shelves filled with pieces of wood, paint cans, and cardboard boxes.

"Hello?"

Silence filled the room. Moving deeper into the building, she thought she heard a child giggle.

"Hello?"

Not minding a quick game of hide-and-seek, she continued walking until she stood at the back of the long, narrow building. There were no windows, but a few rays of sunlight streamed through the cracks in the wooden walls. Through the hazy gray air, she noticed an old, damaged sleigh.

"Is someone in here?"

Seeing no one, she worked her way around the sleigh, moving slowly so she didn't stumble. On the far side of the sleigh, she knelt, looking under it for signs of the children.

A cane and two black boots came into sight. The footwear shifted.

Embarrassed and addled, she stood.

A silhouette of a man passed her an unlit candle. He struck a match, revealing that, in spite of the cane, he was in his twenties. After lighting the wick he shook the match and tossed it into the dirt. "Can I help you with something?" His voice sounded warm, but he looked uncertain of her.

"I...I'm Elizabeth Hertzler." She brushed dirt off her apron. "I...I thought I heard children in here playing. I shouldn't have searched for them this far back into your shop, but it's just...I got caught up in following the sounds of their whispers..." She wiped her hands down the sides of her dress. "From the look on your face, I may never redeem myself."

He gestured for her to follow him. "You'll feel better once I show you something."

They wound through a darker section of the building, making her glad he'd brought a candle. A moment later he popped open a rickety door. The wind blew the candle out, and the sounds she'd heard earlier echoed through the bright sunshine.

She blinked, waiting for her eyes to adjust to the light. The young man placed his hand under her forearm. "Watch your step."

Glancing around as her eyes focused, she expected the fierce white view to retreat and reveal children. Instead, she saw a terrace of some sort. From the eaves of a gazebo hung at least two dozen hand-carved wind chimes.

She stepped closer, awed at the find. "They sound like children whispering and laughing. How is that possible?"

"They're designed to make inviting tones. I've found that what a person hears tends to vary." His brown eyes held no pity concerning her intelligence and no judgment against her behavior. Whoever he was, she was glad he'd been the one to discover her on her knees beside a broken sleigh and not someone more critical.

"Does this Jonah Kinsinger make these too?"

"I do."

Startled, she tried not to look too surprised. "You do?"

He nodded.

"And the large carving from Pete's—you did that too?"

"Yes. Pete said that you liked it and that he gave you my address."

Her conscience pricked when he mistook her for Beth, but something told her not to correct him. The business cards and catalogs they passed out had the store's name and phone number and the name Elizabeth Hertzler. It wasn't the Amish way to promote an individual, so if people knew how to reach "Elizabeth" at the store, that was all they needed to know.

"But I don't understand. I thought you would be old."

"Probably because Pete's called me Old Man since I was five, when he began teaching me how to whittle."

Her nerves were still on edge, and she tried to gather herself. "Your bishop allows you to sell your carvings, including the wind chimes?"

He motioned to a set of chairs under the shade of the gazebo. "You look a bit pale. Would you like to sit for a spell?"

"Very much. Denki."

"Can I get you a glass of water? My place is just beyond those trees."

"No. I'm fine." As she said the word *fine* to describe herself, visions of her beautiful, lonely niece entered her mind. She took a seat. "So your bishop doesn't feel that you're creating graven images?"

"Well, he might have had a few reservations. You'd need to talk to him about that. Over the years I've wondered if his decision was based on favoritism."

As the eeriness from earlier began to fade, she saw a depth in his eyes that drew her like his work had drawn her niece. "Favoritism?"

"When I was injured at fifteen, I couldn't get around well enough to do an apprenticeship, so he allowed me to do something I'd had the ability for since I was young." Jonah shrugged, and a mischievous smile seemed to come out of hiding. "The bishop's my Daed."

"Oh." She studied the intricate details of the wind chimes. "I'm afraid that's not much help to me. I've thought about carrying your work in my store, but your father allowing you isn't likely to convince my bishop."

"I'm not really interested in creating pieces on demand to sell, anyway."

"Not interested? Your work is gorgeous, and it touched the very soul of…" A thought swept through her, scattering pieces of a plan across her like sawdust caught in the wind.

Beth.

Jonah's work stirred her. Called to her. Wakened her. But whatever else it did, it refused to be ignored. Beth could ignore her own needs, her own heart, and forge ahead with life, but she hadn't tuned out the artistry of Jonah Kinsinger.

As she looked at this young man, knowing Beth felt a connection, the plan unrolled inside her.

She stared into his eyes, hoping what she was about to do was the right thing. "Giving it up for a girl, are you?"

Jonah laughed. "I never said I was giving it up." Using his thumb, he pushed his straw hat back a little. The gesture revealed two missing fingers, probably more damage sustained in the accident. "It's not about money."

"I'm sure it's not." Lizzy moved to the edge of the gazebo. The place was an odd mixture—a rather dilapidated building attached to a much newer shop. A beautiful garden area with an expensive gazebo behind the old place. To her left, a recently built cabin almost hidden behind a grove of ancient trees.

And a handsome young man with a skill that calls to my niece.

"Your carving seems to carry life in it."

Somber as a church meeting, he gazed at her. "The piece you wish to sell in your store was a royal pain from the get-go. The tree lay at the bottom of a gorge, and I tried to ignore it for months. But by last winter I couldn't disregard it any longer, so I wrestled it out with my brother's help and took it to my shop." He leaned back against the railing. "And the truth is, I was glad to be done with it. Just as soon not have that experience again. So if you're looking for a carver, I'm probably not your man."

"Is that why there's a layer of dust on your tools and the wood on your workbench?"

"The only thing I made out of that tree was the carving you bought. I cut other pieces with the intention of carving scenes in each, but…it's just not in me. Still, I guess I'd be pleased to sell or put on consignment whatever is in my shop that I've made from other trees."

"This isn't what I expected when I came here. You're supposed to be excited and trying to convince me to get permission to carry these items."

He smiled and cradled one chime in the palm of his hand. "When I was injured, if my Daed hadn't given me freedom to carve, I'm not sure I could have stood it. I was stuck in a wheelchair for nearly a year. Lost all sense of who I'd thought I was. Surgeries and physical therapy were constant and painful. And as selfish as it sounds now, being without two fingers felt totally humiliating, like God had singled me out to mock. My Daed gave me a way to transfer my emotions into a lump of wood." He released the chime, making lovely tones float through the air.

Wishing Beth could hear this man's understanding of life after loss, Lizzy's plan became clearer to her. "I've never married, so I don't have children, but I do have someone I love as if she were my own. And right now she's in that bad place you spoke of. But it's been nearly a year and a half since her loss, and I don't know why it continues to be so heavy."

"Maybe for you it wouldn't be, but for her it is."

A dinner bell clanged loudly.

He motioned to the steps of the gazebo. "Come eat with us, Elizabeth. It's our family's once-a-month workweek gathering. You can meet all sorts of Kinsingers and three other Jonahs. Afterward, I'll load you up with the carvings I do have."

When he spoke her full name instead of her nickname, Lizzy knew the door to her hope stood wide open. As they walked around the side of the building, she saw Gloria waiting for her. "I can't stay." She stared into the crystal blue sky. Part of her felt as if she was about to follow God's leading, and part of her felt like a manipulative woman.

Hoping her plan didn't push Beth further from her, she dared to give her idea a try. "Jonah, meeting you today has been the best treat I've had in a long time. I'm hoping you'd be willing to keep in touch with me by mail."

The way he looked at her, she knew he thought she was a bit off-center. Still, he nodded. "I suppose that'd be fine."

"Good." She stopped at the foot of the steps that led to what had to be his grandmother's place. "Did Pete give you my card, or do I need to get one for you?"

"He passed it to me."

"Even though it says Elizabeth Hertzler, you should write to Beth. I mean…" She tried to word it so she wasn't actually lying. "Beth, Lizzy, Elizabeth—they're all forms of my name."

He raised both eyebrows, looking more skeptical. "Beth." He lightly spoke the name without relaying either question or statement in his tone. "Pete did say you went by Beth."

Her throat seemed to close, but she pressed on anyway, hoping Pete hadn't said anything about Beth's age. "And you shouldn't feel obligated to write that it was good to meet me. I mean, we can say that right now and skip the fluff in the letters. Don't you think?"

Lines deepened as he looked at her much like he had when he'd found her by the broken sleigh.

"Jonah." A tall, gray-haired man stepped onto the porch, and relief that she could stop stammering flooded her. "Will your guests be staying for lunch? We have plenty."

Jonah looked at her. "You're welcome to stay."

"I really need to load up some of your carvings so I can be on my way. Hopefully, I'll be able to talk Omar into letting us carry them in our dry goods store."

Jonah nodded and turned to the man on the porch. "*Daadi,* this is Elizabeth Hertzler from Apple Ridge, Pennsylvania. She owns a store there. Elizabeth…Beth, this is my grandfather, Jonah Kinsinger."

The man descended the steps. "Apple Ridge?" He said the name thoughtfully, and she realized he was trying to think of any Amish he might know from the area. She wanted to avoid that conversation before her letter-writing plan was ruined.

"It's so good to meet you. Your grandson has quite a skill for carving."

The older Jonah smiled broadly. "Can't say he's ever set his hand to anything he didn't become remarkable at."

Jonah smiled. "The favoritism thing I mentioned earlier? Uh, it runs in the family."

Lizzy chuckled. "I really do need to get going."

"Ya, Pete said you kept to a schedule." He turned to his grandfather. "Tell Mammi I'll be in shortly. I need to help Beth load up a few carvings."

Her plan was destined to fail. She knew that. But if it worked for a week or two, that might be enough time for Jonah and his wisdom about loss and dealing with it to reach inside Beth and make a difference. That was what Lizzy wanted most of all—and she was willing to suffer Beth's anger over it.

And if Beth were ever free from all that held her heart captive, she might actually see the man who was standing here.

Seven

The clip-clop of a horse and buggy on the road filtered through the open window of Beth's office. She'd moved the wringer washer outside that morning so she could both wash and hang the laundry before being stuck in this tiny room all day. Now she sat at her desk, shuffling endless amounts of paperwork. Buying-and-selling trips were much more fun than this, but since so many Amish could no longer make a living farming, many depended on her to sell their handcrafted products. She loved being a source of help for her people, but it required her to be behind this desk a lot.

Sitting back, she studied the details of the carving. For the tenth time that hour, she ran her fingers over the tracery. How could anyone make such intricate cuts into a block of wood?

When someone knocked on the door, she came to herself and returned her focus to her work. *"Kumm rei."*

Her aunt opened the door, holding up a stack of letters.

"Denki." Beth pointed to a tray on her desk.

Lizzy placed them in the holder. "Jonah Kinsinger wrote a letter." She took the top envelope off the stack and held it out.

"For me?" Beth stared at the envelope. The bishop hadn't budged on giving them permission. "He's probably wondering what Omar has decided. I don't know what to say to him. I can't do anything to help him sell his work. I did my best to convince Omar. You even gave it some effort."

"I didn't just give it *some* effort." Lizzy pointed the letter at her, wagging it as if it were her index finger. "I went to see Jonah as you asked. I brought some of his work back. And then I showed the pieces to Omar and talked to him about it, just the same as you did."

"I tried to convince him. You straddled the fence."

"He's our head, the top church leader over several districts. Is it our place to try to change his mind and heart? Shouldn't that be left in God's hands? We presented our request, and he doesn't feel he can allow such a thing, at least not yet."

"Omar closed the door, so that's the end of it? It's over?"

"He's a good man, Beth. Always has been. I believe if we're all praying, God will side with whoever's right, and Omar is the kind of person who will hear Him. Now rest in that, and answer Jonah."

"I don't have anything but bad news to share with Jonah."

"That's ridiculous. At what point did you become so negative? You have friendship to offer along with your love of his work. I'd say that's not *all* bad news." Lizzy held the envelope out to her again.

Looking at her aunt's face, she couldn't help but smile. "Denki."

"Gern Gschehne."

Laughing at the sassy way Lizzy chose to tell her she was welcome, Beth watched as she closed the door.

Maybe her aunt was right. She did have friendship to offer. And maybe the old man just needed a friend.

She slid her finger under the seal and realized it was already open. Either it had never been closed properly, or her aunt had already read it. Although either of them opened whatever store mail came in, it wasn't like Lizzy to open Beth's personal mail. But, after all, Jonah Kinsinger was a business relationship.

After pulling out the letter and unfolding it, Beth wondered if he'd written the letter himself or if he'd dictated it to someone, because the printing seemed awfully neat for an elderly man. Then again, each word seemed as perfectly chiseled as his woodwork.

Beth,

It's been encouraging to know that my carving caught your eye and that you hope to sell it in your shop. It's been quite a while since anyone showed this kind of interest.

Maybe that's why I'm not really interested in carving for money, or maybe it's because that one work about wore me out.

I spotted the log a little less than two years ago while riding bareback through the woods. That's a great pastime of mine. I like getting out by myself. Sometimes I pack a tent and a bit of food and meander hundreds of acres for days before returning home.

THE MOMENT I SAW THAT FALLEN TREE, EVEN AT A DISTANCE, IT BURNED INTO MY MEMORY. BUT IT LAY IN A GORGE WITH NO EASY WAY TO GET IT OUT. THE LAND BELONGED TO A WIDOW WOMAN PETE KNOWS. SHE DOESN'T ALLOW CUTTING OF TIMBER ON HER LAND, EVEN WHEN IT'S A FALLEN TREE.

WELL, YOU CAN IMAGINE THAT I'D HAVE MUCH RATHER LEFT IT THERE THAN TRY TO PULL AN ENTIRE TREE UP THE SIDE OF AN OVERGROWN CRAG. SO I LEFT IT.

BUT AS THE MONTHS PASSED, I COULDN'T GET THE RICHNESS OF THAT PARTICULAR TREE OR THE POSSIBLE CARVINGS THAT COULD BE MADE FROM IT OUT OF MY MIND.

I VISITED THE WIDOW AND ASKED IF I COULD CUT THE LOG INTO SECTIONS, BUT HER HUSBAND NEVER WANTED ANYTHING CUT FROM THAT FOREST AREA, AND SHE HAD TO HONOR THAT.

FOR A SECOND TIME, I DECIDED TO LEAVE IT, BUT AS YOU CAN TELL FROM THE PIECE YOU FOUND AT PETE'S, DEAD WOOD HAS A STRONGER WILL THAN I DO.

SO WITH MY CANE IN HAND AND A ROPE OVER MY SHOULDER, I DESCENDED INTO THE CANYON IN HOPES OF BEING MIGHTIER IN MUSCLE THAN I AM IN WILL.

IT WASN'T TO BE — NOT THAT I ACTUALLY THOUGHT IT WOULD. BUT SOME THINGS IN LIFE ARE JUST THAT WAY. THEY DEMAND MORE OF YOU THAN YOU HAVE, AND EVEN

KNOWING YOU'LL LOSE, YOU HAVE TO ATTEMPT IT ANYWAY.
OR IS THAT JUST ME?

WELL, I NEED TO GO BEFORE SUPPER CATCHES
FIRE...AGAIN.

JONAH

Beth paused, soaking up his humor and openness. The carving hadn't caught her eye, as he'd said. It had snagged her heart. She should tell him that. He hadn't told her how he got that log out of the forest. How odd to bargain with an old woman who would let him have the felled tree but wouldn't let him cut it while it remained on her property. And Beth had to set him straight about the piece she'd brought home—she didn't intend to sell it.

She read his letter again.

In spite of the freezing winds that continually circulated inside her, warmth spread across her chest. Her hidden guilt had isolated her in ways she'd never imagined possible, but the letter eased her loneliness a little, and she felt something besides regret and her sense of duty to those around her. Was it possible every hidden part of who she'd once been—her heart, passion, and ability to connect—had not been fully destroyed after all?

Then a memory returned, and she saw herself on bended knee in the pouring rain.

For her part in Henry's death, she should be too numb to want a new friendship. Her relationship with Henry had shown her things she hadn't known about herself. She wasn't good at loyalty, yet she knew without it friendship was simply heartache waiting to happen. If she were capable of true devotion, Henry would be alive. When he died, she'd vowed to remain single forever.

But Jonah was old, and he would never need to test her endurance for commitment. She trusted that as an Amish man, he had plenty of family and friends who possessed strengths he could rely on. Surely even she could give what little he was asking for.

She opened a drawer and pulled out her best stationery.

Eight

*O*n his back porch Jonah sipped a cup of coffee, watching as the first rays of daylight illuminated the canopy of leaves on the massive oaks. The deep greens of summer foliage carried the first hints of changing to gold, yellow, and red. Each year the sight begged him to watch endlessly. The colors of summer slowly faded, allowing the true color of the leaf to shine through. And then one day he'd wake to find their color had grown no brighter, and soon the radiant golds, reds, and yellows would tinge with brown, bringing with it a different type of beauty.

The front door slammed, and someone stomped through his home like a horse, vibrating the house. Jonah angled his head toward his left shoulder. "Coffee's on the stove."

"I have a wife who makes mine, and she does a right good job." His brother walked through the french doors and onto the porch with a cup of Jonah's steaming coffee. "But I thought I'd make sure yours weren't poison."

"Ya, just in case I rise early every day to brew toxins for myself."

Amos sipped the drink and made a face. "Broken buggy wheels, I think it might be dangerous to drink this stuff."

He took a seat in the rocker, and it moaned under the weight of him. At six foot seven inches, his brother was one of the largest men Jonah had ever known. He had the hands of a giant and a heart to match.

"I don't get it." Amos motioned toward the field. "It's a bunch of trees with leaves."

Jonah laughed. "And yet you join me and insult my coffee nearly every morning." Mist rose from the bottom land along the foot of the mountain until the top edge of the fog disappeared into the surrounding air as if it'd never existed. The early morning sun would soon burn off the remaining vapor. In spite of the birds chanting loudly, the morning seemed to hold on to a peaceful quietness.

Amos finished drinking most of his coffee before tossing the drips off the porch. "My gut can't take too much of that stuff." He placed his hands on the arms of the rocker and pushed himself up. "We got work to do. Oh, wait." He dug into his pants pocket. "Speaking of my wife, she checked your mailbox yesterday."

Jonah took the letter.

"It's from a girl." Amos's teasing grin didn't hide the seriousness in his eyes.

Jonah read the return address. "No, it's from Elizabeth Hertzler. You saw her in my driveway about a month ago."

"She was a nice-looking woman but a little older than I'd hoped you'd find."

His brother had shared his opinion for two reasons—to voice his concern and to let Jonah know he supported whatever he wanted. "Go gather eggs for Mammi and Daadi while I read my letter."

Amos left, whistling as he tromped through the house. Jonah ripped open the top of the envelope and pulled out the parchment-looking paper.

Dear Jonah,

It was so nice to receive your letter. It's been a very long time since I enjoyed anything as much as I enjoyed reading about your life. I can understand the desire to camp out in the forest—although I'll admit the idea of sleeping in a tent sounds dreadful, and a forest has too many creepy-crawlies for my taste.

Jonah laughed out loud, and the wind running through the leaves made it seem like the oaks joined him. Her truthfulness by itself kept him chuckling. He hoped Beth could see the majesty of the great outdoors. He refocused on the letter.

It's past midnight as I sit alone in my office. The minutes began ticking by hours ago, and I continue to wrestle with what to share and what to keep to myself. Your carving sits on my desk, and the smoky flame from my grandmother's kerosene lamp casts its glow over your artwork, causing the faces to change as the fire burns unsteadily. And the longer I sit here, the more I want to write what I'm thinking.

I'm glad you shared with me about finding the piece of wood and how you fought with whether to drag it out of the gorge or not. Your carving did not catch my eye as much as it snagged my heart. That log would not let you forget it, and your carving does much the same to me.

I must dare to be boldly open, so I can tell you that your work causes me to dream. Parts of the dreams are disturbing, but I'd forgotten what it feels like to be stirred by life.

I find it a little troubling to think a lifeless object can awaken one's soul, but your work has done that for me. I feel hope once again, and although I don't deserve it, I'm grateful for it. From the moment I saw this piece at Pete's, I never intended to sell it.

You didn't tell me how you got the tree out of the canyon and back to your shop.

Looking forward to hearing from you again,
Beth

"Jonah!" Amos hollered. "Daylight's burning."

Jonah folded the letter and shoved it and the envelope into his pocket. Beth's voice on paper didn't sound like she had in person. When here, she seemed nervous and scattered, but on paper she sounded serene and centered. After he finished at the sawmill for the day, he'd write to her again.

He set his mug on the railing, grabbed his cane, and walked around the side of the house. Her letter was an odd mix of thoughts and emotions. Even in its brevity it conveyed business, open admiration of his work, and hesitation to share the rawness she felt inside. Maybe that was why she sounded so different in her letter than at the farm.

He'd heard quite a few things inside that note, although he couldn't identify them. As the day wore on and he cut fresh lumber and sold from the seasoned stacks, his thoughts returned to the letter. He read it two more times, trying to hear what she wasn't saying. That was what his *Urgrossdaddi* Jonah used to say to him before he died—"If you hear what's not being said, you'll hear the heart of the matter."

She'd written, "The minutes began ticking by hours ago, and I continue to wrestle with what to share and what to keep to myself." Clearly, she'd struggled to break through the reluctance he saw when she'd visited. Maybe her inability to talk openly was why she'd asked for them to exchange letters. In person she'd been just another woman, but her letter seemed to have touched something inside him.

While Jonah drove the horse and buggy home after work, Amos cracked jokes. "Two snowmen were standing in a field. One says to the other, 'Funny, I smell carrots too.'"

Cutting and loading lumber for twelve hours straight was exhausting, but Amos rarely seemed tired at the end of a day.

"You don't always have to entertain me."

In a rare moment of seriousness, Amos became still. "But when you laugh, I feel like I've done something to help ease…" He let the sentence drop and stared out the side of the rig.

His brother's past recklessness couldn't be changed. The incident that dogged Amos would never be wiped out, not even through endless moments of amusement. They both knew that. Jonah had forgiven him long before Amos could look him in the eye again, but Amos seemed to find his redemption through the friendship and loyalty he offered Jonah.

"Nothing needs to be eased, Amos."

Amos scratched his face through his whiskers. "When I grow up, I want to be like you."

Jonah chuckled. "You're the oldest of the family, and even your young uns have given up on you growing up."

"Well, aren't you just full of good spirit today? So, you gonna write some of that charm and wit in a letter to that woman?"

Jonah glanced from the road to his brother.

Amos shrugged. "I saw you reading it again at work. Clearly she has your attention."

His brother's statement forced Jonah to think about his emotions. He couldn't deny he had some odd feelings about her. From the moment Pete had placed Beth's business card in his hand and told him of her strong interest in his work, he'd felt a stirring within. And the pleasure of writing to her, sharing parts of himself that he'd not shared with anyone else, and the enjoyment of reading her letter again and again hinted at a possible connection with her. But in person she seemed more like a nervous chicken than an intriguing woman. He supposed that might fade with time.

"Jonah?"

"Maybe."

He pulled into the driveway and let Amos off in front of his home before driving the rig under the overhang. After putting the horse in the pasture, he tossed feed into its trough.

Gazing across the field, he watched a flock of chimney swifts circle above the horizon. At sunset each day they made an odd twittering sound as more birds arrived. Each year, in late summer and early fall, this ritual took place until the flock nearly blackened the sky. Then one evening they wouldn't show up, and he'd know they'd taken off for South America. They were usually gone by now, but perhaps the delay of fall weather had them remaining longer than usual.

Life's mysteries could no more be understood than the thoughts of a flock of birds. The living was ruled by instincts and God-designed principles His creatures had little say over.

And desire.

He reached into his pocket, feeling the letter. Beth wasn't the only one who didn't want to reveal too much. Walking into his shop and to the old part of the building, he thought back to when he'd lost two fingers, full use of one leg, and more than a year of his life.

His siblings suffered nightmares and guilt, but thankfully, that was all. For the lives he'd managed to save, his loss was worth it. Would he have saved any of them had he known the price beforehand? He ran his palm across the dusty leather seat of the sleigh. When he was a teen, his parents had allowed him to decide the sleigh's fate. He'd refused to get rid of it or to use it, so here it sat, making a grown woman think children were hiding under it. It hid things, all right, but childish games and laughter were not part of its secret.

It would take weeks of work to restore the sleigh, and he'd need the help of a blacksmith. He turned to leave. Some things just weren't worth it.

And some were.

He walked the narrow dirt aisle between the stalls of the old building to his workshop bench. He'd created only one other thing since carving the piece Beth bought. A gift box. He'd made it from the same log, but he'd not yet carved it.

He'd tried. Even now, as his hands moved over the rough-hewn treasure, he couldn't visualize what he should carve. That had been the problem for months. Ready to know the thoughts of the man who'd taught him his craft, he tucked the box under his arm.

He went to the barn and hitched a horse to the carriage. As the horse ambled down the road, Jonah leaned back and enjoyed the scenery. Rolling hills, thick foliage on the trees, lush pastures. While looking out over the fields, he let his memory roll back to the day he'd dragged that fallen tree out of the canyon, and he realized just how much he looked forward to writing to Beth.

Pete's driveway came into sight, and he slowed his rig. A few Englischer customers were leaving the store as he got out of the carriage. He noticed they hadn't bought anything. With the box in one hand and his cane in the other, he climbed the steps and went inside.

"Hey, Old Man," Pete called. "How about shutting that door and turning the sign around? I'm done for the day."

It wouldn't matter if Jonah showed up at midnight; Pete never failed to sound pleased to see him. Jonah did as asked and then walked to the counter where Pete stood. In a few minutes they'd walk to the back of the store, go through a doorway, and enter Pete's tiny apartment.

Pete counted money from the cash-register drawer. "What brings you in this time of day?"

Jonah set the box on the countertop.

Pete laid a stack of tens on top of the drawer and moved in front of him. "This looks like it's from that tree you and Amos dragged from the gorge."

"Ya. I've only finished one project from that so far, the one Elizabeth Hertzler bought. Then I made this gift box, but I can't for the life of me carve anything into it."

Pete lifted the box, holding it in his hands as only a fellow carver would—with reverence and respect. He removed the lid and set it on the countertop before running his fingers across the inside of the box. "Maybe you've forgotten the lesson you taught me years ago."

"I taught you?" Jonah knew the old bachelor was getting on in years, but he'd never seen him confused about anything.

"Yep." Pete inspected the box again. "You put a lot of time into this."

"And I'd like to finish it."

Pete reached under the counter and pulled out a soft leather utility case. He unrolled it, revealing a set of carving tools. "You sat right there." He pointed to an old wicker chair near the front counter. "You hadn't been carving more than a year when you made a freestanding bird on a branch—not no relief carving, mind you." Pete walked to his showcase and unlocked it. He brought the bird to Jonah.

"I'd forgotten about making this."

"I won't never forget. Look at the intricate detail. That's not the work of an ordinary kid, or even a man, for that matter. I asked how you made it so lifelike, and you said, 'All I did was remove everything that wasn't the bird.'" Staring at the carving, Pete smiled, making his wrinkles deepen. "You were as wise as an old man from the start."

Jonah passed him the bird. "Whenever I pick up this box to carve on it, I don't see anything."

Pete returned the bird to the showcase and locked it. "Blank?"

Jonah nodded.

"That doesn't sound like you." He pulled a twelve-millimeter gouge with a number four sweep to it from the leather pouch. "You need to remove whatever is hiding the image from you." He placed the tool in Jonah's palm. "The thing is, you may have to cut into more than the box to figure that out."

Jonah squeezed the tool and thought of Beth's letter. The oddness of that piece of wood lying in the forest, tugging at him, and then Beth's strong draw to it felt…eerie. Yet calmness accompanied the feeling, and memories of dragging the felled tree out of the gorge absorbed him.

The cold winter day. The thick layer of snow on the ground. The exhaustion he felt as he wrestled with the elements. Amos calling to him through the frigid air. The strength of the draft horse. The sense of Christmas wonder that filled him once they'd managed to drag the tree out of the canyon.

As he stood in Pete's store, the blank wood in his hands revealed its hidden image. It would take only a few days to create the scene.

But it might be months before he could make himself carve it.

Nine

*B*eth's arms ached from the day's work as she left her parents' home and walked toward the barn. Church would be held there tomorrow, and her Mamm required every bit of help she could get. It wouldn't do for the windows not to be scrubbed clean inside and out, as well as every nook in the house and the old hardwood floors polished to a shine. After doing a thorough cleaning, they'd set up the benches in the living room, so everything was ready for the long Sunday ahead.

The sun was setting, and the early October air had a nip to it as she hitched her horse to the buggy. After climbing into the rig, she slapped the reins and began the four-mile trip back to her place.

With twenty-eight families in their district, nearly three hundred people—including babies, children, and teens—would attend. Thankfully services came to each household in the district only once a year. Unfortunately, Beth had to work just as hard when the rotation landed at her sisters' and brothers' places, as well as Aunt Lizzy's. As a single woman, her life was not her own. It belonged to all her married siblings, her parents, and her aunt.

A wedding for a sibling had been celebrated every other year for the past decade. Refusing the threatening tears, she tried to choke back the sorrow.

Everyone who loved her gently prodded her to lay grief aside. They wanted her to find happiness again, but she never would. Resigned contentment perhaps, eventually. But she couldn't say that to her family.

She longed to tell someone how she really felt and why. But her thoughts and emotions were simply too heavy and too embarrassing to pass on, so she coped the best she could.

She pulled the rig into the barn next to the shop and stepped out of the buggy with wobbly legs. She led the horse to its stall for the night, dumped feed into a trough, and hurried across the yard and into the dry goods store. Too drained to do any office work, she lit a kerosene lamp and slowly climbed the steps.

She had called this stairway "the dark, wooden tunnel" when she was a child. The steps creaked, and the paneled walls seemed to absorb light rather than reflect it.

After setting the lantern on the stand beside her bed, she lit the gas pole lamp, knowing it would give off more than just light. It'd radiate enough heat to knock the chill out of the air. She took hold of the pole and rolled the lamp with her as she entered her tiny kitchen. A package and letter sat on the kitchen table.

Jonah.

Dismal thoughts vanished, like darkness giving way to the power of a match. Snatching up the letter, she noticed it too had been opened. She was ready for her aunt to stop reading her mail from

Jonah. Because of the shared name and business, she and Lizzy often opened each other's mail. Sometimes it didn't matter who opened it; sometimes they didn't know which of them it belonged to. Neither of them ever minded, but Lizzy knew Jonah was writing to Beth, so she had no reason to continue opening the letters.

She unfolded the letter, and the tart flavor of loneliness lost some of its edge.

DEAR BETH,

I THINK I FOUND YOUR LETTER AS FASCINATING AS YOU FOUND MINE. ███████████████████████ ███████████████████████ AND I HOPE WE'RE ABLE TO CONTINUE WRITING FOR A VERY LONG TIME. IF I WERE BOLD AND DARING, I'D CONFESS THAT YOUR LETTER SEEMS TO INDICATE THAT YOU CARRY A HEAVY BURDEN. BUT SINCE I'M NOT BOLD, I WON'T BRING THAT UP.

His joke did little to ease her discomfort. How had he picked up on that? And what had he written that he decided to black out with a marker?

WHAT I DO WANT TO TELL YOU IS THAT WHATEVER YOU SHARE GOES NO FURTHER THAN ME. EVER.

I HAD AN ACCIDENT SOME YEARS AGO AND SPENT A LOT OF TIME IN A HOSPITAL. WHEN I GOT OUT, I BEGAN

VOLUNTEERING AT OUR AMISH SCHOOL FOR THE DISABLED, AND I CONTINUE TO THIS DAY TO SPEND TIME WITH THOSE WHO DEAL WITH PHYSICAL DISABILITIES.

His life and perspective seemed fascinating. Surely the old man had much in the way of wisdom he could share. Each time she read one line from him, she longed to know five more things.

She opened the cookie jar to see if Lizzy had brought her any goodies today. She had. Homemade chocolate chip. When not cleaning Mamm's house today, Beth had helped prepare both lunch and supper, but she'd not taken the time to eat much of anything.

Munching on a cookie, she began reading again.

BECAUSE OF MY TIME IN THE HOSPITAL AND REHAB, I LEARNED THAT JUST AS THERE ARE UNTOLD TYPES OF INJURIES THAT ALL REQUIRE DIFFERENT TREATMENTS, EACH PERSON ALSO SUSTAINS INJURIES TO THEIR HIDDEN MAN — THEIR MIND, WILL, AND EMOTIONS. THEY'RE JUST AS REAL AS ANY PHYSICAL INJURY, BUT SO OFTEN PEOPLE SEEK HELP FOR THE BODILY DAMAGE AND IGNORE THE NEEDS OF THE HEART AND SOUL.

THE SPIRIT CAN NO MORE BE IGNORED WHEN IT SUSTAINS INJURY THAN A MUTILATED LEG OR SEVERED FINGERS.

Not only was the man interesting, but he made her feel safe, like it might not be wrong to feel and think and experience life differently than most. Was it possible she could share her oddities with him? Her deepest secrets?

Although her outward life matched most every other Amish woman's existence—from the cape dress and white prayer Kapp to her one-room schoolhouse education—Beth had discovered in the hardest way of all that she didn't possess the tender yet powerful sense of loyalty and love that women should.

Was it possible she could tell Jonah Kinsinger the truth about herself and he'd actually hear her? understand her reality? help her find forgiveness for her sin?

It seemed possible he could be that sort of a man. Older people often had that capability. Sometimes the most accepting, loving people in a person's life were their grandparents, only she was unwilling to unload herself on hers. They'd take it too hard. But a stranger? Surely he could hear her without bearing the weight of her shame. And maybe he'd have wisdom to pass on to her, and she could slip free of the dark blanket that lay heavy over her heart.

Excitement, or maybe hope, seemed to surround her.

YOU ASKED HOW I GOT THAT PIECE OF WOOD OUT OF THE CANYON. IT'S QUITE A TALE, AND ONE THAT TELLS TOO MUCH ABOUT MY STUBBORNNESS AND NOT ENOUGH ABOUT MY GOOD SENSE.

I COME FROM A LONG LINE OF STORYTELLERS (YOU KNOW THE KIND: AFTER SUPPER EACH NIGHT THEY SHARE STORIES FROM AS FAR BACK AS THE LIVES OF THE AMISH WHO ESCAPED

THE PERSECUTION IN THE OLD COUNTRY), SO I WILL WRITE THE EXPERIENCE OUT AS MY OWN URGROSSDADDI MIGHT HAVE DONE IF HE WERE AROUND TO WRITE TO YOU.

SINCE I FAILED TO SHARE ENOUGH OF THE STORY LAST TIME TO SATISFY YOUR CURIOSITY, I WILL OVERDO IT THIS TIME.

STRADDLING MY HORSE, I PEERED DOWN THE SIDE OF THE STEEP RAVINE. I'D BEEN TO THAT SAME SPOT SEVERAL TIMES BEFORE, AND EACH TIME I'D ASSURED MYSELF I COULD FIND A SIMILAR TREASURE IN AN EASIER PLACE TO REACH. BUT THERE I WAS AGAIN.

EVEN THROUGH THE FALLEN SNOW, I SPIED THE TREE.

DISMOUNTING, I FELT EVERY PART OF THE FOREST SUR-ROUND ME—THE EARLY RAYS OF SUNLIGHT WORKING THEIR WAY THROUGH THE CLOUDS OVERHEAD, THE MUSKY SMELL OF ROTTING LEAVES HIDDEN UNDER THE LAYER OF THICK SNOW, AND THE MOVEMENT OF CREATURES I COULDN'T SEE. (MOST OF THE CREEPY-CRAWLIES YOU DON'T LIKE WERE IN HIBERNATION.)

AFTER I REMOVED MY CANE FROM ITS HOLSTER, I TETHERED THE HORSE TO A NEARBY SHRUB AND WALKED TO THE EDGE OF THE DROP-OFF.

BUT HERE I STOOD AGAIN, BRACING MYSELF FOR THE BATTLE OF GETTING MY FIND UP THE SIDE OF THIS CRAG.

HOURS SLIPPED BY LIKE MINUTES, AND I WISHED I'D BROUGHT A STURDIER HORSE, ONE I COULD USE TO HELP

PULL THE CARGO OUT. BUT I HADN'T, AND I COULDN'T RE-
LEASE THE LOAD I'D PULLED HALFWAY UP THE SIDE OF THAT
STEEP HILL. MY BODY MOVED AS SLOWLY AS A BOX TURTLE
AS I INCHED THE WEIGHT OF MY LOAD UP THE SLIPPERY
HILL. I CONTINUED TO MAKE SLOW BUT STEADY PROGRESS
AS NIGHT CLOSED IN AROUND ME.

THE CRISP SMELL OF A SNOWSTORM RODE ON THE AIR.
BARE TREE LIMBS RUBBED TOGETHER AS THE WIND PICKED
UP, AND THE RHYTHM OF THE NIGHT SEEMED TO CHANT.

"GIVE UP."

"GIVE UP."

AS THE SYMPHONY PLAYED, OLD MEMORIES ROSE TO
HAUNT ME. THE THING I HATED MOST IN LIFE STOOD BE-
FORE ME, CLOAKED IN DARKNESS BUT AS REAL AND POWER-
FUL AS THE LIFE THAT PUMPED THROUGH ME. IT WASN'T
THIS SINGLE FIGHT THAT CAUSED THE WORDS OF THE SONG
TO HOUND ME. I KNEW THAT. HOW MANY TIMES HAD LIFE
SMACKED ME IN THE FACE LIKE I'D RUN INTO THE SIDE OF
A BARN? BUT GOD AND I WERE IN AGREEMENT—EVERY
VICTORY WAS WORTH FIGHTING FOR.

THE BAD—AND MOST OF THOSE I WORK WITH IN
REHAB HAVE HAD PLENTY OF IT—CAN ONLY FIGHT FOR A
WHILE. PAIN SUBSIDES. INJURIES HEAL. THEN THE DARKNESS
GIVES WAY, LIKE A BULLY FACING SOMEONE TOUGHER. BUT
RIGHT THEN, IN SPITE OF MY PEP TALK TO MYSELF, THE
CHANTING INSIDE MY MIND HAD ME RATTLED.

"GIVE UP."

"GIVE UP."

I KNEW THAT MY FEELINGS WERE LYING TO ME AND THAT I WASN'T ALONE. I SHUT MY EYES, WILLING THE NIGHT'S CLAMOR TO BE A SOUND IN MY EAR AND NOT AN ECHO OF THE PAST IN MY SOUL. SOMEWHERE ABOVE ME I HEARD MOVEMENT IN THE FOREST.

"JONAH!" MY BROTHER YELLED, SOUNDING HOARSE, AND I KNEW AMOS HAD BEEN SEARCHING FOR ME FOR QUITE A WHILE.

RELIEF BROUGHT NEW ENERGY, AND I ANGLED MY HEAD HEAVENWARD. "DOWN HERE."

UNWILLING TO CHANCE LOSING MY GRIP, I KEPT MY HEELS DUG INTO THE TERRAIN. A FEW MOMENTS LATER AMOS YELLED MY NAME AGAIN. WE CALLED BACK AND FORTH UNTIL MY BROTHER'S VOICE CAME FROM THE RIDGE DIRECTLY OVERHEAD.

"DU ALLRECHT?"

"YA. I'M GREAT, BUT I COULD USE A HAND." I TRIED TO SEE MY BROTHER AGAINST THE DARK OF NIGHT, BUT I COULDN'T. "DID YOU BRING THE MULE?"

"THE DRAFT HORSE."

"EVEN BETTER. IT WON'T BE STUBBORN."

"YA, I'LL ATTACH THIS END OF THE ROPE TO HIM, AND HE'LL PULL YOU UP. YOU'LL HAVE TO KEEP YOUR FEET AGAINST THE FACE OF THE CRAG AS MUCH AS POSSIBLE."

Amos tossed one end of a rope over the side of the ravine, but it dangled too far away for me to reach it.

"Uh...I'm not stuck down here. I'm getting what I came for."

The screech of a barn owl came from nearby, and another one responded, but my brother remained quiet for a long minute.

"Fine," Amos finally grumbled. "We won't leave without your precious stump. That's why you came out here alone, wasn't it? You need a better hobby." Amos pulled the rope up and tossed it again, and this time it landed within inches of me. He began mumbling, but his volume assured me he meant every word to be heard. "The best-looking one of the lot, you are. I've been taking your side against the concerns and complaints of the womenfolk for years. And this is how you spend your days? You need a woman!"

"I need what's on the other end of this rope." Although I didn't know why, my gut said it was special. I studied the dangling rope before me and the one in my hand, taut from the stress of the load it held. "Hey, Amos, did you happen to bring two draft horses?"

He hadn't, but we got that tree up the side of

THE STEEP HILL, AND SOON THE HORSE WAS DRAGGING IT OVER SNOWY FIELDS. AND IF LIFE ENDS BEFORE I MAIL THIS LETTER OR LASTS ANOTHER THIRTY YEARS, I'LL ALWAYS BE GRATEFUL THAT PIECE HAS BEEN A BRIDGE FROM YOUR WORK TO MINE.

YOUR FRIEND,
JONAH

Beth's heart thumped like mad, begging for more as she imagined every step of his story. What a beautiful way to share his experience, though the adventure sounded awfully dangerous for a man his age.

She pressed the letter to her chest. He didn't just carve life out of stumps of wood; he carved it into her soul.

Drawing a deep, relaxing breath, she caught a fresh glimpse of the box on the kitchen table. She'd been so interested in reading his letter and so fixed in his words, she'd forgotten about the accompanying gift. Lifting it, she noticed two things: Lizzy hadn't opened it, and Jonah had written a note that read: "From the same tree as the carving you bought." Beth removed the brown paper wrapping and opened the cardboard box.

Inside lay a hand-carved gift box. The image he'd carved thrilled her. She clutched it against herself and hurried down the steps, then ran across the road and let herself in at Lizzy's. The bishop sat across the table from her aunt with a cup of coffee in his hand. Papers were spread on the table between them.

It took only a brief glance to remember her aunt was planning her annual communitywide dinner, dessert, and hayride. Each year she invited all the Amish singles from communities far and wide to come. Those who lived a good distance away would stay for at least one night, often two. For all Lizzy's years of living single, she seemed to have matchmaking in her blood, and many a couple had found each other through these events.

Too excited to ask how the plans were coming, Beth thrust the box toward Lizzy. "Look." She cleared her throat, trying to regain some sense of calm. "Look at what Jonah carved. Did you tell him?"

A look passed between her aunt and the bishop, but Beth didn't care if he minded that Jonah had sent her a carved gift.

Lizzy's eyes brimmed with tears even before she looked at the item. "Tell him what?"

"Is something wrong?" Beth glanced at the bishop.

"The excitement in your eyes and voice." Lizzy rose and cupped Beth's cheeks between her hands. "That's all."

Realizing anew how her sorrow and guilt grieved Lizzy too, Beth hugged her. She'd tried to spare her aunt as much as she could with her silence, but it must not have been enough.

As Beth stepped back, Lizzy wiped the tears from her face. "Let's see what has you glowing." Her aunt peered inside the cardboard box and touched the carved sleigh and its two riders. "No, Beth, I didn't tell him."

Beth brushed her finger along the side of the sleigh. "He even carved sleigh bells just like the etched bronze ones I love so much."

"What didn't your aunt tell him?" Omar asked.

Beth took the box with her as she moved to a kitchen chair. "I know you remember when my family could barely keep food on the table."

"I remember. Blessings galore but hardly any money."

"Well, whenever Daed asked what I wanted for Christmas, I always wanted a sleigh ride. But we didn't own a sleigh, and he must not have known anyone who did, because year after year Christmas came and went without me getting a sleigh ride."

"But he tried other things." Lizzy suppressed a smile.

Recalling half a dozen inventive ideas her father had come up with instead, Beth broke into laughter, and Lizzy joined her. How long had it been since she remembered something fun…and guilt free?

"Ya, he did. One year he fastened a saucer sled behind a horse and put me in his lap." Beth rubbed her head, mocking pain. "If you know anything about saucers, you know we were bound to fly into something at full speed. And we did, but between our heavy clothing and the thick snow, neither of us was seriously hurt."

Lizzy took a mug from the cupboard and filled it with coffee before setting it in front of Beth. "If I remember right, one year he attached a tarp to the back of a wagon, but the rope broke and slung you and your Daed into the road."

"We must have skidded on our backsides twenty feet before stopping." Beth lifted the wooden treasure out of its cardboard box and noticed Jonah had carved scenes all the way around it. When she lifted the lid, she discovered a note.

Dear Beth,

May these scenes fill your mind with serene
thoughts so that good dreams follow.
     Psalm 4:8 — I will lie down and sleep in peace,
for you alone, O Lord, make me dwell in safety.

     Jonah

The note made her feel warm and safe, but holding on to any
good feelings had been impossible this past year. She'd made her peace
with God concerning Henry. That didn't weigh on her. She trusted
Him and His judgment. Unfortunately, she didn't trust her emotions
or judgment.

Without sharing what Jonah had written, Beth tucked the note
back into the gift box. "I should go."

"Don't you want to stay and drink some coffee with us?"

Beth shook her head. "I want to write Jonah. I'll have the buggy
hitched at seven thirty in the morning so we can help Mamm get the
beds made and the breakfast dishes washed before anyone arrives for
church. I'll see you then."

The air around Lizzy vibrated with hope and fear. When Beth learned
the truth about Jonah—which she was bound to do—would she hold

a grudge against her like she'd held on to her grief? The question bothered her, but the risk would be worth the price if it helped Beth more
than it hurt her.

Lizzy had confessed her deception to Omar, and in spite of his
disapproval, he'd not insisted she tell Beth or Jonah. Instead, he'd asked
her to pray and to be very careful to hear God.

Omar stirred his coffee, making a clinking sound against the mug.
"When will it dawn on her that I'm not visiting this often because of
my duties as a bishop?"

Lizzy felt her cheeks turn pink. It seemed too adolescent to be in
love for the first time in her long life. "I'm hoping the two of you can
work some things out first."

Omar slid his hand toward hers, making her heart pound, but
then he stopped and returned it to his lap. His sense of propriety ran
deep. He'd not even touched her hand when they were alone, and he
couldn't touch her when around others—not yet, maybe not ever. His
position as bishop required him to be above reproach, even more than
regular folk.

A lopsided smile etched his ruggedly handsome face. "It's not
enough that I've spent two years earning your approval. Now I need
Beth's too?" There was humor in his voice, but she also heard concern.

"She's the closest thing I'll ever have to a child of my own."

"And she'll always be deeply special to you. She's a part of you and
you of her, but we don't know that you'll never have a baby, Lizzy. You're
thirty-eight. We've seen women give birth well into their midforties."

"Ya, women who have been having babies half their lives. Their bodies are primed, like a pump that leads to a spring-fed well. And mine is a desert."

A tender, adorable smile radiated from him. "Will you mind too much if we can't have a child of our own?"

Lizzy drew a deep breath, basking in the warmth of the newly burning fire within her. "I never expected to find love. I'll be content forever."

"And after I buried Ruth and spent years raising my children, I never considered I might find love again."

Lizzy's heart turned a flip. Did he practice saying the right thing? "I need you and Beth to…to bond. I don't want to lose a child in order to gain a husband."

"You know that I wish Jonah's work didn't feel like a graven image to me. It's not so much the gift box or wind chimes as those statuelike items he makes. Perhaps I should go see his bishop. Maybe I'd come to see those carvings differently."

"But the bishop is Jonah's own Daed. You could spill my secret without meaning to."

A troubled look removed every hint of a smile, and he went to the coatrack. He took his hat and jacket. "How long will you carry out this secret plan of yours?"

"You saw her tonight. She's on the brink of embracing life again, but she needs more time. I just hope the truth doesn't disclose itself too soon. I had to mark through one of the lines he'd written in his last letter to her. He'd written, 'Your voice on paper sounds so much different than it did in person.'"

"Smart man to figure that out so quickly. And he's in the hands of an amateur romantic." Omar winked at her and put his black hat on. "I'd say this pretense won't last much longer." He moved closer, concern evident in his eyes. "And I pray when it ends, that you are not the one who loses. But whatever happens, I understand what you did and why." He dipped his head once, his eyes glancing to her lips, before returning to her eyes. So many words and feelings ran between them that they were not yet free to express. "Good night, Lizzy."

Ten

*F*eeling hungry, Jonah set his v-tool on the worktable in his living room. His shop was functional, but it was also drafty and physically uncomfortable after a long day at the lumbermill. Rather than sitting on a stool at his workbench, he'd brought the wood into his home.

His desire to carve again had been reawakened by Beth's keen interest in his skill. Once he had the tools in his hands, his passion for the craft seeped back in. After completing her gift box, he'd immediately moved on to another project.

He carried a kerosene lamp to the kitchen, where he lit the eyes to his gas stove, then placed the camp-stove toaster over one and a cast-iron skillet on the other one. He grabbed a loaf of bread and put a slice of bread in two of the four toaster slots before getting a carton of eggs out of the refrigerator.

When someone knocked, he hollered for her to come in. The menfolk walked straight in, so his visitor had to be female—his mother, grandmother, a sister, or a sister-in-law. He cracked an egg into a bowl and glanced up to see his grandmother.

"Hello, Mammi. What brings you out at dinnertime on a drizzly evening like this?"

"You received a letter."

He wiped his hands on a kitchen towel. "Already?"

"Actually it came yesterday, and I planned to pass it to you when you came by, but you never did." She looked around his house. "You're carving again."

"Ya, appears so." He shifted. "The letter?"

"Oh, ya." She pulled her arms free of her black shawl and passed him the envelope.

Just as he expected—as he'd hoped—it was from Beth.

"Jonah." His grandmother's sharp tone made him look up. She hurried to the stove and jammed a fork into a piece of smoking toast. She flung it into the sink and stabbed the other one.

He turned off the stove eye. "Only one side is burnt. The other side is still edible."

She huffed at him and turned on the water. "Not anymore." They laughed, and then she gave him that grandmotherly look of hers. "Why don't you come over to the house? I have plenty of leftovers I can reheat for you. We had beef stew. That'll be better for you and warm your insides."

He wasn't as hungry as he was interested in reading Beth's letter. "I think I'll stay here. If I change my mind, you'll know."

She raised her eyebrows but said nothing else. "All right, then. Good night."

As she left, Jonah opened the letter and removed it from the envelope.

Dear Jonah,

What a great storyteller you are. Since I don't have your gift for words, I can't really share what your letter meant to me. When I opened the package, I couldn't believe my eyes. You see, sleighs have always been a dream and fond memory of mine. I'm so excited to have another item made from the wood you dragged out of that canyon. Although I must confess you do sound, as you said yourself, extremely stubborn.

The beauty of that box and of your friendship means so much.

We were very poor during most of my childhood. I had one Christmas wish year after year—to ride in a sleigh. But in spite of his best and sometimes dangerous efforts, my Daed could not make that Christmas dream come true. By the time I turned eight, I understood the constraints of money and made a point to always ask for something my father could provide. So I'd choose something from my aunt's store, like a few yards of fabric for a new dress or a favorite piece of candy. That way he could buy it at cost.

One Christmas Eve after my married siblings had gone home and my younger ones had gone to bed, my father went to my uncle's home to gather the gifts for Christmas morn...or so I thought. At the request of my mother, I stood on the porch, cleaning snow and ice off the steps so my father wouldn't fall when he returned.

I was eighteen years old, but when I heard sleigh bells,

I felt like a hopeful child again. I remember standing in place, absorbing the joy of it. Isn't it funny how certain things mean so much to us for so little reason? What would make a child want a sleigh ride so badly? Or a nearly grown woman feel such joy at the sound of distant sleigh bells?

As the jingle grew closer, I thought my feet might come off the ground. I truly did. All I wanted was to see the sleigh pass, but when it came into view, it slowed and pulled into our driveway. I wish you could have seen my father's face as he finally brought me the one thing I'd always wanted for Christmas.

My mother brought a thermos of hot chocolate out to us and an armload of blankets. The sleigh was not due back to the owner until midmorning, and we rode nearly all night, singing carols and talking of the God who provides. We were able to take my younger siblings for a ride after they opened their presents. But the greatest gift was knowing that my Daed loved me enough to care about a silly girl's childhood Christmas wish.

Under the weight of the last few years, I had forgotten things you have caused me to remember. I'm not sure how, but sadness and guilt have a way of changing a person. You've judged me correctly, though I can scarcely see how when we know so little of each other. I do carry a secret. A horrid one.

I think you must be right, that just as there are physical

injuries that cause permanent injury, so it is with damage to the inner man.

My problem began the day I realized I could not do what I'd promised to do. I wrestled with myself for a while, and then I went to Henry and told him my decision. I was willing to pay the price, but he paid instead, and I shall never be free of that guilt—no more than he can be free of the grave.

I'm healthy in body but still heartbroken in so very many ways. I try to hide that from those who love me—not because I fear their judgment. I have allowed God to judge me already, but I don't want to hurt them.

I began this letter in great joy, but I end it sobbing like a child. It seems you have the power to stir my heart and my memory with your carving. And loosen my pen with the sincerity of your letter.

If I dare mail this letter, I will be surprised. But I have written my secret. Perhaps vaguely, but it is done.

Beth

Jonah eased into a chair. Although he was unsure exactly what she was talking about, her words held the weight of a dozen silos.

"Beth." As he whispered her name, he couldn't visualize the woman who'd sat across from him in the gazebo. The two voices, the Beth from the gazebo and the Beth who wrote to him, were very different. No doubt.

He closed his eyes, seeing nothing but blank darkness. He tried to relax and wait on an image to form, like he did when carving, but nothing came to him. Recollections from the time Beth had visited and the things she'd later written to him swirled like drops of oil in water, but no matter how he looked at it, they wouldn't blend into one person.

The woman in his gazebo said she knew someone who was struggling. It'd be easy to believe this letter was from that person, but would Elizabeth Hertzler have deceived him?

Pulling the card Pete had given him out of his wallet, he thought about calling her. But then guilt covered him. She'd just laid bare her heart, shared the hardest thing of her life to him, and he doubted her?

He glanced at the letter. No, he didn't doubt the woman who'd written to him. He heard her sincerity as she unveiled her soul. He read the letter again and stumbled over the words "my aunt's store."

Her aunt's store?

It was possible the store she now ran had once belonged to her aunt, but…something left him ill at ease. A call would set things right. He looked at the clock. Just past six. He didn't know what her store hours were, but if it wasn't closed already, it would be soon. It'd take him a good twenty minutes to get to Pete's to use his phone.

Willing to take the chance, he slid into his jacket and hat and headed for the barn. The rain came and went in spurts, but his horse made good time. When he arrived at Pete's, the store was closed. He knocked and a minute later saw Pete coming out of his office. Pete unlocked the door.

"Hey, Old Man. What happened to your key?"

"I didn't think to bring it. I need to use your phone."

"Sure. You know where it is. Care to eat a bite of supper with me when you're done?"

"Who's cooking? Me or you?"

"You. Oh, did I mention that I'm glad you stopped by?"

Jonah chuckled and moved to the phone behind the cash register. He dialed the number and waited.

"Hertzlers' Dry Goods."

Nothing in the woman's voice sounded familiar. "Yes, I'm trying to reach Beth Hertzler."

"You've reached her. How can I help you?"

She sounded young and friendly, and he felt rather queasy. "I don't think you're the right person. I spoke to the woman I'm trying to reach and…"

"Oh, well, two Elizabeth Hertzlers run this store. I'm one of them, and my aunt is the other. You must've spoken to Lizzy, but I'm Beth."

His mind ran with thoughts, but he urged it to pick up the pace. As dozens of pieces of his encounter with Elizabeth Hertzler shuffled around inside him, he remembered her saying, "You should write to Beth. I mean…Beth, Lizzy, Elizabeth—they're all forms of my name."

Suddenly feeling like an idiot, Jonah tried to find his voice. "Lizzy?"

"Yes, that's my aunt. The store is closed for the night, so she's not here, but if it's store business you need her for, I'd be glad to try to help you."

A sense of betrayal burned through him, but until he got to the bottom of this, he'd not say a word to anyone but Lizzy about it. "Uh, no, I shouldn't bother you."

"It's no bother. I wouldn't have answered if I wasn't at my desk. Is there an order you'd like to check on or place?"

Tempted to voice the questions that pounded at him, he resisted. Who did she think she was writing to? "No, but thanks."

"Can I get your name and number so I can pass the info to Lizzy?"

"No, I'm good. I don't think I need anything from her after all."

The woman grew quiet, probably taken aback by the oddness of this conversation.

"Good-bye, Beth."

"Bye."

Jonah hung up the phone, feeling like he knew far less now than when he'd arrived.

"Whoa." Pete scratched his head. "For a man who's slow to anger, you sure do look riled."

"You talked to Elizabeth Hertzler face to face, right?"

"Sure did. She's a bit odd for an Amish woman."

"Odd how?"

"All businesslike, maybe? I don't know." He shrugged. "It's hard to explain the difference, but I've had Amish women come in here my whole life. They tend to be quiet when dealing with men. They ask careful questions, barely hinting at the tougher ones inside them concerning some piece I have that they're interested in, and when I answer, they always seem to keep their real thoughts to themselves. The one you're talking about had a polite salesman-type boldness about her. And she didn't mind questioning my methods as the owner of the store, especially when it came to your carving."

"What did she look like?"

"Well, it's been a while, but…I remember she had dark hair. And even though it was August when she was here, her skin was as fair as if it were the middle of winter, so I didn't reckon she spent much time in a garden."

"Her age, Pete. How old was she?"

"Oh, well, why didn't you say so?" He scratched his head again, looking like his memory was being taxed. "Young. A couple years younger than you, maybe more."

Wavering between anger and confusion, Jonah felt his head pounding. "You're sure? I mean, she didn't look a few years older rather than younger?"

"There was no way she was older than you."

As the woman's trickery continued to dawn on him, his face flushed with embarrassment. "Anything else?"

"Not that I remember. What's going on?"

"Not sure, but I can guarantee I don't like it."

"Are you going to try to figure it out?"

"I'll need to think awhile before I know the answer to that."

Eleven

*L*izzy closed the door to the office and phoned Pete's. She knew the minute Beth told her about the strange conversation she'd had with a man who had their names mixed up that Jonah had figured out what was going on. What had once seemed like an opportunity to help Beth now loomed over her as the utter deceit that it was. She'd tried to reach him on three separate days but hadn't been successful. During the last call Pete gave her a set time, saying he'd try to have Jonah at the store then.

As the phone rang over and over again, her nervousness made her feel lightheaded. It'd already stolen her sleep over the past few days. She couldn't blame Jonah for not wanting to talk to her, but if she didn't connect with him today, she'd get Gloria to take her to his place. If she could've gotten away from the store over the last few days, she would have. But regardless if she talked to him today or tomorrow, how would she explain her actions?

Finding it hard to stay on the line, she shivered when someone picked up the receiver.

"Pete's Antiques."

She recognized Pete's voice easily by this point. "This is Lizzy Hertzler. Is Jonah there?"

"He is. Don't want to be, but I cornered him into it. Hang on, and I'll go get him."

Unable to pray, she hoped to find a way to tap into the man's understanding and forgiveness. While rapping her fingers on the desk, she noticed one of the invitations to the fall hayride.

"This is Jonah."

The distance in his voice said even more than his unfriendly greeting.

"Uh, this is Elizabeth Hertzler. Lizzy."

He said nothing. If she could just speak with him face to face, she could find the right words to make him understand. She hated the phone. It just wasn't the right way to communicate heartfelt emotions.

"I know you're angry, and you have a right to be, but I really need us to sit down together and talk. I'm sure you're wondering why I did what I did. And I'll explain everything but not on the phone. I have a fall hayride each year. Single young people from all over come for that. Why don't you—"

"No, I'm good. Thanks."

Lizzy's heart sank. She couldn't blame Jonah. She fought against tears and managed to find her voice again. "I know I wasn't honest, and you're right to be angry." She grabbed a tissue off Beth's desk and tried to hide the sounds of her crying from him.

"However funny you've found this game of yours, it's not."

"Please don't think anyone's been laughing at you. My reasons are complicated, and I—"

"So," Jonah interrupted, "who all knows about this hoax?"

"Me and Omar. He's a close friend and our bishop, and he's had deep concerns about my actions from the start. But for too long I've looked in Beth's eyes and seen nothing but pain, like staring at a wounded doe. I've been desperate to find some way to help her. Then she came home from her buying trip this summer with your carving. Excitement radiated from her eyes and voice for the first time in more than a year, and all she wanted was to get permission to carry your work in our shop or be allowed to market it to Englischer shops."

"And just who does she think she's writing?"

"You. Only a very old you."

"So you led her to believe she's writing to my grandfather."

"Well, no, not exactly. Pete called you Old Man, and that's who she thinks you are. I told her the truth—that you've never married and you live by yourself. She thinks you're a lonely old man. Your work reaches into her and stirs life. You can't imagine what that spark of excitement in her did to me. I didn't set out to trick anyone, but when I met you, I knew you could help."

"I still don't understand why you didn't simply tell both of us the truth about the other one."

"If I'd told you my plan, would you have agreed to write to Beth without revealing who you were?"

"Absolutely not."

"And if she'd known you were a young, single man, I would have met resistance with the strength of ten oxen. She wouldn't have read your letters or written to you."

"Why?"

The office door opened, and Beth walked in. Lizzy covered the receiver. She had hoped for some privacy while Beth was too busy with customers to take any real notice.

Lizzy lowered the phone from her ear. "I'll just be another minute."

"No problem. Mr. Jenkins is here, and I need his invoice." She pointed to the phone and went to the file cabinet. "No need to keep the person waiting."

Unwilling to reveal her secret to Beth or to let go of this chance, Lizzy held the phone to her ear. "Please come to the hayride event. It's this Saturday night. We're having a dinner at five and an evening of hayrides, bonfires, and fun. People start showing up right after lunchtime. A lot of the young people will stay with me until Sunday afternoon, some until Monday. You're more than welcome to stay however long you wish."

Beth moved in front of the desk. "Be honest, Lizzy. Tell that poor soul there'll be plenty of food and very little rest and that, although their goal may be fun, your goal is matchmaking." Her niece raised an eyebrow, seeming to dare Lizzy to dispute what she'd said.

"Mind your manners," Lizzy whispered.

She shrugged and set the file of invoices on the desk, looking through the stack of papers.

"If you're uncomfortable," Lizzy continued, hoping to keep her cover, "you'll blend in with dozens of other people. There are always new people we've never met before. It's the best way to get this sorted out."

Beth rolled her eyes. "And the matchmaking begins."

Lizzy had no doubt that even Jonah heard the disdain in her niece's voice. She lowered the phone. "Could you take your wet-blanket attitude elsewhere for just a minute please?"

"I was just warning the poor girl." She winked at Lizzy before she left, closing the door behind her.

"So now I'm a girl?" Jonah sounded as if he found Beth's description amusing, and Lizzy hoped she was making headway. Still, his voice reflected leeriness and anger.

"Jonah, please don't do anything that will hurt Beth. I know she has to be told, but she's had a spark to her of late, and she's innocent in this. Just come to the event and we'll talk. I doubt if she'll participate. You have wisdom, and I wanted her to hear it, but she wouldn't have if she'd known you were a single guy not much older than she is. Will you come this weekend and give us a chance to talk?"

"Maybe. I need to think about it."

Pete's nephew, Derek, stopped his car outside Hertzlers' Dry Goods. Jonah studied the store, still not sure he should have come. The hitching post had five horses tied to it, and the parking lot held eight parked cars.

"Busy place." Derek put the gearshift in neutral. "Uncle Pete might not see this much traffic in a month sometimes."

Jonah nodded and looked across the street. Long lines of horseless buggies were parked in the field. Two volleyball nets were set up, and young people were laughing while playing the game.

Feeling old and out of place, he flipped the lock. "It looks like the get-together is happening across the road. I'll be waiting for you in front of that house in two hours."

"Uh, yeah, I should be back by then."

Jonah didn't like Derek's sudden uncertainty on their agreed timing, but there was little he could do now. If Pete still had a license, Jonah would have asked him to drive here today. But Pete had eyesight issues that had made him give up driving.

With his cane in hand, Jonah got out of the car and headed across the street to the house. The yards—side, front, and back—teemed with young singles. A couple of older men stood at an industrial-sized grill, smoke billowing from it as they cooked what smelled like chicken. A baseball game was under way in the pasture, a portable dog cage acting as a backstop. The late-October air had a nip to it, and everyone had on sweaters or light jackets.

Before he was halfway across the paved road, Lizzy came out the front door of the house. With a platter in her hands, she went down the porch steps and into the side yard. She passed the platter to a man standing at the grill.

On her way back to the porch, she spotted Jonah heading her way. "You came." Her smile held uncertainty.

"I came. It's a bit busy around here."

"Ya." She stood in front of him, studying his face. "I hope you can come to understand why I did such a deceitful thing."

He remembered the first time he'd met Lizzy. The earnestness in her eyes and voice were obvious. But did she fully realize Beth could end up more wounded rather than less?

When he said nothing, she motioned for them to walk to a set of chairs. A game of volleyball was being played twenty feet away on one side of them, and at about the same distance on their other side was a game of horseshoes. Dozens of young people stood watching, talking, and cheering.

Jonah placed his elbows on the armrests. "Tell me what you'd hoped to accomplish by having me and Beth write to each other."

"When we met, you seemed to understand how to deal with loss and pain. She suffered loss, and because of that, she has walled everyone out. I thought your letters might share some much-needed balance and that by keeping your identity a secret, she stood a chance of hearing what someone has to say."

"And that would make what you've done worth it?"

"I hoped so." Lizzy leaned in. "But I can recognize that it was a careless idea—wrong and hurtful. Even if it's what I thought Beth needed. Can you forgive me?"

"I have forgiven you, Lizzy, but—"

Her hand covered his. *"Gross Dank, un Gott segen dich."* Her eyes brimmed with tears as she gave thanks and said, "God bless you."

"Gern Gschehne. Unfortunately, forgiving you solves nothing."

"I know Beth will be upset with me, and I can't imagine what she'll say or do. But she connected with you through your work, and you two shared letters. How angry can she be?"

"She thinks she's been writing to a grandfather. Imagine her embarrassment and anger when she discovers you lied to her."

Lizzy's mouth moved a few times before she managed to speak. "Did she confide things in you?"

Jonah wasn't about to answer that. "She had a right to choose who she would turn to, Lizzy. And I shouldn't have been pulled into this, thinking it was one kind of a relationship. You offered friendship, remember? Then you made me someone's counselor."

Lizzy stared into the sky and wiped at several stray tears. "You're right."

A flock of young people passed nearby, every bit as flighty and noisy as chimney swifts.

"Is she here?"

Lizzy shook her head. "She's working."

The constant buzz and laughter made him wonder what secret was so strong it could keep Beth from embracing life again. "I'd like to get out of this without embarrassing or hurting her."

A clamor of excited voices caught his attention. A group of five or six girls headed toward them. One glimpse at the girl at the back of the group, and Jonah stopped breathing.

The woman from Pete's store. The one who'd nearly run into him. The one he hadn't been able to forget.

As everything he knew fell into place, emotions tugged at him—shock, frustration, amazement, embarrassment, and even honor that she valued his work so highly.

Her deep blue eyes were the most amazing he'd ever seen, not because of their beauty, but because of the unknown riches he believed lay behind them.

"Look who I dragged out of her office," one of the girls yelled as she tugged on the arm of *the* girl, of Beth.

The games and conversations paused, and people broke into a disorganized murmur of welcomes, claps, and cheers.

"Denki." Beth lifted her chin and made three circular motions with her hands as she bowed. An uproar of cheers rose into the air. "Denki. Ya, if someone drags me, I'll show up." She gave one slow nod. "Now, please shut up and go back to talking and playing."

Her friends laughed, but most did as they were told. The girls surrounding her slowly dispersed, and the sight of black fabric engulfed him.

She stopped at one of the grills on the far side of the yard and spoke to a man. Then she spotted Lizzy and headed toward her.

What would he say to her? How would he and Lizzy tell her?

Beth stopped before them, lifting a hand to shade her eyes from the sun. "Lizzy, Daed said to tell you the meat is almost done."

What Jonah saw in Lizzy's eyes during those few moments explained a lot about her. She loved Beth dearly, enough to take a chance at angering both Beth and him. Lizzy stood. "Honey, I'm surprised you came today."

Beth shrugged. "Susie and Fannie said Daed asked me to come, and then they proceeded to drag me."

Lizzy put her arm around Beth's shoulders. "There's someone here you should meet."

Beth looked right at him, and he saw a hint of recognition flash through her eyes, as if she might be trying to place him. "Hello." The friendliness he'd seen in her when addressing the group was gone; instead she sounded like the businesswoman Pete had told him about.

"Beth." Lizzy's voice shook. "I'd like you to meet—"

Noise exploded among the volleyball players. Beth's brows furrowed, but she held out her hand. Her palm was soft against his rough calluses. He'd thought about this woman every day since seeing her at Pete's. If he'd stood any chance of making friends with her, Lizzy had ruined it.

"Hi, Beth."

Judging by the look in her eyes when she shook his hand, she hadn't heard his name, leaving him torn about repeating it or letting the matter drop for now. It seemed a very inappropriate time to share such awkward and upsetting news. Lizzy didn't seem to know what to do either.

The volume around them rose again.

"Lizzy, I'm going back to the store now," Beth said. "Okay?"

"Already?"

"I did as Daed asked." A captivating half smile graced her lips, and she raised one eyebrow. "Besides…" She slid the letter he'd written from the bib of her apron. After talking to Lizzy on the phone, he'd had to write Beth again. If he hadn't, she might think her openness had caused him to stop writing.

Lizzy looked at Jonah. His insides churned like the stew children made when playing—a concoction of muddy water swirling with dirt and debris, only good for pretending. He didn't want to play make-believe. Never had but especially not now.

With Lizzy watching him, Beth's attention moved to him too. But rather than showing interest in who he was and why he seemed familiar, her features grew cooler.

She kissed her aunt's cheek. "I'll see you tomorrow afternoon, okay?"

"Maybe." Lizzy winked at her.

Beth's lips pursed. "Don't send Daed or my sisters to come get me after supper. I'm not going to the bonfire. Is that clear?"

Lizzy shrugged. "This kind of gathering where I invite Amish from all over happens only once a year, Beth."

"Good night, Lizzy."

He watched her as she headed for the road. "We would have eventually met on our own, you know."

"How?"

"I didn't know her name, but I ran into her at Pete's. He now orders things from her for his store. We would have met properly soon enough. By then she'd be past such grief, and we wouldn't have all the difficulties you've put in our path."

"You don't understand. *I* don't understand. Something changed her, and…" Lizzy shook her head. "I shouldn't have said that much.

But it wouldn't have worked—not since Henry. She's become a brick wall. She's unyielding when it comes to those who might be interested in her. Are you?"

"Am I what?"

"Interested."

"I wouldn't know. Would you expect me to be?"

"You seem a bit intrigued."

"She's beautiful. But a lot of women are." Even as he answered Lizzy, he knew he felt a definite awareness of Beth—had since the day he saw her at Pete's. And now to realize she was the one his work called to, the one writing him letters. His sense of awe grew.

Confused, he watched as Beth continued to make her way toward the road. She walked backward as a group of girls spoke with her. Each time she broke free of one conversation, someone else called and ran closer to talk to her. He couldn't help but chuckle. Just as she made it to the road, the man she'd spoken to at the grill, the one she referred to as her Daed, called to her.

Beth turned. As they talked, her eyes moved to Jonah and settled there. After several long moments she looked at the man in front of her, responded to something he'd said, hugged him, and then crossed the road. But she didn't go inside the store. She walked down a path, opening the letter as she went.

The beauty of the image—huge beech trees holding a golden canopy above her while she read his letter—only added to his confusion. His last letter wasn't warm or filled with stories, and he regretted that. He'd been trying to be fair to Beth while getting free of the mess Lizzy had pulled him into, but now he wished he'd been less distant.

Lizzy cleared her throat. "I'm so sorry for what I've done, Jonah. I only thought of Beth, and even then I aimed for the insights you had to offer that might help her. I didn't really think about all the possible emotional ties."

"I know, Lizzy. Stop apologizing."

"She didn't catch your name, did she?"

"Appears not."

"When I met you, I was willing to do anything to help her. And now I fear I've done the opposite."

"And for good reason."

Twelve

*L*izzy opened her stove and pulled out a pan of rolls. In spite of her many guests, she'd never felt so alone. She'd held on to her optimism that when Beth learned the truth, it might work out smoothly somehow, but now that she'd witnessed her niece's reaction to Jonah, she knew it had been a false hope. Beth had shown no measure of openness toward him, and Jonah might find it easier to break through a solid oak door with his bare hands than to remain—or was it to become?—friends.

Lizzy could blame no one but herself, but she wanted a bit of comfort, which meant finding Omar. It was ridiculous to feel this way. She'd been a single adult, running her own life, for nearly twenty years. Whether her decisions were wise or stupid, she'd borne the weight of them without the arms of a man to shore her up. So why was this ache to be with him so strong that she couldn't ignore it?

Tears threatened, and she grabbed her thickest sweater and slipped out the back door. At the second eight-foot grill, Omar stood without his coat on, basting chicken in barbecue sauce. It seemed a little cool not to have on a jacket. She moved in his direction, and the crowd of young people filling her yard seemed to fade away.

As if a match had been struck at midnight, she understood a dozen things about herself. She wasn't worthy to become the wife of a bishop. She'd been meddlesome and used trickery to cover her deceit.

When Omar's eyes met hers, her composure broke. Tears ran down her cheeks.

He moved to her. *"Was iss letz?"*

The concern in his eyes as he asked what was wrong magnified her emotions. She shouldn't be here, not if they meant to keep their relationship quiet. They'd agreed not to tell anyone until the time was right. Although they weren't sure when that would be, they knew they'd know when it arrived—like knowing a hayfield was ready or the corn was ripe. Now she wondered if that time would ever come, because it seemed that Omar should be free of someone as foolish as she was.

He turned to Stephen. "Can you watch this grill? I'll be back in just a few minutes."

"Ya."

He placed his hand under her forearm and guided her toward the carriage barn. "Kumm." He opened the wooden door, and they stepped inside.

She paced back and forth in front of him. "I saw it, Omar. I saw the reason I meddled in Beth's life. Why I lied to Jonah about who he was writing to. Even why I do these get-togethers year after year. And it scares me."

"What did you see?"

"I thought it was because of what Beth needed. But that's not it."

Her ego lunged forward, urging her not to say more, but she would. "I don't want *anyone* spending their life alone, not if they don't have to. All this time I thought I'd accepted God's providence in the way my life went. I even thought I liked it. But now I discover…"

Omar stood in front of her, blocking her pacing. "That you've been lonelier than you knew?"

She nodded. "Beth was the best thing to ever happen to me. She filled my days like a daughter, and I wanted to prevent her from making wrong decisions."

"All parents have to learn that a child's path must be his or hers to choose, not Mamm's or Daed's to manipulate."

"But what if my life has influenced hers too much? She attached herself to me before she was school age, and even before Henry I was afraid she'd want to follow my lead and live as a single businesswoman."

Omar stepped closer. "I don't think Beth's struggles are because of who you are. I think she's strong enough to get past what's ailing her, with or without your"—he mockingly cleared his throat—"help."

The longer she stood there, the more she knew that Omar deserved someone better. "What am I going to do if Beth gets hurt and it's my fault? Or if she's so angry she won't even talk to me?"

He placed his hands on her shoulders. "Beth's a hard one to figure out, but she loves you."

She lowered her head. "That's not the only reason I'm upset."

He placed his warm fingers under her chin and tilted her face upward. "What else weighs on you?"

Fresh tears broke free. "I'm not worthy to be the wife of a bishop."

"And I'm not worthy to be a bishop, but judging by how God

replied to Moses when he said something similar, I don't think He wants us wasting time moaning about it."

"You need someone better, Omar."

"And there will be times after we're married when you'll think the same thing—that you need someone better than me. I assure you of that."

"Are you hearing me?"

"I am. You're burdened with guilt over your dishonesty with Beth and Jonah. And because of that, you're tempted to ruin all my future happiness."

He placed his hands in hers, making her distress melt into a pool of warm security.

"I love you, Lizzy Hertzler. And I'm glad you're not perfect, because when we marry, it'd be awful to be the only one who's ever wrong. I'll tell you the truth. You wouldn't have wanted to be my first wife, because I thought I was always right about everything. It took a long time for me to see that a head of a household or a head of several church districts can be just as wrong as anyone else."

Desire swept through her at his openness, and she stood on her tiptoes and kissed his cheek. "You're something else nowadays. Ya?"

"I'm something all right."

She chuckled. "I'd better go."

⁂

Jonah had little to say as he sat at the supper table, but he enjoyed the banter. Tables filled every room in the house. The food and laughter during the meal held a pleasure of their own. He lost track of the conversation a few times due to differences in the region's Pennsylvania Dutch. Each state, and sometimes each area, had its own dialect of the language. When not trying to decipher the unfamiliar words, he met a lot of people, including Beth's Daed, a married brother who'd been helping grill meat, and two of her sisters, still young enough to be in their *rumschpringe*—their running-around years.

"I'm not going to the bonfire without Bethie," Fannie, the older of the two sisters, boldly stated to those at the table. "Not again this year."

It wasn't long before ten or twelve of those near her agreed. They'd take a wagon across the road and refuse to leave until she joined them. Jonah wanted to see who would win this battle.

After dinner he stepped out onto the front porch. Sunlight had faded, and a golden harvest moon hung on the horizon. Through a second-story window of the store, he saw the dim glow of a kerosene lamp.

When everyone had boarded a chosen hay-filled wagon, he watched as one wagonload of youth went across the road and parked in the grass under the window where the light shone. They taunted Beth by calling her name over and over again. A minute later she came onto the porch, leaned over the railing so she could peer around the side of the house, said her piece, and went back inside. He might have laughed, but the need to tell her the truth blocked all possibility of levity.

Lizzy joined him on the porch. "What are they doing?" She pointed at two young men who'd gotten out of the wagon. One had a baseball bat, and the other pitched a ball to him, using the side of the store as a backstop.

Lizzy pulled her sweater tighter around her. "Those teens have gotten caught up in their fun-time mood and aren't thinking. Come with me."

He followed her down the stairs and across the street.

"*Schtobbe!*" Her command to stop was interrupted by the sound of breaking glass and a yelp from inside the building. The guys ran around the side of the house, heading for the porch of the store, but Lizzy beat them to it.

"No way. You keep that bat and your wildness out of the store. Gross Dank." She looked through the small crowd until her eyes found Jonah. "Jonah, check on Beth and the damage, please."

He wasn't sure of his motive, but he wasted no time going inside. A second-story window had been broken by the foul ball, so he looked for a set of steps. A glance through one door revealed a small office. His carving took up a third of her desk. He opened another door and found the stairs. With the aid of his cane, he soon stood at the open door of a small apartment, tapping on it.

Beth called out to him from another room. "I don't think the idea of a home run is to hit the ball into someone's home and then run."

She didn't sound angry, but he couldn't really tell.

"Jake Glick, if you want this ball, you'll come in here and help clean up this mess." Her tone sounded like a big sister correcting a sibling.

Jonah eased inside, feeling odd standing in her bedroom, but it was just inside the threshold of the stairway. Her voice came from his right, a kitchen by the looks of it. He moved to the doorway.

"You know, there are better ways of getting my little sister's atten—" Beth looked up and stopped midsentence. "You're not my sister's beau."

"I realize that." He hoped she took his words as he meant them, like a playful tease.

Suppressing a smile, she placed several large pieces of glass into a trash can.

He gripped his cane, easing some pressure off his bad leg. "Lizzy wouldn't let the culprits come into her store."

Beth grabbed the ball from the table and tossed it to him. "For their sake or the store's?"

He caught it, feeling the sting of the force from her throw. "Well, I thought for the store's, but I'm beginning to wonder…"

She blinked, and then a sweet, genuine smile shone through, hinting at the woman he thought her to be. "They'll want that ball back, and now you have it."

Amused at her polite dismissal, he tossed the ball through the broken window. "And now they have—"

"Ouch," someone bellowed from below.

Beth's beautiful eyes grew large, and she covered her mouth with her hand as she moved to the window.

"Denki," a young man's voice said cheerfully.

Beth waved at someone below, and when she looked back at

Jonah—her eyes filled with mischievous humor—they both broke into laughter.

A stack of paper lay on the table beside the lantern. His name was written across the top of one page, but it had no other words. The gift box he'd carved sat beside her pen. He dreaded the thought of telling her who he was, but he had no choice.

Procrastinating, he misdirected the conversation. "You don't do hayrides, Beth?"

She shrugged. "Not anymore."

"You think you've outgrown them?"

"Mostly I fear for those who will think they've found the right person to build a life with before the night is through."

"And you're sure they'll be wrong?"

She shrugged again.

He grabbed a broom from the corner. "I know you have an opinion."

"How can you possibly *know* that?" She placed the dustpan on the floor.

With gentle caution he swept shards into it. "Because your eyes said so."

Her head tilted downward so that she wasn't looking at him, but her aura, as deep and rich as her letters, filled the air. "I can tell you, but you won't like me at all once I do."

Unable to imagine not liking this woman, he chuckled. "I'd like to know."

"The men go because they hope to find a girl who will always be like she is now. They hope her beauty will never change and her attention will stay fully centered on him the way it is tonight. And the girls go in hope of finding a man who will always be as gentlemanly and kind as he is on the hayride." She took a pan full of glass to the trash and dumped it. "True love has more facets than a lifetime can explore. I've seen it. But it's not found in nights like tonight—where strangers meet and sparks fly."

He wondered why she felt so sure of her opinion. "But if it's impossible for love to start through the meeting of two people, where is it found?"

When she raised an eyebrow, seemingly growing leery of him, he knew it was time to stop the small talk and tell her the truth. There wouldn't be a better time.

"I need to—"

"Beth. Beth. Beth." The chant started again, rattling the remaining broken glass in the window's frame.

She growled softly. "I thought they'd left for the bonfire by now." She motioned toward the door. "Go, and tell them I'm not coming."

"The window needs boarding up. It's going to be a very cool night."

"I'll handle it. Just go convince them that they can't annoy me into going."

"But we need to talk."

When a look of concern flashed through her eyes, he knew he'd stepped too close, but she tried to cover her discomfort with a polite smile. "We've talked plenty, but denki."

The wind carried the chant through the window. "Beth. Beth. Beth."

"Please." She elongated the word.

Part of him wanted to leave, to not tell her anything. Not yet. It made sense to wait until Lizzy wasn't so busy with guests and, if Beth had a screaming fit, until there weren't so many to hear her private business.

"Beth," a man called from the foot of the steps.

"Ya, Daed?" she hollered.

"I heard you have a busted window." His heavy footsteps started up the stairway.

She turned to Jonah. "See, I have help with the window. What I need is that crowd to leave me alone."

As he paused, watching her, his moments with her seemed suspended inside him like specks of gold dust—from the encounter at Pete's, to the letters they'd shared, to each second he'd been with or seen her today. He felt more drawn to her than he'd ever imagined possible.

He forced himself to leave, deciding that the best way to reveal the truth was by letter. He'd find Lizzy and tell her to let him break the news to Beth.

Thirteen

Beth moved to the window and watched as the man who'd been in her room stood in the yard, speaking to the group in the wagon, hopefully persuading them to go on without her.

Most of them looked up at her and waved. She smiled and returned the friendly gesture. The buggy pulled onto the main road and slowly gained speed. The nameless man spoke with Lizzy for a moment before she climbed into a wagon and left with the young people. He then walked toward Lizzy's house, and Beth couldn't make herself pull away from the window.

Her thoughts blended into each other. Lizzy's casting net for bringing Amish singles from far and wide drew first-timers to this event year after year, but Beth still couldn't believe he'd come. She had no recollection of his cane, but she remembered the man. His brown eyes, the colliding emotions inside her, the way he'd stood inside Pete's store, studying her as she had studied him. She'd embarrassed herself with how attracted she was to him. At least this time she'd kept her wits.

Through broken glass she kept her vigil. The cane and his slower amble only added to the sense of charm and intrigue he carried. Despite her past and her will, something about him drew her. But she'd felt a spark for Henry too—not nearly as strong, but it had been there.

Mourning Henry had so little to do with missing him and so much to do with guilt. When he was found dead, the police had asked her questions, and she'd answered honestly. But they didn't ask the right ones. The coroner declared his death an accident, and in a court of law it was. But no judge or jury had asked her to testify to her part in his fatal injury.

An odd sadness enveloped her, as if the reality of who she'd become was sinking in afresh. Fear and blame owned her now, and there was no way to buy herself free.

The man moved to the porch and sat, placing his cane beside him and his forearms on his knees. When he looked up at her, it felt like a part of her flew through the window and met a part of him, dancing on the wind for a brief moment.

Refusing to keep staring at him, she turned from the window. She grabbed a wet cloth and wiped a few stray shards of glass from her kitchen table, but thoughts of the man pulled on her.

She eased to the window again, hoping he wouldn't see her. A car pulled into Lizzy's driveway, and he walked toward it.

Her father stepped up behind her. "If he's that interesting, perhaps you should go talk to him."

The man looked up at her again.

Move away from the window, Beth.

He waved and then got into the car before she decided whether to wave back or not.

"Who is he, Daed?" She cringed, wishing she hadn't asked.

"I met him. He seems nice enough, but I don't remember his name or that of any of the other half-dozen young men I met today. Maybe John or Jacob? Lizzy will know."

"Don't you dare tell her I asked." She turned from the window and took the broom in hand. "I was just curious, and she'll pester me until I'm as wrung out as a desert."

Daed struck a match and lit another kerosene lantern. "Not a word from me." He shook the match and tossed it into the sink. "Has she gotten that bad?"

"Since spring. She's sure all sting in my life will disappear if I find someone new. The community's always pushed the singles, but she wasn't like that before Henry."

"We only want our young people to find someone."

"I know, but it's a little silly to say you trust God to find us a mate and then to pressure *us* to find one. Why is that?"

He shrugged. "We're a few bales shy of a wagonload, I guess."

She elbowed him. "Daed, what an awful thing to say about the rest of the community."

"Just about them? Watch it, Bethie girl. I'll leave here without boarding up that window." His smile reminded her of the steadiness of a good man, and loneliness swept through her.

While her Daed moved in and out of her apartment, going up and down the steps with materials to board up the window, she swept the floor several times, trying to make sense of her emotions. Her mind zipped with a hundred thoughts and her heart with too many feelings. How odd to see that man again.

But she had to stop thinking about him. Taking Jonah's letter in hand, she unfolded it again. At least she had a fascinating old man she could share her thoughts with.

DEAR BETH,

YOU ARE WELCOME FOR THE GIFT BOX. FOR A WHILE THE SLEIGH I CARVED ON IT TRIED TO HIDE FROM ME, PERHAPS BECAUSE MY FEELINGS TOWARD SLEIGHS ARE THE OPPOSITE OF YOURS. BUT I'M GLAD IT MEANT SOMETHING SPECIAL TO YOU.

I HOPE YOU'LL ALLOW ME ROOM TO SHARE MY OPINION WITHOUT SHUTTING ME OUT.

I THINK YOUR EFFORT TO KEEP FROM BURDENING OTHERS WITH YOUR PAIN IS ADMIRABLE. YOU CLEARLY HAVE A LOT OF STRENGTH. BUT YOU MUST BALANCE THAT DESIRE WITH WHAT YOU NEED FROM OTHERS. IT SOUNDS AS IF YOU'VE REQUIRED TOO MUCH OF YOURSELF. I ASK THAT YOU CONSIDER SHARING IT WITH YOUR FATHER OR BISHOP — SOMEONE WHO CAN DIRECT YOU TOWARD HEALING.

A SECRET SO HEAVY THAT YOU CAN DO NO MORE THAN REFERENCE IT VAGUELY, AS YOU DID IN YOUR

LETTER, IS TOO HEAVY TO BE CARRIED ALONE. BE CAUTIOUS AND WISE WITH YOUR CHOICE OF WHO TO TALK TO, BUT DON'T LET IT STAY INSIDE YOU FOR TOO LONG. IT'LL EAT UP EVERYTHING GOOD AND GROW STRONGER AS YOU GROW WEAKER. BUT WHEN YOU FACE IT THROUGH THE EYES OF SOMEONE YOU TRUST, YOU WILL GROW STRONGER, AND IT WILL WEAKEN.

YOUR FRIEND,
JONAH

She closed the letter, hoping he was wrong about her true self growing weaker. She feared he wasn't. But he didn't understand. If he did, he'd not suggest telling anyone. With her pen in hand, she began a letter to him.

While waiting on the right words to come to her, she studied the handcrafted gift he'd given her. As she ran her fingers over the beautifully etched scenery, an idea energized her. She'd been thinking too narrowly about how to sell his work. If her bishop wouldn't let her sell the items but his bishop would, she needed to find another store owner who Jonah could go through. She could find the right buyer and negotiate the agreement, and then Jonah could work with the buyer directly after that.

It wasn't the answer she wanted, but it was a beginning point. After a while maybe Omar would change his mind.

"Bethie, I'm all done for now." Her Daed wiped his hands off on a dishtowel. "I'll order glass on Monday and should have you a new window by next weekend."

"Denki, Daed."

The flame of the lamp in her hand wavered, causing the shadows to dance as she followed her Daed down the steps. After telling him good night, she went to her office. She turned the knob on the lamp, giving the fire more wick, then pulled a file of sellers from a drawer and looked for the address and phone number of Gabe Price, a Plain Mennonite who owned a store. He not only bought a lot of Amish-made items from her, but he had great connections to other possible buyers and not just other stores. He also furnished items to a couple of resort owners. Since Gabe only lived an hour from Jonah, her plan for them to work together should be doable.

Surely it was time she pushed a little harder to get her way. She'd given Omar time to work through his reservations. He hadn't. If she made no profit in this plan, he had nothing to hold against her, did he? Jonah's work deserved to be made available to more people. She would call Gloria and go see Gabe Price as soon as she could. After all, if she hoped to talk Gabe into carrying Jonah's work, he needed to see the depth of the old man's skill. She couldn't show him that through a phone conversation.

The hour grew late, and she felt ready to crawl into bed. Although slipping into her nightgown and snuggling under the covers sounded appealing, she wasn't sleepy. She took the kerosene lantern with her and went upstairs.

She really wanted to write a long letter to Jonah. If he didn't want to read all she wrote, he could use the letter to start a fire. Or maybe she should buy a diary and leave the poor man alone.

"He's old, Beth, not bored silly," she mumbled to herself.

In the dimness of the barn, rays of daylight sifted through the cracks in the walls as Jonah studied the sleigh. The broken rig sat in this dreary place year in and year out. How could something as simple as a sleigh conjure dreams of happiness for one and nightmares of defeat for another?

He slid a hand into his pocket, feeling the letter he'd received yesterday. Through her words Beth had carried him to places he didn't want to go, and he wished she hadn't been so deep and personal. At the same time, her transparency made him long for more. She'd been so open, but now a paraphrase of a silly nursery rhyme circled around inside him, squawking like chimney swifts—All the king's horses, and all the king's men couldn't put Beth together again.

A shaft of light rested lifeless against the filthy sleigh. That awful night when Jonah was but fifteen replayed in his mind as it had a thousand times before. The midwinter weather had warmed a bit, but by the next morning the half-melted snow had turned to ice. Three of his sisters and two of his brothers sat packed inside the sleigh, the fastest horse they owned hitched to it. Amos drove, flying across the fields and passing Jonah as he chopped a fallen tree into firewood. Mamm and Daed wouldn't let Amos get on the road, so he drove up and down the long hill, causing the surrounding fields to ring with delight from their siblings.

After several trips Amos brought the rig to a stop, teasing Jonah because he hadn't wanted to ride. Even then Jonah hated the gliding feel of a sleigh. It lacked control, and he wanted no part of it. While Amos teased him, Jonah moved away from the patch of wood to the center of the open field, packed a tight snowball, and threw it at Amos, smacking him hard. Amos slapped the reins against the horse's back and yelled.

The horse headed straight for Jonah, but he laughed as he side-stepped and doubled back. Amos went up the long hill, turned the sleigh around, and charged after Jonah again. He brought the horse around too quickly, and the sleigh hit a patch of ice and swung out wide. The rigging snapped, breaking the connection between horse and sleigh. The horse bolted, jerking the reins from Amos's hands, and the sleigh hurtled down the slope, straight toward a twenty-foot ravine.

Everything became blurry after that, but Jonah remembered it'd been a long, bloody fight to make the sleigh change course and veer into a nearby snowy embankment. And when the struggle was over, only Jonah had sustained more than bumps and bruises.

He ran his hand over the leather seat of the sleigh. The memory had dulled over the years, yet the injury he'd sustained remained. When Beth learned the truth about his identity, would her sense of embarrassment be like a wound that never fully healed?

He'd finished his letter of explanation to her even before hers arrived, but it'd been impossible to place it in the mailbox. How did one hurl a heavy object, even a truthful one, at someone on purpose? In certain ways she radiated aloofness, but if he had any ability to read her, that wasn't who she was. She used her indifference to keep people— suitors, he believed—at bay. She had the breadth, height, and depth within her to connect.

He should have mailed his letter already. A jumble of confused reasons kept him from doing so, but mostly he wasn't ready for the letters to end.

He ran his hand over the sleigh. If it were in working order, it would have the power to bring joy—not to him, but to someone.

The sound of someone entering his wood shop drew his attention. His grandmother's soft voice called to him. "Jonah."

"Back here."

She walked toward him, a beam of light shining from the hand-crank flashlight she held. "Hi."

Since this shop was his haven from a family that stayed too close sometimes, she was one of the few who entered, and she didn't come often. She said nothing, and the sounds of the wind chimes filled the empty space between them.

"Did you need something, Mammi?"

"I just wanted to ask you to supper."

He didn't believe that was all she wanted, but he wouldn't call her on it. "Nah, I'm good. Thanks, though."

She shifted, and after a long pause she finally spoke again. "You've been too quiet for more than a week. I just wondered if you left your voice in Pennsylvania and if we could go back and get it."

He chuckled. "I've just been thinking. That's all."

"About the accident?"

"Not so much."

"I can't know how to pray if you stay hidden."

His grandmother's faith was different from anyone else's he knew. She paced the floors praying Scripture over her family. Before sunrise she whispered specific verses over each member. He'd been little when he first heard her pray for each grandchild's future spouse.

He reached into his pocket and felt the letter. Emotions swirled from deep within, like a whirlpool that led to unknown worlds. "I…I saw a young woman in August. Just for a minute but she stole every thought. I had no idea who she was. Then I saw her again in Pennsylvania."

His grandmother waited, studying him like she always had when something weighed on him.

He shrugged. "She wears black."

Her soft wrinkles bunched in the center of her forehead. "She's in mourning."

"Ya. But she's been mourning far longer than is traditional. Since the man wasn't her husband, it should have been over nearly a year ago."

"That's unusual."

"Beth is unusual. And I can't understand what it is about her that draws me. I'm tired of thinking about her, worrying about her, and yet if she slips my mind for a minute, I intentionally recall memories of her and her letters." He released his hold on the letter inside his pocket. "It's ridiculous. I don't know her well enough for all this nonsense. And what I do know makes the relationship impossible."

His grandmother climbed into the sleigh and sat. "I think it sounds like you found that treasured piece, the one you said you'd know when you saw it."

He'd felt the pull of Beth from the moment he saw her, but he believed he'd felt it long before then. It rested inside his faith during year after year of waiting.

But so much more separated them than the secrets Beth had shared because Lizzy had tricked her. He was convinced she wanted nothing to do with another man. Why else would she keep wearing black? And even if they worked through that, she provided much of the economic stability of her community. She didn't just live in Pennsylvania; her feet were cemented there.

Mammi angled her head. "Is she...who you want?"

"I'm not sure it matters what I want. You were right when you said I'm an idealist. I thought when I found the right person, we'd carve a life together, creating amazing scenes of things we'd both always wanted. I hate how I sound, so over the top with emotions, but I've waited so long, hoping I'd find her. And now everything is all wrong."

Mammi sighed. "If you can't carve the image you want, then carve what you can." She stepped out of the sleigh. "We take what is and trust that God is making things we can't yet see." She touched the place on his hand where his two missing fingers had once been. "You use pieces of wood most people would burn in a fireplace, and you make them into something only you can." She picked up his cane and passed it to him.

"Carve what can be carved." That idea sat really well with him. "You're pretty smart."

"So are you." She gave the flashlight a few hard cranks, making the beam of light grow stronger. "There's supper at our house if you're interested."

"Ya? Is it any good?"

"Better than your burnt toast specialty."

He started to leave but then paused and held the kerosene lantern near the sleigh. Between him and Beth, maybe he should be the first to refuse to hoard broken things from the past. If he could make himself renovate this sleigh, he might find it had more to give than bad memories and haunting voices.

Fourteen

Gabe Price walked beside Beth as they left his office. "How soon before you'll know?"

Beth's heart pounded with excitement, and she glanced at Gloria, who rose from her chair in the waiting room.

Beth kept her tone even, her emotions in check, as she put on her winter jacket. "I'll talk with Jonah Kinsinger as soon as I can reach him. He may need a while to think before responding, but I expect to have an answer for you within a week."

Gabe walked with her as they went to the van. The early-November air made her shiver.

He opened the door. "Sounds good. I hope this works out."

She slid into the vehicle. "Me too."

Gabe closed the door, and Gloria started the engine. Beth waved and managed to keep her excitement under control until they were out of his driveway.

"Yes!" Beth stomped her feet in quick succession. "Can you believe this? If Jonah agrees to these contracts, it'll be the best deal I've ever made for an Amish craftsman."

"I've always said you got confidence, Bethie girl. Bold, brassy gall. That's all I can say."

"Ya, but look what I came away with." She pulled the contracts out of her bag. "You know my next question, right?"

"Hmm, let me think about this. It'll have something to do with going to Jonah Kinsinger's place."

"If he had a phone, I'd call first, but even if we can't catch him at home, we can leave the information at Pete's. Maybe Pete can tell us where to find him."

"Who are you talking to? There's no way you're heading back to Pennsylvania without a face-to-face with Jonah, even if we have to stay at the closest motel and try again tomorrow."

"We've been traveling together for too long, Gloria. What else can you tell me about myself?"

"That you're not hungry, but I am. That you won't need a rest room for another four hours, but I do. That you probably slept no more than three hours last night getting ready for today, and on the way home you'll fall asleep. And that you pay well enough that I'm willing to drop everything almost anytime you need a driver."

Beth drummed her fingers on her canvas briefcase, ready to tell Gloria she knew about her longstanding agreement with Beth's parents. "Well, you have more incentive than just what I pay you, don't you?"

Gloria glanced from the road to Beth and back again several times. "You're not supposed to know about that."

"What, am I eighteen and on my first business trip again?"

"How long have you known?"

"Since I was eighteen and going on my second trip."

Gloria broke into laughter. "They love you, you know."

The joy of the deal faded, and she managed a nod. She knew. The problem was she'd kept so much of herself from them once she began having trouble with Henry that they no longer knew the real her. Even when in the room with them, she missed the closeness she'd once cherished.

"Your family couldn't stand letting you go on these trips without a chaperone."

"So they sweeten the pot because you're the safest driver they know, and you report back to them if I start some ungodly behavior like eating without a silent prayer before and after the meal, right?"

Gloria chuckled. "You have a dry sense of humor. Sometimes I don't know if you're teasing or perfectly serious. They trust me to keep you safe. That's all they really want."

"Well, then, let's safely travel to Jonah's place. You know where he lives?"

"I know. Do we need to call Lizzy and say we're extending the trip by a few hours?"

"I guess we do. I wasn't sure how this would go with Gabe, so I didn't tell her we might go on to Jonah's. You stop as needed for food and rest rooms. You call. You drive. I'll work."

Beth opened her briefcase and removed paperwork. The next time she looked up, they were passing through the little town of Tracing and were near Pete's Antiques. The roads twisted and curved until Gloria pulled into a driveway.

"That's the house Lizzy went to," Gloria said, pointing. "Then she went into that shop."

Beth slid the files and contracts into her briefcase. "I need to talk with Jonah alone, but you can't stay in the van the whole time. If he's home, I hope to be a while."

"Your aunt sure liked him. Sounds to me like he's good at working his way into the hearts of Hertzler women."

Beth opened the door. "You coming?"

"I'll wait here for now. We'll change plans as needed."

***

Driving the rig toward home, Jonah listened while Amos shared humorous stories from their day at the lumbermill business. The moment Jonah guided the horse and carriage into the driveway, he spotted a van. It looked like the same vehicle Lizzy had used when she visited, although there was no shortage of white work vans in these parts.

Before he could direct the horse to swing the buggy wide so he could see the license plate, his grandmother burst through the door and hurried down the steps. The intensity on her face caused him to stop the rig.

"Beth's here," she said. "Arrived about forty minutes ago."

He couldn't name the emotion that thundered through him— hope, unrest, anxiety—but his insides felt caught in a hailstorm. "Beth or Lizzy?"

"She's wearing black. That's Beth, right?"

He passed the reins to Amos. "Ya. Where is she?"

"Since I thought she was the one you told me about, I sent her to your place. Her driver is inside with me."

Without asking any of the questions he wanted to, he headed for his cabin. Cold air circled around him and dead November leaves crunched under his feet as he walked to his house. Smoke rose from his chimney, and he wondered if his grandfather had started a fire for her. If his *grossdaddi* had walked into Jonah's home, she already knew the man writing to her wasn't who she'd thought. He said a silent prayer and went inside.

Beth sat in a ladder back at the worktable in his living room, her attention on the carving in front of her. She held one of his many finished crossword magazines in her hand.

The moment she looked up, emotion drained from her face, and she reminded him of the stark beauty of tree limbs in winter.

He crossed the room. "Beth."

Her blue eyes reflected unease as she laid the magazine down. He removed his hat and set it on the table.

"I'm Jonah Kinsinger."

She stood. "What?" Disbelief colored her whisper.

"I have to tell you a few things that will be hard to hear at first, but I see no reason for us to end our friendship because I'm younger than you thought. It's still me, Beth. And the woman I've been getting to know is really you." He pointed to the carving. "I understand that you like my work."

"*Your* work?" She grabbed her satchel and pulled out one of his letters. "This Jonah Kinsinger?"

"Ya. There was a mix-up, and I didn't know I was writing to you, and you didn't know… Well, I realized something was wrong the night I called the store. Remember the odd conversation you had with—"

"What?" she interrupted, but he doubted she actually wanted any information repeated.

"It's not as bad as it sounds. I was shocked too when I learned of the misunderstanding."

Confusion, embarrassment, and horror were written on her face.

Pursing her lips, she cleared her throat. "Yes, well, I…uh." Her voice wavered, and she cleared her throat again. "I brought an offer for you to consider." She tossed his letter onto the table and reached into her satchel. "It seems"—she licked her lips and drew a deep breath— "that, uh, we have a man interested in your work."

"Beth, I'm sorry, but there's an explanation. Don't hide behind your work. Can we talk about this?"

With her eyes on the contracts in her hand, she held them out to him. "No, but thank you, anyway."

Her voice regained some evenness as she fought to remain calm. She'd shut him out. Professionalism stood in her stead. He could see feelings and thoughts running through her, but she refused to share any of them with him. He began to understand why Lizzy would resort to deception to circumvent her will.

Reluctant to point a finger at the person who had tricked them both, he tried again. "Miscommunication caused the letters to start."

"Not a problem. We have it all settled now, don't we?" While holding the contracts out to him with one hand, she covered her eyes with the other for a moment, visibly shaking. Then she lowered her hand. "Take a few days and look that over. The deal would be between you and Gabe Price. If you have any questions, you can call Lizzy. I can relay any information to her."

"Beth."

She looked him directly in the eyes, anger starting to outweigh the hurt and embarrassment. "Do not try to act like this was all a mistake. Clearly I'm still gullible at times—something that won't happen again, I promise that—but I'm not inexperienced when it comes to men and deceit."

Men and deceit?

Feeling as if she were on the brink of really talking to him, he cringed when he heard his front door open.

"Hey, Jonah."

Jonah didn't turn around. "Now's not a good time, Amos. Please close the door on your way out."

Beth raised an eyebrow, defiance clear as she sidestepped him. She grabbed her satchel and coat. "Hi." She smiled at Amos, one of those professional looks Jonah was learning to despise. "We were discussing some work, but we're through."

"No we're not." Jonah moved closer but remained to the side. He didn't want to block her, only to get her to look at him. "You have a right to be angry. Say what you're feeling, but don't act like it's no big deal. It's still me, Beth. I made the carvings. I answered your letters. I've been getting to know you."

"A deceived part of me and a part I would not have chosen to share if I had known the truth. Which of those do you request to bow to your will?" Her matter-of-fact tone struck him like a physical blow.

Speechless, he watched as she walked out the door.

Once past the threshold, she paused and faced him. "That's a good offer, the best I've ever negotiated. If you don't intend to accept the work, please don't leave Gabe Price hanging. He needs to know by next week. Can I trust you with that much?"

"You can trust me with anything."

She rolled her eyes, but he saw the threatening tears before she turned and went down the porch steps.

Amos blinked, looking too stunned to move. "Sorry. I didn't mean to interrupt."

"Your timing stinks. She was so close to…" He stopped. Nothing that had happened was Amos's fault.

"Close to what?"

"Screaming, yelling, being honest."

"If that's what you've been looking for all these years, you've got strange taste in women." Amos sighed. "Well. If you want to provoke her, go after her."

The sensible part of him wanted to let her go. She deserved time to adjust and let the weight of her response settle. But if he let her go, would they talk later, or would her freshly poured cement wall have hardened? Guessing the answer, he worked his way down the steps and across the yard, leaning heavily on his cane.

Beth stood at the foot of his grandmother's steps, telling her goodbye as the driver descended the stairs.

With dead leaves scattering as he walked, she had to hear the unique scrape of his cane as he approached, but she didn't turn around. He stopped right behind her.

"You're being guarded and evasive, and that has its place. But we'll both be better off if you'd share what you're thinking."

She spun toward him. "Don't do this," she whispered. "Haven't I suffered enough humiliation without you asking for more?"

"Just take a walk with me, and we'll talk."

"Oh, I've shared plenty with you already, thanks."

He stood within inches of her, but he wasn't sure he'd ever been farther from anyone in his life. "Beth, I know you're not intentionally being cold—"

"Cold?" Her voice showed the first hint of real desire to lose control, and she leaned in even closer. "A piece of advice—never underestimate how cold I can be."

Jonah leaned back as if slapped. "I guess I'm learning that."

"And now we're leaving."

"Beth, don't go like this. I went to the hayride…"

She shot him a look of bitterness. "I'm done."

"I'm not. Come on, Beth. I went to the hayride to figure out what was going on. When I had the chance to tell you, it felt wrong to blurt it out. I needed more time to explain everything."

"It would've taken you thirty seconds to say your name clearly."

"You seemed content enough not to know it. Why is that?"

"Fine. You're completely in the right, and I'm completely in the wrong. I'll send no more letters, and I'll receive no more from you. Is that clear?" Her poised indifference was unsettling. "Gloria, please unlock the van door."

"You can hide behind black for the rest of your life." He stayed in step with her as she moved to the vehicle. "Others may not see what you're hiding, but you have to look into that darkness every day."

The anger and fight drained from her, and he didn't know how to move her in the opposite direction.

Without so much as a glance, she got into the van.

Fifteen

*G*loria kept her eyes on the road and asked nothing as Beth sobbed. As the miles passed, her embarrassment faded, and memories of the night Henry died began to haunt her. She'd been so stubborn, so unkind. He'd begged for another chance, promises flowed from his lips, but she fought herself free and left—never to see him alive again.

"Gloria, go back."

Her eyes were large. "You sure?"

"Yes." But how could she face Jonah? He'd tricked her, and he knew too much. "No...keep going."

Visions of holding Henry's soaked, cold body against her own and her desperation for the nightmare to end engulfed her. She couldn't carry the weight of leaving like this. Not again.

"Go back."

Gloria glanced from the road to her but slowed the van. Soon they were in the Kinsinger driveway again.

"I don't know how long I'll be," Beth said. "I need to find peace between him and me before I can go."

Gloria pulled the vehicle directly in front of Jonah's place this time instead of his grandmother's. "I'll wait here."

"Denki."

"You're welcome."

Beth got out, but before she closed the door, Gloria called to her. Beth bent to look through the window.

"Are you sure he's safe?" she asked.

Thinking someone should have asked that question about Henry, Beth nodded. "I'm sure of it."

She moved to the front door and knocked.

"Kumm," Jonah's voice called.

Easing inside, she spotted him at the kitchen sink, his back to her as he filled the percolator with water.

"I'm fine." His voice filled the room with warmth. "I'm not hungry right now, but thanks. And I told you she was unusual. I know I shouldn't have pursued her when she was so mad, so don't even say it." He turned slightly and glanced toward the door. All of his movements stopped.

"Unusual?" She tried smiling but couldn't manage it. He knew so much about her. She felt as though she stood before him without her hair pulled under her prayer Kapp. "Is that the Ohio Amish way of saying 'troubled'?"

It was his turn to be startled. "I can't believe you came back. Did you leave something?"

She shook her head, all her words lost for a moment, and watched him set the coffeepot on the stove and light a flame under it.

His movements were as tranquil as crystal water flowing down a lazy stream. His back and shoulders looked strong, and she could envision him fighting the terrain and elements to pull that log out. She wondered if he was the man he appeared to be, the man he sounded like in his letters. She knew most men weren't like Henry, but she'd been attracted to him when they began their relationship, and she didn't know if she could trust the power of what she felt for Jonah.

She smoothed her apron. "You don't seem bothered by the clash we had, so if you're okay with things between us, I probably should head on home. I just… I was worried, but…you're fine. I'm fine."

He smiled. "Up to you, but I make really great coffee."

"I can't be here that long."

"Man, what is it about my coffee that makes everyone feel that way?"

The emptiness inside her eased a bit. He knew part of her secret, and she hadn't been destroyed by it. "Jonah, I came back because I need us to end peacefully, okay?"

"I admire that, Beth, and I understand. But I see no reason for our friendship to end, even if peacefully."

Her skin tingled from the awkwardness she felt. "There's no chance you didn't get my last letter, is there?"

He slung a dishtowel across his shoulder and shook his head. "I got it."

She shuddered. "Great."

Why did I share so much? From now on she had to do a better job of controlling and hiding her loneliness.

A tender smile crossed his face as he pulled two mugs from the cabinet. "So you thought I was cute, huh?"

Mortified, heat rushed through her body. Of the many things she'd written about, describing the reaction she'd had when she saw the nameless man at Pete's Antiques might have been the most frivolous. Then, like a teenager with a first crush, she'd expounded in her letter on the impression "the stranger" left on her when he came to Lizzy's supper and hayride event. "Well…not so much anymore."

His laughter eased the tension between them, and even with her lingering embarrassment, she knew she'd done the right thing in coming back. The aroma of coffee began to permeate the room, making the place feel warm and welcoming.

"How'd the mix-up happen?" she asked, already knowing the answer. Lizzy was the linchpin between them since her visit. She had to be in the center of it all.

He shook his head and said nothing. Leaning back against the counter, he set his cane next to him. For the first time she noticed he was missing two fingers. He had an appealing ruggedness about him, a presence that pulled on her. When she lifted her eyes, he seemed to look straight into her soul. She couldn't imagine what he must think of her.

He looked from her to his hand. "A sleighing accident."

She nodded. "The reason we have opposite feelings toward sleigh rides."

"That'd be it. At first I was a self-conscious teen who tried to hide my hand. As time passed, I realized everyone is damaged in one way or another."

"Some of us more than others." She lowered her eyes to the countertop, unable to look him in the eye. "And we all have to learn to get by with the limitations we're left with."

"That's only partially true, Beth. When I was injured physically, I went through surgeries and physical therapy. All of it was painful, but if I'd refused to have the operations and hadn't fought to regain use of my leg and arm, I'd be in constant pain and truly crippled, not just reliant on a cane."

She tried to comprehend, but her divided emotions still battled inside her. His pain was different from hers. But what she did understand slipped past her barriers and felt like a soothing balm on a painful burn. Maybe there was freedom to be found, even for her. Had she allowed her injury to do more damage to her than it should have?

The answer scraped away the freshly applied salve. When it came to Henry's death, she was no innocent casualty.

"I...I'm glad you got the help you needed, Jonah." She wanted to shake his hand, thank him for being gracious, and leave, but she couldn't make herself budge.

"Beth, healing isn't some special gift designed just for me."

His gentle warmth felt hauntingly familiar. He clutched his cane, went to the stove, and turned off the eye under the coffeepot. It seemed no time had passed since she'd walked back into his home, but since the coffee had finished percolating, she realized they must have been talking for fifteen minutes or more.

Jonah turned back to her. "In that sleighing incident...I was the only one who got physically hurt. But for a long time, my siblings suffered emotional trauma because of my injuries. It's been thirteen years since the accident. Shame or regret still crops up in Amos or one of the others. We talk it out, get some perspective, apply fresh forgiveness where needed, and keep moving on."

His words made her ache for that kind of openness with someone. When she thought she was coming to see the old man she'd been writing to, she'd planned to tell him about the night Henry died—not all of it, but maybe enough to lift some of the weight. Easing the solitude of her secret might help, even if she knew a pardon didn't exist for her. "For everything you know about me, there's much, much more that you don't."

"Beth." His gentle voice circulated through her blood, reminding her of a hundred dreams she once imagined for her life. "That day at Pete's, when we saw each other, I felt it too. I've thought of you so many times since then. Are you going to close me out because I don't know you when you're the one not giving me that chance?"

She went to the kitchen table and picked up the letter she'd tossed there earlier. She always carried letters with her when traveling, an old habit in case she needed to reference some information or address a question. But in Jonah's case, she'd kept them with her because she enjoyed rereading them. Walking back to where he stood, she pulled it out of its envelope and opened it. "Did you mark out this line?"

He took the letter from her, studied it for a few moments, and then laid it on the counter in front of her. Without giving an answer, he opened two small tin canisters, added a spoon to each, and slid them her way. One contained sugar and the other powdered cream. "You're changing the subject. We were talking about you, about us."

She picked up the letter and lightly shook it. "You want honesty from me, but you can't give it?"

He took two mugs from the cabinet and moved to the stove. "Your aunt knew we needed each other's friendship. She saw that in both of us, but we agree she went about it completely wrong." He held out a mug of steaming coffee to her.

She didn't take it. Instead she nudged the letter toward him again. "What did the line she marked out say?"

He set the cup on the counter in front of her. "I think it said that your voice on paper sounded much different than you sounded in person. I noticed it in the first letter from you, but I thought maybe that's why you asked for us to write."

Beth's throat ached from the effort of bottling emotions she didn't want. Without meeting her, Jonah sensed more of who she was from a letter than others she had known since childhood did. Tears choked her, and she wished she hadn't asked about the marked-out line. "I should go."

He met her eyes but said nothing for a moment. She felt so transparent and couldn't sort out if it thrilled her or frightened her.

"I understand. You know what I'd like, but it's ultimately your choice." The finality in his voice dug deeper into the canyon of doubt inside her. He took a sip of his drink. "I'll miss hearing from you, Beth."

She stared at the black liquid in her cup, not wanting to see the message in his face again. "If you were an old man, I'd be a nice girl to write to, one who could help you earn money selling your carvings.

But you're not old, and I can't chance what might happen if I don't walk away. There are boundaries I can't cross."

"That's how you've been coping, I know, but I don't believe that's who you want to be."

A sob escaped her, and she turned her back to him. To her right stood a set of french doors, framing a view of rolling pastures, sprawling oaks, and a huge moon, highlighting the work of a God larger than her pain. "I felt drawn to a man once before." She whispered, but she knew by Jonah's silence that he'd heard her. "Only a little compared to...us. But it dug two graves—his and mine."

Jonah stepped closer. "Can you tell me what happened?"

She'd come this far. "There were two Henry Smuckers. The one I agreed to marry and the one who showed up soon after I said yes to his proposal. The latter came out of hiding whenever he didn't like something."

It was several minutes before she could say more, but Jonah waited.

"The longer we were engaged, the more things Henry didn't like about my life. He wanted to control my every thought, every feeling. Accused me of caring too much for my family. He especially resented my feelings for Lizzy and my Daed. He demanded I give up the store. At first I avoided family gatherings, worked fewer hours—anything that might make him feel more at ease. No matter what I changed for him, it wasn't enough. His complaining turned into yelling. Then he started getting rough with me—nothing huge, just quiet ways of leaving bruises on my arms. A day or two later he'd be the Henry I fell for...warm, endearing, funny. He said he knew he needed to change, and if I'd help him, he would. But the closer we got to our wedding, the worse he became. I could see only misery ahead. I wanted to remain loyal, but I couldn't marry him. I grew more distant, indifferent, and when I no longer cared whether he needed me or if I was being selfish, I told him I was done. And I didn't care what it did to him."

She turned to face Jonah and drew a deep breath. "He wasn't from Apple Ridge, but he was staying with one of his uncles when I went to see him. It had been pouring rain for days. We stood on the porch, and I told him I couldn't marry him. At first he was kind and understanding, trying to convince me to change my mind. Then he grew angry and began threatening me. He lifted me off my feet and banged my back against the side of the house, demanding"—she looked Jonah straight in the eye—"*demanding* I marry him. I broke free and ran for my buggy. He chased me, begging me not to leave him, swearing he'd change. But I told him it was too late. He threatened to spread lies, said he'd break my Daed's heart and ruin my business and…" She wiped a tear from her cheek. "Suddenly I could see that his problems were deeper than insecurity and uncontrollable anger. He needed real help, but I just wanted out. As I climbed into the buggy, he…he jerked me out and then dropped me. I slid through the muck in the yard. When he grabbed me off the ground, I kicked and lashed out with all my strength. I…I guess I caught him off guard, because he went down to his knees in pain." She rubbed her eyes. "Dear God, forgive me. While he was still down, I said horrid things one person should never say to another." She closed her eyes. "And while he screamed promises from the mud, I left."

"And Henry?"

"The next day he was found downstream—dead, drowned. Before daylight his uncle brought me the news, and I went to where they'd found him. I knelt in the rain, holding him, with no way to change the past. The muddy, frothy water roaring nearby was unusually powerful from the previous days of rain. When the police arrived, I told them about our fight. One of the officers said they'd need to investigate but that I should protect Henry's family and my own by keeping the argument and the breakup to myself. It didn't take long for them to verify that Henry was still alive when I left him and that I was home when he came up missing. Another officer, a detective, I think, said he'd found a spot on the creek bank where it looked as if it had caved under Henry's feet. There were claw marks in the mud nearby that showed where Henry had tried to get ashore, so they didn't believe foul play or suicide was the cause. But they told me again that it wouldn't help anyone to share what Henry was really like or the hurt he was feeling when he died. I understood it would hurt everyone I loved to learn the truth. And I kept thinking if I'd been more loyal, been the kind of person who'd stand by my fiancé no matter what, then he wouldn't be dead."

"Beth, you're blaming you for protecting yourself. Can't you see that?"

"I should have seen his problems sooner. When his issues were serious, I should have been strong enough to help him. But as I stood at Henry's grave site the day he was buried, covered in bruises no one would ever see, I knew it didn't matter what I should have done, only what I would do. Make sure never to let it happen again."

"You question your loyalty, but didn't his proposal come with an unspoken promise of love and protection?"

She didn't answer. The logical part of her understood that, but the hardness that she felt inside didn't yield to reason. "None of that matters now. I try to do what's right. Try to respond to those around me like before Henry's death, but it's not the same."

He dumped a spoonful of sugar and one of powered cream into a mug. "And ever since, you hide from your future behind black." He stirred the coffee. "Henry had problems, the kind we almost never hear of among the Amish. But you did the right thing not marrying him." He walked to where she stood and held out the mug to her. "The right thing, Beth."

"How could it be right if I carry Henry's blood on my hands?"

"The only blood on you—whether his or yours—is what he spilled every time he hurt you."

His words sliced through the lies she couldn't find freedom from, leaving her staggering at the revelation that someone else knew her secret—and didn't find her guilty. "I...I need to go."

"Then take a few sips while I get something I want you to have."

She took the cup. Her chest ached from the tears, but she was glad to have finally told someone. She drew the warm mug to her lips and drank. The flavor was both customary and keenly rare.

Like the man himself.

Breathing in the aroma, she couldn't imagine what he'd used or done differently to make it so delicious.

He came back into the room with a letter in hand. "It's the one I wrote to you after I came to the hayride. I mean every word, if you can manage to hear it."

She kept both hands wrapped around her mug. "No more, Jonah. It's too much, and I can't take it. Lizzy shouldn't have thrown us together. I just gave you every reason you need to let me go." She held the drink out to him.

He took the cup, but with his index and middle finger of that same hand, he continued to hold the letter out to her. "Take the letter. Mostly it says what I've already said here today, but you'll be able to hear it better when you've had more time to adjust to who you've really been writing to. Just tell me you'll read it, and I'll let you be. I hope to hear from you, though."

"You won't."

In spite of her assurance, she eased the letter from his fingers before she turned and left.

Sixteen

*B*eth and Gloria rode home in silence, the joy of the business deal gone. Despite Beth's anger with Lizzy, Jonah's voice continued to work its way through her, as if they stood in the same room. His letter tormented her, begging to be read, but she left it sealed.

After one stop for food and gas, they continued on. She hadn't eaten, and between pondering what Jonah had said and thinking about how ridiculously wrong Lizzy was to have pulled such a stunt, she couldn't manage to hold a conversation with Gloria.

The hum of the tires against the pavement continued mile after mile, and her emotions finally began to settle. The lull of the van slowly overtook Beth's anxiety, and she grew drowsy. As sleep eased over her, sleigh bells rang, and children's laughter echoed. Darkness filled every corner of where she stood. It matched her clothing. It matched who she'd become, and she couldn't see a way out. The tinkling sound of bells and laughter came from a place ahead of her.

Feeling her way through the darkness, she walked and walked. Her palms bumped against a heavy wooden door, but it swung open easily, and she stepped onto a snow-covered field. The moon glistened on the white backdrop. A man appeared in front of her. A beautiful sleigh held several children of various ages—how many she couldn't tell. The man's hand stretched toward her, but she refused. He motioned for her, unable to cross some unseen barrier.

She knew this place. Fear jolted through her.

Demanding her body to wake, she slowly became aware of the car seat beneath her, but the sound of sleigh bells continued. Willing herself to breathe deeply and become fully conscious, she seemed to be awake several long moments before the jingling faded.

Beth sat up, watching the silhouettes of night pass by until Gloria pulled into Lizzy's driveway. Even though it was past midnight, going to her aunt's house after a trip was the routine, one Beth couldn't avoid or Lizzy would come to her. That would be especially true since Gloria had called Lizzy after they'd left Gabe's to say they were going to Jonah Kinsinger's.

Beth wished she knew how to share the mix of anger and humiliation circling inside her, plus the confusing situation Lizzy had heaped on her.

Gloria stopped the van.

Beth gathered her things. "I don't know what all you report back to Daed, but this situation with Jonah is personal, and I'm twenty-six."

"One day I'd like to understand how you had such a row with a man you'd never met before, two of 'em, in fact, but I won't say a word to anyone." Gloria looked at her. "You okay?"

"I'm not sure," Beth mumbled, wishing she knew the answer. "Do you believe people need surgery and physical therapy for emotional or soul wounds?"

Gloria put the van in Park. "I never thought about it in those terms, but, yeah, I do."

"Jonah believes it. He thinks if I'd quit trying to hide long enough to face what's killing me, I might find happiness again." Beth paused. "If you held a secret, an awful one that would hurt everybody, would you tell your family or pastor?"

Gloria ran her palm back and forth over the steering wheel. "I've known you for a long time, and I don't want to say anything that would hurt you, but the truth is, if a secret was doing to me what it's done to you, I'd tell. I guess you should ask yourself if holding on to the secret isn't hurting people just as badly as telling them the truth."

Beth had thought she was sparing her family, Lizzy in particular. "Go on. I'm listening."

"Isn't it the same amount of pain either way? Only you're doling it out little by little over a lifetime and allowing it into the future as well as the past." Gloria pushed a button, turning on an overhead light. "How long will you punish yourself?"

"I don't know. I can't see ever getting past it, really."

"Then why did Christ die?"

Gloria's words hit hard, and Beth wondered if somehow the answer she needed rested in that simple question. "I've asked Him to forgive me."

"With a tender spirit like yours, I'm sure that part came naturally. But if you continue to carry the guilt, it's like what He did is not sufficient. As if you're telling God that His gift of mercy is not powerful enough to help *you* forgive you."

"But I…" Beth fidgeted with the canvas carryall, unsure what word to use to complete the sentence.

"Sinned? Blew it? Made a stupid mistake? Did something you can't undo? It's all covered."

It's covered.

The words entered Beth, echoing over and over again. She ached to be free of her past, but that wasn't going to happen. Could she at least stop hating herself over it?

She whispered a thank-you to Gloria and got out of the van. Lizzy stood on the porch, watching as Beth climbed the steps. With no words to express her feelings, Beth went inside without speaking.

Lizzy closed the door behind them. The large open space of the kitchen and sitting area was warm and inviting. The fireplace roared with flames, and the air carried the aroma of stew and cornbread. Sometimes Beth didn't know if Lizzy was her mother, aunt, sister, or best friend. In one way or another, she was each of those.

"I'm sorry, Beth."

Beth turned and faced her aunt. "I don't even know what to say. You had no right. But you knew that when you began this."

Lines of regret creased Lizzy's face. "I…I just wanted to help, but Jonah's right—I was wrong to trick you. Once I started, I couldn't make myself tell you."

Beth threw her satchel onto the couch. "What you did was so much more cruel than just leaving me alone. I wrote personal things to him, Lizzy. The kind of stuff I'd never have told someone his age. Then I showed up at his place with no clue what I was walking into. Why would you do that to me?"

"I'm so sorry."

"No." Beth peeled off her jacket and tossed it across the arm of a chair. "The question is why, Lizzy. Not how do you feel about it."

Lizzy's hands had an almost undetectable tremble as she gestured toward Beth. "You liked his work, and—"

Beth stepped forward and placed her index finger against her aunt's lips, shushing her. "Why?"

Lizzy's eyes filled with tears. "Because I was scared for you. You wouldn't let me inside that dark place where you hide, and you refused to step outside of it. Because you think you want to be alone the rest of your life, and you don't know what it's like. Jonah's work was the first thing to interest you in such a long time, and I grabbed on to it." Lizzy broke into tears. "Because I thought he might make you feel something again, and I feared for your future more than I feared your anger."

The weight of Lizzy's worries settled over Beth, and her aunt's emotions tangled into so many of her own. Beth's fears began when she realized the lines between trust and distrust, love and apathy, controlled anger and meanness were so thin a person could cross over with no effort at all.

Feeling weary, she moved to the sofa. Lizzy melted into a nearby chair, and neither one spoke. The dancing flames in the hearth slowly faded, leaving mostly embers in their stead.

Beth reached for Lizzy's hand. "I forgive you, Lizzy." She squeezed gently before letting go. "And I understand making poor choices and keeping secrets. Besides, I can't honestly blame you. I've been a mess for so long."

"You're just a little lost. Losing Henry was powerful hard on you. You'll find love again. I know you will."

"Lizzy…" Beth's chest ached with the truth. "I wasn't in love with Henry, not by the time of the accident. We had quite a brawl about it hours before he died."

Her aunt's eyes filled with shock and tears, but she remained outwardly calm. Beth had no doubt Lizzy would weep over the news when she let herself. Beth should have never tried to protect everyone. If she hadn't, most of the pain of her failed relationship with Henry would be behind them.

"I'm taking off work tomorrow. I need to tell Daed and Omar things I should have told them long ago."

A box of Christmas crafts sat on the other end of the couch. Beth moved the container to the floor, took off her shoes, and stretched out. She was worn out and should have gone home to sleep, but she and Lizzy needed each other tonight. "You didn't start making Christmas cards as you planned."

Lizzy shrugged. "After Gloria called, I wasn't in the mood to be creative. I still have six weeks to get them made and delivered."

Beth released a sigh she'd been holding since before Henry died. "I haven't seen or felt Christmas in years. Sometimes it doesn't feel like it will ever come again."

Lizzy covered her with a blanket and sat on the coffee table next to her. "You'll start enjoying Christmas again. I know it. Just look at the steps you're taking."

"It's taken me too long, and yet it's not been nearly long enough."

"You weren't ready sooner. But it has been long enough." Lizzy took the straight pins out of Beth's prayer Kapp and lifted it from her head. "How did things go between you and Jonah?"

"Embarrassing. Awful. Awkward." Beth closed her eyes and yawned. "Lizzy?"

Her aunt kissed her forehead. "Ya?"

Sleep pulled on her. "I don't want to wear black anymore."

"I'll loan you anything you want while we make you new clothes."

"I love you," Beth mumbled as sleep took over. Even as sleigh bells began to jingle in her awaiting dream, she felt Lizzy tuck the blanket around her.

"I know you do."

Seventeen

*I*nside Lizzy's home Beth watched her family, awed at the power of love. The kitchen table had been extended to make room for the whole family. Sunday afternoon conversations ran like threads through a homemade dress, each one helping to hold the family together. Her mother glanced at her and winked while feeding a grandbaby a spoonful of applesauce.

Beth's Daed placed a piece of pie in front of her and sat on the bench seat beside her. "How'd we do?"

She ran her fork through the butternut squash pie and took a bite. "My part is perfect. Yours...not so much."

"But we blended our ingredients, Bethie girl."

"And mine is perfect."

He chuckled. "Then I guess my part isn't good enough for me to help you make desserts later this week for our Thanksgiving meal."

"Oh, no. As a new cook, you have to help." She squelched a giggle and leaned her shoulder into his. "You need the practice."

Two weeks ago she had sat down with him and the bishop and

told them everything. It'd been the first time she'd seen tears in her father's eyes. Since that day Beth and her family had been taking the first steps on a journey to find healing.

Not long after meeting with Omar and her Daed, she'd returned to Henry's grave one last time, a severing of ties of sorts. She'd gone there so many times since he'd died, not out of love and only partially out of guilt. Like so many other things, her reason for going was clearer now. During each visit she'd woven a rope that kept her tied to that cemetery.

Whether intentional or not, Henry had begun a cycle of fear—fear of displeasing him and fear of his anger. Before the breakup she'd been anxious over ending the relationship and fearful of what he'd do, fearful of what their families and the community would think of her. Oddly, his death hadn't stopped what he'd begun. Before she'd worn her first black dress, fear had splintered into a hundred pieces inside her, and each one turned into a painful ulcer. To keep anyone from touching those spots, she'd pulled away before they got a chance.

Now, she understood, that was her past. Today she was new, with hope and promise for tomorrow. She wanted to stop fear from ruling her. She'd begun that process, but she imagined it would take a while to find all the places where splinters still hid.

The only thing truly missing from her life was the pleasure of writing to Jonah. She might write him one day, but she needed to sort through her thoughts, problems, and emotions on her own first. She was rebuilding herself—a better self.

Her rebuilding work wasn't the only thing keeping her from writing to him. Since he'd been pulled into her life through trickery, she hesitated to reach out to him. Still, she should touch base with him. She might discover that he was waiting for her to contact him as he'd said before she left his home, or she might find that after he thought everything over, he'd changed his mind about her.

There was only one way to find out.

***

Jonah finished applying another coat of lacquer to the sleigh, then set the brush in a can of turpentine. He'd realized he'd been doing the same thing with the sleigh that Beth had been doing by wearing black—not letting go of the past nor truly entering the future.

In spite of all the work he'd done to the sleigh, including taking it to the blacksmith's and having the runners reworked, it wasn't finished yet. But it would be, and he'd give it to Beth as a Christmas present. He hadn't yet figured out how he'd get it there. Even if the snow was perfect and he were willing to drive it, which he wasn't, it couldn't be driven all the way to Apple Ridge, Pennsylvania. But he still had time to figure it out. With each new coat of paint or lacquer, he prayed for Beth.

He walked to the mailbox, hoping the carrier had already run. Four weeks had passed without a word from her, but he kept checking. He'd asked that none of his family get his mail for him. Otherwise, after he checked the box, he had to check with his sister-in-law and grandmother to see if either of them had picked up his mail. Until Beth, he appreciated them bringing the mail in.

The dreary early-December sky spat the first sleet of the season. It wouldn't amount to much, not right after Thanksgiving like this. He'd been using his time to help at his family's lumberyard, to work on the sleigh, and to fill orders for Gabe. It felt good and right to use his carving skills again, but he had questions for Beth, legitimate business ones, and he couldn't call her. He'd told her he wouldn't reach out, and he wouldn't. She had to make the first move. If his grandmother's prayers were as powerful as he believed, and if Beth was truly the one for him, as he believed, then he'd just have to wait.

He opened his mailbox, seeing a couple of envelopes stuck between junk mail advertisements. Closing the box with his elbow, he flipped through the letters. Energy shot through him at the sight of Beth's handwriting. He tore the envelope open.

Dear Jonah,

I hope this letter finds you well. I'm holding my own, having gone through—as you call them—several surgeries. The physical therapy isn't nearly as bad as I thought. My Daed and I have had a lot of long talks. Omar, our bishop, is a kind and gentle man, who comes by my office two afternoons a week. He was one of Henry's uncles here in Apple Ridge. He thought he'd seen shadows of Henry's darker side, but he kept hoping he was mistaken.

Omar's counsel and understanding have been deep and helpful. I carry my past with a sense of peace and faith in God's mercy toward both Henry and myself.

How you stepped into my darkness, bringing a light no one else could, I'll never know. But I want to thank you.

I spoke with Gabe, who said he talked to you last week but that you had a few questions he couldn't answer. Please feel free to call the store at any time.

Gratefully yours,
Beth

As pleased as he was for permission to contact her, she sounded formal and professional. He should expect no less, he supposed. She'd been as injured in her relationship with Henry as Jonah had in the sleigh accident, only his injuries had not been hidden nor left to fester. Teams of skilled professionals, along with his family, openly addressed each issue month after month, year after year, until he was as healed as he'd ever get.

Sliding the letter into his pants pocket, Jonah walked toward the barn. This was what he'd been hoping for, an invitation to call her. He saddled his horse and headed for Pete's. After arriving he talked with his friend briefly, then lifted the receiver to call Beth. As he dialed her number, hope worked its way through him.

"Hertzlers' Dry Goods."

Her voice moved into the empty spaces of the last few weeks, filling him with contentment. "Hi, Beth. This is Jonah."

"Hello, Jonah." The sound of papers being shuffled came through the phone. "What can I do for you today?"

Not treat him like a client would be a start, but after she'd revealed her pain to him, he understood her defenses. She wasn't in the same place he was. He knew what he wanted from this relationship. He'd waited so long for her. Years.

"You said I could contact you with any questions, and I have a good many."

"You received my letter already?"

Deciding how much restraint to use, he leaned one forearm on the counter next to the cash register. "I've had it all of thirty minutes."

She chuckled. "If I were your boss, I'd be furious at such a delay."

He heard more warmth in her voice and felt confident that open honesty without pressuring her was welcome. "I needed time to saddle a horse and get to Pete's. Not all of us have a phone on our desk… or even in our barn."

"Get a faster horse."

The touch of banter held the promise of all he knew they could be in time. "I like the horse I have, thank you."

"I knew the contracts would be confusing. They're written as separate agreements so you can choose which requests you wish to fill."

Sensing that he should stick to business for now, he asked a few questions, and she answered. When he felt a nudge inside him to shift the conversation, he changed the topic. "So how are you doing, Beth?"

"Me? That's been the topic of conversation too much lately. I even wrote you a letter about all the me stuff."

"Yes you did, and I'm very thankful for that. So then tell me about your Thanksgiving and what's happening with your store."

She didn't respond, and he wondered which she'd do—remain professionally distant or share some small part of herself with him. Either way they were making progress.

"Thanksgiving was really good. I think it's the first time I've tasted a meal in ages." She paused, possibly giving him a chance to talk, but he waited. "It feels like I've missed joy for far too long." She drew a slow breath. "Mamm and Daed and I talked for hours. My Daed helped me make his favorite dessert. It seemed so odd to have a man in the kitchen actually cooking, but it healed something inside both of us. It's crazy at the store right now, and it will be like running a race until we close at noon on Christmas Eve. How about you?"

"The actual work in the lumberyard itself is slow this time of year, but pricing jobs to clear timber off of land is fairly busy. People need money to get through the winter months, and we pay in advance. I had the best Thanksgiving I've had in a very long time." He paused, wondering if he should say what he wanted. He decided it might not be wise but to chance it anyway. "My family—they're all great. But this Thanksgiving had a new hope…concerning us."

She grew quiet again. "Ya, I…I felt those hopes too."

Her quiet, restrained confession made him feel much like he had when he'd started building his cabin—full of promise but no strength against the elements just yet.

"About those contracts, Jonah." She veered the conversation back to business. "Do you understand the requests concerning each cabin? The construction will take place in phases. The first phase includes the twenty cabins they want ready for occupants by May first."

"Gabe wants me to carve on the back of chairs, the mantels, free-standing objects, cabinets, and something called Aeolian chimes."

"Aeolian chimes are the same as wind chimes. The owners of the resort know Gabe, and they're asking if you'll do these things. You're not obligated to do any more than you want, but the price they're willing to pay is incredible. I have Amish craftsmen making the cabinets, tables, chairs. That part of the deal will work out whether you choose to carve designs on them or not. Your first job is to choose what you're willing to carve, but once you decide, it has to be done for each cabin. The owners' top choice is for you to do the backs of the chairs, the cabinet doors, and the mantels to match. They're going for an upscale rustic look. It'll be beautiful. They'd like to pick a base color for the fabric used in each cabin for things like kitchen chair cushions, couches, and throw pillows. I didn't know if the color the interior decorator chose might affect what scenery you'd carve or not."

"I don't know either. I've never thought about it."

"Well, there are a couple of ways we can work this. You can create the carvings, and the interior decorator can choose a color that coordinates with whatever scenery you chose, or you can choose a color from a scheme first. I wrote the contracts so you had the freedom of choice, not the decorator."

"What's your favorite color, Beth?"

"It's not black, okay?"

"Better than okay. So what is it, and why?"

The conversation unwound like a spool of thread, magically sewing pieces of their lives together in the process. As the hours passed, she occasionally put him on hold while she tended to store business.

He didn't want to end the conversation, so he waited. Although most Amish avoided phones except for business, no one would object to their talking like this.

Each time she came back on the line, they seemed to be in a better place than before. He could hear people come into her office and ask questions. When she left the office a couple of times to help, with each beat, each movement, he understood more of who she was.

The physical distance between their two lives still nagged at him. Her roots were deeply planted in Apple Ridge. The community relied on her, and she adored her family and her work. He was part of a family-owned business that had been passed down for generations, and he was needed. Jonah, three of his brothers, and his Daed each had a specific job, and it took all of them to keep the mill profitable. He'd built more than just his dream cabin on acreage his grandfather had given him—on the very spot Jonah cherished most of all. He'd made a home for himself.

By the time he and Beth hung up, Jonah realized that for all they'd worked through to get to this point, they still faced a huge issue. He needed a solution.

It had been dark for hours when he finally walked into Pete's kitchen.

"I guess if you stay on the phone long enough, I gotta cook the meal." Pete chuckled and pointed to the plate of food on the back of the stove.

Jonah turned a chair around and straddled it. "I got a problem, Pete."

"Women'll do that to a man." The old bachelor winked.

Forty years ago Pete had come close to marrying, but for reasons he wouldn't talk about, it never took place. He grabbed the plate of food and a fork and set it in front of Jonah.

Jonah took a bite of mashed potatoes. "Ya, but this one's worth it."

"Well, you know what I always say about problems."

"Start at desire and work from there."

"Yep. So bottom line, no fantasy nonsense, what do you want?"

"Beth Hertzler to be my wife." As soon as he said it, he got a bad feeling in his gut. "Scratch that. I'd like to be the husband of Beth Hertzler."

"Don't see the difference."

"In one scenario she's mine. In the other I'm hers."

"Still lost here."

"You'll have to trust me. I think I know the solution. Thanks."

Pete scratched his head, looking confused. "Anytime. Are you gonna tell me?"

"I need to move to Pennsylvania and be her husband, not have her move here to be my wife."

"That's a lot to give up for a woman. I don't recommend it."

Jonah shrugged. "If she'll have me, my mind's made up. I just don't know how I'll leave the business."

Eighteen

Beth held the phone to her ear, feeling the customary war between caution and desire. Silence lay between her and Jonah like newly fallen snow, and she struggled to find the right words. Her store closed Thursday at noon for Christmas Eve, and Jonah wanted to see her.

Part of her longed to go to Ohio and spend time with him as he'd asked. The rest of her wanted to slow everything down to a pace she didn't find so scary—something more like the laziness of sunset in midsummer rather than nightfall in winter.

Over the last three weeks he'd sent long, deeply moving letters, and he'd called her most evenings after the store was closed. He'd carved her the most beautiful set of ink pens she'd ever seen in her life, and he'd sent a year's supply of refill cartridges with them.

The more she got to know him, the more she knew she was falling in love. How could she not? If he were only half of who she believed he was, he'd still deserve to steal her heart. She hoped her heart was worthy. Even in the letter he'd given her at his home, he'd written things as deep and personal as she had written to him before she knew who he was. And she knew he truly was the man she'd thought him to be through his letters.

Lillian Petersheim walked into the office with a small stack of twenty-dollar bills in her hand and closed the door behind her.

"Hang on, Jonah." Beth held out her hand for the cash and counted it. "What do you need?"

"Ones and fives."

Beth went to the safe.

Jonah had been in the area on lumberyard business last weekend—pricing the clearing of timber from nearby land—and he and his brother had dropped by the store. Unfortunately she'd missed his visit. She and Gloria had gone into Lancaster to handle a supply-and-demand issue that needed Beth's attention firsthand.

It still struck her as odd—and heartwarming—that he didn't seem the least bit frustrated about not seeing her. Instead, he seemed to enjoy staying for dinner at Lizzy's. Her aunt sent word to Beth's parents, and they came over as well and spent the whole evening getting to know Beth's carver. Her easygoing Daed grilled Jonah and came to the conclusion he really liked him. That reassured her, but on occasion Beth still found doubt and fear lurking inside her.

She passed the bills to Lillian and picked up the receiver. "You still there?"

"Yep," Jonah replied. "In Ohio. And the question on the table is, will you join me here for Christmas?"

Silence reigned, but she was no longer surprised by his willingness to wait for her to find a voice for her thoughts. She wasn't sure she was ready to meet his family. That would shift their relationship from friendship into expectations of marriage.

If they lived in the same area, they could see each other on Christmas or any other day without anyone thinking much about it. More than likely they'd ride home together after singings; at other times he'd bring his rig to the edge of her property so she could slip off to meet him without anyone knowing. If Jonah lived close, they'd have the same friends and would have gathered for games at rotating houses, no matter what the season. That's the way courtships usually worked, allowing singles the opportunity to socialize without it meaning a declaration to marry. But when a young woman traveled four hours on Christmas Eve to see a man, it would cling to the family members like molasses—making everything it touched sticky and altering its flavor.

"Beth." Jonah's assuring voice finally broke the stillness. "If you're not at ease about this, we'll visit another time."

She'd expected him to pick up on her reluctance. He seemed to know her well, which only strengthened people's ability to hide their true self and manipulate others, didn't it? She cringed at the distrust that still crept from a hiding place and tried to rule her.

Regardless of her issues, it hurt to imagine how he must feel, knowing she wasn't returning the invitation. "I…I'm sorry, Jonah."

"Not a problem. But it's an open invitation."

"You don't mind?"

"Not if it takes a decade. Well…let's make that half a decade."

And as she said good-bye, she recognized another piece of her hesitation. She'd have to give up the business she helped build, and she didn't know if they'd ever find a solution she could live with.

⁂

Beth helped the last customer to her car, her arms full of packages. She closed the trunk and refused the tip the lady offered.

Snow swirled through the air, dulling visibility as the woman's red taillights faded into the distance. Beth couldn't remember the last time it snowed during Christmas. She buttoned her woolen coat. The glow from Lizzy's house across the street—kerosene lanterns, gas pole lamps, and the fireplace—shone clearly against the gray and white of the snowy midday.

For days her longing for Jonah had increased during every lull, and now that the store was closed for Christmas, the rest of the holiday would be one long roar of silence.

An hour ago she'd given the sales help their bonuses and sent them home. They wouldn't return until the store opened on Monday. Lizzy hadn't come in at all that day. She and Beth's Mamm were busy baking the Christmas Eve meal for most of the Hertzler clan.

As Beth stood watching Lizzy's home, she noticed Omar's carriage. His horse wasn't attached to the rig, indicating he hadn't stopped for a quick visit. Clearly he intended to spend hours at Lizzy's with Beth's family. And it dawned on her what she should have known months ago—her aunt and the bishop were more than friends.

Darkness and freezing temperatures surrounded Beth as fear of life and love tried to tighten its grip again. At thirty-eight years old her aunt had the courage to open her heart to a man who'd once been happily married, who, as bishop, bore a heavy responsibility before God, and who had a grown family and grandchildren. She guessed that he was eight years older than Lizzy. The whole situation sounded very scary to Beth.

She moved to the store's porch steps, dusted snow off, and took a seat. Why did concerns and fears constantly try to overrule her belief that love was worth it?

Thoughts and dreams and hopes swirled inside her. If she had faith instead of nagging fears, she'd find a way to get to Jonah's, even if she didn't arrive until midnight. She wouldn't worry about how much the gesture would reveal or what his family would expect from the relationship. She'd simply go and enjoy and let life be filled with unexpected moments.

"Dear God...I want what sounds so simple and feels so impossible—to trust in Jonah, in myself...in love...in You."

Several thoughts rushed through her. Pieces of Bible verses drifted first one direction and then another, like the downy flakes in front of her. Memories of the parable about the man who'd been given only one talent—one piece of money—and hid it, afraid of losing what little he'd been given, came to her. The idea of the man receiving something of value from God shook her. Was anything more important to God than love? Giving it. Accepting it. Investing it. She couldn't recall a time when He ever hinted it should be buried.

The man in the parable hid his value out of fear. *That* she understood, and once again she determined to stop. If Jonah had refused to keep moving because of his injury and pain, he'd never have carved that piece she'd discovered. He kept moving regardless of the pain, and it seemed she shouldn't keep her life on hold because rogue fears cropped up here and there.

Ready to embrace all of life, she went inside the store and called Gloria. After making plans and packing, she went to Lizzy's.

While waiting for Gloria to arrive, Beth talked with her family and exchanged gifts. Lizzy and Omar couldn't keep their eyes off each other. Lizzy caught Beth watching them and gestured toward the bedroom. Beth followed her.

Lizzy had barely passed through the doorway when she turned. "I…I wanted to tell you something. Omar asked me to marry him this afternoon."

"Hmm, he's still here, and the two of you are glowing, so I guess you said yes."

"We've been talking about it for a while, but he officially asked today. I told him you had to be the first to know. Can you believe I've finally found love?"

Tears stung Beth's eyes, and she hugged her aunt tightly. Lizzy had carried unspoken aches for years. Arm in arm they left the room.

"Ah, you told her," Omar said softly.

"Ya." Lizzy stared into his eyes. Beth headed for the living room to give them a moment of privacy. When she looked back, her aunt and the bishop stood toe-to-toe, holding hands and whispering things no one else would ever know. Omar kissed Lizzy on the cheek, and Beth wondered if they might marry before the wedding season. The rules altered for those who'd lost a spouse; they could marry whenever they wanted. Omar had been single for many years, and Beth knew he'd cherish Lizzy as the great find she was.

An hour later Beth sat in the passenger's seat of Gloria's van, waving to her family as she and Gloria pulled out of Lizzy's driveway. Snow continued to fall throughout the long, quiet drive, and Beth gazed out the window while chatting with Gloria. It felt magical to have snow on Christmas, but she wished it would stop.

The weather continued to slow their drive on Highway 22, but a little over four hours into the trip, Gloria merged into the far right lane to cross the Fort Steuben Bridge.

"I hope your surprise visit doesn't work out for you like it did for Jonah," she said.

"It won't," Beth replied. "He said the Kinsinger family spends Christmas Eve at his grandparents' place, although he goes to Pete's for a while first."

"Maybe we should stop by there on our way, just to be sure."

"Sounds like a good idea."

Brake lights shone through the white fog ahead of them, and the van fishtailed as Gloria brought it to a halt, barely missing the vehicle in front of them. Surely they could make it all the way to Jonah's. It was only fifteen, maybe twenty, more miles, but unease made Beth's skin tingle.

Beth looked behind them. Three or four cars almost locked

bumpers before regaining control. Ahead of them, traffic on the bridge was barely moving.

Gloria craned her neck, trying to see beyond the cars in front of them. "If the snow gets any thicker, we may both be staying with his grandparents tonight."

"I really don't think you should try to go back tonight. Will staying be a problem?"

"Ronnie won't be home until suppertime tomorrow. I'd like to be there in time to have a Christmas meal waiting. This is supposed to let up by morning, so we're good."

"Is it hard having a truck driver for a husband?"

Gloria wrinkled her nose. "Honey, *anything* can be hard—having a husband gone all the time, or underfoot all the time, or no husband, or…whatever. The answer is to build a life around those things. If I sat around waiting on him, I'd get unhappy. So would he. If he gets home tomorrow and I'm not there, he'll start supper, knowing I don't get mad when he's gone and he needs to return the favor. It works."

They slowly inched across the bridge and continued on Highway 22 until the Ohio River was miles behind them. Just as Beth started to relax, brake lights flashed ahead of them, and a couple of cars slid off the road. The sound of metal crunching made Beth's stomach lurch, but Gloria managed to stay on the road as she stopped the van.

"What happened?" Beth asked.

"Not sure, but it doesn't look good." Gloria turned on the radio. "Maybe there will be a report."

The minutes inched along almost as slowly as the cars crammed together on the highway. Finally a traffic report let them know a tractor-trailer had jackknifed miles ahead of them.

Even as they crept onward, Beth knew what they had to do. Once they turned off Highway 22 and began driving the back roads that lead to Tracing, the journey could be even more unpredictable.

She stared at the snow-covered roads. It seemed wrong that an object as feathery light as a snowflake could collect into something keeping her from Jonah, especially when she was this close.

"Gloria, we can't keep trying to ignore the weather. We need to find a motel."

Gloria sighed. "I think you're right. But with this weather, an empty room may not be as easy to find as it sounds."

Beth studied an information sign ahead, trying to read what hotels might be close. "It'll be easier to deal with than getting stranded in a ditch."

Nineteen

Like every Christmas Eve, before going to his grandparents' house, Jonah sat across the table from Pete. But tonight Jonah stayed longer than normal, hoping to hear from Beth. He'd called her, but twice the phone was busy, and since then no one had answered. She'd be with her family by now, and he should leave. He knew that. Still...

"Care for a game of chess?" he asked.

Pete's day-old whiskers formed odd patches as he smiled. "Think you got the Christmas magic on your side this year?"

"Nope, but I'm all for giving an old man a break once in a while."

"Giving an old man..." Pete leaned across the table. "Listen here, Jonah Kinsinger, you're the Old Man."

"Then give me a break. And stop calling me Old Man in front of other people. It's caused me nothing but grief lately."

The phone rang, and Jonah almost knocked the table over jumping up to answer it.

Pete laughed. "You're right. You don't have an ounce of Christmas magic in you."

Jonah hurried into the store, glanced at the caller ID, and grabbed the phone. "Merry Christmas. I was hoping you'd call."

"Probably not hoping *I'd* call," Lizzy said.

"Well, Merry Christmas to you too, Lizzy, but I was hoping you were Beth."

"I figured that the first time we met."

Jonah chuckled. "Where is she?"

"In Ohio, stranded in a motel off Highway 22."

"She went somewhere on business on Christmas Eve? In this weather?"

"No. She went to see you."

"Me?" As the news sank in, he felt he housed the excitement of Christmas.

"The two of you need some serious help with your romantic gestures, which is why I'm intervening. I thought Pete might own a tractor or you might have some way of reaching her."

He wasn't sure he did have a way to get to her. He didn't know anyone who owned a tractor. He had a sleigh, but it needed a specific type of snow to work. "Do you know what motel she's in and where?"

While Lizzy shared the info, Jonah took notes.

"I'll give it try. Merry Christmas, Lizzy."

"Merry Christmas."

***

Beth looked at the small, dreary motel room. Concrete block walls, cold stale air, and the tinny sound of the cheap television Gloria was watching made the disappointment sting even more. Blasts of frigid air found their way around the door that led directly outside. She removed the pins from her prayer Kapp and bun and, unwinding her hair, sat on the edge of the bed.

Gloria held out a small bag of chips. "It's all the vending machine had left."

Beth shook her head. "They're all yours." With her coat still on, she slid between the cold sheets and pulled a blanket over her head. Gloria flipped from one news station to another.

Though she didn't feel sleepy at all, Beth closed her eyes anyway. When the sound of sleigh bells jingled over an anchorman's voice, she figured she must be sleepier than she'd thought.

The television went silent. "Did you hear that?" Gloria asked. "Santa must be coming to this old motel."

Beth sat up. "You hear sleigh bells too?"

"Sure do."

They moved to the window, but the frost kept them from seeing outside. Gloria shrugged and returned to watching television. Beth slid into her boots and added a wool scarf over her head before she opened the door. A blast of freezing air ripped through the room, stealing what little heat they had. She stepped outside and closed the door behind her.

The sound of sleigh bells rode on the night air like magic, and she looked in the direction the noise came from. She expected to see a dad in a red suit playing Santa for his stranded children on Christmas Eve, but no one came into sight.

As she listened, she realized the sound was coming from the back side of the motel.

She closed her eyes, letting the snow drift around her as she remembered so many childhood years of dreams and hopes. Memories of all the times her Daed came up with a substitute for a sleigh ride warmed her. The longer the sound went on, the lighter her heart felt. So her plan to see Jonah hadn't worked. This was a substitute year, but now that she fully trusted him and knew she loved him, they'd fulfill the real dream soon.

She opened her eyes. Through the dark night and white cloud of swirling snow, she saw a horse pulling a black sleigh with an Amish driver.

Is it possible?

Beth blinked.

Jonah.

Her heart pounded madly. Jonah pulled on the reins and slowed the horse until the sleigh came to a halt. He looked straight at her, and her mind jammed with too many thoughts to process.

His beautiful smile didn't say nearly as much as his brown eyes. "Merry Christmas."

Tears brimmed, and she couldn't find her voice.

"I knew if I kept circling the motel, you'd come outside." He held out a basket. "My mother sent dinner."

She moved closer and took the basket. The aroma of a Christmas feast filled her.

"Of course, you're welcome to come home with me." He patted the seat beside him. "Or we can stay here and eat…if I'm invited."

Stay here?

Beth shook her head. "No. I mean, yes. But…but no."

He laughed.

She drew a deep breath. "You're invited to stay, but I'd much rather you go. I…I mean…taking me with you, of course. Oh, and Gloria too."

He leaned forward. "Are you rattled, Beth Hertzler?"

She nodded, and tears warmed her cheeks. Was she dreaming? "How…"

"Lizzy called Pete. I just happened to be there…waiting and wishing you'd call."

In her mind's eye she saw children in the sleigh—just for a moment. She heard their laughter, but she couldn't tell how many of them there were. She saw a white prayer Kapp or two and a couple of black felt hats. In that moment she understood why she'd begun hearing the sleigh bells of her childhood again. For her, it was the sound of hope and love. It rang inside her as she slept, trying to remind her that love was alive and worth whatever it took to hear it when awake. But she couldn't have started hearing them again without Jonah.

An overnight bag sailed above her head, and Jonah caught it. Gloria took the basket of food from Beth. "I'll keep this. You go."

Jonah placed the bag on his far side. "You're welcome to join us," he said to Gloria.

"No thanks. I'll turn in early and hit the main roads first thing tomorrow. I have a feast to hold me over until then. I'll come back for her on Sunday." Gloria passed Beth her prayer Kapp and pins. "You enjoy your Christmas."

Beth hugged her. "I will. Thank you for this, and call Lizzy for me. I'm sure she's sitting by the phone in the office, waiting to hear what happened."

"I will."

Beth climbed into the sleigh. Jonah lifted a blanket, and she slid in beside him. The seat, as well as the blankets, was warm. She looked at Jonah for an explanation. He showed her the power source for the two electric blankets—a converted car battery.

"Pete loaned me the blankets. I had the rest." He made a clicking sound with his tongue, and the horse moved off, gaining speed.

Within minutes they were beyond all signs of town life. As they glided along the back roads, going up and down the hills that dominated the area, Jonah told her where the sleigh came from and why it was ready for use that night.

He then slowly shared his secret—the pain of resenting his siblings, Amos most of all, as Jonah suffered surgery after surgery. And the horrid, guilt-filled days when he felt like he wouldn't have saved any of them if given the same situation again.

Beth studied the man beside her, needing to hear every word he shared. "When Henry died, it was easy to forgive him. But how did you get past the pain to deal with your anger and resentment against Amos?"

"Well, time and medicine and family would have eventually helped, but during the worst of it, I caught a glimpse of how Jesus let go of His anger. Just a fraction of a second, mind you, but I saw Him on the cross, looking beyond the people who'd put Him there and to the Father He trusted. It seemed that He didn't hold the people accountable because He wasn't looking at them. When in the worst pain, He kept his focus on everything above."

His words circled inside her, and she snuggled closer. They passed through the small town where Pete's store was located and continued on toward Jonah's.

The batteries ran out of energy, and the blankets stopped giving off heat. The wind chill grew bitter. When Beth shivered, Jonah urged the horse to go faster. Soon he pulled into his driveway and headed for his home.

"You're awfully quiet, Beth. I don't think you've strung two sentences together since I arrived."

The fields were covered in snow that wouldn't melt for months yet, but the land underneath would respond to the first signs of spring, and it would become rich with nutrients as the snow slowly melted.

How could she share all that was in her mind and heart?

Jonah stopped the sleigh in front of his house. She caressed his cold cheek with the palm of her hand, wishing he could read her mind.

He studied her. "I won't forget the gift of you being here for Christmas." He moved in close, and she was sure he was going to kiss her.

"Jonah!" a man yelled.

She jolted, and Jonah smiled. "It's just my brother. When it comes to us, he has really bad timing."

"Will he always?"

"Always?" Removing the blankets, Jonah stood. "Did those words hint of a promise?"

Beth nodded.

He stepped out of the sleigh and helped her down. "Is it too soon to ask?"

She shook her head, and his smile seemed warmer than a hearth at Christmas.

Amos barreled toward them. "I'll take care of the horse. The womenfolk insisted we clear a path from your cabin to Mammi's, so you now owe us."

Beth pulled the woolen scarf tighter around her head, suddenly uncomfortable without her hair pinned up or her prayer Kapp on.

"I'll pay you guys back. Don't you worry about that." The mocking threat on Jonah's face spoke of his deep friendship with his eldest brother. "Amos, this is Beth Hertzler. I do believe she might be around quite a bit in the future if you don't scare her off."

Amos shook her hand, looking like his huge grin might soon give way to tears. Then he poked Jonah. "Me? What about you?"

"Take the horse and go." Jonah lifted her overnight bag from the sleigh. "I have something I need to ask Beth."

Amos took the reins. "I started a fire in the fireplace and in the wood stove in your bedroom more than an hour ago. Got coffee started a few minutes ago and lit a lamp in each room."

"Now that was useful. Thanks."

Jonah planted the end of his cane firmly into snow. With her overnight bag in one hand and his cane in the other, they went up the steps and into the cabin. The warmth of the room made her body ache from cold, but the place felt like a dreamland.

Jonah held her bag, looking completely at ease. "I'm not sure where you'd rather stay tonight. You're welcome to sleep here, if you won't get lonely, or at Mammi's."

"Here, if you don't mind."

"Here it is. I haven't stayed at Mammi's since I was a teen. She'll enjoy this." He carried her bag down a hallway.

Beth followed him but stopped long enough to peer into two empty rooms along the way. Neither had one stick of furniture or anything else in them, but they were bedrooms. She was sure of it. One for girls and one for boys. He'd built this house in the hope of having a family.

He stepped into a large bedroom and set her things on the bed. "The wood stove at the foot of the bed will keep it warm all night."

Looking at the exposed beams, she tugged at the oversize scarf on her head, loosening it, but keeping it on. "This is so gorgeous."

When he turned to face her, she gazed into his brown eyes, a little uncomfortable at the desire that ran between them.

His face told her he felt the same power. "I'll check on the coffee while you get settled in."

As the soft thump of his cane moved across the wooden floor and down the hallway, she longed to hear that sound every day for the rest of her life. Slowly running her hand along the rough-hewn logs of the cabin's walls, she left the bedroom and headed down the hall. "Jonah?"

He stopped at the end of the hallway.

"This whole place feels like you...I mean, like the carvings."

"Not everyone would think that's a great thing, you know," he teased.

"I'd never ask you to leave it."

"You don't have to ask. I've already decided. Home will be in Pennsylvania."

"You're part of a family-owned business."

"I've been mulling that over lately, and now I've got my eye on a cousin of mine who for years has made ends meet doing odd jobs. He's even worked at the mill when we've needed help, and I feel certain he'd jump at a chance to work at the lumbermill full-time."

"But you built this house expecting to always live here."

He moved closer, and her heart thumped like a dozen racing horses. "I can build another one, and I have no shortage of siblings willing to buy or rent it. Or, if we economize a bit, we could keep it for visits." He slowly reached for her hair, which cascaded from the loosely worn shawl that covered her head. His eyes moved over her face as he rubbed a lock between his fingers.

Suddenly aware of the quiet, empty home surrounding them, Beth eased back a step.

Jonah cleared his throat. "You should pin yourself together and join me in the living room."

Her cheeks burned, but she managed a nod. When her hair was in place and her prayer Kapp on, she walked down the hallway.

Jonah held a cup of coffee out to her. "I can't believe you're here."

"That sleigh ride…" She lifted the mug from his hand, but it was the man she drank in. "It was beyond all my best dreams."

"I was leery of driving a sleigh, but it turned out moderately worth it." He gave her a lopsided grin.

She lowered her eyes and took a sip of her drink. Did he know how much he stirred her—how he reached into the most hidden, dark parts of her soul and brought light and warmth?

He eased the mug from her hands, set it on the countertop, and stepped within an inch of her. "I love you, Beth. Everything I know about you. Everything I don't know. I love *you*." He intertwined his fingers with hers. "Will you marry me?"

Feeling a bit dizzy, she nodded. He lowered his face to hers. Within a breath of her, he paused, and then he gently pressed his lips against hers.

Her whole body trembled, and he pulled her into a hug, holding her as if she were a delicately wrapped gift. "You won't make me wait too long, will you?"

"I'd marry you today if I could."

He took a step back. "You surprise me, Beth."

"Me too."

He smiled that gentle, calm smile of his. And then he kissed her.

There was a loud knock on the door, and Amos hollered, "Coming in."

Beth's cheeks burned as she and Jonah put space between them. While Amos shut the front door, she peered up at Jonah and drew a shaky breath. "Pennsylvania, Jonah," she whispered. "Definitely, Pennsylvania is the place to live."

Jonah laughed. "That's what I said. That way your friends can break our windows instead of knocking on our door."

They laughed.

"Kumm." Jonah held out his hand. "It's time you met the rest of my family."

Book 2

The CHRISTMAS SINGING

A Romance from the Heart of Amish Country

CINDY WOODSMALL

One

*C*old darkness and the sugary aroma from the cake shop below surrounded Mattie as she slid a solid-colored dress over her head and tied her white apron in place. The Old Order Amish here in Ohio didn't wear the black aprons—a difference she enjoyed—and only those involved with baking wore the white apron from the waist down. After brushing her hair, she fastened it up properly and donned her prayer *Kapp*. Who needed a light or a mirror to get ready for the day? She'd been wearing similar clothes her whole life, and the Ohio Amish pinned up their hair in much the same way as she had back in Pennsylvania.

Now, cake decorating—that required good lighting and great attention to detail. And her favorite season for making specialty cakes—Christmas—was right around the corner.

Ready to take on a new day, she hurried down the rough-hewn steps that led into her shop, lit a kerosene lantern, and pulled on her coat while going out the back door. Before getting to the woodpile, she paused a moment, enjoying Berlin's lights. Illuminated white bulbs hung like beacons against the dark night. Although she missed her *Mamm* and *Daed,* this was home now, not Pennsylvania.

She scanned the silhouettes and shadows of nearby homes and shops. The golden full moon had a silky glow around it, a ring almost as clear and defined as the moon itself. What would it look like if she designed a cake with a halo?

Eager to make notes, she loaded wood into the crook of her arm and went inside. She dumped the logs in the bin and then stirred the embers in the potbelly stove and added kindling. Before her first customer arrived, she'd have the place toasty warm.

The shop was old and narrow, but Mattie loved it. When the previous owner, a man who sold saddles and such, decided to sell his place a few weeks before she moved here, her brother James had helped her buy and remodel it. They'd torn out all the old counters, workbenches, and shelving.

The ceiling, floors, and walls were made of unfinished, exposed wood. She'd put in a huge display case along the left wall, and a couple of small tables sat to the right. Stainless-steel sinks and a gas-powered commercial oven and refrigerator filled the back wall. Her work station, where she pieced together and decorated her cakes, sat a few feet away. Even in cooler weather, keeping the place warm without electricity wasn't much of an issue with the heat radiating from the oven and the wood stove. Hot summer weather was a little more problematic, but the many windows helped.

She began searching for her spiral notebook, which she often referred to as her brain. The pages of her combination sketch pad, scrapbook, and journal were covered with drawings, doodles, and pictures from magazines and newspapers. It'd been a gift for her twelfth birthday, and although the gift giver had broken her heart seven years later, she still appreciated the book. Her day planner was in the back of it, with the types of cakes she needed to make, due dates, and all her clients' names and phone numbers. Without it she wouldn't know how to run her store.

She knelt and looked under her work station. It was there, maybe two feet away. Reaching as far as she could, she touched the edge of the thick binder and grabbed it. Now where did she leave her pencil?

Is it behind your ear, Mattie Lane? Gideon's voice washed over her.

She shuddered, detesting hearing him inside her head, especially with the added use of the pet name *Mattie Lane. Lane* was not a part of her given name or her surname. When they first broke up, his voice had played constantly in her mind, but after three years these whispers from the past were rare.

They'd been good friends most of their lives. He was three years older than she, and it had stung when he began dating at sixteen. But worse than seeing him with other Amish girls was seeing him with *Englischer* girls. At eighteen, he'd stopped seeing others and told her that he'd decided to wait for her.

Their first date had taken place on her birthday, Christmas Eve, and she'd attended her first singing with Gideon. The magic of Christmas seemed to surround both of them as their voices rose in celebration of Christ's birth and the blessing of being together. Nothing in her life had ever compared to the emotion of that night, not even owning her own shop. For the next three years, they enjoyed the glorious Christmas singings together.

And then she caught him.

Her heartbreak had been compounded by confusion. *Nothing* had prepared her for his betrayal.

Pushing those thoughts away, she found a pencil lying next to the sink and jotted down notes about the halo. Then she made herself a quick breakfast. Before she'd swallowed the last of her coffee, she had four dozen muffins and four dozen cupcakes in the oven.

The cowbells hanging on the door chimed numerous times throughout the morning, and by noon she had sold the usual amount of baked goods for this time of year and had taken three new cake orders—for a birthday, a bridal shower, and a summer wedding. She couldn't think of anything more exciting than running Mattie Cakes.

She went to the phone and dialed her Mamm. One of the things she loved most about owning a shop was the permission to have a phone handy. She called her Mamm at least once a day.

Few women were as remarkable as her mother. She'd been forty-seven when she got pregnant with Mattie. But Mamm's health issues progressed from inconvenient at the time of Mattie's birth to life threatening by the time Mattie turned sixteen. Mattie had spent much of her life fearing she'd lose her mother. But when Mattie hesitated to move from Pennsylvania to Ohio, her mother had refused to let her stay in Apple Ridge.

After ten rings the answering machine clicked on. Since Mamm was seventy and her phone was in the shanty near the barn, Mattie rarely reached her on the first try of the day.

At the beep, Mattie said, "Good morning, Mamm and Daed. This is your adoring, favorite daughter calling." Mattie chuckled. "Being the only girl has perks... Anyway, I'm having a great day, and I want to hear about yours. I'll call back at two thirty. I hope you're dressed warmly. Love you both." If Mattie established a time she'd call back, Mamm never failed to be in the phone shanty, waiting to hear from her. Daed had set up a comfortable chair and a gas heater out there. She talked to her Daed too, but he didn't stay on the line long.

The bells on the shop door jingled again, and a cold blast of November air burst into the room.

Mattie's almost-five-year-old niece came barreling through the door, bundled up in her black winter coat and a wool scarf over her prayer Kapp. Mattie wondered if Esther had walked the half block from her house to the shop by herself or if the little girl's mother was trailing behind, pushing her two youngest children in a double stroller. Esther also had four older siblings, but all of them were in school during the day.

"Mattie Cakes!" the young girl cried.

Mattie chuckled at Esther's excitement. None of her nieces or nephews called her "Aunt Mattie" these days, but she found this nickname adorable.

Esther ran to her, clutching a silver lunch pail. "You didn't come home to eat, so I brought you some food."

"Denki." Mattie wasn't surprised when Esther held on to the pail. Her niece loved toting things.

Esther began her routine inspection of the store, beginning with the sink full of dirty cooking utensils. She enjoyed coming to the shop, and Mattie hoped that in seven or eight years, Esther might want to learn the trade. Esther's older sisters didn't seem to have any desire to make cakes.

Sol walked in, carrying a bow, a quiver full of arrows, and his camouflage duffel bag. He set it all behind her work counter, looking more confident than he used to. "Hi." He flashed a quick smile before looking down. Sometimes shy, he didn't keep eye contact for long.

They'd begun seeing each other on special occasions more than two years ago. Now they saw each other regularly, and unlike Gideon, Sol found getting along with young women a challenge. He was reserved and tended to mumble, but Mattie and Sol liked being together.

When the bell on the door jingled again but no one came in, Sol hurried to open it for Mattie's sister-in-law as she pushed the stroller into the room.

"Did you forget something, Mattie?" Dorothy asked. "Like coming home for lunch?"

Mattie glanced at the clock. "Sorry. I didn't realize how much time had passed."

Dorothy sighed. "I've heard that before."

"And you'll hear it again," Sol mumbled. A grin sneaked across his face as he stole a glance at Mattie. She wanted to hug him, but he liked to keep his distance before a hunt. He didn't bathe or shave for a day or two before leaving, not wanting to scare off the wild game by smelling of soap or aftershave.

Mattie held out her hands for the pail. "Thank you very

much, Esther. If your Mamm doesn't mind, I think you should pick out a cupcake."

Esther gave her the pail and gazed up at her mother.

Dorothy hesitated, probably calculating all sorts of mom things—like how many sweets Esther had eaten this week, if she'd had her fruits and vegetables today, and if Mattie was spoiling her. "Oh, all right."

Esther clapped and hurried to the display case housing the decorated cupcakes. "You made turkey cakes!" Each one had a tiny turkey head made of marzipan and tail feathers of icing.

"*Ya,* I did."

Dorothy stood near Mattie's work station and craned to see the display case. "You made so many."

"It's Thanksgiving next week. People have placed orders for most of those and will pick them up late this afternoon. I'll make even more for tomorrow's orders. The Englischer girls and boys have class parties before they're out for the holiday next week. This year I've gone an extra step. The feathers are not only a different color from the frosting, but they have a mildly different flavor too." Mattie opened the wood stove and stoked it before adding another piece of wood. "I think it's some of my best blending of colors and tastes yet...for cupcakes designed to look like turkeys."

Dorothy set the brake on the stroller and moved to a stool. "I still don't understand why you go to that much trouble for something that will be devoured in less than two minutes."

"Only the cake is gone. The memory will last much longer, perhaps days or a month or a lifetime. Just look at Esther."

The four-year-old was talking to herself, or to the cakes, as she tried to choose one.

Dorothy's face eased into a smile. "I guess I do understand. You know, come to think of it, James and I still talk about the ten-year anniversary cake you made for us." Dorothy sighed. "But we want to see you more. You sleep here and skip meals. At least hang the Out to Lunch sign and come eat with us."

Sol pulled a flashlight out of his bag and made sure it was working before taking a seat on his usual stool at the far end of her work station. "Would you feel better if she gave her word that she'd try to come home for lunch from now on?"

Dorothy laughed. "Ya, it would make me feel better…even though I know it won't change a thing."

Mattie held up her hand as if taking an oath. "I will do my best not to lose track of time and to follow all your advice."

"Wait until you have little ones and are trying to herd them toward the table," Dorothy teased.

Sol winked at Mattie. They were in agreement on this topic—they'd definitely marry one day, but it'd be a while.

Dorothy turned to her. "So what has you so preoccupied this time?"

Mattie grabbed her notepad. "Look at this." She opened the spiral-bound book and tapped the rough sketch of her halo cake. "Wouldn't this be an unusual wedding cake?"

Dorothy leaned in, wearing a slight frown. "I suppose if I were an Englischer, it'd snag my interest. Is that a net? Is it edible?"

"Oh, ya. And it's not a net. It's a halo…of sorts."

"How on earth will you get it to surround a cake in midair like that?"

Mattie splayed her fingers and waved her hands over the notebook. "I can do magic."

Dorothy chuckled. "Ya, magic that takes weeks of hard work."

A car horn tooted. Sol stood. "That's my ride."

"What zone are you headed for?" Mattie put several cupcakes in a bakery box.

"C." He shoved his flashlight into his duffel bag.

She was sure he'd told her the zone before, but she didn't try to keep his hunting schedule straight any more than he tried to keep up with the type of cake she needed to bake next.

He slung the bow and quiver over one shoulder and his duffel bag over the other. "We're going to a campsite in Hocking Hills. I have several tags, so I hope to bring back a few deer."

"The venison will come in handy this winter at the soup kitchen." She passed him the box of goodies.

"Denki." He studied her for a moment, grinning. "Don't get into any trouble while I'm gone."

It was his way of telling her that he cared. "I won't."

He opened the door. "See you in a few days."

"I'll be here." Mattie returned to her open scrapbook, wondering if she could fashion the framework for the halo out of hardened sugar.

Dorothy sighed. "Isn't there a limit on how much wild game the local charities will accept? Sol told James that he's going on a seven-day hunt less than a week after Thanksgiving."

"Ya. He is." Mattie pointed at her chicken scratch of a sketch. "I think I know how to make the halo. What if I made an edible dowel from my crispy rice concoction and anchored—"

"Something's wrong." Dorothy cut her off.

"With the halo idea?"

"No." Her sister-in-law placed her hand on the notebook. "I know Sol builds pallets from his parents' house, but even so, how does he manage to get off work so much?"

"As long as he meets his quota each week, he can spend

the rest of his time doing whatever he wants. He works long hours some days so he can take off when he wants. Is that a problem?"

"No…" Dorothy turned pages in the book without looking at it. "Honey, everyone in the family likes Sol. But…"

Mattie folded her arms, ready to defend herself. With seven big brothers, she knew how to stand her ground. "But what?"

"I keep waiting to see in you the zest that young people in love always have. It seems there's no more now than when you started courting two years ago. Am I wrong?"

Mattie shrugged, hoping to keep the conversation short. "Sol has all the traits I could want in a husband. Zest isn't on the list."

Dorothy leaned in. "When you love someone enough to marry him, you find him fascinating. You love being in the same room with him. You desire to bear his children. You have a bond that's so powerful you'll gladly overlook the things about him that will drive you crazy years later."

"What Sol and I have doesn't fit that description, but our bond is strong. Maybe letting each other pursue outside interests is more important than you think."

"He's not one of your brothers, Mattie. After fourteen years James and I still arrange our days to get as much time together as possible." She looked up at Mattie. "He draws me, Mattie, and I, him. People in love should have that."

Mattie once had that kind of relationship with Gideon, and Dorothy knew it. What she didn't understand was that Mattie and Sol's relationship was much better, at least for her. "Dorothy, I know you want the best thing for me, but you have to trust me. Sol and I are very happy."

Dorothy nodded, not looking convinced, but Mattie wasn't bothered by what she or the rest of the family thought. She knew what being with Sol meant.

The bell jingled, and more cold air rushed inside along with Willa Carter and her son. Excitement danced inside Mattie. The whole time she'd worked on Ryan's birthday cake, she looked forward to seeing his eyes light up when he saw it.

"Happy birthday, Ryan." She closed her notebook and set it aside.

"Mattie!" Dorothy lifted it off the wood stove. "Think... please."

"Oh, yes. Thanks." She thought in English and used it easily these days, a result of having regular contact with her non-Amish customers and friends. She turned to the little boy. He was so cute in his blue jeans and cowboy hat. "How old are you today?"

Ryan held up four fingers. "I'm this many!"

Mattie stepped out from behind the counter. "You are so big!" She turned to Mrs. Carter, who was jamming her car keys into her bright red purse. "How are you today?"

"Frazzled." She unbuttoned her plaid coat. "I forgot this place sat so far back from the other stores, and I parked halfway down the block."

Dorothy shifted her stroller out of the center of the floor. "We'd better go."

Mattie grabbed a small dessert box and moved to the case of cupcakes, where her niece stood. "Did you decide which one you want?"

Esther pointed one out, and Mattie boxed it up. "Here you go."

"You eat the lunch we brought," Dorothy whispered.

"Okay." Mattie mocked a loud whisper in return.

Esther shook her little forefinger at Mattie. "I'm comin' back to check after I have my cupcake and milk."

"You do that." Mattie held the door for them before returning her attention to Ryan. "Come." She went to the refrigerator, and as she removed the plastic cover from the cake, the smell of chocolate wafted out. She carried the cake over to Ryan.

Ryan gasped. "Mommy, look!"

A smiling teddy bear stared up at them. The three-dimensional bear had come out just as she'd hoped, and the look in Ryan's eyes made every hour of effort worth it. This wasn't her first time to create a bear cake, but she'd used the new specialty tips that had arrived earlier in the week, and the results looked even better than she'd imagined. The bear's claws, paws, and facial features nearly jumped out of the box.

"It's perfect, Mattie." Mrs. Carter's smile reflected appreciation. "When my girlfriend told me about your shop, I never expected such excellent work."

The pleasure of this moment would linger with Mattie for a long time. "Thank you."

"I have a daughter turning thirteen next month. She ice-skates, does ballet, and plays basketball. Think you could design a cake around one of her activities?"

"Sure." Mattie grabbed her scrapbook and flipped it open. "Or I could do one that showcases all three." She showed her several pages.

Mrs. Carter pointed at a triple-tier cake. "That one."

"I can put a different sport on each tier."

"She'll love that!" Mrs. Carter turned away quickly, scooping up Ryan, who had begun to race around the small store.

Mattie jotted down a few notes, feeling exuberant, then set the book aside. "I'll call you next week, and we'll make specific plans. Let me help you with this cake." Since Mrs. Carter was parked so far away, Mattie moved Ryan's cake to a stainless steel utility cart and grabbed her coat.

Mrs. Carter secured the squirming boy in one arm and pulled out a check she'd already written.

Without glancing at it, Mattie slid it into her coat pocket and wheeled the cart toward the front of the store.

"I hate asking you to leave the store unattended, but he is so wound up."

"I don't have anything baking in the oven, so it'll be fine."

Sol sat in the front passenger seat, half listening to the conversation between Amish Henry, his brother Daniel, and the driver, Eric. All were a little younger than he and eager to be on this trip.

Eric turned down the radio. "So my neighbor, the one with two hundred acres who hasn't let anyone hunt on it for more than thirty years…"

That caught Sol's attention. "Thirty years?"

"Yeah, he's always been real picky about who he lets on his property, but he said we could hunt it. Says the deer have really been ripping up his cornfields the last few years."

"Let's do it!" Amish Henry said.

"There's a catch," Eric said. "His mother is elderly and doesn't want to hear gunshots or have hunters stomping around on the land, so we'd be limited to Christmas Eve and Day, because they'll be away visiting relatives then."

Reality overtook Sol's moment of excitement. "I'm out. I can't go on Christmas Eve. That's Mattie's birthday, and she's got a thing about us attending the Christmas singing."

"Must be nice to have a girl," Daniel said. "I might give up hunting altogether if I had one."

"Not hunt at all?" Sol laughed. "If that's what she wants, you've got the wrong girl."

Eric clicked on the turn signal. "Why don't you hunt just in the morning on Christmas Eve and Christmas Day? You could probably tag your quota and still be back before noon. Come on, man. It'll be great."

"Ya, maybe." Sol tapped the dessert box that held the cupcakes. "I want to talk to Mattie before I agree to anything."

Eric pulled into the parking lot of a fish-and-wildlife store. "I need to get a few things."

They all piled out with him. Sol didn't need anything, but it never hurt to look around. He went to the knife case to see if they had anything new.

"Can I show you a particular knife?" the man behind the counter asked.

"Nah, I'm just looking. Thanks."

A girl stopped beside him, and his peripheral vision told him she was Amish. She pointed at various knives. "He'd like one of every kind he doesn't already have." He recognized the voice. Katie King.

Sol's insides knotted, and he stepped away from her. Their eyes met, and she smiled. She had dark hair and even darker eyes. He'd always thought she was pretty. But looks weren't what mattered to him. It was the way two people fit into each other's lives that really meant something.

His gut twisted with nerves, and he wished she'd leave. Mattie had never once made him uncomfortable, even when they first talked after the singings. She was the one who had approached him each time, but she did it in a reserved way— not staring or saying anything that he didn't know how to respond to. He'd never asked to take a girl home from a singing. Mattie, in her quiet, self-assured way, had asked him.

Katie put one hand on her hip. "I sure see you out with your friends a lot. I guess you shy guys have to stick together. It's a shame though, ya?"

Sol shrugged, not at all sure what answer she was fishing for. He never knew how to carry on a conversation with someone like Katie—all bubbly and blabbering about nothing at all. Mattie said what needed to be said and talked about things that made sense.

Amish Henry stepped out from an aisle, looking as if he wanted to rescue Sol but wasn't sure how. "You about ready?"

"Ya." Sol nodded. "Bye." He started to leave.

Katie stepped in front of him. "I think it'd be neat to climb a tree stand in the early morning hours and wait for dawn."

Sol wished Mattie would suddenly appear. He didn't understand women at all. Was Katie just being silly? He took another step back, studying her shoes, which were half covered in mud.

Katie angled her head, catching Sol's eye. "I hope you have a good trip." She turned and walked off.

Sol drew a deep breath, wondering if he'd ever get over some people making him feel as if he had a ten-pound block of ice in his gut.

Amish Henry adjusted his black felt hat. "I think she was hoping you'd ask her for a date."

The words jolted Sol. Her small talk and mannerisms made no sense to him, but maybe Amish Henry was right. He watched her leave. "Nah. She just wants to sit in somebody's tree stand."

"If that's what she wants from you, she'll never get it. Climbing into your tree stand? No way."

Sol laughed. "*Kumm* on. Let's find Daniel and Eric. We've got a long way to go before we can set up camp."

Two

After getting the cake into Mrs. Carter's vehicle and bidding her and her son good-bye, Mattie saw someone coming out of Today and Forever Books, where Mackenzie worked. They hadn't had a girl chat in weeks, and Mattie had been wanting time with her. She scurried toward the store, pushing the service cart along.

She parked the cart out front and stepped inside. Mackenzie stood behind the coffee shop counter, serving someone. She had on just enough makeup to give her color and wore a yellowish-gold sweater with a turkey on it.

Mackenzie glanced up, almost as if sensing she were there. "Hey!" Her friend's long, straight brown hair swayed as she came out from behind the counter and toward her. The store belonged to Mackenzie's grandfather, and as the current manager, she could take a break without asking anyone's permission. "Tell me you have time to visit over a whole pot of coffee."

Mattie hugged her. "I have time to visit over a pot of coffee."

"It's about time. I was going to come to Mattie Cakes when I caught a minute. We need to talk about the cake to celebrate our shop's thirtieth anniversary."

"Love the idea." Mattie slid out of her coat and tossed it over the back of a chair.

Mackenzie took a seat at the small round table. "Anyone scheduled to pick up an order today?"

"Not until almost closing time, and I've already finished preparing everything. But if you want to talk about my making something for the store's anniversary, I don't have my brain with me."

Mackenzie laughed. "I thought you never went anywhere without your notebook."

"Oh, I do…because I forget everything all the time. The day will come when I'll be working in the shop, a customer will walk in and give me a funny look, and I'll realize that I'm in my nightgown because I forgot to get dressed." Mattie laughed. "That's a real fear I have."

"Now I know what to get you for Christmas. I'll buy you a flannel nightgown. That way, if you do forget to get dressed, you'll look cute anyway."

"That's your best solution? That's just sad." Mattie tried to keep the grin off her face. "The answer is to come by my shop early, before any customers can arrive, and make sure I'm dressed."

"Before the sun's up? Sorry, but we're not that good of friends." Mackenzie's eyes lit up. "Okay…I'll loan you paper so we can talk about that cake I want."

Mackenzie stood and went into a back room.

The aroma of fresh-brewed coffee in the old wooden bookstore reminded Mattie of her shop, and the smell of books, both old and new, mixed together in a delightful scent.

Mattie looked at the coffee shop's display case, noticing how few muffins and cupcakes were left. Mackenzie's grandfather came by Mattie Cakes at nine thirty each morning and bought several dozen freshly made muffins and cupcakes. She made muffins only for herself and this store. Otherwise she was all about cakes.

Mackenzie sat down with paper, pen, two cups of coffee, and a basket holding cream, sugar, and stirrers. Mattie glanced at the clock.

"You need to get back?" Mackenzie asked.

"Not for a bit yet. When I called Mamm this morning, I left a message saying I'd call back at two thirty."

Mackenzie flipped her silky hair over her shoulder. "You say you forget everything, but I've never known you to forget to call your mom when you said you would."

Mattie poured a tiny cup of cream into her coffee before

stirring it. "Mamm means a lot to me, and with her health problems…I feel a need to stay connected. I always have. Plus, I appreciate her wisdom. When the time comes that she's not here, I can still rely on what she has taught me."

"I've never even thought about losing my mom. That seems morbid to me."

"My mom's seventy now, and her health's been delicate my whole life, so I've had to face the possibility of losing her."

"Isn't it emotionally exhausting to live as if she's going to die?"

"It's been a challenge to find a balance between caring and being burdened. But I think we've found it. The trick is not to let the power of what might happen tomorrow ruin today. She was diagnosed with lupus when I was sixteen, and she taught me how not to let her illness pull me under. But those lessons didn't come easily."

Mattie and Mackenzie talked for a long time, eventually discussing the type and size of cake Mattie needed to make as she took notes on loose-leaf paper. Mackenzie refilled their coffee mugs time and again. Mattie took another quick look at the clock and stood. "I need to go call Mamm now."

"You can use our phone."

Mattie went behind the counter and dialed her Mamm. Her mother picked up before the first ring finished.

"Mattie, sweetheart, is that you?"

"Ya, Mamm, it's me."

While she talked, a strange aroma caught her attention—chimney smoke, she guessed. Most of the nearby Englischer homes had fireplaces or wood stoves, but they were used more often in the evenings. The scent seemed strong. "Ya, Mamm, I'm coming home for Thanksgiving next week, and James and Dorothy want you and Daed to come for Christmas again this year."

"Is Sol coming with you for Thanksgiving?"

"I think he'll come this time. I'll know for sure in a few days."

Mackenzie slipped on her coat and went outside. Mattie continued talking with her Mamm, but she noticed a small group of shop owners standing outside without their coats. Some stared toward the sky. Others appeared to be talking intently.

Mamm wanted to know all about the cakes she'd been making and how she and Sol were doing, and most of all she wanted to be reminded over and over when they'd see each other again. "Next week, Mamm. I'll be there late Wednesday and stay until late Saturday."

Mackenzie tapped on the window, motioning for her.

"Mamm, I need to go." She'd barely gotten the words out of her mouth when her mother said good-bye and hung up. That was her Mamm. She loved to talk to Mattie, but she never wanted to hold her up if she needed to work.

Mackenzie stepped inside. "Mattie, there's smoke coming from somewhere down the block."

Concern charged through her. She put on her coat and gathered the scattered papers filled with diagrams and notes for the cake. When she stepped outside, she saw black smoke billowing from the direction of her shop.

Mattie's heart burned as if it were on fire. She ran down the sidewalk with Mackenzie right beside her. She turned the corner where her place sat off the main road. Flames licked the walls and roof.

"No!" Tears sprang to her eyes.

Mackenzie pushed numbers on her cell phone.

Through one of the first-floor windows, Mattie saw movement inside. A flash of burgundy caught her eye, reminding her of the dress her niece had on that morning.

"Esther!" Mattie threw down the papers she was carrying and took off running.

"Wait." Mackenzie grabbed her arm and stopped her. "You can't go in there."

Mattie jerked free and ran inside. "Esther!" She couldn't see anything but thick gray smoke. Turbulent flames lashed out but did nothing to light her way. "Esther!" Heat seared her dress, and her lungs burned. Wondering if Esther had tried to get away from the fire by going upstairs, Mattie dodged flames and embers and hurried to the second floor.

Three

The empty, almost-finished home echoed as Gideon built the doorjambs. Nothing felt as good as having the strength to work. It was something he never took for granted. Not anymore. Today he could hold a hammer and make a nail disappear into wood with little effort. But what about tomorrow?

He ignored the question and placed a level on one side of the closet doorframe, making sure the casing was aligned correctly. He struggled to keep the wood in place as he shifted from one tool to the next. Work on an oversized closet like this required two men, but the rest of the Beiler Construction team labored to get a new home dried in before winter. If snow or rain hit before the house was complete enough to keep the weather out, they'd have to replace damaged particle board, framing, and insulation, and all work might have to stop until spring.

His brother had promised Beth and Jonah, the owners of this house, that Gideon would be the one to complete it, including the punch list. He still had a ways to go on the job.

"Hello?" Jonah called.

"Master bedroom," Gideon answered.

Jonah's distinct tempo echoed through the unfinished place. He was only thirty, but as a teenager he had been injured in a sleigh ride accident that left him walking with a cane. "I came to lend a hand." Jonah already had on his tool belt. "I've cleared my schedule with the boss, and I have the rest of today and most of tomorrow to be your assistant."

"Good. I could use it."

Jonah was an artist by trade. He carved beautiful scenery into wood, bringing it to life, but he'd been a lead carpenter while building his previous home. And then he met the woman he lovingly referred to as "the boss." Now Jonah had little time to devote to working on the new home he and Beth would live in. After they were engaged, Jonah had spent another year living in Ohio, fulfilling contracts by carving doors, chairs, mantels, and cabinets for a cabin resort near him. As soon as he'd finished that job, he'd moved here to be near Beth. Since then he'd spent his days carving large items to sell and helping Beth and her aunt Lizzy expand and operate the dry goods store.

Without needing instruction, Jonah steadied the far side

of the closet's doorframe while Gideon leveled and nailed it into place.

They each added the needed hardware and then hung the folding wooden doors. It took a bit of effort to get them on the runners and operating smoothly.

"So what's next, hanging more doors or doing trim work?" Jonah asked.

"Baseboards and window casings. Can't hang doors. There's some sort of holdup on those," Gideon teased. The problem was that Jonah hadn't yet found the time to carve scriptures on them, and Beth didn't want them hung until they were completed. Jonah was capable of carving beautiful scenery, but since this would hang inside his home, he needed to use caution so that no one in the church considered the visual adornments a graven image.

Jonah laughed. "I've assured my fiancée I'll get to them by the time she and I have two or three little ones running around. But regardless of how busy it gets, it feels so good to be living here now. Beth said you moved from here and lived elsewhere for a couple of years, right?"

"Ya." Gideon hoped Jonah wouldn't ask anything else. He did his best not to lie to anyone, but he had secrets to keep. Falsehoods weren't the only thing he detested. He'd hated living in a city away from everything familiar and only returning for the Christmas holidays.

"Jonah." Beth's voice came through the Amish intercom—PVC piping sticking up through the floor and running underground to the store. "Are you at the house?"

Jonah moved closer to the pipe and spoke into it. "Ya. You need something?"

"I'll walk over. I just wanted to be sure you were there."

"We're in the master bedroom."

"Denki."

Gideon chuckled while measuring the length of the wall. "I've always thought Beth had a good head on her shoulders for business."

"She does. She's amazing at it."

Gideon took note of the length of the wall and released the tape measure. "Then how come every time I turn around she's asking you for your opinion? It's like she can't make a decision lately without your input."

Jonah slid an uncut baseboard onto a makeshift bench. "In any serious relationship, if you don't gather your partner's opinion before making a decision that impacts you both, you're just storing up trouble for the future."

Gideon scoffed. "If you figure out a way to avoid trouble in relationships, let me know, okay?"

He measured the board and marked it. Sometimes watching Beth and Jonah interact was like sitting on the porch of an old, run-down trailer while looking at wealthy neighbors. It didn't matter how much he loved them, the reality of their happy relationship chafed.

Three years ago Gideon had let go of the woman he loved. The only woman, really.

He set the wood on the miter box and lowered the battery-powered saw to the board. He never talked to Beth or Jonah about what he had done or why. Actually, he never talked to anyone about it. His family had put together pieces of the truth, but no one discussed it.

Despite Gideon's secretive nature, Jonah seemed to see past his silence. Jonah's perceptiveness was one reason he'd won the heart of the once-wounded and distant Beth Hertzler.

Gideon could only imagine what it'd be like to have the privilege of marrying *the one*. He'd found his *one*. Thoughts of Mattie Lane tormented him. She was…

He stopped his thoughts cold. "Good grief," he mumbled, trying to focus on the work at hand. He took the wood to the base of the wall.

"Having one of those days?" Jonah grabbed one end of the plank, and they set it on the well-placed shims.

"I guess." Gideon hammered nails into his end of the baseboard while Jonah steadied the other end.

Beth's steps echoed through the empty rooms.

Jonah looked up and gave her a welcoming smile that ended quickly. "Something wrong?"

"Remember me telling you about my cousin Mattie, the one I wanted to make our wedding cake?"

Gideon kept pounding in nails as if he had no interest in hearing this conversation. The fact was, he always wanted to know what was happening in Mattie's life. But he could bet money on what Beth was going to say next. Mattie had once again turned down their offer to pay her way home for the wedding and had declined making a cake for their big day.

She didn't return to Apple Ridge often. He knew she had too much business in Berlin, Ohio, to close up shop and come here for a wedding. Even if she could hire someone to fill in for her, she wasn't likely to do so, not even for Beth. He could thank himself for that. Mattie Lane avoided him at all costs. She didn't have to be the one to leave home. He'd left, and he hadn't planned on coming back.

Beth cleared her throat. "Her place burned to the ground this afternoon."

Gideon wheeled around. "What happened?"

"I don't think anyone really knows."

"But Mattie Lane must have some idea how it started."

Beth glanced at Jonah. "She's in the hospital, unconscious."

Dizziness hit Gideon full force, and the hammer in his hand fell to the floor with a thud. *God, not Mattie Lane, please.* "What happened?"

"I can't say for sure. Her sister-in-law called the dry goods store. Aunt Lizzy's taking a message to her parents."

"Beth," Gideon said, "did Dorothy give any indication of how Mattie's doing?"

"She said she has only minor burns, but she inhaled a lot of smoke."

"Smoke inhalation can do as much damage to the insides as flames do to the outside. I don't understand. Her place had excellent smoke detectors."

"How would you know?"

Gideon had made sure Mattie's brother had installed good ones, but he wouldn't tell Beth that. "Go on, Beth."

"Oh, ya." Beth shook her head, as if to refocus her thoughts. "Dorothy said a friend of Mattie's told her that Mattie wasn't at the shop when it caught on fire."

"Then how did she inhale so much smoke?"

"When Mattie arrived, she thought her niece was inside, so she ran into the building, but the shop was empty."

"That's just like her, risking her own life to help when it's not even needed." Gideon wasn't far from having a raging fit.

Beth tilted her head, studying him. "I don't understand you. If you feel this strongly about her, why'd you break up with her to date other girls?"

He rubbed his forehead, trying to control his emotions.

"Even though we aren't together, that doesn't mean I don't care about her well-being. I want what's best for her, and until now that's exactly what she's had. Ya?"

Beth's face creased with lines of concern. "Ya. She loved building up her business and getting better at making decorative cakes." She chuckled. "From the time she was little bitty, she used to get into such fixes, and you always managed to get her out of them." She turned to Jonah. "Mattie is six years younger than me, about three years younger than Gideon. Her ability to create cakes seems boundless, but she can be as flighty as a sparrow."

Beth grinned at Gideon. "Remember when she was fourteen and she won the Hershey's Cocoa Classic contest for her age group? She was so excited that a few minutes after the announcement, she walked straight into a metal pole and about knocked herself unconscious. You grabbed her before she hit the ground and carried her all over those grounds searching for the medic."

Gideon hadn't thought about that in years. "That's classic Mattie Lane." He drew a breath, knowing he had to see her, even at a distance. "Listen, I know you want your home done in time for the wedding to take place here, but I need to check on her for myself. I won't hang around. I just...need to see her."

"We're fine." Jonah picked up the hammer in front of Gideon's feet. "You do what you need to."

Beth pressed a small piece of paper into his hand. "This has the name of the hospital and her room number."

Gideon hurried to the dry goods store and wasted no time calling driver after driver, trying to find someone who could drop what they were doing and take him to see Mattie Lane, hopefully one who didn't mind pushing the speed limit a little.

⁂

Sol went ahead of the other three hunters, going deeper and deeper into the woods. He could hear them talking as they trailed behind.

He took a deep whiff of the air around him. Cold and earthy. He loved the outdoors. The restlessness of the nocturnal creatures after the sun began to slip behind the horizon. The brilliance of stars at this time of year. The beauty of being in a tree stand as dark yielded to the first rays of the sun. The exuberance of the animals at daybreak.

He wished Mattie would come with him just once. They didn't have to hunt. A perfect spot on a hill or in a tree stand and a pair of binoculars was all she'd need to learn that everything worth doing in a day didn't take place inside her cake shop.

He spotted the clearing of the campsite some twenty feet

ahead. As soon as he arrived at the camp, he quickly set up his tent, and while the others put up theirs, he gathered wood and started a fire. The campsite had level ground, a fire pit, and a creek that provided both fresh water and the gurgling sound he loved to hear while falling asleep.

Within an hour they'd had a simple meal of hot dogs and were sitting around the fire ready to talk about nothing.

"Hey, Sol." Amish Henry sat on a nearby rock with his forearms propped on his knees. "The three of us have been wondering about something."

"Ya, what's that?"

"You couldn't get a girl before Mattie, and now that you have her, others are looking your way. It's like you had to get a girl to catch the eye of a girl."

Nothing felt as right as having Mattie. He had someone to think about wherever he was and someone to go home to.

"You know, what Amish Henry said is true," Daniel added.

Sol hadn't really thought about it but had noticed a few girls looking his way during singings and at church services. "I've never asked to take a girl home from a singing. Not even Mattie."

"Plenty of older single guys were ready to fight over her," Daniel said. "What'd you do different?"

"Nothing. When she came up to me after the singings, I

talked to her. She didn't mind that I didn't have much to say. I wanted to ask to take her home, but I couldn't. Not then. I think I could now. Maybe it's not having a girl to get a girl as much as having confidence."

"Ya," Daniel said. "You're confident you're not interested in anyone else, and suddenly other girls are looking your way."

"Wait," Amish Henry said. "You mean *she* asked *you*?"

"Hey," Sol said, trying to change the subject, "Mattie packed five cupcakes." As Sol rose to his feet, he noticed shafts of light splashing here and there. "I think I see flashlights coming toward us." Sol strode that way. "Hello?"

"We're looking for Sol Bender."

A beam of light flashed in his face. "You found me."

"We've been looking for you since four o'clock. Mattie's brother sent us…"

Their voices muffled in his ears. The night air closed in around him, and everything that had seemed right about coming here became heavy.

※

After forty-five minutes of calling every driver he knew, Gideon found one. Twenty minutes later Gary arrived at the dry goods store, and they began the trek to the hospital in Berlin. Gary flipped radio stations and tried to engage Gideon in conversation the whole way, but it was the longest, most miserable six-hour trip he'd ever made.

Thoughts of Mattie Lane tormented him. He didn't care how cliché it sounded—there was not another woman like her.

She had a smile that all but swallowed her. When she was tickled about something, which happened often, her cheeks turned a color similar to her reddish-blond hair. It wasn't a blush as much as her enthusiasm glowing from within.

She had a gentle side and would do anything for those she loved. Even as a little girl and teen, when she was given the slightest chance to get free of the heaviness and concerns over her mother's chronic illness, Mattie Lane radiated joy—like sunlight streaming through storm clouds.

But when her mother had become seriously ill six years ago, Mattie Lane struggled. She'd deny it, but he knew the truth, had witnessed it time and again—the tragedies of others weighed more on her than on most folks. And he imagined that the destruction of her property would be crushing.

Gary yawned as he entered the hospital's parking lot. It'd been dark for most of the trip here, but the clock on the dashboard said it was only eleven. He stopped the car near the front of the hospital. "I'll park and then go to the waiting room on her floor."

"Thanks." Gideon jumped out and hurried through the automatic doors. He barely took note of anything as he rode the elevator to the third floor. He walked past the nurses' station, found Mattie Lane's room, and opened the door.

His chest physically hurt when he saw her. She didn't look like herself at all. Her face was pale, and she wore no prayer Kapp. A large patch of gauze was taped to the side of her neck, and it continued down past the edge of her hospital gown. A small white tube hung from the side of her mouth, and a larger beige one was attached to her arm. A plastic apparatus on her right index finger glowed.

"Hello," said a female voice, and he looked up. The woman, wearing a blue uniform, stood at the head of Mattie Lane's bed, messing with a bag of liquid. She smiled. "Visiting hours are over. I sent the rest of her family home awhile ago."

"I came as soon as I heard, and it took me hours to get here."

"Ah, then I suppose you can stay for a little bit."

"Is...she okay?"

"She will be."

"Are you sure?"

"Yes," she said quietly. "Dr. Grady said she's a lucky young woman. Emotionally traumatized, but she sustained relatively few physical injuries."

Relief hit so hard it made his legs weak. A machine behind her head indicated that her heart rate was strong and steady. And other than the gauze traipsing down the right side of her neck and shoulder, she didn't have many outward signs of wounds. But fresh fears began to surface.

"Any internal injuries?"

"I can't give out that kind of information, but I can say that she's had every necessary test run and is receiving the proper treatment."

"Has she woken up?"

"Yes, for a few minutes here and there, but she's groggy from being put to sleep for some of the tests. I imagine she'll be released in a day or two."

Gideon sank into a chair, whispering thanks to God as the woman left. He missed Mattie so much it hurt, but he'd done the right thing. He knew he had.

Her face reflected pain as she shifted. Her eyes opened for a brief second, then closed again. "You're here," she whispered hoarsely.

"I'm here, Mattie Lane."

A faint smile crossed her lips, and she reached for him. His heart thudded wildly, latching on to these few moments. Desire for a life with her swept him away, and needlelike pinpricks ran over his skin from his head to his feet.

Just a few more moments with her—surely God would grant him that much.

He took her limp hand in his and was rendered powerless by the connection. It'd been so long since he'd felt the soft, delicate skin of her fingers. Confusion enclosed his thoughts. What was he doing? He'd broken up with her for good reasons, ones that stood almost as insurmountable today as they were then.

Almost.

She squeezed his hand. His mind went crazy with longing. But a clear vision of what little he had to offer her splashed icy water on his hopes.

"S…s…" Her eyes fluttered but didn't open.

His mouth went dry. She wanted Sol Bender. Of course she did, and that's how it should be. Maybe her feathery light smile moments ago hadn't been because she'd seen or heard him. Who knew what she was aware of or thinking as she drifted in and out of consciousness? No matter who she called for, Gideon had to get out before she opened her eyes and saw him. Easing her hand onto the bed, he stood.

"Gideon?" she whispered.

Finding it hard to breathe, he turned to leave. A man wearing camouflage gear stood in the doorway. He swallowed hard. Gideon had opened the door for Sol to walk into Mattie's life, yet jealousy clawed at him.

Had Sol heard Mattie whisper his name?

Gideon shifted. "The reports were vague, so I came to check on her."

Faint recognition of some sort went through Sol's eyes. "Have we met?"

He forced himself to hold out his hand—this man was Mattie's future, after all. "Gideon Beiler."

The expression on Sol's face showed disbelief. "You're kidding me."

Embarrassment smothered Gideon. How could he possibly justify being here?

"Sol Bender." He finally shook his hand. "She and I are together now, have been for a while."

Gideon swallowed hard. He racked his brain, trying to think of the right thing to say. "I know it may not seem like it, but I'm glad for her."

Skepticism entered Sol's eyes before he went to the far side of the bed and touched the back of her hand. "Mattie?"

She didn't respond. But her smooth face and rhythmic breathing indicated she was sleeping peacefully…obviously soothed by her boyfriend's presence.

"Mattie?" Sol repeated as he cradled her hand, but she didn't rouse.

Gideon felt like an intruder, but he couldn't make himself leave.

Sol peeled out of his hunting jacket. "You can stay if you want to," he mumbled. "But she's not going to like that you're here. It'll just add more stress." Sol gently brushed hair off her forehead.

Gideon steadied the ache inside his chest. He'd done the right thing to end their relationship. He was sure of it, and if given a chance to do that time over, he'd set her free again. But that didn't make seeing her in love with someone else any easier.

Four

Mattie stood in front of her brother's home, her mood as dark and cold as the night surrounding her. The street lamps peered through the fog as Sol loaded her bags into the rig. She'd shared Thanksgiving earlier today at her brother's place. Dorothy had made quite a feast, but Mattie had barely stomached eating. All she could see in her mind's eye was the ruins of Mattie Cakes.

Her brother put a fresh car battery in the floorboard and attached wires to it so the headlights worked. "I know you don't want to go back to Pennsylvania right now, but there's nothing you can do here until we get the issues settled with the insurance company, and that's going to take about four weeks. Then we can look for a place to rent and convert it into a usable bakeshop until we can rebuild this spring." James put his hand on her shoulder. "Besides, Mamm wants her only daughter to come home for a while after all that's happened. And I think maybe you could use a little time away from here."

She gazed at where Mattie Cakes had stood only a week earlier. Through the foggy night air, she could see the jagged, charred remnants of her shop two hundred feet away. She was grateful the flames and sparks hadn't set any other buildings on fire. But the old wood Mattie Cakes was built with had ignited like a box of kitchen matches, and her ovens, pans, utensils, and supplies had melted or been damaged beyond repair. The worst loss was her scrapbook with all her notes, pictures, and magazine cutouts of specialty cakes.

Dorothy hugged her. "As soon as we get the insurance straightened out, we'll buy the materials to rebuild. Then in the spring we'll have a shop raising to rival any barn raising you've ever witnessed."

"Denki." Mattie held her tight, not wanting to leave the place she now called home. But she released her and climbed into the rig.

Her parents had made the trip here last week, visiting her in the hospital every day until she was released. Then Mamm had returned to Pennsylvania a couple of days ago, needing to get ready for the traditional Thanksgiving meal at her home with her six other sons and their wives and children. But once Mamm got home, she couldn't rest with Mattie elsewhere, so she beckoned her daughter to return to Apple Ridge. Mattie's siblings were concerned about Mamm and were also urging

Mattie to come—without any further delay for Mamm's sake. So here she was, at the end of Thanksgiving Day, miserable, and yet packed and headed to Pennsylvania.

No one expected to be able to rebuild the shop in the dead of winter, but she wasn't staying in Pennsylvania until warmer weather arrived. She'd managed to talk Mamm into letting her return to Ohio in time for Christmas so she and Sol could attend the Christmas singing together.

Sol climbed in beside her. He took the reins in hand and slapped them against the horse's back as she waved to James and Dorothy. The clip-clop of the hoofs against the pavement echoed in the quietness, and she settled back in her seat. Sol eased his hand over hers as he drove toward Strasburg, where they'd meet up with a driver who'd agreed to take her to the train station. Later, a woman named Gloria, who often drove her cousin Beth, would meet Mattie at the station in Pennsylvania.

Mattie tried to steady her pounding heart by reminding herself that the journey ahead was simply keeping the promise she'd made to come home if Mamm ever needed her. But the rampant thudding inside her chest reminded her that giving one's word was much easier than keeping it.

As soon as she arrived in Pennsylvania, she needed to finish contacting all her clients to cancel their orders. All her records had been lost in the fire, but she'd called every person she could remember in order to cancel orders that had been made. Her thoughts were too cloudy to recall everyone. It'd be awful if someone showed up at her store expecting a cake and saw the shop in ashes.

If she could find a place in Berlin to keep working, she would. But baking decorative cakes required ample workspace and a large oven. Dorothy's kitchen couldn't accommodate Mattie's needs, nor could Mackenzie's shop. Mattie didn't want to cancel all the orders for the next four to six months, but she could think of no solutions, and she was heartsick over it.

The midnight jaunt to Strasburg left Mattie feeling as if she were a character in one of those old movies playing in the Englischer homes where she used to baby-sit. Danger always lurked in the misty darkness.

Even under the shroud of night, Sol looked capable and relaxed. She wished she could be more like him in that way. "As skittish as a horse on a highway" defined her personality of late, but changes in plans, even unfair ones, never shook Sol.

He glanced her way and smiled.

"Would you sing for me?"

He put his arm around her shoulders, and she moved in closer while he sang, *"Welcher nun Gott mill lieben thun."* As he sang, she considered the lyrics—"Whoever now wants to love God, let him first love his brother. Lay down his life for him, as Christ gave Himself for us in death…out of love and mercy."

Was Sol trying to tell her that she needed to be more gracious about having to go home? Irritability churned inside her as it had ever since she woke up in the hospital. She had to constantly fight the urge to gripe or cry about everything.

He pulled in front of the driver's home, brought the rig to a halt, and turned off the lights. "You'll be back before you know it."

The front door of the home opened, and Sharon Wells held up one finger. "Be there in just a few." She disappeared into her home again.

Sharon had driven Mattie to and from the train station whenever Mattie needed a lift. It was too far to drive a rig to the station in Alliance, and not many drivers were willing to take her there at one in the morning.

Another round of sadness swept through Mattie. She longed for the comfort of her shop, its vanilla scent and the warmth of the oven. "Could you please think of something soothing to say?"

Sol removed his hat and scratched his head. "Your folks asked, and you agreed." He got out of the rig, went around to her side of the buggy, and opened the door. "They've paid for two drivers and a train ticket. You can't get cold feet now."

That didn't make her feel any better, but she knew that he intended for his no-nonsense explanation to be comforting. She climbed out as he grabbed her bags. "You didn't pack much."

"I'd have even less if Mackenzie hadn't given me a stack of magazines to take with me. Most of my belongings were in the attic room of my shop. I've already told you that."

"Yep, you did. I was just making sure you hadn't left something behind." He set the luggage down.

She chuckled. "You are such a liar, Sol Bender. You know good and well that you simply forgot I'd told you."

He swallowed her in a gentle hug. "Who is going to keep me straight while you're gone?"

She waited for the strength of his arms to absorb some of her nervousness. "No one if you know what's good for you."

He tilted her chin upward. "No matter how long you're gone, I'll be as faithful as if you were standing next to me."

Sol wasn't much of a talker. He usually said what he needed to express in quips or shy smiles. But he understood what she needed from him. She wiped fresh tears off her cheeks. "I'm so sick of crying."

"Well, we agree on that at least." He was teasing her, but she was sure her recent behavior had taxed him. "Maybe you need this trip, Mattie."

"Oh, you just want to get rid of me so you can return to your hunting free of all guilt."

He kissed her. "Can't blame a guy for trying."

She backed away and pulled an envelope from her purse. "This is the number to Hertzlers' store. It'll be the easiest way to get a message to me." She'd given him this information twice already, but if she knew Sol, he'd already misplaced it. He was a lot like her when it came to misplacing things. But on nights like this, when she needed his help at one in the morning, he never muttered the slightest complaint.

Sharon came out of her home and unlocked her van.

Sol put her luggage in the trunk and closed it. He stifled a yawn as he waited for Mattie to get in the passenger's seat. She waved, and he held up four fingers, representing the weeks she'd be gone.

Her frustration surfaced again. Mattie Cakes stayed so busy during the holidays, and she loved every minute of it. She'd miss all the hustle and bustle of getting brightly decorated cakes out the door to become a part of people's feasts and celebrations.

She'd thought that coming to Ohio three years ago was God giving her beauty for ashes—the shop and Sol. But now Mattie Cakes was nothing but ashes, and Sol's favorite thing about her—her ability to remain on an even keel emotionally—had also gone up in smoke. Had she displeased God somehow and this was His way of getting her attention?

At least one good thing would come from this change of plans. She'd be able to make the cakes for her aunt Lizzy's and her cousin Beth's weddings. Lizzy was actually Mattie's step-aunt. Lizzy and her siblings came from the second marriage of Mattie's grandfather. As a widower, he'd married a younger woman, so now the siblings and stepsiblings ranged in age from Rebecca at seventy to Lizzy at forty.

Even though Lizzy was forty, she never had a beau until she and the widower bishop fell in love. It was an odd coincidence that Beth and Lizzy, who'd run Hertzlers' Dry Goods together for years, were getting married less than two weeks apart.

Beth was more than a decade younger than Lizzy and had buried her first fiancé. Mattie had never seen anyone take the death of a loved one harder than Beth had. But two years ago Beth had met Jonah Kinsinger, and shortly after, it was revealed why she had shut herself off from everyone after Henry died. He hadn't been who he pretended to be, and when Beth realized it, she ended their engagement. Whether by accident or on purpose, later that night he drowned in a river.

Henry and Gideon had more in common than Mattie wanted to admit. Both men hid parts of who they were from everyone. Gideon wasn't abusive like Henry, but she was floored by his interest in non-Amish women.

She watched the lights in the distance as the driver headed for the train station. Regardless of her sadness over losing her business, she was looking forward to meeting the new man in Beth's life. Somehow Jonah Kinsinger had brought truth and healing to Beth, and Mattie intended to hug him for it.

As the lights of various towns came and went, she wondered what had changed Gideon. She'd known him his whole life. Beth had been caught by surprise at who Henry really was, but he hadn't grown up around them. Gideon's grandmother's farmhouse sat across the street from her parents' place. When they were little and he stayed the night with his grandmother, they waved at each other from their bedrooms and talked on the two-way radios until one of them fell asleep. As teens they used sign language…and the two-way radio. Once they'd even sent messages back and forth tied to the mane of a horse. Because he lived with his parents in a different district some twenty miles away, they didn't attend the same Amish school or the same church, but she'd been certain she knew the real Gideon.

She used to think that marrying him would mean spending the rest of her life with her best friend. As it turned out, he wasn't a friend at all—not to her and probably not to himself either.

It wouldn't affect her one way or the other, but she couldn't help wondering if he'd changed any in the last three years.

Five

With a fresh supply of screws in hand, Gideon left the dry goods store. Cold air seeped across the land as if someone had opened a huge freezer. While he strode across the parking lot, he studied the outside of Beth and Jonah's unfinished home, mentally calculating what he needed to finish.

After several holdups due to supplies and weather, he couldn't afford another setback. Workwise he had lost only half a day when Mattie was hurt. But emotionally he'd yet to regain his footing. Something hard inside him had dislodged when he feared for her safety, and he needed to get it back in place. Since he hadn't told her the truth about why he broke up with her, she might always hold a grudge.

Determined to accept his fate, he tried to focus on the job in front of him—finishing Beth and Jonah's place. The couple could have their wedding at her parents' place and live in Beth's apartment above Hertzlers' Dry Goods until the house was completed. But Gideon had given his word he'd finish it on time.

Car tires crunched against gravel in the store's parking lot. Gideon glanced behind him, and his heart threatened to stop.

Mattie Lane sat in the car with Beth's driver for the store. Jonah had mentioned that Gloria brought Mattie home from the bus station early this morning.

Relief at seeing her strong enough to be out once again washed over him. But he still would rather not face her. Had Sol told her about his visit to the hospital?

Trying to avoid looking Mattie's way, Gideon went up the wooden steps and into the house. A layer of chalky dust covered the walls, ceilings, and particle board floors. Kitchen cabinets stood in the center of the room, waiting for him to secure them to the newly finished walls. Leftover wood trim was stacked along one wall. Tubs, sinks, and commodes were still in their boxes, sitting in odd places, along with various types of hardware. But right now he intended to hang a few doors.

The cold and empty disarray of the place made him feel as if he'd stepped inside his own soul. In all his planning and calculations to set Mattie free, he hadn't anticipated what his life would be like if he survived the cancer. He'd spent the better part of two years in a hospital, much of it quarantined. Not one doctor had expected him to beat the blast crisis phase. The journey from the day he was diagnosed to today had changed him so much he no longer recognized himself.

Ignoring the weight of that thought, he kept his outward movements as normal as any other day, hoping to convince anyone who might see him—like someone from Beiler Construction stopping by or the visitors Beth, Jonah, and Lizzy regularly gave tours to—that he was fine. But he couldn't fool himself. His dry mouth and clammy palms spoke truth. His mind hadn't let him sleep the last few nights, and his heart couldn't decide whether to race or to stop beating altogether.

The destruction he'd faced since learning he had chronic myelogenous leukemia seemed infinite. When he was first diagnosed, he was in early chronic phase, and his survival rate was ninety percent, so he quietly traveled to Philadelphia for treatment, thinking he could keep it from Mattie until he had a clean bill of health. But while in treatment, his abnormal white cells had exploded in growth, and with it his chance of survival plummeted. So did he, but he'd shored himself up as best he could, while keeping his diagnosis from everyone in Apple Ridge. The battle with cancer had stolen nearly every piece of who he was. If anyone could destroy what little he had left, Mattie Lane could. She hated him for cheating on her.

Regardless of how she felt, he had to find a way to peacefully deal with her over the weeks ahead.

After moving two freshly carved doors from the back porch to the appropriate spots to hang them, he put on his tool belt and went into the master bathroom. Gideon attached a set of hinges to the frame of the doorway, then used his foot as a prop to help balance the door while tapping the pin into the hinge with a hammer.

"Gideon," Jonah called as he entered the home.

"Master bathroom."

When Jonah came to the room, Gideon opened the door he was trying to hang just enough to let Jonah enter.

With a cane in one hand, Jonah held out his other hand for the hammer. Gideon gave it to him, glad for the help. He dug into his tool belt and pulled two more hinge pins.

Jonah took them and tapped one into place. "I think you should get the kitchen cabinets in place next."

"But you haven't finished carving on them."

"There's been a change of plans. We'll put them up as is."

"Okay, but why?"

The sound of female voices caused Gideon to shift his attention to the window.

Mattie Lane and Beth were heading this way. Mattie was dressed like an Ohio Amish woman now, with the stiffer oval prayer Kapp and a sage green apron that matched her dress. Like him, she'd joined the Old Order Amish faith about two years ago. It was below forty with the wind blowing, and she wasn't wearing a coat.

Her eyes grew large with pleasure as she studied the new home, and a part of him he'd buried long ago rattled against its confinement. She pointed out various details and smiled as she hugged Beth.

Mattie Lane. Energetic. Vibrant. Talented. Poised. And beautiful inside and out. She was also scattered, easily distracted, and had a jealous streak the size of Pennsylvania. When it came to ending their relationship with a lie, he used her jealousy against her to set her free from his doomed future.

Jonah's cane thudded against the particle board as he moved closer to the window. "Look at them, Gideon."

"I did." The familiar hardness took control again, and he turned back to his work. "I saw two half-giddy women gabbing ninety to nothing."

"Ya, sharing encouragement and excitement. Menfolk would never do that…except maybe with a girlfriend or wife."

"The day a man needs that kind of nonsense is the day he might as well accept that he's not really a man at all."

Jonah laughed. "Not a man, eh?"

The sound of the front door swooshing open started a war inside Gideon.

If she knew he had come to the hospital to see her, he could discount his rash action by saying he'd overreacted to hearing that she'd been hurt. But his nervous shaking reminded him that he had deeper secrets to keep and a heart to guard.

Hers.

Gideon motioned toward the bedroom door. "I'd like to get that door up next." *And close it.*

Gideon grabbed the door and laid it on the sawhorses so he could get the hardware on it.

"Jonah?" Beth called.

He stepped toward the doorway, and the women entered.

Beth looped her arm through her fiancé's. "And this is Jonah."

Mattie Lane's hands were tucked inside her folded arms, probably in an effort to stay warm, but her smile embraced Jonah. "I think she might be just a tad in love with you."

Gideon tried to pull his attention back to the job at hand— mounting hardware on the door.

"A tad is not nearly a success," Jonah said. "Mattie Lane, right?"

The use of her pet name caused Gideon to cringe, and he looked up.

The smile on her face faded. "Why would you call me that?"

Jonah glanced at Gideon, and Mattie noticed him for the

first time since entering the room. Her pale blue eyes stayed glued to him, as if she were too shocked to move. Gideon hadn't realized he'd used that name when talking to Jonah, but he'd called her by that nickname since she was twelve, telling her that a day with her was a journey all by itself—a trip down a one-of-a-kind country road, Mattie Lane.

Finally she nodded. "Gideon."

"Hi." All the months of aching for her that had painstakingly turned into years rushed from their buried place and leveled him.

She looked back at Jonah. "It's just Mattie." She held out her hand and shook Jonah's. "I'm so glad to finally meet you. Beth's told me a lot about you in her letters." She entered the room and peeked into the full bathroom. "I'm completely awed by this home. You've done an amazing job."

Jonah shoved his hammer into his tool belt. "Gideon's been doing everything from the contracting to the finishing carpentry while I've spent the better part of this past year helping Beth and Lizzy expand the product line for the dry goods store."

Mattie glanced at Gideon as though he were some half-remembered acquaintance from her past. She shifted her attention out the window. "You have a perfect view of the store."

"And look." Beth took Mattie to the PVC piping that was

the conduit for the Amish intercom. "It's a direct line from the store to here. The workers can easily contact us this way."

Mattie chuckled. "I could've used one of these between Mattie Cakes and my brother's place."

"The intercom system was Gideon's idea," Beth said. "He dug the trench to lay the pipe and installed it for us."

An unfamiliar look entered Mattie's eyes, as if anything to do with him disgusted her. She moved to the bathroom door. In bold scroll Jonah had carved "Charity endureth all things."

"What a beautiful carving." She rubbed her arms.

"Ya. Jonah's work is what drew me to him," Beth said. "I saw a scene carved on a small stump in a store in Ohio and wanted to purchase more just like it for our store."

Gideon took off his coat and held it out to Mattie. "The heat will be in working order next week."

She shook her head. "Denki. But I'm fine."

"Oh," Beth exclaimed. "I was so excited to show you around, I didn't even notice you were freezing."

"I took off my coat in Gloria's car. She had it really hot in there while we were running errands in town for Mamm, and I forgot to grab it before she drove off."

Beth frowned. "Seems like you would've thought about it the moment you got out of the car."

Mattie shrugged. "One would think…"

Gideon knew that when Mattie had one thing on her mind, like seeing Beth, she didn't notice much else until she was in a fix and needed rescuing.

Gideon thrust the coat toward her. "Take it, Mattie Lane."

Her eyes flashed with an anger much deeper than anything to do with her refusal to borrow his coat. "Do not snap orders at me, Gideon." She spoke each word slowly, issuing both a boundary line of how to treat her and a threat of a volcanic-sized eruption.

Gideon couldn't help but chuckle. She'd outgrown being overly nice to everyone, and he was glad to see it. "Finally standing up for yourself. Good for you."

She moved toward the doorway. "Beth, I'd like to see the rest of your house. And Jonah's new workshop."

When he realized his comment had come off as an insult, he flinched. Beth's brow creased with concern before she placed her arm protectively around Mattie's shoulders. "Sure."

Jonah motioned for the women to go on without him.

Gideon stepped ahead of them. "I'm sorry. That was rude. I can't believe I blurted that out."

After staring ahead for several long moments, Mattie turned to Beth. "Can I have a minute with Gideon?"

"Ya. Sure." Beth took Jonah's hand, and they went down the hallway.

Now that they were alone and could speak freely, Gideon would soon know whether Sol had told her about his visit to the hospital.

She studied Gideon. "I've always had a backbone. Any confusion I had about when to use it was your fault, not mine."

He wasn't sure exactly what in their past made that statement true, but he nodded. "I ask your forgiveness for thinking otherwise."

The Amish ways forced her to forgive him, so he felt no sense of release when she said, "Forgiven."

He held out the coat. "In that case…"

Her eyes, sizing him up, carried disrespect. He still didn't know if Sol had told her about his visit. She wasn't as easy to read as he'd expected.

She took the coat from him and slipped it on and, after buttoning it, waggled her shoulders as if enjoying its warmth. "Anything that keeps you uncomfortable while doing the opposite for me works for me. Thanks."

She shoved her hands into the pockets and left.

Gideon sighed. He had set her free, and she'd prospered from it. She'd gone to Ohio and built a successful business and met Sol. He'd expected her coolness toward him, but he was beginning to question if he could ever be content with it.

*M*attie got up from the dinner table and began stacking plates. Oddly enough, after barely stomaching the Thanksgiving meal yesterday with her brother and his family, she'd enjoyed having leftovers today with her parents.

Her mom stood.

"Mamm, take your cue from Daed, and sit." Mattie patted her mother's thin, delicate skin.

Daed's gray hair had the shape of having worn a hat all day. "Ya, Rebecca. What other child do you have who'll wash dishes?"

Mattie laughed. "The price one pays for having so many sons."

Mamm sat back down at the table, her eyes bright in spite of the new wrinkles weighing on her eyelids. Mattie's brothers had been right. She'd needed to come home and spend extra time with their mother.

"Verna came by today while you were out," Mamm said.

"She was bent on seeing you. I promised her you'd walk over there tonight."

Mattie put the dishes in the sink, wishing her mother hadn't told Gideon's grandmother she'd visit. She'd seen Gideon ride bareback past the front window a few minutes ago. While he was working on Beth and Jonah's home, he was probably staying with his grandmother rather than trekking back and forth from his parents' place.

His winter jacket hung on the coatrack in the front hallway, and he could go the whole winter without it for all she cared.

"Mattie?" Mamm called.

She turned. "I don't want to go tonight. Can it wait until tomorrow?"

"I suppose. But I gave my word, and you're obviously feeling well enough to walk across the street."

Daed shifted his chair away from the table. "I agree with your Mamm. I don't want us to have to make up an excuse for why you're not up to seeing her."

Mattie stared at Gideon's coat, hating the idea of having to be nice to him.

Mamm followed her gaze. "What's wrong?"

Unwilling to burden her mom with petty emotions that should have been long dead by now, she kissed her cheek. "Not a thing. I'll go see Verna."

"She'll be so pleased."

She put on the coat Gloria had dropped by the house a few hours ago, then grabbed Gideon's. Crossing the narrow street, she coached herself on how to speak gently. She climbed the two stone steps, knocked on the door, and waited.

Verna opened the door. "Mattie." She hugged her warmly. *"Kumm mol rei."*

Mattie stepped inside, warmth and the smell of dinner surrounding her. "It's good to see you. How are you?"

"Fair to middling for a woman my age. I sure was sorry to hear about your cake shop. I remember a couple of years ago when Gideon told your brother about—"

"Mammi Beiler," Gideon interrupted. He stood at the kitchen table with a plate of pancakes and bacon. "Kumm eat." He set it on the table.

"Oh, he fixed a meal for me. I'm having breakfast for dinner because yesterday I sent all the Thanksgiving food home with his Mamm. I should go see if it's any good before it gets cold." Verna went to a chair and sat.

Gideon walked to Mattie and held out his hand for the coat. "Thanks."

He didn't look like the man she'd once loved. That man had been carefree and gentle. This one seemed hardened and weary. Maybe trying to keep an Amish girlfriend while dating Englischer girls did that to a man.

She gave it to him. "Denki for the use of it."

"Not a problem."

"It's clearly mealtime, and I should go." She turned to Verna. "Good to see you. Maybe you can slip over one morning before I go home. We could have hot chocolate in front of the roaring fire like we used to."

"And maybe some oddly shaped coffeecake?" Verna asked.

Mattie laughed. "Sure. But if they come out oddly shaped these days, it'll be intentional on my part."

"That reminds me." She stood. "I have something for you. Wait right here." She headed for the stairs. "Make yourself comfortable. I'm going to be a few minutes."

Gideon moved to the stove. "Care for some hot tea?"

"No." The word came out harsher than she'd intended. It wouldn't have been easy to be nice to him under the best of circumstances, and she was far from her best self.

He stole a sideways glance before grabbing the kettle off the stove. He reached into a cabinet and pulled down the delicate china cup she'd always used when visiting here. He rinsed and dried it. "I know it's been rough for you lately." He set a variety of tea bags on the table and poured hot water into her cup.

She dumped the cup of steaming water into the sink. "Please don't act like you're my friend."

The muscles in his jaw tightened. "I didn't mean to offend you."

That was the problem. Everything about him offended her. "How's Ashley?"

Surprise reflected in his eyes for a moment. "I haven't seen her in a while."

"Ya." She wrinkled her nose. "It's hard to keep the decent ones around when you keep cheating on them."

Hardness entered his eyes. "Give it a rest, Mattie Lane."

She took a seat across the table from him, wishing she was in Ohio baking and decorating cakes. And wishing he'd stop calling her Mattie Lane.

They both stared at the kitchen table, and she wondered if he was thinking about the same thing she was—the day she caught him with Ashley.

It'd been Christmas Day. They'd attended the annual Christmas singing on her birthday the night before. She'd enjoyed it as much as ever, except Gideon hadn't been his usual fun-loving self. When he hugged her good night, he said he was really tired and wouldn't come over on Christmas. Actually, he'd been using exhaustion as an excuse for weeks, and he'd said the doctor thought he might have mono. So she'd wanted to do something special to help him feel loved until he was on his feet again.

She spent all day making a beautiful Christmas cake to take to him, and she wrote a love letter as part of her Christmas present. She hired a driver to take her the twenty miles to his parents' home in Plainview.

With his gifts in tow, she arrived at his parents' place. Gideon lived in a tiny house less than a stone's throw from his parents, but as a single woman, she couldn't visit him there.

When his mother opened the door, she stammered something about Gideon not being around and reluctantly invited her in. Mattie tried to have their usual relaxed conversation, but Susie was obviously upset.

Mattie wondered what was going on. If Gideon didn't feel well enough to come to her place on Christmas Day, why wasn't he at home resting? She visited for a minute before leaving the cake.

She hadn't been willing to leave her love letter with his parents, so she went to his little home across the yard, intending to shove it under the door. When she reached his doorstep, she heard voices. She started to knock on the window of the door but then caught a glimpse of him through the curtains. He was holding a woman with long, free-flowing black hair, dressed in jeans and a silky gold jacket. An Englischer.

Jealousy flew over her. Nothing was as insulting as a Plain man wanting a fancy woman. Mattie followed the ways of their people, and he was supposed to respect and honor that, not go chasing after something…someone different.

She opened the door. Gideon and the girl jumped, looking as guilty as forbidden lovers caught in the act. "What's going on?"

"Mattie." Gideon was breathless. "What are you doing here?"

"Answer my question. What is going on?" She said each word deliberately.

The woman began to cry. "Tell her, Gideon."

He rubbed his forehead, a habit he had when trying to figure out what to do. "Okay, Ashley, I will."

The girl's eyes widened. "You're finally going to tell her the truth?"

Finally? How long had Gideon been seeing this Englischer woman?

"Go on home and rest. I'll be over later tonight." He escorted Ashley to the door.

Once she was gone, he turned to Mattie. "I…I'd hoped we could get through the holidays before…"

Mattie's head spun, and her body felt as if it had turned to lead. "Tell me now, Gideon. Right now."

"I…I think it's best if you see other people. You've never dated anyone else. And I need to be free too."

Mattie shook all over, trying her best not to cry. "What? Why?"

"It's the way it needs to be." His voice wavered, and he cleared his throat. "I'm sorry."

He had feelings for her. She could see that even as he broke up with her. But they weren't enough for him. She'd seen him with Englischer girls before. She'd only been fifteen the first time she saw him getting out of a girl's car. But he always had some excuse—she'd had a flat tire, and he'd helped change it before she gave him a lift, or she was a stranger dropping by his house to see if he wanted a free puppy.

The night she saw him with Ashley, she had no choice but to set him free and go live with her brother as quickly as she could pack up all her baking equipment.

For three years she'd put her heart and soul into building a new life. And she'd done everything in her power to avoid thinking about Gideon. But seeing him now, in the flesh, brought back memories of all she'd held dear. She'd loved him. But what can be done when the one you love doesn't feel the same way?

Mattie looked up from the kitchen table, wishing she'd accepted that cup of tea after all. "I've met someone."

Gideon's jaw clenched. "I'm happy for you." He brushed his hand along the edge of the table. "That being the case, can we let go of the past and get along as friends?"

"I'll try." She played with her empty cup. "I will."

Verna came into the kitchen with a stack of used cake pans. "I've been collecting these for years. Didn't know why, 'cause you had plenty of your own. But now maybe they'll help." She set them on the table in front of Mattie.

"Oh, Verna, this is so kind of you." Mattie lifted each one. There were heart-shaped, round, rectangular, Bundt, square, and ring pans. "Denki."

Tears clouded her vision. The pain of losing her shop and everything in it still rattled her very soul.

Gideon stared into his mug, looking uncomfortable. "I know you'll consider that what I'm about to say are the words of a man who thinks everything and everyone can be replaced. But you'll rebuild. Whatever the insurance company doesn't cover, the communities—both here and there—will."

She should simply nod, but the need to tell someone who would understand pressed in hard. "I lost the notebook."

It seemed that grief and disappointment ran through his eyes, and she found a measure of comfort in his compassion for her loss.

After he'd given her the notebook, they'd spent years going places to get ideas for creating cakes and had filled the book with rough sketches they'd drawn and pictures they'd cut out of cake-decorating magazines. She could feel his laughter wash over her as they went through museums, trying to draw ideas as they came up with them when neither one of them was any good at freehand art.

He used to take her to Front Street in Harrisburg, and they would stroll along the Susquehanna. Watching the river was what gave her the idea for her rough-ride icing, which was a huge hit with customers. Then the two of them would eat at the Fire House Restaurant, a renovated fire station built in the eighteen hundreds. Between Gideon's ideas and other sites in Harrisburg, she'd garnered a lot of her cake-making ideas.

As she sat across from him, remembering so many of their dates, she realized how self-absorbed she'd been. Did they ever do something he enjoyed?

She looked up and met his green eyes, wanting to acknowledge that maybe she had played more of a part in their breakup than she'd admitted. But she couldn't say it, not without asking why he hadn't talked to her about what bothered him in their relationship *before* he cheated.

"I guess the notebook was a little like us—years in the making and destroyed in just a few minutes." Mattie gathered her pans. "Well, I'm just a bright spot right now, aren't I? I think I'll take my gloom elsewhere for a bit."

Verna hugged her. "You'll feel better in a few weeks, and you'll get back on your feet again in a matter of months. You always do."

Between her mother's health issues and Gideon's betrayal, she'd faced her share of difficult times in life. "You're right. I always do."

Seven

Wind pushed against the enclosed buggy, making it rock unsteadily, as Gideon drove toward Zook's Diner under the dark morning sky. He pulled onto the gravel parking lot, hopped out, and looped the strap around a hitching post.

The aroma of breakfast foods filled the air even before he opened the glass door. He walked through the tiny convenience store attached to the diner and headed straight to the pass-through that separated the restaurant from the kitchen. The place had the typical look of an outdated diner: cement floors, well-worn Formica tabletops, and a long counter with accompanying swivel chairs. It probably hadn't had a face-lift in sixty years.

Roman, a strapping young Amish man a few years younger than Gideon, looked up from his wheelchair. "Finally, a customer!" He grinned. "Aden's been cooking since four this morning. But it looks like the weekend following Thanksgiving Day is going to be slow this year. What can we get for you, Gideon?"

Aden, Roman's identical twin, gave Gideon a brief nod as he stood at the sink, washing pots and pans.

"I'll take the house special." Gideon wasn't hungry, but how could he fail to support a diner that was so rural it had almost no business on the busiest shopping weekend of the year? The Hertzlers' store stayed covered with customers on days like this, but Zook's sat in the middle of nothing, ten miles away. "Five of them, to go."

"Now we're talking." Roman wheeled himself to the take-out containers and placed five of them in his lap. Aden went to the icebox and pulled out a carton of eggs.

Gideon figured he could drop off the breakfasts at the Snyder place, where the crew of six men were trying to get the house dried in. Even though some were bound to have eaten already, they would still devour these breakfasts in no time.

"Aden, I have a proposition for you."

Roman looked to Aden and then to Gideon. "What is it?"

Since Aden struggled with a stutter, Roman did most of the talking for him. Gideon wasn't sure whether Aden liked it that way or the outgoing and talkative Roman just never gave his brother a chance to speak. But whatever the dynamics of that relationship, Aden stayed in the shadows, cooking, and Roman waited tables and charmed customers. But Aden's real skill wasn't as a short-order cook. He was a quite talented artist.

Gideon pulled his billfold out of his pants pocket. "Remember when you drew some sketches of cakes for Mattie's portfolio?"

Aden gave a lopsided grin. "Y-ya."

"You heard about her cake shop burning down, right? And that she's come home for a bit?"

"We heard," Roman said. "Is she doing all right?"

He wasn't so sure she was. "Considering everything, ya, I think so. But the portfolio, which she's been adding to since she was a kid, burned in the fire."

Aden stopped scrambling the eggs. "I'm sor- sor-"

"Ya," Roman interrupted. "He's sorry to hear that. We both are."

Aden flashed a look from Roman to Gideon. Roman nodded. "Oh, ya. So what can he do for you?"

Gideon rested his forearms on the counter. "I was hoping you could remember some of the things you drew, and anything else you remember seeing in her portfolio, and would draw them again fresh."

"Sure," Roman said. "He'd be glad to. I bet he remembers

everything he saw in that book, but it's been a while since he looked at it."

"I'm pretty familiar with what all was in there, so I might be some help."

He'd looked at her portfolio several times since they'd gone their separate ways—not that Mattie had a clue. Her brother James did, as well as Dorothy. But he was confident neither of them had ever mentioned his visits to Mattie. She didn't want to know anything about him, and they respected that. He had no desire to alter the course of her life, but in his pitiful stabs at protecting her, he couldn't help but keep up with her life.

Roman rolled his wheelchair out of the kitchen, carrying five takeout boxes stacked on top of one another. "Why don't you give him a few days and then you two get together and take a look at what he's got?" Roman went to the cash register and rang up the food items.

"If that sounds good to you, Aden, that's what we'll do."

Aden nodded.

Gideon passed Roman two twenties.

"What I don't get is why you're helping her out. You two ended things years ago—and not on very pleasant terms." Roman grabbed a roll of quarters and broke them open into the change drawer.

"Sometimes a man needs to redeem his past. And for the

record, this transaction is just between us. When the portfolio is complete, Aden, you can take it or mail it to her, and leave my name out of it." He eyed the talkative one. "Okay, Roman?"

"People always think I share everything I know." He counted out the change and passed it to Gideon. "I can keep a secret just as well as my brother." Roman pulled bills out of the register and laid them on the shelf above the cash drawer. "Just you—"As the door to the restaurant opened, he dropped his sentence and froze in place.

Gideon turned to see the distraction. A young woman stepped inside, carrying what appeared to be a very heavy cardboard box. She looked a little familiar, but Gideon couldn't place her. Her small, circular prayer Kapp and her flowery blue cape dress that showed below her heavy coat told him she belonged to the Old Order Mennonite sect.

He glanced at Roman and saw insecurity in his eyes, erasing all hints of his outgoing personality. He backed his wheelchair away from the cash register.

Gideon looked at Aden, and his usual lack of confidence faded as he caught her eye. Smiling, Aden came out of the kitchen and walked directly toward her.

"Morning, Aden." She returned his smile.

Aden took the box, his eyes fixed on hers. "M-m-morning, Annie."

Clearly, Aden didn't want Roman speaking for him when it came to this young woman.

She lowered her head, a pink blush rising in her cheeks before she peered around him. "Hello, Roman."

Roman's fingers tightened on the hand rim of his wheelchair. "Is something wrong with Moses?"

Now Gideon remembered who she was—one of Moses Burkholder's granddaughters. She didn't live in Apple Ridge, but she came here when her *Daadi* Moses needed her.

She took off her coat. "He's down with bronchitis, but the doctor says he'll be fine in a week or two."

Moses was a silent partner in the diner. Without him, the Zooks would have lost their family restaurant. Aden and Roman's grandfather had built this place years ago and had run it without electricity. When regulators mandated that electricity had to be installed to meet new legal codes, Moses stepped in and became a partner. Members of the Old Order Amish church couldn't have a business with electricity, but they could co-own a place with a Plain Mennonite, who could have electricity installed.

Gideon pondered the opposite reactions the Zook twins had to Annie. Of all the Old Order Amish and Old Order Mennonites he'd known, he'd never heard of anyone crossing the line from one sect to the other—not even to court, much less marry. It was forbidden, and if one of them was interested in her, it could cause a rift between her grandfather and the Zooks, perhaps destroying the family business as well as the years of trust between them.

If Gideon understood anything about love between a man and a woman, he knew it could grow where it wasn't planted and thrive without anyone nurturing it—like poison ivy. And it could make a man just as miserably uncomfortable.

"Roman." Gideon nodded toward the cash.

"Oh, ya." He passed him the money.

Gideon shoved it into his pocket, grabbed the takeout boxes, and said good-bye.

Regardless of what was going on with these three, Gideon had his own battle to focus on—the one of avoiding Mattie Lane.

Mattie sat in Beth's office at Hertzlers' Dry Goods, using the community phone to make calls. If Mattie used the phone shanty at home, Mamm would fix her a favorite meal or start making her a new dress. Whenever Mattie was doing business on their property, Mamm was on the move. So each time Mattie thought of someone who'd ordered a cake from Mattie Cakes, she came here to call them and let them know she was out of business, probably until April. She wished she had a better way of reaching everyone, because relying solely on her memory could cause someone not to be ready for a big event.

Once a piece of information concerning a client came to her—like an address, a relative's name, or a husband's first name—she called directory assistance to get the phone number. She dialed Mrs. Gibbons, an Englischer who'd ordered a cake for her parents' sixtieth anniversary. This was Mattie's third phone call of the day, and each one was difficult to get through. She explained the situation to her, and just like all the others she'd spoken to, Mrs. Gibbons was kind in accepting that she couldn't fill the order. But every client asked what caused the fire. When she explained she'd left the place unattended with papers near the wood stove, they seemed satisfied with the answer. What she didn't tell them was that in her pleasure at seeing Ryan's excitement over his cake, she might have laid her notebook on the wood stove before leaving the store for more than an hour.

Being creative was fun. But for her the flip side of creativity was being scattered, and she *really* didn't enjoy that part.

Lizzy quietly slipped into the room and went to a file cabinet. Mattie finished her phone call and put the receiver in its cradle. "Seems to me the more you add on to this store, the busier you get. You're not getting ahead, Aunt Lizzy."

"I said the same thing the other day," she teased.

Her aunt always seemed to look a decade younger than she was, but now she absolutely glowed. Lizzy's dark hair had very few strands of gray, and her sparkling brown eyes said she'd never been happier. Mattie wondered how amazing it must feel to be forty and getting married for the first time.

Maybe she would be that happy by the time she reached forty. It felt as if it'd take that long, anyway.

She caught a glimpse of movement across the yard and glanced that way.

Gideon.

She'd once loved him—his energy, his sense of humor, his dedication to God, family, and work.

He had a stack of two-by-fours on one shoulder and a huge bucket of paint, maybe twenty gallons, in his free hand, carrying them as if they were no heavier than an umbrella.

Beiler Construction belonged to Gideon's grandfather and then to his Daed, who had several sons, but the business was in serious financial trouble by the time Gideon graduated from school at twelve. Even as a scrawny kid, he poured his energy and heart into the business, as did his brothers. By the time he turned seventeen, no worker was more powerful or capable.

Over the years she and Gideon had discovered some of the problems Beiler Construction had with supplies, contracted labor, and scheduling projects. She'd cherished those times of talking over business issues while on a date or sharing a meal with his family. She had come up with some helpful solutions, and it'd made her feel valuable to him. And to his family.

But somewhere along the way, Gideon decided that she didn't mean enough to him.

Lizzy followed her gaze. "Is something wrong?"

Mattie cleared her throat, trying to think of a cover. "Just wondering if the house will be done in time." That was true enough, wasn't it?

"I'm sure it'll be done sufficiently."

Wondering what had caused Gideon to change his mind about her was a subject she'd put away a long time ago, and she refused to start rehashing it now. As long as she was on this earth, she wouldn't know the answers to lots of things, and that was one of them.

"Do you have pictures of the types of cakes you're making these days?"

Mattie shook her head. "When I find something similar, I'll show it to you. With the big day in two weeks, I have no time to lose." She didn't even have the right cake pans for what she hoped to make for her aunt.

"I don't want anything fancy," Lizzy said. "But I'd like it to be memorable."

Mattie suppressed a smile. She heard this sentiment regularly when making cakes for the Amish. "I'll do just that. And I want your cake to be quite different from Beth's. What did you have in mind?"

"Omar's eyes always light up when people have one of those enormous cakes like you made for your parents' anniversary a few years ago. I was going to try to make it myself, but since you're here, I'll gladly turn that responsibility over to you. Is it possible to make one like that?"

"Unfortunately, that large pan was charred and warped in the fire. I could bake several smaller ones and put them together."

Lizzy frowned. "You can't keep doing that forever. You need new pans. If you'll order them, I'll be glad to pay for them."

"I can't let you do that."

"You most certainly can, and I'll not hear another word about it, or I'll go straight to the bishop."

Mattie laughed. "You're going to take full advantage of marrying the bishop, aren't you?"

Lizzy moved around to Mattie's side of the desk. She cupped Mattie's face in her hands. "Seriously, let us replace those pans."

She'd forgotten how pleasant it was to be treated special by Lizzy. "Denki."

"So where do we buy them?"

"I don't know." Gideon had special-ordered them from a

man who'd never made cake pans before. All she had to do was find the courage to ask Gideon for the man's name and number. "I'll see what I can find out."

"Sounds good to me. I need to get back to work, and you need to get busy finding some answers."

"Denki, Lizzy."

"It's good to have you back, Mattie." She closed the door behind her.

Mattie didn't want to ask Gideon for help, but she couldn't afford to lose time searching for someone else to make the pans. She put on her coat and walked onto the main floor of the dry goods store.

"Hey." Beth stopped sorting books. "You leaving?"

"I need to ask Gideon a question, and if he has an answer, I may need to use your phone again. I'm trying to avoid doing business at home because Mamm stays on her feet the whole time."

"Come back whenever you need to. If the store is closed, just bang on the door. I'll hear you."

"I'm sure you're looking forward to living somewhere other than above this store."

"I'm looking forward to getting married." She raised her eyebrows. "Where we live isn't that important right now."

Mattie laughed. "Must be nice." She waved. "I hope to see

you in just a bit." She left the store and walked across the parking lot and the lawn and into Beth's new home. "Hello?"

"In the kitchen," Gideon groaned.

When Mattie walked in, he had a large kitchen cabinet balanced between the wall and his shoulder. One hand was stretched up as high as he could reach on the front of the cabinet, his face was turning red, and his arms were shaking.

"Could you do me a favor?"

His predicament and his nonchalant question didn't exactly match, and she found it quite amusing. It was obvious her answer needed to be yes, but something playful in her, or maybe the need to aggravate him, came out of hiding. "Maybe."

"Mattie Lane," he growled.

She laughed. "Well, what is it?"

He nodded toward the floor, and she noticed a broken deadman brace. "There's another one on the back porch." He gritted his teeth under the weight of the cabinet.

She ran to get it and hurried back. She propped the T of it as he'd shown her years ago. Then she crawled onto the makeshift countertop and helped hoist the cabinet into place and held it steady while he got one nail in—hopefully into a stud, or the cabinet would fall.

She closed her eyes while the hammer banged away.

"We did it." Gideon rubbed his shoulder. "That'll keep it

from falling while I get the screws in." He offered her a hand down.

She hesitated, confusion churning. Taking his hand could be a mistake, one that might unleash thoughts and feelings she couldn't allow. She shooed him away and hopped down. "Where's your helper?"

"The crews are at another home, trying to get it dried in before bad weather hits." He used his level to get the cabinet just right, and then with a battery-powered screwdriver, he sank two long screws into the cabinet and wall.

"The business must really be behind schedule."

"Might be the worst yet." He removed the brace and set it aside.

Memories of their brainstorming about scheduling issues stung her heart for a moment. She'd loved those times—looking for solutions, laughing at some of the ridiculous predicaments Beiler Construction dealt with, and letting him vent his frustrations. Apparently he hadn't felt the same way.

Mattie rubbed her hands together, trying to warm them. "Why are you installing cabinets anyway? Does Beiler Construction do that now?"

"No. That's why this cabinet job wasn't likely to go well no matter how many hands were here. But my oldest brother decides who'll be where these days."

"John? That's your position. You earned it."

He shrugged, obviously not interested in talking about John taking over as the lead contractor of Beiler Construction. He dusted off his shirt. "Denki for your help, Mattie. If I'd tried to set the cabinet down, it would've toppled and gotten damaged, and I couldn't keep holding it up."

She dropped the subject of John. It wasn't any of her business who was the walking boss of Beiler Construction, but if Gideon were running it, no one would be finishing a job by himself.

He folded his arms, leaned against the counter, and narrowed his eyes at her. "I was in a bind and asked for help, and your answer was 'maybe'?"

She barely managed to keep the grin off her face. "It was tempting to see how long you could last. When you said you needed a favor, it was all I could do not to ask, 'Now?'"

The amusement in his eyes made her long for the days when she was the one who'd mattered most to him. Uncomfortable with her thoughts, her mirth vanished.

She pulled a scrap of paper out of her coat pocket and laid it on the counter. "The reason I'm here is to ask if you have the name and number of the man who made those custom-sized pans for me."

"Ya." He pulled out the tape measure and started working again.

"May I have it?"

"Now?"

She resisted laughing. "No. I could wait until you're asleep tonight and toss a rock through your window."

"Again?" He mocked gaping at her. "Didn't we get into enough trouble the first time?"

"Uh, I didn't get into trouble. Only you did. Actually, I think my Daed was quite proud that his only daughter could throw a rock that far and that hard at twelve years old."

"What was the deal with you throwing a rock and me getting in trouble for it? I was asleep!"

"Mammi Beiler said it had to be your idea, and since you were older, I was totally under your influence."

"Whatever," he teased.

Her heart pounded, enjoying the nostalgia they so easily shared. She reminded herself of who he was and cleared her throat. "The man's name and number?"

"Sure. Dennis Ogletree. I met him on a job site one time, and we've stayed in contact. He's a machinist by trade. He can make the pans in less than a day once he gets to the project. I'm just glad to see a spark of life returning to your face."

"Do not say the word *spark* to me, please."

His familiar lopsided smile that held more compassion than humor sent fear running through her. Getting along with women came effortlessly to him, and she was a fool to be drawn in so easily.

A hint of a thought darted across his face before he took a wristwatch out of his pants pocket and glanced at it. He grabbed a carpenter's pencil off the countertop.

While he wrote down the information, she noticed a small bucket filled with a bundle of fall flowers sitting on the floor near the washroom. Since it was the end of November, they had to come from a florist.

"Aw, Beth's getting flowers from Jonah. How sweet."

He glanced up, his face flushed. She hadn't meant anything by her observation, but he certainly seemed uncomfortable.

He slid the paper across the counter toward her. "You should go call him now."

"You think he's home in the middle of the day?"

"You won't know until you try." He gestured toward the door, clearly trying to hurry her along.

She studied the measurements he'd jotted down under the name and phone number. "Are these the size pans I should order?"

"It's what I ordered before."

"Denki." She put the paper into her pocket while going toward the door.

"No problem."

When she went outside, she saw a car pull up near the house. She continued down the steps and toward the store. The driver tooted the horn and hopped out. She had short black hair and wore dangly gold earrings and a bright red sweater with a yellow and red scarf. She was stunning, and Mattie couldn't help but think that she strongly resembled the girl Mattie had caught Gideon with three years ago. But she was too young to be Ashley.

"Is Gideon here?" she asked Mattie.

His desire to hurry her out the door suddenly made perfect sense. He didn't want her to know he was still seeing Englischer girls. She'd kept her mouth shut about it when they broke up. Did he think she'd make trouble for him now by telling the church leaders or his family? It was broad daylight, and he wasn't exactly sneaking around, so people had to know, didn't they? "He's inside."

The girl reached in and tooted the horn again. He came out onto the porch, the container of flowers in hand.

"Oh, they're beautiful!" She scurried up the steps and threw her arms around his neck.

Mattie's eyes caught Gideon's, and she wondered if he had any idea how disappointing his behavior was. Would he ever mature and either join the faith or leave it? And would she ever grow out of caring?

Eight

Gideon got into Sabrina's car. She maneuvered the flowers as she climbed behind the wheel, then passed them to him and started the engine. Soon they were pulling onto the road.

The look in Mattie Lane's eyes made him want to slither away. Living a lie was so much easier when she wasn't here to see him. If his life had gone down the path he'd expected, she would have understood the reason for what he did to her, and she would have forgiven him.

Sabrina held out her hand, palm up. "We don't see each other often enough."

He put his hand in hers and squeezed it before letting go.

"So who was the cute blond chick?"

"Chick?" He tried to sound jovial. "Is your generation using that word now?"

"My generation? You're not that old."

He couldn't think of one humorous thing to say, and he only had the energy to be honest. "I feel old."

"Yeah, Ashley used to say that too."

Weariness engulfed Gideon as he remembered his friend.

Sabrina pulled into the cemetery and parked the car. "I can't believe it's been two years." She gripped the steering wheel and stared at the headstones. "It's so unfair."

He got out and went around to her side of the vehicle. After opening her door, he passed her the flowers. "Kumm."

They ambled through the beige grass, and dried leaves crunched under their feet. When they came to Ashley's headstone, Sabrina removed an old arrangement and replaced it with the new one. "We didn't forget you." She brushed her fingertips along the top of the headstone. "We'll never forget," she whispered. She moved to Gideon's side and wrapped her arms around him. "Do you still miss my sister?"

"Not the same way you do, but ya."

"Nothing was ever the same after she was diagnosed."

He squeezed her tight. Even now, in spite of how much they'd talked about Ashley and her painful journey, Sabrina couldn't manage to say the word *leukemia*. "How's your family?"

"Coping better, but a piece of everyone who loved her died when she did."

"I know."

His heart had never been heavier.

If he explained his motives and reasoning to Mattie for what he did, she'd feel differently, and maybe she'd regain a tiny measure of respect for him. But he wouldn't do it. He refused to chance opening a door for her to return…or to risk watching her learn the truth and then not come back to him.

Sabrina tugged on his coat. "Come on. I'll let you buy me lunch at Zook's."

The weathered headstones stood stark and lonely as he and Sabrina drove toward the exit, and suddenly he was filled with a desire to grab on to life while he still could. But such longings weren't meant for people with a death sentence. What could be gained by reaching for something he couldn't hold on to?

Even as he asked himself that question, he knew the truth—he didn't want to take hold of something for forever. Only God knew how many days he had on this earth. Gideon trusted Him with the keeping of every sunrise, sunset, and all that was in between. He trusted Him concerning every battle, and he knew the power of the Cross. Those were the big issues, and Gideon had peace concerning his days and the end of them, but that aside, he still craved one thing—a little time with Mattie.

Sol stood in the tiny shed he called a workshop, behind his Daed's house, hammering out his frustrations by attaching stringers to yet another pallet. But his mind wasn't on the work. His thoughts lingered on Mattie...or, more accurately, on what Katie King had told him yesterday about her.

Mattie had been gone less than a week, and he felt all out of sorts. Displaced, he guessed. He had to talk to her, if just to regain his bearings. Yesterday he'd gone to King's Harness Shop to use their phone and call her at her Mamm's. But no one answered.

While he was there, Katie had braved the cold winds to walk from her house to her Daed's shop so she could tell him some news about Mattie.

"I was helping Daed, and I couldn't help but overhear the conversation when James Eash stopped by to call his mother." Katie had smoothed her dress time and again. "In response to something his Mamm said, James said it was hard to believe that Mattie and Gideon were able to work in the same house together."

When she'd said those words, Sol had felt a storm of emotions he couldn't begin to decipher.

"That struck me as an odd conversation. I know I've heard James mention that name before, but I don't know who Gideon is. Do you know him?"

After swallowing hard, Sol had said, "We've met."

"James also said he wasn't surprised that Gideon was doing whatever he could to help her replace all her pans."

Sol's jumbled emotions had funneled into one: irritation. First the man broke her heart, and then when she was clearly in a relationship with someone else, he decided to treat her right. "Maybe I should visit Mattie…make sure she's doing okay."

"That's sweet, Sol."

"I hope I can find a driver on such short notice."

"You know, my family's going to Lancaster tomorrow. Daed has some business there, and the rest of the family is going to visit relatives. We have to go through Apple Ridge on the way."

"Think your Daed would mind if I hitched a ride with you and your family?"

She'd grinned. "I know he won't. He's got an order to drop off at your Daed's place. He could do that tomorrow and pick you up while he's there."

Tired of replaying yesterday's events over and over, Sol put another board on the pallet and nailed it into place. There was no way Mattie would get involved with Gideon again.

Was there?

Through the tiny window of the shed, Sol saw a large white van pull into his Daed's driveway. The driver turned off the engine and leaned back, waiting for his passengers to disembark.

Benuel King, Katie's Daed, got out of the van, and his wife and five children followed suit. Sol's father came out of the house, and the two men opened the back of the van and pulled out two leather horse collars and the rigging, which they carried to the barn. Katie's Mamm and four siblings went inside the house with Sol's mother.

Katie stood on the driveway, looking at him through the shed window. She pointed at herself and then his shed, asking if he minded her coming over. He hesitated but motioned to her. He didn't want to talk with her, but she didn't make him as nervous today, probably because he was in too foul a mood to care what she thought.

Katie meandered into the shed, her brown eyes studying every inch of the small room. "Do you always work with the doors open and the kerosene heater running in winter?"

He put the unfinished pallet under the workbench. "Most of the time," he mumbled.

"You don't like being closed in, do you?"

He hadn't thought about it, but she was right. He shrugged rather than answer.

Katie shoved her hands into her coat pockets. "I shouldn't have said anything to you about what I overheard James saying on the phone. I feel like such a gossip."

"Why *did* you tell me?" Sol put his hammer on its peg to avoid looking at her.

"When Mattie first moved here, the single men went wild,

all wanting a chance with the new girl. But it was obvious to me that she had her sights on you."

Katie made him sound as if he were a buck grazing in an open field and Mattie had bagged him. He turned to her. "You sound jealous."

She froze for a moment, and he could see remorse reflected in her eyes. "It's true. I have been for so long, I guess I jumped at the first chance to make you see her in a bad light." She closed the gap between them. "But I'm not a bad person, Sol. I'm not jealous because of her success or because she turned the heads of all the other guys. What bothers me is that you started talking to me before she butted in. After that, you never even noticed me."

Three years ago it never dawned on him that Katie was interested in him. He'd thought she was just being her silly self, talking about nothing. Seemed odd she'd still be miffed about that, but he wasn't interested—not then or now. "I'm sorry. I didn't realize you felt that way."

"Are you upset with Mattie over what I told you?"

"I'm not going to Apple Ridge because of some one-sided piece of a conversation you overheard. I just want to visit her." He looked at Katie, realizing he no longer was the bundle of insecurity he'd always been around girls. For the first time he didn't feel nervous and miserable. He felt confident, just as he did when sitting in Mattie's cake shop talking to her.

He saw their Daeds returning from the barn and walked toward the door.

Katie grabbed the sleeve of his coat. "You let her hold too much power over you."

Sol gently pulled her hand free of his coat. "You don't look so good in green, Katie."

Mattie hitched her Daed's horse to a carriage and led the old girl to her front door. "Wait right here." She patted Jessie Bell's head and hurried into the kitchen to grab her sample cakes and head for Beth's.

Mamm stood at the table, wiping it down.

"Mamm, it's clean. Go rest." Mattie kissed her cheek. "Please."

"There's something sticky." Mamm scrubbed a spot as if trying to remove tar. Her gray hair had lost its luster long ago, and her pale skin had deep lines. She didn't need to stay in the kitchen the whole time Mattie was baking, but Mamm wouldn't have it any other way.

Mamm had gotten up with her before dawn this morning, helping her look through the stack of cake magazines Mackenzie had sent with her. The glossy pages had all sorts of pictures of wedding cakes, and they'd poured hours into looking through them and flagging the ones to show Beth and Lizzy. None of the images quite matched what Mattie wanted to make for them, but it would give the brides-to-be a few ideas so she could begin to make plans.

Mamm had stayed by her side while she prepared four types of cakes and frostings. Mattie intended to surprise Lizzy, Beth, and Jonah with samples of flavors she could make for their big day. She planned on stopping by Omar's on her way to the store to see if he could come to this surprise tasting too.

Taste-testing events were fun. The couples tended to enjoy each flavor of cake and frosting. But then they had to keep tasting and talking about the cakes until they could decide which one was their favorite.

She'd made Beth and Lizzy each a cake from a favorite flavor of theirs, then she'd added Belgian chocolate and buttercream filling to one and chocolate ganache with vanilla pastry-cream filling to the other. After that she made two cakes from flavors that were a bit more romantic in her estimation— an orange coconut cake with orange syrup and buttercream icing, and an apricot-praline cake with Bavarian cream filling.

Mamm had watched, cleaned up after her, and even offered suggestions, but she didn't have the energy to keep up with someone Mattie's age.

When Mamm stopped scrubbing her table, Mattie took the rag from her and put it in the sink. "Kumm." She took her by the hand and led her into the living room. "You prop up your feet and read awhile, okay?"

Mattie counted each year that her Mamm lived as a blessing, one she never took for granted. But sometimes they were too close for their own good. Moving away after she and Gideon had broken up hadn't been easy, but it'd been good for both of them.

Mamm had nearly died when Mattie was sixteen. She'd spent months in the hospital, battling lupus, and she'd had some close calls after that. At the time, Mattie had stopped everything to become her caretaker. But Mamm had slowly regained her strength, and she'd been holding her own since then.

Mamm slapped the arms of the chair. "Oh, I should go to the grocery store and get more supplies for you while you're at Beth's."

"You've done plenty. I'll get whatever we need." She didn't know how to handle the next few weeks where she'd need days of long hours to get Beth's and Lizzy's cakes made, but working in Mamm's kitchen wasn't the answer.

"Mattie," Mamm fussed, "the grocer is in the opposite direction of Hertzlers'."

"I know that, and I'm fine." She passed her a paperback book. "Promise me you'll rest."

Mamm's blue eyes stayed steady on her. "You're the one who was injured. And you're dealing with the shock of your shop burning."

Mattie sat on the ottoman near Mamm's feet. "Look me in the eyes. Do I appear to be falling apart?"

She shook her head. "No, but I heard you crying a few times after you crawled into bed."

"But the busier I stay, the better I feel, as long as I know I'm not wearing you out while I do it, okay?"

"You're sure you don't need me to—"

"I'm positive. What I need is for you to trust me."

Mamm patted her knee. "You always were a sweetheart."

"You too." Mattie squeezed her hand and returned to the kitchen.

She grabbed her mother's four cake carriers before getting into her carriage and heading to Hertzlers' Dry Goods. She'd ordered the pans from Mr. Ogletree Saturday evening, and he'd said she could pick them up at Lizzy's place after lunch today. So Beth and Lizzy were expecting her, which was good, but the cake-tasting venture would be a complete surprise.

Nine

A few hours after the deliverymen installed the gas-powered refrigerator and oven, Gideon finished hanging the last door. His joints ached, and a bone tiredness that he hadn't experienced in a long time wearied him. Maybe he was pushing himself too hard to finish this house, or maybe his symptoms were recurring. He'd beaten all the odds, and every routine medical test said he'd been clear of cancer for more than a year, but his kind of leukemia could come back at any time without warning.

Refusing to walk in fear, he whispered prayers of trust. Minutes ticked by, and Gideon began singing praises to God. Soon the aches stopped looming like a huge monster. Peace settled over him, and he was able to concentrate on the work at hand.

The cabinets and countertops were in place, and yesterday the heating guy had put in the wood furnace in the basement. The plumber would be here tomorrow to add the faucets and commodes and hook up the water. Gideon still had a pretty long to-do list, but he'd accomplished a lot in the last couple of days.

After leaving the cemetery with Sabrina, he'd squashed the desire for a little time with Mattie and had dived into work…as he'd always done when he had the strength. But working like crazy wasn't enough this time. He wanted to be with her today more than he wanted a promise of life tomorrow.

Conversations filtered into the master bedroom. It sounded as if three or four people had entered the front door.

"Oh, just look at this place!" Beth exclaimed. "Gideon?"

He walked down the hallway to the kitchen.

Jonah peeled out of his coat. "We have heat."

Beth, Jonah, Lizzy, Omar, and Mattie Lane were taking off their jackets. Mattie set a large paper bag with handles on the counter. Beth turned toward him. "How have you gotten so much done since I was here yesterday?"

"He's barely slept," Jonah offered.

Without looking at Gideon, Mattie reached into the bag she'd brought.

"Seems like his loss is your gain." Omar winked at Beth.

At times like these, Gideon was glad Bishop Omar didn't know his secret. But living a lie was exhausting.

"Kumm." Beth motioned for him. "Mattie made samples of wedding cakes, and I wanted to taste them in our new home. You have to try these and help us decide."

"Maybe he has other plans." Mattie shot him a quick look. "Ones that don't include hanging out with Plain old us."

He looked at the others to see if they had caught her barbed meaning, but they seemed too interested in the cakes. Clearly she was disappointed in him for leaving with an Englischer girl the other day. She probably wished he'd leave again, but his stubborn side refused to give her what she wanted.

Mattie pulled a small spiral notebook out of the bag, and her eyes grew large. She looked straight at him, as she had so many times in the past. At this moment she seemed void of anger, and it moved him.

"Missing something?" he asked.

"I didn't think to bring plates."

"I'll go get some from my place," Lizzy said. She and Omar put on their coats and hurried out the door.

Mattie set the notebook on the counter, pulled out a cake carrier, and looked into the bag again. Lines creased her face. "I didn't bring napkins either."

"The store has rolls of paper towels." Beth grabbed her coat. "I'll be right back."

"Thanks." Mattie turned to Gideon. "Can we start a fire in the hearth? You know, for a more special atmosphere."

"Sure. It's got a gas starter." Gideon went to the woodbin.

"Oh, no. Beth, wait."

Gideon turned to see Mattie hurrying to the door, trying to catch Beth, but she was halfway across the parking lot.

"What else did you forget?" Jonah asked.

"Forks to eat with and a knife to cut the cakes."

Jonah went to the door and then paused. "Anything else?"

She rolled her eyes. "Look, I've never done one of these outside my shop, and I had all this stuff there."

Moving logs to the fireplace, Gideon chuckled. "This is why I call her Mattie Lane. A day with her is a journey all by itself—a trip down a one-of-a-kind country road."

She gave Jonah an apologetic shrug. "I guess I am Mattie Lane after all."

Jonah laughed. "I'll be right back."

The house became quiet again. Gideon turned on the gas and lit a flame under the logs. He dusted off his hands and stood. "Did you remember the cakes?"

"Of course." She held up a cake carrier and frowned. "Wait. I...I only have one. What'd I do with the other three?" She looked into the paper bag. "I know I loaded four cake carriers in Mamm's kitchen. How could I not have them?"

"Because when you're on Mattie Lane, magical things happen."

She pursed her lips. "I don't like that lane, and clearly you don't either. I don't want to pull everyone else along that path with me."

He wanted to tell her that he'd always loved being a part of her world. But if he did, he'd have to explain why he'd broken up with her. "Maybe they're in the rig."

Her eyes lit up. "Ya, maybe." She put on her coat, then looked at him with concern. "What if I put the cake carriers on the carriage's sideboard when I left Mamm's? They'll be scattered all over the road."

"One step at a time, Mattie Lane. Kumm." He opened the door for her, and they went to the hitching post. The air smelled of snow, and a car parked at Hertzlers' Dry Goods had a pine tree strapped to its roof, reminding him that Christmas was less than a month away. The weeks leading up to Christmas always went by so quickly, as if a week equaled one day instead of seven. He wished that by some Christmas miracle time would slow and these days with Mattie nearby would last forever.

They went to the passenger side, and he opened the door of the rig. "Oh, good." A beautiful grin removed all the stress from her face.

She grabbed two cake carriers and passed them to him and then took out the last one and slammed the door to the rig. "I drive myself crazy sometimes." She studied him. "Did my forgetfulness drive a wedge between us and I was too scattered to know it? You can tell me the truth."

He couldn't move. At the time he'd been so sure of himself,

confident of his decision to lie in order to free her. Now a glimpse of insight into what he'd done to her chipped away at his certainty. "No, Mattie. I promise."

Her blue eyes stayed glued to him, and his heart pounded. *"Gut."* She nodded and walked back to the house.

He followed, wondering if he should tell her the truth. She needed to be set free from thinking he hadn't cared for her, but how could he do that without revealing his deception? He always figured she'd understand one day. But her question of self-doubt haunted him.

Beth and Jonah returned, goods in hand. "Look." She held up a handmade Christmas card. "We've received our first card of the season. It's addressed to Jonah and me." She put it on the fireplace mantel before turning to Jonah, satisfaction and joy radiating from her.

Lizzy and Omar walked in, each carrying a small box of items. "Plates." Lizzy held them up. "We also brought mugs, coffee, and the fixings."

"Great." Mattie opened the carriers and doled out a slice of cake to everyone in the group. "This first sample is praline-and-apricot yellow cake with Bavarian cream filling." She handed a paper towel to each person.

"Oh, I love apricot yellow cake," Lizzy said.

The moans and aahs over how good it was made Mattie Lane smile.

"Isn't it delicious, Gideon?" Beth asked.

"Ya." He hated that his tone sounded flat, but no part of him cared about cake right now. He stood mesmerized and bewildered at all he felt for the one who'd made it.

"Denki." A slight smile graced her face. She put another type of cake on Beth's plate and then Lizzy's. "Next is strawberries-and-cream vanilla cake layered with vanilla pastry cream and chocolate ganache."

Beth dug her fork into it. "Oh, that is too good." She scooped up another bite and held it in front of Jonah.

He opened his mouth, and she gently fed it to him. "Incredible."

The happy couples gathered at the far end of the counter, talking about the different cakes and flipping through magazine cutouts in the spiral notebook. A few minutes later Mattie dished up the third type of cake, explained what it was, then added the fourth type, describing it also.

Beth, Jonah, Lizzy, and Omar moved into the living room, discussing the textures, colors, and flavors. Was this his opportunity to talk to Mattie alone for a few minutes?

"Your baking skills are even more impressive than I expected." Gideon hoped to relax her with some friendly conversation.

"Denki. Give a girl nothing but time to work on cakes, and it's amazing what she can accomplish."

Her response quickly stopped his effort at small talk.

Omar returned, holding up his plate. "Lizzy and I know which one we want."

Mattie wiped her hands on her apron and opened her notebook. "Which one?"

"The apricot-and-praline yellow cake with the Bavarian cream."

"Perfect." Mattie jotted down notes.

"We know too." Beth came in, licking her fork. "The strawberries-and-cream vanilla cake with the vanilla pastry-cream filling and the chocolate stuff."

"Ganache," Mattie said. "I thought you'd like that one."

Jonah pointed at his plate with his fork. "But that orange coconut cake with the buttercream icing is almost as delicious."

Mattie added notes about Jonah's second choice. "Got it. Denki."

"Look." Beth set down her empty plate as she gazed out the window. "It's snowing." She grabbed Jonah's and her coats. "Jonah, remember the year it snowed on Christmas Eve, stranding me at a motel, and you rescued me?"

Jonah grinned while putting on his coat. "Nope."

Beth laughed. "You do too." She took him by the hand. "Kumm." The back door slammed shut as they went outside.

Lizzy laughed. "Omar, do you mind if we join them?"

He held her coat while she slid her arms into it. "Of course not."

Lizzy turned to them. "Mattie, Gideon?"

"No, but denki." Mattie wiped her hands on her white apron again, watching Beth try to catch snowflakes in her hands. "I need to clean up."

Gideon shifted. "I think I'll get a bit more work done too."

Lizzy and Omar went out the back door.

Mattie focused on him, her light blue eyes reminding him of all they'd once shared.

Maybe he needed to address the Sabrina issue and put to rest her insecurity about why he broke up with her.

Gideon reached for his tool belt on the counter, then hesitated. "I think you need to know a few pieces of information I left out when we broke up." Even as he said that, he wondered just how much to tell her.

Mattie placed the leftover cake on a clean plate. "Seems to me it's long past time for you to clarify anything. But if you need some type of resolution, go ahead." Now that she'd concluded her cake-tasting event, her tone reflected what she really felt—like moving a pan from a cold back burner to a heated front one.

She handed him the roll of paper towels. Then she took the empty cake containers down the hall and stepped into the wash house.

He followed her, leaving the door open behind them. The almost-finished room had two mud sinks, a wringer washer, and a couple of stools.

Now that they were alone, all the reasons he'd broken up with her echoed in his mind. He silently prayed, hoping the right words would come to him.

Mattie Lane dumped the cake carriers into one of the sinks. "We actually get along pretty well when I manage to forget about your dating habits, although they are a little hard to block out when I'm face-to-face with the newest habit."

He stared at the paper towels in his hand. "That was Ashley's sister. Sabrina."

She wheeled around. "Gideon, how could you?"

"It's not like that, Mattie Lane. For one thing, I joined the faith two years ago and wouldn't go against our ways by dating outside the faith. Have you never asked anyone what I'm doing these days?"

"No," she snapped. "And the other thing?"

"Ashley died, and—"

She gasped. "I'm so sorry. What happened?"

"Leukemia."

Mattie's brow wrinkled. "How awful. I'm truly sorry."

"She had it when we met."

She peered at him, and he could see the light of understanding creep into her eyes. "Are you saying that you began to care for her…when she was sick?"

He shifted the paper towels into his other hand. "She was scared and needed a friend."

"So you ditched me?" Her eyes flashed. "You tossed me out like an old shoe?" She yanked a paper towel off the roll with such vengeance he nearly dropped it.

He knew when he'd used her jealous nature against her that she'd probably walk off and never look back. But now he needed her to understand he hadn't tossed her aside because he preferred someone else.

He rubbed the back of his neck. He should tell her he never thought of Ashley as more than a friend. But then what would he give as the reason he broke up with her? "The truth is—"

"Wait." She held up a hand. "Just because I happen to have crossed your path again, don't feel you need to make up a different story about what took place."

"I'm not doing that."

She wiped the cake carriers with a wad of towels, doing the best she could to clean without water. "The problem with liars and cheats is that they lose all credibility."

This was not going at all the way he'd hoped. Instead of his assuring her the breakup wasn't her fault, he was simply reopening old wounds.

Mattie finished scrubbing the cake carriers and set them in the sink. "I'm really sorry about Ashley," she said, her tone less harsh. "But at this point, I'm not sure you're even capable of telling me the truth."

"I am, Mattie Lane. With all my heart."

She tossed the frosting-covered paper towels into the second mud sink and looked up at him. "It's ridiculous, but I still want to believe you when you tell me something. But I can't. I just can't."

He avoided her steady gaze. "It won't do any good for me to try to explain if you're not going to believe me."

"I do believe you about Ashley." Her tone was typical Mattie Lane—a bit high-strung, yet tender-hearted and resolute. "And when I saw Sabrina, I noticed that she looked a lot like Ashley, so I believe you about her too."

That was a start. Gideon took a deep breath, wishing he could reveal the secret he'd been harboring. "I need you to know that our breakup had nothing to do with your not being good enough or perfect enough."

She scoffed. "Nearly three years after the fact, you're going to give me the line 'It wasn't you; it was me'? You must think I'm vulnerable and frail because my shop burned down."

"Don't be sarcastic. It doesn't suit you."

"Ya? Well, what does suit me, Gideon? Because whatever

it is, you suddenly seem to think it's your place to find out and fix it."

A van pulled up in front of Hertzlers' store, and a man got out. The lines of frustration faded from Mattie Lane's face. "Sol's here."

Once again, Mattie's beau showed up at an awkward time. "Were you expecting him?"

"He's supposed to be hunting." She pursed her lips together, suppressing a smile as she gazed out the picture window. "But whatever he's doing, I trust him in ways I thought I'd never trust again." She turned to Gideon. "Was there something else you wanted to tell me?"

He shook his head. "I suppose not."

She tucked a few stray strands of hair into her prayer Kapp and hurried out of the room.

Mattie still thought he'd fallen for Ashley and broken up with her because of it. The only thing this conversation had accomplished was that she knew he wasn't dating Sabrina.

He watched through the window as she slid into her coat while hurrying across the yard. Sol grinned and embraced her. Gideon's knees threatened to go weak on him, but he refused them that right.

Jonah tapped on the open door. "I saw Mattie out there. I suppose that's Sol."

"Ya."

"You doing okay?"

Gideon collapsed onto the stool in the corner of the wash house. "I wanted to tell her the truth."

Jonah closed the door. "What truth?"

Gideon rubbed clammy hands down his trousers. Even though he hadn't known Jonah much more than a year, he considered him a trustworthy friend. And it'd feel good to share his secret with someone. "Three years ago, in the fall, I started feeling strange. I was tired all the time, had night sweats, couldn't get rid of a cold, and spiked a high fever regularly for no apparent reason."

"Serious stuff."

"Ya. The first time I mentioned my symptoms to Mattie, she was alarmed, practically beside herself with concern, so I downplayed how I felt. Her mother has had health issues all of Mattie's life, and when she almost died about six years ago, Mattie struggled. She barely slept, and when she did, she had nightmares."

"Beth told me about that."

He scratched his brow, remembering how dark and confusing life was when he couldn't share his concerns with the one person he needed most. "After going in circles with doctors who couldn't figure out what was wrong, I went to a new doctor. He diagnosed me to be in the chronic phase of a rare form of leukemia." His throat closed up.

Jonah shifted his cane from one hand to the other. "I...I didn't know. "

"No one does, except my family, and I swore them to secrecy." He cleared his throat. "I told people I had out-of-town jobs, and I went to a cancer center in Philadelphia for treatment. That's where I met Ashley...Sabrina's sister. She'd had leukemia for years and was a volunteer at the clinic. We became friends. She believed we'd both get well, and I was almost convinced. But rather than me getting better, the cancer jumped to the worst possible stage—the blast phase."

"But you didn't tell Mattie what was going on?"

"I hated the idea of telling her. Still, I decided to tell her after the holidays. But on Christmas Day, Ashley came to my house, needing to talk. She'd received new test results, and her prognosis was grim. She'd been positive of a cure, regardless of the nightmare roller coaster she'd been on for so long. While I was consoling Ashley, Mattie walked in. She saw us hugging and wanted answers."

"What did you tell her?"

"That she needed to date others."

"Why would you say that?"

"Ashley's type of cancer was much easier to beat than mine,

and when her cancer returned, her whole family went into a tailspin. I knew I didn't want to drag Mattie down that road with me. Letting her think I cared for Ashley freed her to build a life of her own rather than watching mine deteriorate."

Jonah took the stool beside Gideon. "All this time you've let her believe you care for someone else?"

"I couldn't see any other way of protecting her…so I lied. I said I wanted to be free." But he hadn't been free. His heart had remained her captive. "Even though I'm in complete remission right now, the disease could return tomorrow. Or next year. Or a decade from now."

"Or never," Jonah took off his jacket. "You should've let Mattie make her own decision."

"She'd just turned nineteen the day before. A kid, really."

"And what were you, all of twenty-two?"

"Barely. I have no doubts that if she had known the truth, she would have stayed by my side." Gideon clenched his fingers together. "I'd never try to get her back. But watching her with someone else is killing me more than the cancer."

Jonah folded his hands together and stared at them. "Remember when you told me you found it odd that Beth, who's spent more than a decade making her own decisions, constantly asks my opinion about things?"

Gideon nodded. "You said that when two people are a couple, they need to get each other's opinions before making any decision that impacts both, or they'll store up trouble for their future."

"Regardless of the purity of your motivation, you've brought problems on Mattie and yourself."

Gideon shook his head. "I know I've hurt her. But staying with me would have brought her even more pain. There's no telling what it would have done to her."

"You think you were guarding Mattie's heart. But it sounds to me as if the only thing you protected her from was making her own choices."

Like a workhorse whose blinders had been removed, Gideon saw beyond the narrow path directly in front of him. He viewed a landscape that had once been fertile soil growing lush greenery but now was parched and desertlike with multiple shades of brown.

The cancer hadn't done that. He had.

And because of his actions, Mattie had moved away, found good soil, and replanted her life.

One question remained. What should he do now?

Ten

*A*fter embracing Sol, Mattie waited in the yard of Beth's home while he took his overnight bag to her carriage tied outside the store.

A light snowfall swirled around her, making everything look peaceful and charming, but Gideon's confession had rattled her. On the one hand, relief that he wasn't nearly as shallow as she'd thought lapped over her. On the other hand, disappointment that he'd chosen Ashley over her still stung— even if he had bonded with the Englischer girl out of compassion. At least his sketchy account of what had happened between the two of them lined up a lot better with who she'd always thought him to be, a kind and deeply caring man.

He should have told her the truth about Ashley *before* she caught them together. And when he broke up with her, why didn't he tell her about Ashley's illness? What had he been thinking?

Gideon had always been complicated. She used to think of

him like an oak tree—the magnificent, stretching limbs didn't compare to the complex root system.

Sol walked toward her, and she tried to clear her mind, not wanting Sol to see the conflicting emotions on her face. She wished she felt nothing for Gideon. But wishing it didn't make it real.

The man in front of her was the opposite of Gideon in every way. He said what he thought, always simple and straight-forward. She liked that about him. He wasn't full of twists and turns that could confuse or hurt her. She wished she could return to Ohio with him now and not look back. Since the cake-tasting was over, maybe she could pop back in and tell them a quick good-bye. Then she'd leave and keep right on moving…in every possible way.

She opened her arms, gesturing across the land. "Welcome to Apple Ridge."

"Denki." He glanced at the road. "I'm so glad you're here. Do you realize I don't have the address to your house?"

"So how did you find me?"

"The driver knew how to get to Hertzlers' Dry Goods, so our plan was to stop by and ask someone in the store where you lived. But here you are."

"I'm wrapping up a cake-tasting event for my cousin and aunt and their fiancés."

He placed his hands on her shoulders, looking bewildered, but his smile gave him away. "So how'd we manage two years of courtship without my ever coming to your folks' place?"

She put her arm around his waist, not feeling the least bit of warmth emanating from him through his wool coat. "Because they always visit us. And you would have been here for Thanksgiving this year…if the shop hadn't burned down. But you'll see my childhood home soon enough. Why don't you bring the rig up to the front door? I'll tell everyone a quick bye, and we'll be on our way."

He frowned, a moment of disbelief flashing in his eyes. "You don't want me to step inside and meet your cousin and aunt?"

Not really. She'd have to introduce him to Gideon, which would be awkward. But it'd only take a few moments. "Oh, ya. Sure." As they climbed the stairs to Beth's home, they parted a bit.

"Are you hungry?" she asked.

"No." He reached for her hand.

Holding hands was out of character for Sol, but she didn't question it. "Did I see other Amish in the van when you were dropped off?"

Lines of frustration showed on his face. "Ya. I rode with the King family. They're on their way to Lancaster. Since they have the only Amish community phone now that your cake shop is gone, I had to go there to call you, but no one answered at your folks' place."

"You could've used the phone at Mackenzie's store."

"Ya, then I'd be a spectacle to the Englischers. Besides, if I'd gone there, Katie wouldn't have told me that her family was coming through Apple Ridge so I could hitch a ride."

Guilt nibbled at Mattie's heart, and she couldn't manage to smile at him. While he'd been doing something very sweet by coming here, her thoughts were a tangled mess over Gideon. "That's quite a ride just to visit me."

"Ya. All I can say is I must be crazier about you than I realized. Hunting was no fun with you gone, and my nerves are raw from being closed up in a vehicle with her."

Her gut twisted with shame. He was being as straightforward and honest as ever, and she wanted to be like that for him too. She tugged on his hand. "Sol."

He stopped, and the sincerity in his eyes weighed heavily on her. She needed to at least brace him. "Gideon Beiler is inside."

His expression didn't change, but his gaze pierced her. "Inside the house? What's he doing here?"

"Working. He's the builder, and he's trying to finish it before their wedding."

He nodded and motioned toward the door. She reluctantly opened it, and they went inside.

Beth, Jonah, Lizzy, and Omar were in the kitchen, polishing off the cake crumbs on their plates. She introduced Sol around, and he shook each person's hand. When Gideon walked in, Sol stole a look at her. Her tongue was too thick to speak.

"We keep running into each other, Gideon." Sol shook his hand.

Gideon's jaw clenched. "Sol."

Confusion circled inside Mattie. "When did you two meet?"

"At the hospital the night you were injured." Sol said it casually while taking her hand in his again.

Mattie glanced from Gideon to Sol, aggravated that neither of them had told her. But this wasn't the time to talk about it.

"I hear you're a hunter," Jonah said. "Bagged anything of late?"

"Not really." Sol glanced at Gideon. "The woods are busy these days. When too many hunters crowd the same spot, no one goes home with anything."

Anger flashed in Gideon's eyes, but whatever he was thinking, he held his tongue.

Sol's veiled message hadn't bypassed anyone, and the room vibrated with discomfort. Embarrassment flushed Mattie's face. She wasn't some soft-eyed doe caught in Sol's cross hairs. She pulled her hand from his. "We need to go."

"Sure."

They said their good-byes and left the house. Mattie bit her tongue, determined not to say a word until they were in private. She strode across the lawn and the store's parking lot, removed the tether from the hitching post, and climbed into the rig. Sol got in beside her.

She took the reins and tapped them on the horse's back. "That was uncalled for."

"What?" He looked totally innocent.

"Comparing me to a deer. I'm not prized game, Sol."

"I don't think he picked up on it."

"Of course he did, and so did everyone else."

He shrugged. "I don't care."

"I do." When the horse flinched, she knew she needed to tone down her voice. "And why didn't you tell me Gideon came to the hospital?" She pulled out of the parking lot, taking a different route toward her home so they'd have time to settle this.

"You were under enough stress at the time without me adding something unimportant to you."

"Make up your mind. You didn't share it either because it'd be stressful for me or because you didn't think it mattered."

He stared out the frosty side window for several minutes. "Do you know what this is?"

"What?" she snapped.

"Our first argument." He propped his arm on the door of the carriage.

Until now she'd not thought about the fact that she and Sol never quarreled. She and Gideon had on numerous occasions. At various times they played, worked, and fought hard.

With passion and gusto—that's what Gideon used to call it. And then he'd smile, causing her heart to melt as he confessed that he wouldn't want it any other way...until Ashley came along.

Sol tapped his fingers on the fake wood on the dashboard. "Who is Gideon seeing these days?"

She shrugged. "I'm not sure."

"But you'd like to know."

"I didn't say that."

"True. But you didn't say, 'I don't care,' either."

She slowed the rig, pulling into a Mennonite church parking lot, and came to a halt. "I want to say it."

His features were lined with hurt. He scraped frost off the window with his fingernail. "You told me you let Gideon go because you refused to marry a man who had feelings for someone else. You wanted all or nothing. Remember us talking about that?"

"Ya."

"Here's the problem, Mattie. I feel the same way. I'm not

interested in making a big fuss if you have feelings for someone else."

"But I…I like who we are." Tears filled her eyes.

Sol cradled her face. "I do too. But your answer tells me I may have spent too much time thinking you're in love with me."

She pulled away, wiping her cheeks. "Are you breaking up with me?"

"No." He leaned back on the seat. "I hope that never happens." He brushed the back of his fingers down her face. "But I'd like you to sort out your feelings."

She tried not to gape at him. "Gideon's a cheater and a liar. You and I are good for each other."

"I think he regrets breaking up with you." Sol rubbed her tears off his fingers. The disappointment in his eyes cut her. "He beat me to the hospital when you were hurt, and he looked pretty shook up that night."

Her heart raced at the thought of losing Sol. "What are you saying?"

His amber eyes tugged at her heart. "I'll be in Ohio on Christmas Eve. I hope you'll be there for the singing. If not, we'll both know I'm not the one for you."

"I'll be there several days before then. I promise."

Eleven

With keys in hand, Gideon went up the stairs of Beth and Jonah's place.

Beth followed him, carrying a couple of bolts of fabric. "Sorry about coming by the Snyder place and interrupting your work. More than needing you to unlock the place, I don't want to walk across the floors until you verify they're dry enough for Mattie to get in here and work."

After finishing the floors, he'd purposely kept all the keys, trying to ensure that no one walked on the floors until they were dry. He slid the key into the deadbolt and turned it. When he opened the door, a strong smell of lacquer greeted him. Four days ago, two days after the cake tasting Sol had interrupted, he'd thoroughly cleaned the unfinished floors and then shellacked them. He'd locked up the house, leaving two windows slightly open, one in the wash house and one in the master bedroom. But that wasn't enough to disperse the smell.

At the time he did the floors, he hadn't known Mattie needed Beth's supersized oven to bake Lizzy's wedding cake.

He knelt before entering and pressed on the floor in different spots. "It's not the least bit tacky." He stood and motioned for her to go in ahead of him.

"Good." She stepped inside. "Sorry about the miscommunication. It never dawned on me that you were ready to do the floors this soon."

"It's not a problem for me, just for Mattie."

"She's been doing what she can from her home—making the fondants and preparing some of the smaller decorations. But her Mamm insists on helping, and Mattie doesn't want her to be on her feet much more. It'd be better if she can work here from now on."

Wondering if Sol was still in Apple Ridge, maybe even staying with Mattie's parents, Gideon put a key into Beth's hands. "You ladies can both come in and out as needed."

"Denki." She slid the key into her coat pocket and pulled out a sheet of paper. "This is a list of what I need to have done before the gathering."

While he read over it, Beth went down the hall and into the master bedroom.

"I think most of these things could wait a few days," he called out.

He really didn't want to spend time in the same house as Mattie, trying to protect the lie he'd told.

Maybe Jonah was right. Had he not protected Mattie at all? Still, telling her now was unacceptable. She and Sol were together, and he'd never do anything to change that.

But Jonah's words lay heavy across his shoulders, like a two-ton support beam that needed to be anchored in place, not toted around by a mortal man.

At the time of his lie, he'd considered it acceptable, even honorable—like Rahab, who betrayed her own city through a lie and brought favorable treatment to her whole family. Gideon had chosen to betray himself in order to open the door to good things for Mattie.

A lie would've been unacceptable if he'd wanted to get away with something for selfish purposes. But he hadn't profited from the lie. On the contrary, he'd paid dearly for it.

Beth walked back into the room, carrying the bolts of fabric. "What did you say?"

"I said I think I could wait on this list until after Lizzy's wedding."

Her lips hinted at a slight pout. "But Jonah's family is arriving at the end of the week, and I want everything comfortable for them. They'll be tired after coming all this way. I'd like to at least have all the shelves up in the closets and pantry, blinds or curtains on the windows, and gas night-lights installed so they don't hurt themselves if they get up in the dark." She held a piece of fabric near a window for a moment. "The pegs need to be made and inserted into the wainscot before Jonah's family arrives. And—"

"I read the list, Beth." Gideon lifted his tool belt off the countertop. "Go run your store. Or make curtains. Or something."

"Good idea." She took a few steps and stopped. "You will be nice to Mattie, won't you?"

Gideon chafed at the question. "Not a problem."

Beth pulled the door closed behind her.

He decided to start in the kitchen. Whatever he accomplished in adding shelves and such would make Mattie's preparation for the gathering easier. If he put in some extra hours now, he might get done and be out before she arrived.

Gideon had installed one shelf in the pantry when the front door opened. The sound of pans clattering to the floor indicated it wasn't Jonah. Gideon took a deep breath and went to the foyer. Stooping, Mattie gathered several pans.

He grabbed one, and she gasped, falling onto her backside. "Good grief." She got to her feet. "You startled me."

"Sorry, Mattie. I guess you couldn't hear me coming over the rattling of pans."

"Jonah said you were working on another job for a while."

"I was, but Beth came by with a list of items for me to finish."

Scowling, Mattie went into the kitchen. "Sounds like Beth and I need to talk. She can't expect us to work together like this."

"That's what I told her. But my protests fell on deaf ears." He picked up the rest of the pans and followed her. "Do you need help bringing more stuff in?"

"No. Whatever I managed to remember to bring, I can tote myself." She laid her small spiral notebook on the counter.

Gideon had seen Aden at Zook's Diner that morning and asked him about the drawings. He said he was nearly finished re-creating what he remembered. Gideon reminded him of some of the cakes she'd done that he knew about, and Aden promised to do his best to sketch them.

Mattie's countenance softened as she fiddled with the pages in the notebook. "I'm leaving for Ohio as soon as I can after Beth and Jonah's wedding." She lifted her eyes to his, and the sadness in them bothered him. "Whatever is happening between us here isn't good for me and Sol."

Gideon held her gaze, wishing he could have one day alone with her. Just one day to keep in his memory for the rest of his life. One day with no lies or anger or hurt between them—nothing except forgiveness and friendship.

"I understand." He cleared his throat, trying to make his voice sound normal. "I'll work in another room and leave you in peace."

He hung shelves in one closet after another. Hours passed, and the house smelled of cake and frosting, but Mattie Lane wasn't whistling. She used to whistle. Whenever he stopped making a racket, he heard her sigh and mumble.

A loud thud came from the front of the house, followed by a cry.

He rushed from the far end of the house into the kitchen. Mounds of frosted cake lay on the floor, and spatters of it clung to Mattie's face and dress.

She had her hands on her hips, and anger flashed in her eyes. "I lost all my cake stands in the fire. No one owns anything nearly large enough for a cake this size, so I tried making my own." She wiped cake off her face and pointed at the toppled stand. "I was sure it wouldn't break, but I didn't realize it was out of balance until I added the third layer."

"It must have been somewhat balanced if it held up until then."

Her eyes filled with tears. "I'm missing too many things to do this. The right potholders. My cooling racks. Cake stands. The measurements may have been the same, but these pans are deeper and heavier than I'm used to. I haven't reached for one thing that feels right. It's all different and awkward..."

Gideon stepped around the cake mass and opened the cabinet below the sink. He pulled a disposable cup out of a package and then filled it with water. Putting a firm hand on her shoulder, he guided her toward a stool and passed her the water. She seemed on the verge of hysteria, and he wanted to assure her. "Mattie Lane, you are strong enough to—"

"Ohhh," she growled, cutting him off. "Please don't treat me like I'm going to break from stress. I'm not that fragile, Gideon."

Her voice was filled with emotion, and pink tinged her cheeks. She'd been dealt a lot of blows in life, and he realized he'd always considered her fragile—a delicate, mysterious seedling in need of perfect soil, sun, and water.

She went to the sink, wet a washcloth, and began wiping splotches of cake and frosting from her dress, visibly shaking. But her emotional reaction didn't make her weak, and he'd been a fool to think it had.

She sighed, and a gentle, sad smile graced her beautiful face as a tear fell. "It might be my fault the shop caught fire."

"Whatever happened, it was an accident."

Her chin quivered. "I think I may have left our notebook on the wood stove."

Our notebook. The phrase worked its way into the recesses of his loneliness, bringing relief.

How strange life was. As she opened up to him the way she

had years ago, Gideon saw more than the hurt and disappointment pressing in on her. He saw strength. Wide and high and deep. And so very tender.

She ran her hands over her wet cheeks and sniffed. "Okay, enough of this." She pursed her lips. "Onward and upward." She rolled her eyes and gestured at the cake. "Or onward and downward, as the case may be."

He got a pan out of the sink to put the mounds of cake into, but Mattie Lane grabbed two forks and sat on the floor. She waved a fork over the highest area in the center. "None of this part touched the floor."

Blinking, he took a fork and sat.

She wrinkled her nose. "Remember our first cake?"

He chuckled. "We thought it was supposed to be an upside-down backside cake, right?"

The smile on her face spoke of friendship. "The Bundt cake that we thought was called a Bum cake." She laughed. "Mamm helped me bake it. After it cooled, we had the brilliant idea to make it the perfect Bum cake. I dumped it out of the pan onto a chair, and you sat on it."

He tugged at his pants as if airing them out. "It needed to be a lot cooler than it was when I sat on it. I remember that much."

Her laughter bounced off the walls of the empty home, refreshing his weary soul.

He pointed at her. "And again, I got in trouble, and your family thought you were adorable." He hadn't really gotten in trouble, but his grandmother did lecture him that at ten years old he should know to eat food, not sit on it.

She jabbed her fork into the cake. "Admit it, Gideon. You liked taking the blame, as long as it kept me out of trouble."

He didn't need to confess that, but he saw the truth of it more and more. If he'd seen her as the capable young woman she really was, would he have lied to her?

He took a bite of cake. "I remember the cake you made when we were teens. It was so hard that Beiler Construction used it as a cornerstone when we built a new house."

She laughed. "It wasn't that bad! Besides, you passed me the baking powder and said it was baking soda."

"Oh, ya, sure. Blame me." He swallowed a piece of cake, enjoying these few moments. Memories of them as children faded as ones of their courtship took over. "Remember when we came home all wet from our first canoe trip down the Susquehanna?"

Her eyes grew large, and she chortled. They'd gone down the river with a group of strangers, and a snake had dropped out of a tree onto an Englischer guy. The man panicked, tipping over the canoe. "We always were the talk of the community. What was it your grandmother used to call us?"

"Huck Finn and Becky Thatcher."

"Ah, right." Mattie lifted her chin to constrict her neck. "You kids remind me," she said, mimicking his grandmother's high-pitched, elderly voice, "of two peas in a pod. Life is just a blink, and you two sure know how to make it count."

After a hearty round of laughter at her imitation, quietness surrounded them, and her blue eyes smiled at him.

She stretched out her legs and leaned back against the cabinet. "It's good to see you laugh, Gideon. You've changed. Not so much in ways I can point my finger at, but it's there inside you. A hardness of some type that rarely gives way to the man I once knew. I guess losing Ashley took a lot out of you."

His heart palpitated, feeling as if weights were being lifted from it. "I'm so sorry, Mattie Lane."

She tilted her head, studying him. "Ya, I believe you are. We could wipe the slate clean now if you like."

"How so?"

"We can pretend you broke up with me the right way."

He tried to imagine being barely twenty-two again with the news he'd gotten and what he'd do differently this time. But he didn't know the answer.

She pointed her fork at him. "Regardless of how it happened, I'm actually glad I moved to Ohio to start my shop."

He stared at her, waiting for her to say she was also glad she met Sol.

She stood and washed her hands and face in the sink and then grabbed a towel.

"You seem to really like living there."

"Ya, I do. But I chose to start my business there for two reasons: it was far removed from you, and my parents peacefully accepted the change because I could live under the safety and affordability of James's roof. Not sure there's much calling me back now that the shop burned."

He propped his forearm on his knee, trying to sense her thoughts. Since she hadn't mentioned Sol, he wanted to believe that he didn't matter that much to her, but maybe he was seeing what he wanted to see. Even if it was true, Sol was better for her. Gideon had broken her heart once. If she came back to him and the cancer returned, he'd end up hurting her even worse.

Gideon stood. "Mattie Lane," he said softly, "if Sol's not the one, please don't settle."

"What?" She locked eyes with him, confusion evident.

"You didn't mention him as a reason to return."

"Oh." She got a large bowl out of the sink, knelt beside the mound of cake on the floor, and started tossing bits and pieces into it. "It's just that his job could be done anywhere, so we wouldn't have to live in Ohio."

"He builds pallets for a corporation, right?"

She glanced up. "How would you know that?"

Gideon couldn't stomach telling her another lie. "I asked your brother James about him once."

She raised her eyebrows and waited, letting him know that his answer was not sufficient.

He shrugged. "I needed to be sure you were seeing someone safe."

She returned to dumping cake in the pan, but a slight smile crossed her face. "I'm very safe with Sol. You don't need to worry about that." She stood and carried the bowl to the trash can. "I'm going to be here all night making fresh cakes. I'll need kerosene lanterns."

"I can get some at the dry goods store. You need anything else?"

"That should do it."

"How about a new cake stand?"

"No, I'm fine. I'll just scale back my fancy plans a bit this time." Her eyes met his. "Denki, Gideon."

Her thank-you seemed to hold a dozen messages—gratefulness that they'd patched up what they could between them and that he'd helped her release some of her frustrations over losing her shop. But it also seemed to carry a message of finality, as if they'd gone as far as they ever would in this relationship—two friends who'd go their separate ways all too soon.

With a pastry bag in hand, Mattie stood in Beth and Jonah's finished home, working on their wedding cake. The pleasure of creating and decorating it bounced around inside her with as much energy as was displayed in the rest of the house. Voices echoed off the walls as people came in and out like travelers at a train station.

Lizzy and Omar had married last week, and their wedding cake had been lovely. She'd used dark beige fondant with light beige icing for their apricot-praline cake. The rope design she'd run along the sides and the flowers of the same color on top had accomplished the desired look.

Beth and Jonah had chosen the strawberries-and-cream vanilla cake with chocolate ganache and vanilla pastry-cream filling, so Mattie had used a white fondant with deep red flowers draping down the side.

But it was the cake she'd made for tonight's prewedding

dinner that pleased her most. Unlike the other cakes, she'd been able to work on this one with her Mamm, keeping the hours to a minimum and spread out over a week. She expected Beth and Jonah to get a kick out of how she'd decorated tonight's cake.

Gideon had come to the house one evening on an errand for his grandmother, and even seeing it in the early stages, he seemed awed by her imagination and skill.

Tomorrow was Beth and Jonah's big day. As excited as Mattie was to be a part of their wedding, she and Gideon had already spent too much time together. And neither would get away with disappearing during any part of the festivities. Jonah had chosen him to be the Amish equivalent of a best man, and she was Beth's equivalent of a maid of honor. By Amish tradition those positions had to be filled by unmarried people. Since all of Beth's and Jonah's siblings were married, that role fell to cousins and close friends.

She had to get away from this place as soon as possible.

Lizzy backed in the door, carrying armloads of folded white tablecloths. Another round of cold air surged inside. "The bride's table goes there." Lizzy directed the half-dozen men helpers as easily as she ran her store. They quickly set up lacquered wooden picnic tables and benches in the main living area, and Mattie helped Lizzy dust them until they virtually glowed in the light of the kerosene lanterns.

Several men entered, carrying stacks of folding chairs.

"Those need to be set up in the basement, leaving a center aisle for the couple to walk down," Lizzy ordered.

At Lizzy and Omar's wedding last week, Mattie had managed to avoid being around during the Choosing—a time late in the afternoon when single girls of the age to be courted lined up in a room, and the single men entered one at a time, from oldest to youngest, and chose a girl to pair up with for the rest of the festivities. She'd disappeared during that time, using the excuse that her Mamm and Daed were exhausted and she needed to take them home. Her Mamm told her that when Gideon attended weddings after Mattie left, he'd used that same trick, taking his grandmother home.

Had he not dated anyone since Ashley died? Since he'd joined the faith, he wouldn't have dated an Englischer women. And part of joining the faith was agreeing to seek a wife within the Amish community. She pushed those thoughts aside, demanding her mind to get off Gideon and what his life had been like the past three years. All she had to do was get through the wedding tomorrow and the cleanup the next day, and she could keep her distance from him until she boarded the train at midnight on Monday, which would put her in Ohio a full four days before Christmas Eve.

Mattie helped Lizzy spread the white linen cloths over the long rectangular tables set up in the main room. They lit kerosene floor lanterns as the evening grew darker, making the rooms much brighter.

"Hey, Lizzy," someone called from another part of the house. "Could you come here?"

"On my way."

Lizzy hurried off. Mattie easily tuned out the goings-on around her so she could remain focused on putting the final touches of frosting on the cake. She wished tuning out her thoughts about Gideon were as simple. She'd forgiven him for his misconduct, and now they got along just as well as they always had. Too well.

He'd been really helpful lately, designing and building cake stands to her specifications. He'd also built her a set of professional cooling racks that he said he'd ship to Ohio when the time came. He was the man she'd fallen in love with—giving and caring.

She couldn't remember the last time Sol had offered to help her with anything to do with her making cakes. But that's not who she and Sol were. They made a good couple because they worked well independently and then scheduled time together around their busyness. Lots of couples did that, probably most.

A loud thud resounded through the house, and she jumped, almost smearing the delicate green leaf she'd been working on. "You're supposed to be setting up tables and benches, not tearing the house down," Mattie said loudly, teasing whoever had dropped the piece of furniture.

"Sorry." A male voice echoed back at her.

Mattie switched pastry bags and added a tiny red flower to the side of the wedding cake.

Jonah walked in, carrying a bench. "You seen Lizzy?"

Mattie's aunt flew into the room before she could answer. "Where does this one go?"

"The second bedroom."

"Denki." Jonah nodded and kept going. Lizzy followed.

Beth came in the back door, juggling several large pots and pans that would be used to serve the wedding feast. "There's four inches of snow out there. It's gorgeous." Beth put the pots on the stove and moved to the counter to admire the cake. Again. "It's more lovely than I could've hoped for."

"It hasn't changed much since the last time you saw it."

"I know, but it looks prettier every time I swing through here." Beth rinsed her hands in the sink.

Lizzy came into the foyer on her way to the front door. "We're on schedule, Beth."

"You're amazing," Beth called after her. "That means we'll be done setting up for tomorrow in about five minutes, and everyone is going to Lizzy's to eat. You're going to join us, right?"

"Ya, but I need to do a few more things. I'll walk over as soon as I can."

"More? It's remarkable already."

"Denki. But I'll be the one who decides when I'm done," she teased. "Now, go away so I can finish."

Beth laughed. "Wow, it's a good thing I know you love me."

The racket in the house slowly died down until it became silent. Mattie moved to the kitchen window, watching large white flakes swirl against the dark sky. The shortest day of the year was fast approaching. She stepped onto the back porch. The night air smelled of Christmas.

"Mattie Lane."

Gideon's voice scattered her but also warmed her.

She turned. His gaze held hers, and she tried to lower her eyes.

"We ran out of seats, so Lizzy sent me after one of the benches. Jonah said to tell you it's perfect weather to hitch a horse to the sleigh, so we're doing that after dinner and taking turns going for rides."

Was he asking her to go for a sleigh ride with him? "I can't." She was desperate to keep her distance from him.

He nodded.

"But I could use a hand getting the cake to Lizzy's." She went inside to the wash house and took the celebration cake out of hiding.

Gideon studied it, nodding. "That's really something."

The large sheet cake had edible stencil cutouts and sculpturing that portrayed scenes from Beth and Jonah's story—Jonah in a shop, carving; Beth seeing the carving for the first time; and them writing to each other. Since Beth had thought she was writing to an elderly man at the time, Mattie put a few words on one of the tiny sheets of edible paper.

Dear old man ~

Then she'd made a happily-ever-after scene in which Jonah rescued Beth in a sleigh on a snowy Christmas Eve.

Mattie sighed. "What a love story they've had. And it's only the beginning."

It was a stark contrast to her and Gideon; they were nearing the end of their story, a final *the end*. She'd go to Ohio. He'd stay here. They'd barely catch a glimpse of each other after this trip, and it would likely be under different circumstances, since one of them might be married.

"So." Mattie set the celebration cake on the kitchen counter beside the wedding cake. "Did you come on foot or in a rig?"

"Can't carry a bench in a rig."

"True. After you deliver the bench, could you come back in a rig? The cake isn't so big I can't tote it, and I know Lizzy's is less than four hundred feet from here, but it's a little slippery out there, and I'd like to get this to her place without it landing upside down in the snow."

He chuckled. "I'll be back in a few."

Mattie went to the sink and washed her empty pastry bags and the multitude of tips, along with the rest of the dirty dishes from the day. While she was wiping down the countertops, someone knocked on the front door. She opened it to find Ashley's sister. Sympathy for the young woman tugged at her.

"Is Gideon here?" Sabrina didn't appear too happy, but she looked festive in her red coat.

"Not at the moment. But he'll be back shortly. Come in."

"Thanks." She stomped her snowy boots on the doormat, then came into the house.

"You do know he doesn't live here, right?"

"I know. But he's been here every time I've stopped by since he started working on this place." She peeled out of her coat, revealing decidedly non-Amish attire of stretchy, tight black pants and a hot pink sweater that accentuated every curve from her low neckline to the tops of her thighs. Mattie felt like a brown mouse next to her. She took off her gloves, stuffed them into her coat pockets, and stretched out her free hand. "I'm Sabrina."

"Mattie."

Something akin to shock passed through her eyes. "You're Mattie Lane?"

She took Sabrina's coat and hung it on one of the pegs by the front door. "Ya."

She fluffed out her short black hair. "I saw you here a few weeks ago, didn't I?"

"Ya, you did."

She smiled. "Ashley never liked that he broke up with you. She'd be pleased that the two of you are back together."

That was just odd. Why would Ashley disapprove of Gideon ending a relationship with another girl? "We're not back together. I'm going home to Ohio in a few days."

"Oh. Sorry."

"I'm sorry about your sister."

Her eyes clouded. "He told you?"

"Ya."

Sabrina sniffled and then gave a small smile. "Wow. This place has never smelled so good."

"That'd be the cakes I made today." Mattie led Sabrina to the kitchen.

Her mouth fell open when she saw the two cakes. "These are remarkable. Gideon told me you made cakes, but he never said you were this good."

Why would Gideon say anything at all about her? "Well, I've improved a lot." She took the almost dry pastry bag from the drainer and patted it with a towel. "He...talked to you about me?"

"Only all the time. It's one of the reasons I like him so much. He's got a really good heart. Not many out there like him." Sabrina's eyes widened. "Sorry. I guess it's out of line to say that about an old boyfriend."

"I've met someone else."

"Ashley warned him you would. She told him to be honest with you."

Honest? Feeling as if she was missing entire segments of this conversation, she wanted to ask Sabrina to clarify what she meant. "She sounds like a good person."

"She was. She believed with all her heart that she and Gideon would both beat that awful disease. But there's no predicting who will beat it." The girl's voice grew thick.

Mattie's breath caught in her throat, and her mind ground to a halt. *Both?* Gideon had it too? Suddenly it dawned on her that she'd never once asked Gideon how he met Ashley.

Sabrina returned her attention to the wedding cake. "Did you go to school to learn how to do this? Or does it come naturally to you?"

Her words garbled in Mattie's brain, and she couldn't respond. Everything around her seemed to be happening in slow motion, as if she were in a dream. *Leukemia?*

Gideon walked inside. He stopped short when he saw Sabrina. "Hey there. What are you doing here?"

"I have to leave on my trip tomorrow, and I wanted to see you first."

He shot a glance at Mattie. Then he led Sabrina to the front door, helped her into her coat, and took her arm as they went outside.

Mattie inhaled a halting breath. She poured herself a glass of water, trembling as she gulped it down.

He had cancer. Missing bits and pieces to understanding Gideon dangled just out of reach. She could see the scraps now, but they made little sense.

Reeling in shock, she tried to review the events of three years ago, overlaying what she'd perceived had happened with this new perspective.

What had he done?

Thirteen

*G*ideon walked Sabrina to her car. No stars were visible, and the air seemed pitch black as white snowflakes fell all around them.

Sabrina opened her trunk and passed him a present. "You can't open that until Christmas, but since I won't be in town to deliver it then, I'm going to have to trust you."

He bounced the package up and down. "At least I know it's not another five pounds of fudge."

She laughed. "Ashley made me promise you'd always get a Christmas present. She thought it'd help remove some of the sting of loneliness that swallows people in your position."

She was right. Battling cancer had an unbearable isolation to it. Not wanting to get sucked down that hole, he teased, "What, you mean a man without a girlfriend?"

"No, silly. Although I just met your Mattie Lane."

"She's not mine, not anymore."

"Maybe it's not too late."

"It was too late years ago."

"There's always a chance for Christmas magic. You tell me that every year."

"Not in this case. Mattie's going to Ohio to build a life with her guy, and I'm staying here."

"I'm sorry."

Her words summed up his own feelings. He'd always love Mattie.

He held up the package. "Thanks for bringing this. Now go. Have enough fun in Europe for both of us."

"Merry Christmas, Gideon." She hugged him before hopping into her car. He waved as Sabrina pulled out of the driveway.

Something grabbed his arm and jerked him. When he turned, Mattie's features were taut, and her eyes held disbelief as frigid winds thrashed at her dress and apron. "What have you done?"

His thoughts splintered into a dozen directions, trying to figure out what she was referring to. "About what?"

"How could you?" Her muted shriek came from deep within.

He swallowed hard, fearing Sabrina had revealed his secret.

And he also had a distant, uncontrollable hope that she had.

He took Mattie's arm to keep her from falling on the slick ground. "Let's go inside."

She pulled away, slapping at his arms through his thick coat. "Stop babying me," she hissed.

He held up his hands and backed away. "Okay."

She jerked a breath into her lungs. "I want you to tell me the truth. Can you do that?"

"If I do, it'll open doors to things we've both locked away. Just let it be."

"I want answers, Gideon." She balled her hands into fists. "Truthful ones!"

He nodded. "Okay, I promise, nothing but complete honesty."

She glanced heavenward, disgust and hurt written in her eyes. After a few moments she focused on him, looking a little more in control of her emotions. "What did you do three years ago?"

He took off his coat and put it around her shoulders. She stared at him without moving. He tugged on the collar of it. The temptation to say, "I've loved you for a lifetime, Mattie Lane," was almost too strong to conquer. Instead, he said, "After months of feeling bad and going to doctors who were no help, I…was diagnosed with leukemia."

Horror filled her features. "Gideon." Her whisper held deep

pity, and he was reminded of another reason he'd lied to her. He didn't want her to stay by his side out of pity. "Are you still sick?"

He shook his head. "No, not right now."

Relief flickered in her eyes for a moment.

"I'd planned on telling you about my illness after the holidays. But then Ashley came to me with devastating news." He steadied his voice as best he could. "She was cancer free one day and facing a grueling battle the next. What hope did I have...what life could I offer you? You arrived at my place minutes after she told me her latest diagnosis. Knowing my cancer had gone from a bad stage to a worse one, I...did what I thought would be best for you in the long run."

Her face contorted with confusion. "Did you love me?"

"With every breath I've ever drawn."

"Then why, Gideon?" She sounded close to hysteria.

"Imagine we were in a buggy traveling together and an eighteen-wheeler was gunning for me. All I could think of was getting you out, Mattie. Getting you to safety."

"Do you have any idea what you did to me?" she screamed, shaking her fists in the air.

"Ya. I spared you. I was in isolation for nearly nine months after a bone marrow transplant. I came so close to dying time and again and was too sick to hold up my head; I couldn't work. The treatments cost an incredible amount of money. Every penny I'd saved for our life together is gone. A government program had to take over covering the medical costs. I was powerless to do anything worthwhile…except that I'd let you go before it got that bad." He drew a breath, trying to close the dam of pain before they both drowned in it. "You were brokenhearted when your mother was diagnosed with lupus. I couldn't bear to put you through all that again with me. I didn't want you trapped in a life you'd seek rescue from."

"Rescue? Do you think I wanted to be saved from Mamm's illness?" She held her hands open, thrusting them palms up as she spoke. "What? Do you think I'd have chosen to have a different Mamm just so I wouldn't have to go through that hardship?"

"No, of course not. But your Mamm's health has always been fragile, and you've had a heavy weight on you since you were little, long before she got lupus."

"Open your eyes, Gideon Beiler." She waved a finger in his face. "Sure, I've grieved for Mamm, but because of her fragility, I learned how to embrace each day with her as if it might be our last. I learned how to love and give without allowing her illness to pull me under."

"But it did take its toll, day after day, year in and year out."

"Tears and sleepless nights are not signs of weakness. Jesus wept a few times in His life, and He was awake a lot while others slept. Does that mean He was too weak to cope? Or was He showing the depth and power of His compassion?"

Gideon wished he could make her see his point, but no counterargument came to him.

Mattie ducked her head, fighting tears. "It's impressive that you had the strength to shut me out and go through that journey on your own, but you needed to have found the strength to let me in." She lifted her chin. "Look at who I am. I spend months planning and preparing cakes that are marred with the first slice and devoured in minutes." She drew a shaky breath. "But having something that I've worked on taken apart doesn't make me give up. It's the thrill of creating it and the joy it brings to others and the memories it gives that matter. That's who I am. I wouldn't have given up on you out of fear of what the future might bring. I would have done my best to make our lives a beautiful creation while enjoying whatever time we had."

He heard sleigh bells in the distance. Someone was coming toward them. This conversation would end soon, and he wasn't sure when they'd have another opportunity to speak so openly.

She stepped close and tugged on his shirt. "But I have no idea who you are. I haven't for a really long time." She took his coat off her shoulders and held it out to him. "I'm sorry about everything you've been through. But in your effort to protect me, you killed the one person who mattered the most to me—you."

"Hello." Jonah brought the sleigh to a stop a few feet away from them.

Beth clapped her gloved hands. "You two have taken too long to come to Lizzy's, and we've come to get you."

"Wait, I'll be right back." Mattie disappeared into the house and moments later came out wearing her own coat and carrying the celebration cake.

"What's that?" Beth asked.

Mattie passed it to her. "It's a gift for you and your guests to enjoy tonight. But I'd like to go home. Would you mind dropping me off?"

"Of course not," Jonah said.

"I can't really see all the detail right now," Beth said, examining the cake in the dark, "but I can tell it's exquisite."

"Mattie Lane," Gideon whispered, "don't go like this."

She ignored him.

Beth lifted a blanket. "Kumm. We'll drop the cake off at Lizzy's and be on our way."

Jonah helped Mattie into the sleigh. "Gideon, will you take Mattie's horse and rig home so she'll have it for the morning?"

"Ya." He stood alone as they drove off, knowing that the only thing more devastating than having a serious illness was the destruction wrought while trying to cover it up.

Fourteen

Mattie's head throbbed as she sat at the bride-and-groom table next to Gideon, trying to eat. Six hours ago in the basement filled with loved ones seated on folding chairs, Jonah had walked Beth down the aisle in this house—their home. Beth wore a crisp burgundy wine cape dress with a sheer white cape and apron in place of the usual black one. Mattie had on the exact same outfit, as did the other girls in the bridal party.

Traditionally, Amish couples got married in the home of the bride's parents or an uncle, so today was very unusual—like Beth and Jonah themselves.

Beth sat across from Jonah, and Gideon sat between Beth and Mattie. The placement of who sat where was a tradition that had probably begun hundreds of years ago, possibly longer. But Mattie couldn't take much more of being paired with Gideon.

Her thoughts were a jumbled mess. The idea of Gideon

going through treatment without her support tormented her. She felt as if he'd just received the diagnosis, and the realization that he'd shut her out while trying to protect her made everything worse.

What was she supposed to think...or feel? He'd broken her heart, and, unknowingly, she'd been furious with him while he spent two years battling for his life.

Beth leaned behind Gideon, who was chatting with Jonah, and caught Mattie's attention. "Gideon will lead the first round of songs, so be sure to tell him some of your favorites."

Mattie did her best to keep a smile pasted on for Beth's benefit, hoping not to dampen her cousin's celebration. "I think I'll choose some sad, pitiful dirges," she teased, "to match your mood today."

Beth laughed.

When Mattie sat forward, her eye caught Gideon's, and it was all she could do to keep from bursting into tears. He'd betrayed her—both of them, really. When the main part of the meal was over, a multitude of women removed dirty tableware. Lizzy cut the cake and dished it onto dessert plates, and Beth's sisters-in-law and aunts served everyone. Mattie enjoyed the *ooh*s over Beth and Jonah's wedding cake and received compliments galore once people took a bite of it. Whatever else Gideon had destroyed or stolen, he hadn't ruined the part of her that was a cake maker and decorator.

A distant, fuzzy thought tried to enter her consciousness, and she turned to Gideon as if studying him would bring clarity. He said he'd asked her brother James about Sol, but when? There was no way Gideon had talked to James on her phone at the store. And until her shop burned, James never went to the Kings' store to use their phone. Had Gideon spent his limited strength and money to come to Ohio to check on her?

He turned to face her, and she knew he had. How many times had he come to Berlin in the last three years?

"Just think about our canoe ride down the Susquehanna... and the wild dance that man performed before he tipped us over," Gideon whispered.

She allowed a weak smile to surface. Is that what got him through—thinking about their good times?

The endless questions were on her last nerve, and she wished they'd stop.

In a few minutes she could leave this spot and maybe be able to breathe again. By tradition, when the meal ended, close family would wash dishes and clean up while the bride and groom, their friends, and the other guests visited or freshened up. In an hour or so, everyone would reconvene for songs and rounds of snacks. She scanned the room, looking for her escape.

Mamm was going into a spare bedroom with a stack of wrapped gifts. That'd be a quiet, out-of-the-way place to hide for a bit. When Beth and Jonah got up to mingle, Mattie knew she could disappear without being missed. She wound her way through the crowd, but before she got to the closed door of the bedroom, her Mamm opened it and stepped out.

Mamm grinned, shutting the door behind her. "Sorry, Mattie, this room is off-limits to anyone trying to take a peek at the gifts."

Mattie fought the desire to shrink into her mom's arms and weep.

Mamm's smile faded into concern. "Mattie, sweetheart." She cupped her face with her soft hands. "I thought you'd feel better today."

Tears welled in Mattie's eyes, and Mamm took her by the hand, led her into the room, and locked the door behind them. "You came home early last night and went straight to bed. And now you're sad. What's wrong?"

Mattie wiped her tears. "Gideon didn't break up with me because of someone else. He lied about her, about a lot of things."

Mamm stared wide-eyed. "Are you still in love with him?"

Mattie couldn't answer her. She went into the half bath and rinsed her face, the cool water easing the burning in her eyes. "I might have thought I was yesterday, but how can I be?" She buried her face in a towel, trying to get control. She took a breath. "I don't know who he is."

"I was disappointed in him when he broke up with you. Truth of the matter is, I was really angry that he'd hurt you." Mamm tightened her hands into fists and shook them before she smiled. "And if I'd seen him out and about, I might've scolded him, but he left Apple Ridge about the same time you did. During the first two years, I heard he returned for two or three days around Christmas. Then about a year ago, he returned for good, and I was at Verna's when he came in. He didn't look anything like the man who'd left here. But I talked with him for a bit. I don't remember what it was about, but I saw…" She tapped the center of her chest. "I saw with the same part of me that sees God, and I knew right then that whatever took place between you two, he's the same man he's always been—patient, kind, and trustworthy."

Mattie scoffed. "I'm pretty confident he's not trustworthy, but I think…" She twisted the hand towel into a thick rope and moved from the tiny bathroom to the edge of the bed. "I *know* he still loves me. He's never stopped loving me."

"But you care for Sol now."

"At least he's not a liar. Gideon deceived me when he broke up with me. He was sick, Mamm, and he didn't want me to know."

"Sick?" she whispered. "Oh." A faraway look entered her eyes. "Now it all makes sense, doesn't it?"

"Don't you see? His confession, which he made only because he was cornered with the truth, makes him a fraud and a hypocrite."

"Oh, Mattie, sweetheart." Mamm's face crumpled, sadness and understanding shadowing her smile. She sat beside her. "If I could have spared you, my little sweet-sixteen girl, and your Daed from having to know about and cope with my illness, I would have."

"What? No you wouldn't."

"Ya, I would've. And even though your brothers were married with homes of their own, I'd have spared them the heartache too if I'd known how. It may be the one dream shared by everyone struck with illness. If we could find a way, we'd keep our loved ones from shouldering the strain and hurt, from having their quality of life jerked away from them."

Unable to accept what her mother had said, Mattie went to the window. Last night's fresh layer of snow was marred and ugly because of people shoveling it out of the way, driving rigs across it, or walking through it. She felt like that snow looked. But life caused people to have to move about, and that meant mucking up the once-pristine landscape.

Mamm came to her side and put her arm around Mattie's waist. "I always thought that his wanting to see other girls was a lie. I've asked your brothers and their children who are your age, and no one ever saw him with another girl. They say he's never gone to singings…except the Christmas ones. Even then, he came and left by himself."

She'd loved their first date, when he took her to the Christmas singing, so much that she'd made him promise he'd always go until they were married. And it sounded as if he'd kept that promise, even when she wasn't there to see it.

Mattie closed her eyes. "Why didn't anyone tell me?"

"Because it wasn't our place. All we had was our speculation, and you assured me that you didn't want to talk to Gideon about anything, that you just wanted to move to Berlin. So we let you. It was a year later when we saw him looking so poorly and attending a singing by himself. By that time your new business was taking off, and you were starting to see Sol, and we thought you were happy."

Her self-righteous attitude melted. "What am I supposed to do? I'm with Sol."

"Then explain that to Gideon. He set you free to do just that, didn't he?"

"I didn't want to be set free."

Mamm lifted Mattie's chin and looked into her eyes. "Mattie, do you love Sol?"

She wished Mamm hadn't asked that. "I care for him a lot. But I'm not ready to marry him tomorrow."

"Next year then?"

She shrugged. "Maybe."

"It's okay to hate the sin of lying, but have mercy on the man who loves you more than himself."

She blinked her eyes, trying not to cry. "I can't hurt Sol."

"If you love him, don't let anything stop you from marrying him. But if you marry him for the wrong reasons, you *will* hurt him for years and years. And you'll hurt yourself and Gideon too." Mamm took her hand. "Now, kumm. I need to finish bringing presents in here, and you need to be fellowshipping with Beth and Jonah's guests. Everyone here is buzzing about the cakes you made for these weddings."

Her Mamm was so proud of her, but if she could see how selfishly her daughter acted at times, it'd wound her. When Mattie had moved to Ohio, she'd wasted no time starting to date others. What she should've done was take a little time to figure out why Gideon suddenly wanted to be free of her. But no, not her. She was too proud and too busy reorganizing her dreams to waste any time on him.

Halfway down the hallway Mattie tugged on Mamm's hand, and she stopped. Mattie hugged her. "Denki."

"Gern gschehne."

As they left the hallway, Mattie saw Gideon across the room, standing near a window, talking with Aden Zook. In spite of his sin, his heart had been in the right place. And she did know who he was.

He glanced up, and a timid smile touched his lips.

"Mamm, I need to see Gideon."

"Sure, honey. You go on."

Mattie walked toward him. After excusing himself to Aden, Gideon met her halfway.

"I understand now."

Surprise crossed his face. "You do?"

"Ya. But I still have to go back to Ohio next week."

The look in his eyes intensified. "That's what I've wanted all along, Mattie Lane."

Sadness held on so tight she felt numb. "Is that really all, for me to know the truth and return to Sol?"

His face showed no emotion that she recognized. "Pretty much, ya."

Raising her eyebrows, she waited.

"It's silly, but I thought it'd be nice if we had one day together without anger or grief, just one day to be who we used to be."

"That would've been nice." But one day alone with Gideon without anger or grief would most certainly undo her. She slid her hand into his. "You stay well. You hear me?"

He squeezed her fingers tenderly. "Anything for you, Mattie Lane."

Fifteen

Something woke Gideon, and he rolled over, opening his eyes. The room was dark, and he wondered what time it was. Peace stirred, moving about in him like a construction team laying the foundation for a new home. Mattie knew everything and had forgiven him. That alone would sustain him after she left.

Something thudded against his window. He rose, slipped into his pants, and went to look out. Remnants of a snowball slid down the glass. He opened the window, and below, bathed in silvery moonlight and standing in several inches of new snow, Mattie gazed up at him. A horse stood behind her with Beth and Jonah's sleigh attached to it.

"Mattie Lane, what are you doing?"

She lobbed a snowball straight up into the air and backed away when it almost landed on her. It dropped inches in front of Jessie Bell, and the horse neighed, shaking her head. Mattie bit her bottom lip, smiling up at him like it was Christmas. "One day, Gideon Beiler. You asked for it, and you've got it. We have from now until I leave at eleven tonight. That's about nineteen hours to wreak some havoc as we travel down Mattie's lane."

He could hardly believe his ears. Or his eyes.

She pulled a rolled-up piece of paper out of her pocket. "I spent most the night working on this list." She held the top of it, and it unrolled from her head to the ground. "Number one: Go for a sleigh ride." She jingled the bells dangling on the horse's back. "Number two: Go tobogganing." She pointed at a long sled inside the sleigh. "Number three: Return here, and *you* fix us breakfast. Number four: Hire a driver and go to Harrisburg to watch the Susquehanna." She held up a pair of binoculars. "And I do mean *watch*. Not fall into it. Number five: Have lunch at the Fire House Restaurant before taking a tour of the historic district and visiting the State Museum of Pennsylvania. Number six: Go ice-skating on Miller's pond." She lowered the list. "Hey, do you still have my ice skates?"

"I'm wearing them right now."

She rolled her eyes. "Now, we're going to skate on Miller's pond if it's solid enough. If it's not, only you will go skating while I time how long it takes before the ice cracks and you have a cold swim."

"Thanks, Mattie."

She giggled and propped one hand on her waist and motioned impatiently with the other. "Well, hurry up. Nineteen hours isn't much time."

He dressed, and while hurrying down the steps, he put on his coat, scarf, and hat.

He opened the door, and she flung a snowball at him. He bent to scoop up a handful of snow, and when he stood, she was hiding behind the horse.

"No fair, Mattie Lane."

"All is fair inside the magical, mystical land known as Mattie Lane. How do you not know that by now?"

*

Mattie squeezed the pastry bag, draping thin loops of gold icing onto the Christmas cake. Her brother's home smelled of the holiday feast they'd have for dinner this evening, featuring turkey and stuffing, black-eyed peas, sweet potato pie, and green beans.

Her niece had her own pastry tube. Esther hummed and chatted while squirting mounds of icing onto a batch of cookies. The little girl had not moved from her kneeling position on a kitchen chair for nearly an hour. "Mattie Cakes, do you make your own birthday cake every year?"

Mattie tried to focus her mind, which was still suspended in a fog somewhere between Berlin, Ohio, and Apple Ridge, Pennsylvania. She'd hoped that going through her usual Christmas Eve traditions would lift the grief and confusion, perhaps scrub away some of the desire for Gideon, but that hadn't happened yet. "Ya, I do, sweetie."

James marched into the house, carrying a load of wood, and stomped snow off his boots. "Well, there are two of my favorite girls." He dumped the logs into the bin next to the open hearth. "Where are your big brothers and sisters, Esther?"

She put her index finger on her lips. "They're in their rooms with the doors locked, wrapping presents."

Mattie's eyes met her brother's, and they chuckled. Why did Esther act like the location of her older siblings was a secret?

Dorothy walked into the kitchen, carrying her youngest one on her hip.

James went to his wife, and they spoke quietly for a moment before sharing a long, lingering kiss. Esther glanced up, smiled at her parents' show of affection, then returned her attention to her cookie.

James walked to the edge of the table, amusement on his face. He lifted one of Esther's gooey cookies. "This much icing gives new meaning to the name *sugar cookies.*"

Esther glowed. "You like it, Daed?"

"These will be my all-time favorites." He set it down. "But not until after we eat our dinner."

Dorothy placed an empty mug in the sink. "Esther, have you made your bed?"

"I'm helping Mattie Cakes."

Dorothy looked to Mattie with a raised brow.

Ever since she'd returned from Pennsylvania, the only way Mattie had found any Christmas cheer was through her niece's innocent excitement. "It's true. She's telling me right where all the dots and curlicues need to go."

"And she helped me put my very own cake in the oven." Esther bobbed her little head up and down. "I get to decorate it after it's cool."

Dorothy flashed Mattie a look that was somewhere between gratitude and *you've got to be kidding me.*

James scooped his daughter off the chair. "We're going to have to rename you Mattie Cakes Two." He tapped her nose with his forefinger, making Esther giggle with delight.

Dorothy pulled a clean burp cloth out of a drawer. "But all bakers have to make their own beds and straighten their rooms, even on Christmas Eve."

Esther's eyes grew wide. "Is that true, Mattie Cakes?"

Mattie leaned in and kissed the top of her niece's head. "If your Mamm said so, it must be."

Esther hopped down from her father's arms and ran upstairs.

Mattie set the pastry bag with gold icing aside and picked up the one with red icing. "You know, she was in my attic room at the shop several times, and my bed was rarely made up."

Humor danced in Dorothy's eyes. "You don't want to know my response to that, do you?"

James plopped into a chair at the kitchen table. "Go ahead. She can take it."

Dorothy gave a sheepish grin. "I know this isn't true. It's just the first thing I thought when you said you didn't always make your bed."

"Well, out with it."

"I'd tell Esther, 'And you see what happened to her shop, don't you?'"

James laughed, then stopped short, mocking a guilty look for being amused.

Mattie couldn't help but chuckle. "You have a morbid sense of humor, Dorothy Eash."

"I do, don't I?" She sat beside her husband and put her youngest in the nursing position under a fold of her cape bodice. "Will Sol be here in time for our noon meal?"

Mattie glanced at the clock. Eleven fifteen, and she already thought the day would never end. "Today is the one day of the year I *can* expect him to come see me. He went hunting this morning, of course, so he might be a little late. But I bet he's here before we're finished eating so we can go early to the Christmas singing tonight."

The mirth faded from James's face. He pressed his index finger onto a crumb on the table. "You don't seem at all disappointed that he went hunting on your birthday or that he goes on more hunts than Daniel Boone."

Mattie squirted red frosting on the cake. "He does his thing, and I do mine. What's wrong with that?"

"Nothing," James said. He glanced at his wife. "Dorothy and I just want to be sure you're thinking clearly. Every brother and sister-in-law you have has been praying for you every day for years…especially since you and Gideon broke up."

Mattie pushed the cake away, her smidgen of a lighthearted mood gone. "I appreciate your prayers, but I don't need your advice or your meddling."

"Okay." James angled his head, catching her eye. "Just answer one question, and I'll never bring up this topic again."

She scowled at him. "Then by all means, ask it."

"What draws you to Sol?"

Frustration burned like hot coals in Mattie. "He's a good man who will never break my heart."

"I agree." Dorothy folded the burp cloth with one hand

while holding her baby. "It's impossible for him to break what he can't touch."

Dorothy's words left Mattie weak. She sank into the chair beside her sister-in-law, grief surrounding her as if she were buried in a snowbank. She could have a comfortable life with Sol. It would be void of passion and gusto, but it would be a long, smooth road.

The doorbell rang. Mattie looked through the kitchen window and saw a white truck. "Does FedEx deliver on Christmas Eve?"

James glanced outside. "I guess so."

Mattie hurried out of the room, glad to get away from the prying questions. She opened the door and found a small package on the doorstep. "Merry Christmas," she called to the man in the navy and purple uniform.

He waved while hurrying back to his truck. "Merry Christmas."

She picked up the box. The package was addressed to her. Eager for something to lift her spirits, she took it into the kitchen.

"Who's it from?" Dorothy asked.

"It doesn't say." Mattie got a knife from a drawer and slid it across the packing tape. Inside a layer of plastic bubble wrap, she saw a book. She pulled it out of the layers of protection.

A hand-drawn image of herself with a pastry bag in hand, decorating a four-tier wedding cake, graced the cover. Chills skittered up her spine. In the bottom left corner of the picture, the name Aden appeared in tiny letters.

She dropped into a chair and opened the book. The inside front flap had *Mattie Cakes Portfolio* scrawled on it. She gingerly turned the pages. Aden had meticulously drawn numerous cakes with familiar designs, using colored pencils to give each area the correct shade. At the bottom of every page, he'd written the name of the cake design and where the idea came from, as well as the year she first made it.

Her heart filled with emotions too big for her chest, like the Grinch's had in that kids' movie she'd seen years ago while babysitting. "Look at this."

James and Dorothy moved behind her, looking over her shoulder.

"How could Aden know all this? When I lived with Mamm and Daed, he came over a few times and made sketches of various stages of my work. But he never saw all these."

"Maybe he remembers them from your old scrapbook," Dorothy suggested.

She turned another page. "This is unbelievable. That man has more talent than I realized." She flipped to the next page, and her heart nearly stopped. "I made that cake in September.

There's no way Aden could have seen it." She looked up at James and Dorothy. "You're the only ones who could've told him about it."

"Wasn't me," James said. "I don't remember ever seeing that one."

Dorothy brought her infant out from the flap of her cape. "I need to put this little guy down for his nap."

"Dorothy, wait." Mattie stood. "You know something."

She looked to her husband as if asking to be rescued, but James just shrugged. Her face contorted into an apology. "That must be Gideon's doing."

Mattie's heart skipped. "But a few cakes I made last year are included, up to a few months before the shop burned. How would he know what to tell Aden to draw?"

Dorothy juggled her sleeping baby on her shoulder. "He, uh...used to come by here sometimes."

Mattie shot a glare at her. "I figured that out before I returned here, but I never saw him."

James stroked his beard. "He didn't want to upset you. He always stopped by while you were gone and asked how you were doing. If you left your book here, he'd take a peek at it. He'd do it casual-like, as if he was just curious, but we knew the truth."

And so did Mattie—Gideon loved her more than she'd ever hoped for. "Why didn't you tell me?"

James went to the stove and poured a cup of coffee. "You'd been here about a year when he made his first visit. It only took a glance at him to know he was as weak as a kitten. We never talked about it, but when I saw him so sick, I finally understood why he broke up with you." He took a sip of the hot, black liquid. "You were seeing Sol by then. Mattie Cakes was growing by leaps and bounds. And I respected what he was trying to do."

"We just want you to find the right man," Dorothy said. "If that's Sol, we're happy for you. He's a nice guy. We don't care for him the way we do Gideon, but we'd be honored to have him as a brother-in-law…if…"

"If what?"

James set his cup down hard. "If you haven't chosen him merely because he's a great guy who is incapable of breaking your heart."

With her heart pounding so hard she thought it might explode, Mattie looked through the book again. The fog that'd been so thick for more than a week began to lift. As hard as she'd tried to love someone else, her heart still belonged to Gideon.

But it was too late now.

"Knock, knock," Sol called as he came in the front door.

And she knew what had to be done. "Excuse me." Mattie went into the living room. "You're back earlier than I expected."

"I know. My watch stopped, and I wasn't sure of the time, so I came on back. It wouldn't do to make you angry on the one day we both know belongs under your rules."

"My rules?" she whispered. Was that all that motivated him to be here for the family Christmas Eve meal and her birthday?

She wondered if he remembered their first date. Or the first cake she'd made him. He probably didn't think such things mattered. And he'd be right. It didn't make any difference, because she wasn't in this relationship to be honored or loved. She just wanted companionship and convenience. Someone to spend a little time with when they finally looked up from the things they were passionate about—cake making and hunting. A man to tell others she was seeing while she kept her heart a safe distance from him. He didn't even know how to search for it. And she didn't blame him.

But Sol deserved to find someone who loved him the way she loved Gideon. Her Mamm was right—if she stayed for the wrong reasons, she'd hurt Sol, Gideon, and herself.

She picked up his coat off the couch and hung it on a peg. "Sol, could you sit with me for a few minutes?"

He removed his camouflage-colored toboggan. "Sure." He sat on the couch. "This doesn't sound good, so get to the point. Aim for the target and shoot."

She tried to focus all her thoughts and emotions into one

sentence that would make sense. "I'd rather have one day of giving love and being truly loved than a lifetime of convenient and comfortable."

He raked his hands through his unwashed hair. "Gideon."

"I'm sorry."

"I knew when I came to the hospital and saw him holding your hand that it'd be easy for him to win you back."

"And you cared enough to come to Pennsylvania to check on me."

"That should count for something."

"It does."

"But not enough?" He searched her eyes, looking for answers.

"I'm sorry," she repeated, feeling as if she needed to say it a thousand more times.

He sighed. "I've learned a lot from being with you. Even figured out how to talk to girls." He gave a slight chuckle. "Maybe now I can go to singings on my own and carry on a real conversation."

She touched his hand. "If you do, I'm sure you'll find the right girl for you."

"It won't be Katie King." He shuddered, and they both laughed. "If it doesn't work out with Gideon, you know where to find me."

"Ya." She smiled. "In a tree stand with a bow, gun, or muzzleloader." She pressed her apron with her hand. "Can you forgive me?"

He stood. "Maybe next week." His lopsided smile let her know he'd be fine without her. He grabbed his coat and went toward the door.

"You could stay and eat with us."

"I'm not hungry. Tell your family Merry Christmas for me." He gazed into her eyes. "And be happy, Mattie."

"Denki." She closed the door behind him, praying he'd find the right woman. Within minutes peace for him removed her concern, and her thoughts turned to Gideon.

Sixteen

The cold night air didn't stir, and the stars shone brightly in the clear sky as Gideon walked from his rig toward the Stoltzfuses' barn. The lyrics from "Silent Night" reverberated around him. It was the one night of the year that they sang some of the songs in English.

The promise he'd made to Mattie Lane was only half the reason he came to the singings every Christmas Eve. The other half was his hope that she'd return to him.

But it was time to let go. She knew everything she needed to, and she'd chosen Sol. On the one hand, that was what he wanted for her. On the other, he longed to spend whatever time he had left on this planet by her side.

He'd considered not coming to this singing, but he needed a way of saying a final good-bye to the hopes and dreams of sharing a life with Mattie Lane.

He opened the small door inside the huge sliding door and

walked into the barn. Much as they did in church, the females sat on benches on one side, males on the other. This time they were facing each other, and he took a seat on a bench toward the back.

Omar, who came to every singing as part of his responsibilities as bishop, brought him an *Ausbund,* an Amish book of songs written in German. He put one hand on Gideon's shoulder and squeezed.

Everyone now knew about his battle with leukemia. After his secret was divulged to Mattie, he had no reason to keep living a lie. He confessed his sin to the congregation, and Omar, as the church's authority figure, forgave him. Gideon had to show signs of repentance, and Omar's edict said he must be the lead carpenter on a new mission home. Every two to three years, the Amish community collected money and worked together to build a place for a homeless non-Amish family. These mission homes were a way of helping the poor and building good relations with Englischers.

Gideon had intended to help build the house anyway, and Omar knew it. Making him the lead carpenter was an honor— one that would help put the name of Beiler Construction in the news. Omar knew that too.

Gideon closed his eyes, grateful to finally be forgiven for the lie he'd told. Never again would he be so foolish as to think he could control anyone or anything through false words. He'd speak truth always and pray for God's strength over those who might struggle under the weight of the truth.

He joined in on the chorus.

"Silent night, holy night. All is calm..."

The girls stopped singing and stared at the back of the barn, whispering. Some of the guys stopped too, turning to see what had their attention. Gideon looked behind him.

Mattie Lane.

She smiled warmly, and he knew...she'd come back to him. He went toward her, and she opened her arms. He wrapped her in a tight embrace. Tears stung his eyes, and he couldn't find his voice.

She backed away, caressing his face with her hands. "Mackenzie brought me in exchange for me promising that I'd tell you the full truth."

"You can tell me anything."

"I love you, Gideon Beiler."

He pulled her close, not caring about the unspoken rules of proper behavior. Unable to find his voice, he pressed his lips against hers. He still had no idea how much time he had left—maybe a lifetime.

But whatever God gave them, it was enough.

3-Layer Strawberries-and-Cream Cake

2 cups sugar

1 small package strawberry gelatin

1 cup butter, softened

4 eggs

2¾ cups cake flour

2½ teaspoons baking powder

1 cup milk

1 teaspoon vanilla

½ cup strawberries, puréed

Preheat oven to 350°. Grease and flour three 9-inch, round cake pans. In a large mixing bowl, beat sugar, gelatin, and butter until fluffy. Add eggs one at a time, beating after each. Mix the flour and baking powder together, and add to the sugar mixture in two parts, alternating with the milk and beating after each addition. Fold in vanilla and puréed strawberries. Divide equally into the three cake pans.

Bake for 25 minutes. Cool for 10 minutes in the pans, then remove from the pans and cool completely.

Filling:

1½ cups heavy whipping cream

2 tablespoons sugar

$^1/_2$ teaspoon vanilla

$1^1/_2$ cups fresh strawberries, sliced

Beat the whipping cream, sugar, and vanilla until stiff. Cover the bottom and middle cake layer each with $^1/_3$ of the whipped cream and $^3/_4$ cup sliced strawberries. Set aside remaining whipped cream.

Frosting:

$^1/_2$ cup butter, softened

8-ounce package cream cheese, softened

4 cups powdered sugar

2 teaspoons vanilla

$1^1/_2$ cup fresh strawberries, halved or quartered

Beat the butter, cream cheese, powdered sugar, and vanilla until creamy. Spread frosting around the sides of the cake. Make a pretty piping of frosting along the top edge of the cake. Gently spread remaining whipped cream on cake top. Decorate top with strawberries.

Orange Coconut Cake

$1\frac{1}{2}$ sticks unsalted butter, at room temperature

$1\frac{1}{4}$ cups sugar

4 eggs, at room temperature; separate yolks and whites

2 cups cake flour

2 teaspoons baking powder

$\frac{1}{4}$ teaspoon salt

$\frac{1}{2}$ cup buttermilk or coconut milk

1 teaspoon coconut extract

1 teaspoon grated lemon zest

Preheat oven to 350°. Grease and flour two 9-inch, round cake pans, *or* place parchment paper circles coated with flour in the bottom of the pans.

Beat butter until light and fluffy. Gradually add sugar, beating constantly until thoroughly mixed. Add yolks, one at a time, beating well after each addition. Sift flour with baking powder and salt. Add the dry ingredients to the butter mixture in two parts, alternating with buttermilk *or* coconut milk. Beat in the coconut extract and lemon zest.

In a separate mixing bowl, beat egg whites until medium-firm peaks form. Fold one third of the egg whites into the batter, then fold in the remaining whites.

Divide batter between the pans, and bake on the middle rack of the oven about 30 minutes. Cool in pans on a wire rack for 10 minutes. Remove from pans and finish cooling completely. Decorate with buttercream frosting.

Orange Buttercream Frosting
1 cup unsalted butter, at room temperature
16-ounce bag powdered sugar
4 teaspoons grated orange zest
orange food coloring

Whip butter and sugar together until perfectly smooth. Add grated zest one teaspoon at a time and blend well. Add orange food coloring one drop at a time until the desired shade is achieved.

RECIPES PROVIDED BY SHERRY GORE

Sherry Gore is the author of *An Amish Bride's Kitchen,* the editor of *Cooking and Such* magazine and *The Pinecraft Pauper,* and a contributing writer for the national edition of *The Budget.* She is a member of a Beachy Amish Mennonite church and makes her home in Sarasota with her family.

Sherry enjoys corresponding with reader friends everywhere. She can be contacted at www.SherryGoreBooks.com or via e-mail at TasteofPinecraft@gmail.com.

Acknowledgments

To Jeffry J. Bizon, MD, OB/GYN—Much like your patients, I rely on your expertise and on your tender, caring spirit. Whether you have been in the middle of a busy workday or enjoying downtime with your wonderful family or finishing another umpteen-mile run, you have always made time to answer my numerous questions, even before my first book was contracted. My gratitude to you and Kathy is deep.

To Rachel Esh, my energetic and good-humored Old Order Amish friend—I'm so grateful that you're open to my many questions, that you're willing to make time to return my calls, and that you own a dry goods store with a community phone! You keep showing up in my books because you are a fascinating and unique person. I hope you never change! Thank you for inviting me into your life.

To everyone at WaterBrook Multnomah, from marketing to sales to production to editorial—You are incredible!

To my expert in the Pennsylvania Dutch language, who wishes to remain anonymous—May an unexpected someone cross your path who gives as selflessly to you as you have to me.

Book 3

The DAWN of CHRISTMAS

A Romance from the Heart of Amish Country

CINDY WOODSMALL

To our dear, lifelong friend Catherine Logan

*Your faith is strong and stalwart, yet you understand
the winds of change that sweep through the soul.
You've spent a lifetime going out of your way
to help those who need or seek a transition.
You've tirelessly planted seeds of hope and courage
in every person blessed to come into contact with you,
and since I was a teen, I've considered it a privilege to call you a friend.*

*As my youth fades a little more each day,
and I see the past with perfect clarity,
I honor your wisdom and counsel and strength even more today.
You own a piece of my heart.*

One

*M*uffled voices drifted through the living room, but Sadie couldn't make out the words. She sat in a ladder back, avoiding Daniel's gaze by staring into a fireplace with its few fading embers. Family members, hers and Daniel's, peered at her with eyes full of pity and shock.

When Daniel had made his intentions known, folks whispered behind her back that little Sadie Yoder had finally snagged someone's attention and she better hold on for dear life. She knew that was true, but she hadn't cared what people thought, not one whit. Daniel Miller had moved to Brim from Tussey Mountain a year earlier, and he'd fallen in love.

With her.

Her, of all people. The one best known for being a quiet stick of a girl who caught no man's eye.

Every day that passed she'd thought her heart might explode from the joy of falling in love. When he'd asked her to marry him, well, she'd all but fainted from the excitement.

Daniel wasn't just any man. He was above her in every way. He was handsome and had a deep voice, strong shoulders, and a way of winning people's respect. At twenty-four, only five years older than she, he already had an established horse-trading business. She'd fully believed in him and felt honored he'd chosen her.

Now... |

She lifted her eyes to meet his, and heartbreak stole her breath. If her legs could carry her, she'd get up and walk out.

"Forgive me." Daniel's lips barely moved, his whisper meant for no one but her. He looked as shocked and hurt by his behavior as she was.

She turned her attention back to the stone fireplace. It stood silent, the pile of gray-and-black ashes smoldering from a fire that once burned hot. A perfect depiction of her life.

A blur of crisp magenta folds swirled in front of her, and her cousin Aquilla knelt beside her chair. Aquilla's perfect oval face radiated beauty. Her blond hair framed her head like a halo, and her green eyes were mesmerizing. And all of it was able to steal Daniel's heart before Sadie caught a hint of what was happening.

"Please, Sadie."

Please? What was Aquilla thinking? Did she hope Sadie could also be convinced of her lie? Or did she want Sadie to have the power to erase their betrayal? their indulgence? their sin?

Daniel had been a perfect gentleman with Sadie, but what she'd witnessed less than an hour ago proved he was not unfamiliar with a woman's body. She could still see his hands embracing Aquilla, caressing her in a way that would haunt Sadie for years.

She had invited Aquilla two months ago to come from out of town to help prepare for the wedding. What a fool she'd been.

Aquilla clasped her delicate hands over Sadie's stained ones. "It wasn't as it looked. I promise. You misunderstood."

That was a lie. One Aquilla had already repeated a few times, no doubt hoping it would save her from gossip and from looking like the betrayer she was. Sadie kept her gaze fixed on the fireplace, wishing she could escape like smoke up a chimney. Everyone would leave later, but how many would be unsure of what she'd actually seen? This would be her only chance to defend herself against Aquilla's lies to Daniel's family, but the words begged to stay hidden.

A mere hour earlier Sadie had been making last-minute alterations to her wedding dress. As daylight grew faint, she'd needed a new propane tank for the gas pole light in her bedroom. She hadn't even known Daniel had arrived for a visit. As she'd crossed the backyard, she'd breathed in the fall air and enjoyed the red and yellow leaves of maple and birch trees.

Then she'd opened the shed door. In a moment of time, as quickly as the hope of being loved had come to her, it had fled. Every hope of marrying Daniel shattered. The laughter of their future children silenced.

She'd run back to the house, fleeing a truth she could not escape. Once inside, she'd slammed the door tight, locked it, then fallen against the frame and wept. When she'd looked up, dozens of her relatives and Daniel's were staring at her. She'd forgotten they were there to help prepare for her and Daniel's wedding day.

Daniel and Aquilla had pounded on the door, demanding she let them in.

Sadie's *Daed* had hurried to her, asking what was going on, and she'd whispered what she'd witnessed. The emotions that crossed her Daed's face mirrored her own. He'd been the one to encourage the relationship, nudging the two of them together from the moment Daniel had arrived in the community. When Daed had opened the door to Aquilla and Daniel, Sadie had expected their guilt to be evident on their faces. But they'd looked only upset, and Aquilla's first words were a lie she didn't even stumble over.

Aquilla's eyes had glistened with tears, and her angelic face radiated sincerity. "I fell off a stepladder, and he caught me." She'd turned to face everyone in the room. "She's insecure about Daniel, imagining her worst fears concerning him." She'd wiped tears from her face. "Why would I want the only man she's ever dated when I can date anyone I choose?"

Immediately the heads of loved ones had begun to nod, and murmurs rippled through the room. Daniel had stood by quietly, neither denying nor confirming Aquilla's account. Her cousin had skillfully planted doubt in everyone's mind, and in so doing, Sadie felt what little strength she still possessed drain from her. It wasn't Sadie's nature to defend herself, to stir anger and resentment when the argument would still leave people unsure of who was right.

If given time, would Daniel take up Aquilla's lie too?

Sadie closed her eyes, trying to reconcile what was happening with what was supposed to take place tomorrow. She pulled free of her cousin's hand and rose, hoping her legs would not fail her. Standing mere feet from Daniel, she stared into his eyes, remembering how they'd grown so close over the past months, talking for hours, laughing at things only they shared. She studied him now. Who was this stranger? What did he see when he looked at her? Did his heart break for all he'd forsaken?

He gazed at her. "I swear to you on my life, nothing like this has happened before or ever will again."

She was tempted to believe him. But how could she be sure? Did he mean what he said, or would he say anything to end this nightmare?

She'd never know.

What she did know was that her family believed she'd remain unwed forever if she didn't marry Daniel. Even rebellious teens weren't gawked at or gossiped about like a woman who had never married—at least until the woman was past thirty. Then everyone accepted her fate without further discussion.

Daniel angled his head. "Don't call off the wedding, Sadie," he whispered. "It'll cause a scandal. And there's no sense in trying to weather that."

Visions of him with Aquilla tore at her again. His mouth pressed against Aquilla's, his hands under her dress, roaming over her body. The pain struck again, so deep, so intense, Sadie longed to ease it. She only needed to nod, and he'd embrace her. Relief would rush through him and their families, and everyone would surround her with words of hope and encouragement. Her pain would ease.

But would it ever go away?

She feared not. Doubt would fade when she was in his arms, then grow as bright and scorching as an August sun when she wasn't.

Could she live with that? The seconds ticked by as she studied him, and anger grew in Daniel's eyes.

"Despite what you thought you saw,"—Daniel took a step back, talking loudly enough for most everyone to hear him—"Aquilla has told the truth, and I'm begging you not to call off the wedding over a misunderstanding."

His words hit hard, and she felt the weight of judgment from her family and his bear down on her. Trembling, Sadie struggled to catch her breath. She wasn't strong enough to cope with a broken heart and the fallout of people's disappointment in her if she chose to call off the wedding.

But was she strong enough to marry a liar?

Two

Four years later

S adie rode in the front seat next to the hired driver. Her lips were pressed into a thin line. Summoned. Just like that. She'd been sent for.

She held the letter from her parents, the one they had sent to her boss and trusted advisor. Loyd Farmer had given it to her mere hours ago, his elderly hands trembling in their usual manner.

At least this mandatory family gathering wouldn't be held at her parents' or siblings' homes in Brim. There would be no chance of encountering Daniel.

Thankfully, she hadn't been required to return home but a few times over the years. She could thank her Daed for that. He'd believed her about Daniel's betrayal and had managed to stir up pity for her from the church leaders so they'd leave her alone, allow her to move away, and permit her to go on Mennonite mission trips. Normally, the church leaders would be heavily involved in an incident like the one with Sadie and Daniel and Aquilla. They'd hear all sides and render a verdict. If Sadie had been able to convince the church leaders of what she'd seen, the lovebirds would've been shunned for at least six weeks. But two things stood in her way: an eye for an eye wasn't God's way, and it was her word against Daniel's. Aquilla would have verified Daniel's account of that day. Sadie only had God as her witness. So rather than start a fight she couldn't win, she put the matter in God's hands. Her Daed had appealed to the leaders, telling them that whether Sadie saw Daniel and Aquilla together or simply thought she did, she was broken over her loss. Daed's argument had been convincing enough that they'd let him have final say over Sadie. She respected her Daed for what he'd done, and she owed him a lot, but she liked who she had become because of the extra freedoms she enjoyed. She couldn't give them up now.

Still, her Daed had beckoned her, and in the blink of an eye, she was compelled to head to Apple Ridge, where her mother's family lived. But this wasn't a good weekend to be gone from her job as the floor manager of Farmers' Five-and-Dime. Although they'd probably be fine without her, the Fourth of July weekend was one of their busiest times.

One would think Sadie could get out of bending to her parents' demands by now. With Loyd and Edna Farmer's guidance and support, Sadie had moved into a house in Stone Creek with two Plain Mennonite girls and had gone to work for the Farmers in their variety store.

Sadie had learned that the Stone Creek Mennonite group did mission work at a remote mountain village in Peru. She'd never expected to be able to go with them. It just wasn't done in her community. But her Daed had not opposed her, and what Amish church leader would deny a broken woman the right to serve God by caring for those less fortunate?

None, she'd discovered. Not a one—even if they were not sure what Sadie had seen that day in the shed.

Since her Daed and the church leaders had given her so much leeway for four years, Sadie had expected by now to be free of having to buckle under her parents' wishes. But the opposite seemed to be true. Her Daed had been writing to her more of late and calling her regularly, all with strongly worded pleas for her to return to her Amish roots and live under his roof.

The letter in her hand bore a polite command from her Daed—and he'd sent it to her Mennonite employers. It was a shrewd move on her parents' part. They knew Loyd and Edna would support them and that Sadie wouldn't argue with the elderly couple. And her Daed had chosen neutral ground for what she believed to be the beginning of the latest battle to get her home. She took comfort in the fact that her parents had not pulled the church leaders into their struggle. If they had, she'd have been called home to Brim instead of to her grandmother's place.

The driver pulled onto *Mammi* Lee's driveway. Sadie stared at the old house, dreading what lay ahead of her.

She wasn't the same dedicated-to-the-Amish woman they'd raised her to be, but she couldn't tell them that. All she could do was aim to honor them to the best of her ability and hope her excuse of broken-ness from Daniel's betrayal would continue to give her the freedom she needed.

Her *Mamm* came out of Mammi Lee's house, a smile on her face and worry in her eyes. Sadie opened the car door, praying for wisdom and strength to get through the next three days and then return to the life she loved.

She embraced her mother. The warmth radiating from Mamm brought tears to Sadie's eyes. For a moment she wished that circumstances were different. But no, she would return to Stone Creek. The only question was whether she'd do so with peace and love reigning between her and her parents, or if they'd be at war. Of course, there was one other question...

Whether she'd leave as a member in good standing with the Amish or be excommunicated.

Levi stood at the kitchen counter, cracking two eggs simultaneously and dumping the yolks and whites into a bowl.

"How do you always do that?" Tobias stood on his tiptoes, peering into the container.

Levi tossed the shells into the sink, wiped his hands on the kitchen towel tucked into his pants, and passed him the last egg. "Try it."

Tobias smacked the egg against the bowl. Eggshell slid into the bowl while the contents oozed onto the countertop.

Levi chuckled. "Close enough." Running the flat of his hand across the counter, he scraped the mess into the bowl and dug out the pieces of eggshell. He rinsed his hands, dried them, and handed Tobias a fork. "Here, you scramble them."

With twelve eggs in the bowl, Tobias would be busy for a few minutes. In the meantime Levi started a flame under the camp-stove toaster and put four pieces of bread on it.

Tobias gazed up at him, eyes shining. "I love you."

Levi tousled the boy's hair. "You'd better, or no more eggs for you."

How could this sweet boy's mother have left him so suddenly? If Levi could, he'd look her in the eye and demand an answer to that question. For a moment anger stirred, but he tried not to let it pull him under.

The back door slammed. "Do I smell toast?"

Tobias grinned at Levi's brother. "And soon it'll be eggs too!"

Andy came into the room, both eyebrows raised. "Are you ever going to cook that boy anything but eggs?"

"Nope. It's healthy and easy." Levi flipped the bread over, toasting the other side. "Like some smart guy once said, 'If it ain't broke, don't fix it.'"

"No picking on Levi." Tobias grinned. "I don't know anybody that's got an uncle like mine."

"Good answer." Levi loved the kid. He was a pain in the neck at times, but Levi had never seen another like him.

Andy peeled out of his dirty shirt and tossed it toward the doorway of the washroom, then moved to the sink and flicked on the water. "I'll wash up and take over. You still have time to get cleaned up and make it to tonight's singing."

Levi grabbed a plate and put four pieces of toast on it. "Thanks, but I'm not going." Using a potholder, he removed the camp-stove toaster from the flame and set an iron skillet in its place.

Andy scrubbed his hands and arms up to his elbows, washing off caked-on mud. They usually avoided work as much as possible on Sundays, but one of them had to tend to their small herd of horses. "I think Daniel's coming tomorrow, so I took time to get the horse barn in order."

"He's not going to pay us a penny more for those horses because our barn looks good. Still, I'm sure the horses appreciate it, especially since they're spending so much time under the shade trees in this weather." He dumped the raw eggs into the hot skillet, making it sizzle.

"The fine art of sarcasm. Think maybe it's time to give it a rest?" Andy turned off the water and took a dishtowel off the hook.

"Not for a second." Levi stirred the eggs with a wooden spoon.

Andy retrieved three glasses from a cabinet and the milk from the fridge. "You should go tonight."

Levi wrapped a potholder around the handle of the cast-iron skillet and lifted the pan, deciding just how much sarcasm to fling back at his brother. "Are you confusing me with someone who cares what you think?"

Andy grinned. "I'd never do that." He set three plates on the table.

"You do know that's why Mamm brought a stack of clean, well-pressed clothes for you yesterday? She's hoping you'll go tonight. I think it's time you met someone."

Levi dumped the steaming eggs into a bowl and set it on the table. "And I think it's time you minded your own business."

"Tobias, why don't you go to the bathroom and wash your hands?"

Levi wasn't fooled. His brother had just washed up in the kitchen, so there was no reason Tobias couldn't do the same. Andy wanted Tobias out of earshot. The boy scurried down the hall and into the bathroom, slamming the door behind him. His little-boy voice came through the closed door. "Sorry. Didn't mean to do that."

"Not a problem," Andy hollered, then turned to Levi. "Look, we've covered this before. You can't keep avoiding women because I got a bad shake."

A bad shake? Andy's life had been mutilated, and he'd bear the scars in plain sight for the rest of his days.

Levi set the toast and butter on the table. "I understand Mamm and Daed pushing me. But I thought you and I had this resolved."

"I never said it was settled. I left you alone for a while, but you've had enough time."

"Excuse me?" Levi focused on his brother, eyes wide. "Do I live under your roof for *my* sake?"

"No. You do it for mine." Andy snapped at a fly with a kitchen towel. "And I appreciate it. But it's a holiday weekend, and that's when the best singings take place. New girls from the other districts will be here to visit family and meet available men. Go have some fun for a change."

Levi wasn't interested. He'd witnessed one too many women say they were in love, only to walk away later. He was five years younger than

Andy, and he'd spent his childhood shadowing his big brother. If Andy had a good day, Levi did too. So when Andy fell in love and married Eva, Levi felt as if he could lasso the moon. Eva became a sister to Levi, and she'd loved Andy. Levi knew she had. So what caused Eva to break her vows and leave her family?

Something similar had happened to Daniel too. Andy had been in the thick of losing Eva during Daniel's courtship and wedding plans, so Levi was sketchy on the details, but this much he knew: Daniel's fiancée had left him. At least the woman walked out *before* they were married, if only a few hours before. Daniel said she had accused him of being in the arms of another woman, and he admitted he'd been in a room alone with her cousin. But he claimed he never laid a hand on the girl. The last Levi had heard about it, Daniel said his former fiancée had hightailed it somewhere. Maybe Illinois, Peoria, or Peru.

Eva's departure was worse. It'd left Andy without a wife and Tobias without a mother. And they would stay that way since an Amish man could not remarry as long as his former spouse was alive. No exceptions.

"*Kumm* on, Levi." Andy rubbed the center of his forehead. "Please go. I need a break from Mamm's pleading eyes. She's fretting over this. You know she is."

Tobias ran back into the room, holding up his hands to his Daed. Andy pulled a chair out for his son. "You had hands under all that dirt, didn't you?"

The boy nodded and took a seat. "I've been thinking 'bout all these singings everybody keeps telling Uncle Levi to go to. Maybe he doesn't want to go there to meet girls."

"*Ya.*" Levi sat. "I think he's onto something, Andy."

Tobias folded his little hands, preparing for the silent prayer. "Maybe he'd like the idea better if, instead of girls, you'd put a herd of horses in the barn where the singing takes place. He likes them just fine."

Andy looked at Levi, trying not to laugh.

Levi sighed. "Tobias, you got this all wrong. I like girls."

"You do?" Tobias's big brown eyes were filled with innocence.

"I do." Levi turned to his brother. "Fine. I'll go."

Still, he had to figure out a way to settle this issue for his family and his impressionable nephew. But how?

Three

Sadie steadied her breathing. She'd tried to avoid angering her father. After her arrival yesterday, she'd tiptoed through all the conversational land mines, avoiding each potential explosion. Until now.

Daed wagged his finger at her. *"Duh net schwetze."*

She pursed her lips, determined to obey him and not speak—not in English or Pennsylvania Dutch. She ached for the grief she had caused the man who had embraced her so warmly yesterday. The one who had spent a lifetime telling her to listen to God's voice no matter what anyone else said. The one who had understood her need to get away from Brim. There was no doubt that he had a fierce, determined love for her. But now he was angry. And probably afraid. According to him, she had grown up as the sweetest-natured and most obedient daughter. But something in her broke the day she saw Daniel's body entwined with Aquilla's, and there was no going back, not even for her Daed's sake.

Mammi Lee pursed her lips and shook her head. "Sadie."

Her grandmother's voice had never held such sorrow and disappointment. Her family's reaction hurt. So much for being loving and respectful over the long weekend and for not stirring up any arguments. And today was only Sunday.

As soon as she'd arrived, her parents and grandmother had asked her a lot of questions. She'd tried to be honest without giving away her plans to return to Peru with the mission team after Christmas. She figured there would be an opportunity to ease into that conversation closer to December. But while dodging questions about the lease on the home she rented with her friends, her Daed had picked up on her reluctance and pressed her. Before she knew it, she had told everyone about South America. And she was talking about staying there for another year. Maybe two.

Daed focused on her. *"Was iss letz with du?"*

His accusing tone frustrated her. "There's nothing wrong with me. Some of my earliest memories are of you holding my hands while we prayed. You taught me to pay attention to God's leading. That's what I'm trying to do."

He shook his finger at her again. "I told you to be quiet."

"And then you asked me a question." Her voice went up a few decibels. Why was it easier nowadays to live with strangers than visit with her family?

"I've put up with more than enough since you and Daniel parted ways. I've allowed much more freedom than I should have, because I blame myself for having encouraged that relationship. But we both have to accept what happened and start fresh." Daed studied her, then nodded as if answering a question he'd asked himself. "You need to work out your notice at that store and with your roommates. I want you home by Christmas, and I will *not* discuss this again."

Sadie looked across the small kitchen to her mother and grandmother, beseeching them to defend her. Mammi Lee lowered her eyes, but disappointment and hurt clouded her mom's face. Mamm wiped a stray tear, clearly distressed.

Her parents had come all this way to share some time with the Lee side of the family, and even though her mom and grandmother had been cooking all day for a family gathering tonight at an uncle's place, no one would be in a mood to go after this heated argument.

The three stood there, staring at Sadie, wanting her to repent of her dreams. She swallowed hard, trying not to feel broken. "I tried to change the subject and not say anything to upset you. If you don't want to know, please don't make me answer your questions."

"You're our daughter and a baptized member of our community." Mamm pulled a tissue from the hidden pocket of her black apron. "How can we not ask questions?" She wiped her eyes.

"It's time for you to come home." Daed crossed his arms. "A new Amish family has moved to Brim from Ohio. They have seven unmarried sons. Five are of marrying age. If you were home—"

"Daed, stop." Her parents didn't understand her any more than she understood them. All she wanted was to use her faith in Christ on the mission field. Was that so wrong?

Daed rubbed the back of his neck, breaking his stony stare. He turned and went into the next room.

Mamm cleared her throat and pulled a roll of aluminum foil out of a drawer. "Let's line a cardboard box with this and put the food in it." She sidestepped Sadie, speaking to Mammi Lee. "That way, if any of our dishes spill, it won't leak onto our dresses."

Mammi Lee left and returned with a large box. "It may take two this size to pack up all the food."

They acted as if no one had just trampled over Sadie's plans. Why couldn't Mamm see past Daed's fears and think for herself? Why did she have to agree with him every time?

A humid breeze drifted across the room, and the great outdoors called to Sadie. She longed to sneak away, saddle a horse, and ride across fields of green, with no one seeing her but God—an opportunity she didn't have often in Stone Creek.

"Sadie," Daed called.

She went through the tiny *Daadi Haus* and into the living room. He folded the newspaper in his hand and pointed at the couch. She sat and waited.

The balmy air carried the aroma of gardenias, and she could imagine all the wonderful fragrances she'd experience on a long horseback ride.

"I'm sorry I lost my temper. I'll warn you now that I'm losing patience with your stubbornness. And I should." He tapped the newspaper on the arm of the chair. "You've got to stop running. Daniel hurt you deeply, and his lies have only made it worse. I understand that. But it's time to come home and find someone else."

She bit her bottom lip, wanting to correct him. Yes, Daniel had crushed her, and his lies humiliated her, but she'd quit pining over him years ago. What had happened between them had freed her in a way nothing else could. But if she told her Daed that, he'd be more determined that she return home.

His voice droned on and on.

During her three short visits to Brim since leaving, she'd been careful to say little, hoping not to stir up any trouble. She'd never shame her parents or siblings or community by leaving the Order, but she didn't fit easily inside the church anymore. She was best on her own, listening closely for God's voice. He hadn't yet let her down. If He had, she would be married to a lying cheat. So until God gave her direction, she'd do her best to keep the peace with her family.

She took a deep breath and focused on the simple pleasure of being at her grandmother's.

The smell of spices hung in the air, hinting at the promise of tonight's feast at her uncle Jesse's house, less than a mile away. The Amish didn't celebrate the Fourth of July, because doing so would celebrate a war and the killing that comes with war. Still, it was a national holiday, so they often used it as a time to gather with family. Some Amish youth would attend the town's show of fireworks.

"Are you even listening to me?"

Sadie's thoughts jerked back to her father. The honest answer was no, so she shook her head.

He slung the newspaper onto the floor. "Whether three hundred miles from home or on a different continent or in the same room, you make talking with you ridiculously difficult. Which is the way you want it, right?"

"Okay." Mamm walked into the room. "The food is packed up. It's time to go."

Daed stood. "Sadie will stay here. The family will ask her questions, and I don't like any of her answers. It's not a good influence for the younger ones."

Mamm blinked. "After she came all this way to be with the family?"

It was Sadie's turn to be shocked. Mamm never questioned Daed.

Her father tucked in a section of his shirt. "If she had been paying any attention to me, I'd have let her go. But since she's determined to heed only her own thoughts, she won't miss spending time with her cousins."

Daed's judgment was nearly her undoing, but she held her tongue. Without another word he went to the door and held it open while her mom and grandmother toted their baked goods from the house.

Sadie couldn't believe he was leaving her here! She was a twenty-three-year-old woman, not a child. If her father insisted on grounding her from the festivities with her family, she'd be tempted to saddle up Mammi Lee's horse Bay and enjoy a ride. It'd be nice to spend a few hours pretending that nothing owned her except freedom.

Mamm came back into the house and walked over to her. She lingered, looking as if she wanted to divulge a secret.

"I'm fine, Mamm. Go on before Daed gets angry with you too."

Mamm smiled. "He's not as bad as he sounds when he's trying to reason with you. He could complain to the church leaders, and they'd pull you home by your apron strings. But he hasn't. For the last two years he's feared that if we didn't get you home, we'd lose any chance of you returning to your roots."

"I don't want to hurt anyone, and I'll visit when I can, but I don't believe I'm meant to live in Brim."

"You thought you were at one time." Her mother's eyes glistened with unshed tears. "Are you sure it's God's call you hear and not your own?"

Sadie looked out the window, praying for the right words. The emerald leaves on the gardenia bush swayed in the breeze, and a robin disappeared between the thick greenery, probably nesting. Did God want her in Peru, or did she simply long to be as far away as possible from the memory of her greatest pain?

"Sadie?"

She lifted her eyes, hating that tears had begun to well in them. "Can anyone be positive about such a thing?"

Mamm cupped Sadie's face in her hands. "You'd like the Lantz men from Ohio. Two have already found wives." She grinned. "But the one I think would be perfect for you isn't seeing anyone."

"Ya, and how do you know that? Because he says so...like Daniel did?" Taken aback by her own words, Sadie winced. Maybe she wasn't over the pain as much as she'd thought.

"Child." Mamm's singular word was filled with compassion and dismay. She kissed Sadie's forehead. "We'll be home after midnight."

"Give everyone my love." She swallowed hard, unsure if she meant the words or if she was using them as a jab. It was absurd that she wouldn't be at her uncle's home to give them her love.

She flopped onto the couch and stared at the wall. The sunlight faded, and darkness began to deepen. The hands on the mantle clock marked the passing hours. Was everything she longed to do wrong? Or was her Daed overreaching his authority simply because he could? Well, he *could* as long as she honored him by obeying.

The desire to ride swept through her again, but when her Daed had left her behind, he'd intended for her to stay in the house.

A few fireworks popped and crackled in the distance. She sat up and lit a kerosene lantern. The dim yellow glow made a large circle around her. She went to a table and picked up her grandmother's German Bible. A tattered cloth bookmark stuck out of its pages, and she opened it to that spot—Hebrews, chapter 1. She returned to the couch and read, stopping from time to time to think and pray, hoping the words would speak to her.

Four

*L*evi walked from the flaming bonfire in the Stoltzfuses' backyard toward the barn. He'd known the evening would end like this, with him leaving alone while others watched.

"Levi?"

He turned to see Ruth Esh.

Even under the dark sky, her eighteen-year-old face glowed with pink hues, probably because of her forwardness at following him. "I wanted to wish you a happy Fourth."

That's not all she wanted, and he knew it. She'd like him to offer to take her home.

"I hope you enjoy your off day tomorrow, Ruth." He tipped his hat. "G'night."

She continued standing there, brushing off mosquitoes or rubbing spots where she already had been bitten.

He squelched the desire to walk off. "The insects are less likely to bother you if you're near the fire."

"It's barely after nine. Don't you want to stay a little longer? The Stoltzfuses have lawn chairs set up on the back hill facing the town. They said we'll be able to see some fireworks...and afterward maybe you wouldn't mind taking me home."

His horseless carriage stood outside the barn, lined up with two dozen others. But all he wanted to do was leave the rig here and ride home bareback.

Levi admired her courage in asking him right out. "That's really nice of you, but I need to go." He tipped his hat again, hoping she'd walk back to the group. "Evening."

"Bye."

The moment she turned toward the house, he strode for the barn. Once in the dark building, he lit a lantern. Dust floated in the air, easily seen in the soft glow of the lamp. A long row of bridles hung on a dirty plank wall, held up by ten-penny nails. Horses lined the feed trough, grazing on hay while waiting for their owners to return and hitch them to their carriages.

He wanted to bridle Amigo and see what the thoroughbred could really do. Elmer Stoltzfus wouldn't mind if Levi left his rig here and borrowed a bridle. He took one off the wall and walked through the dimly lit barn until he found Amigo. He slid the bit into the horse's mouth.

He led the animal to the lantern, extinguished the flame, then climbed up bareback. He'd take the route where he wouldn't be seen along the way. Maybe he'd stop by the creek and toss a few stones before calling it a night.

When his pocket vibrated, he pulled out his phone. Levi was allowed a cell phone for work purposes, as were others who needed them for business. If he followed the Old Ways, he'd have tucked the phone in a drawer when he got home from delivering a gazebo last Friday night. But he liked being able to text with friends. Amigo's uneven movement made it a little challenging to read the message, but he saw enough to know his younger cousin was harassing him about leaving the singing alone...again. If Matthew had any sense, he wouldn't be engaged at nineteen years old to a girl who was seventeen. They couldn't possibly know themselves well enough to make a lifetime promise.

Levi had been given a gift: insight into the gamble involved with loving a woman. No wonder the apostle Paul said that if a man could stay single without sinning against God, he should do so. His family had witnessed firsthand that women were not worth the risk. So why did they always press Levi on the subject?

Frustration circled, and Levi gripped the phone as if wanting to squeeze the life out of it. He clutched the reins and urged the horse to go faster and faster. The muggy night air felt cool against his skin. After a few moments several loud booms rang out. *Fireworks.*

Without warning, the horse reared up on his two back legs, whinnying, and the phone flew out of Levi's hand.

"Whoa!" He tugged on the reins, trying to bring the animal under control, but the air vibrated with another round of fireworks. Amigo reared and kicked higher and faster.

"Easy, boy." Levi's voice wavered like Jell-O being shaken, and Amigo bucked harder. The darkness around Levi blurred, and when the horse began to spin, Levi was no longer sure where the road lay and where the patch of woods was. Amigo came to a sudden stop, and Levi sailed over the horse's head.

He landed with a horrid thud. Pain shot through every inch of him, and he couldn't catch his breath. He tried to relax, hoping that he just had the air knocked out of him.

God, please.

His breath returned with a vengeance, and he sucked in heavy air. But pain ricocheted through his back, and dread surrounded him even more than the darkness of night. He needed help, but he could feel consciousness slipping away. Was he going to die here, a place where no one was likely to find him until Old Man Hostetler decided to cut his hay again…sometime next spring?

It hurt to breathe. A sharp pain skittered up and down his torso and to the top of his head. He felt as if he were rolling on shards of glass. But he couldn't move.

He needed help, and he could get it…if he could get to his phone.

Anxiety grew like a shadow from the ground and stood over him, looming all around as if it were strong enough to snatch his life right out of him.

Levi pried his eyes open, almost startled when he didn't see a menacing Grim Reaper above him, poised to strike. The black sky reminded him how sinister the world felt at times, but then the stars looked like white marbles that he could hold in the palm of his hand.

If he lived through this night, he'd look back on this moment and recall seeing the universe in all its majesty and recognizing he was only a powerless man staring into the vastness of an all-powerful God.

The sounds of night faded as he slipped into darkness.

Jonah eased into the bedroom, a cup of hot tea in hand.

Beth opened her eyes for a moment. "I'm awake." His wife sat upright, holding her head.

Jonah adjusted the pillows. She sank against them and then held out her hands for the mug.

With her eyes closed, she took a sip. "As soon as my head stops spinning, I'll be fine."

He sat in the chair beside her, admiring her beauty even after such a hard few days.

She blinked and then focused on him. "Oh, honey, stop looking so sad. It had to happen. We were both perfectly healthy for a year leading up to the wedding, and we've had seven months of wedded bliss without so much as a cold, even through the long winter months of serving hundreds of customers. So it's no wonder you picked up a stomach flu and shared it with me. I'll be fine by tomorrow."

"I was better in twenty-four hours. You're going on three days."

"My goal is to have these symptoms linger until you feel so guilty you'll never share another virus with me."

"You accomplished complete dishonor on my part the first minute you turned pale."

She chuckled.

He loved her laugh. Her voice. Her heart. Her tenacity and stubbornness and exuberance and…

Jonah took her hand in his and kissed the back of it. She had no idea what she did to him, and his desire to take care of her, to protect her from all harm grew stronger every day. But a man could not share these feelings with a woman like Beth. She didn't want to be taken care of. She wanted to make strong decisions and carry them out. And that's what she did and had been doing since long before they met.

Still, this illness concerned him. He cleared his throat. "I want you to be seen tomorrow."

"I'll be seen. I'll wake up feeling better, and customers will see me all day."

"Beth, don't be difficult. You know what I mean." He'd feel better once she saw the doctor. Doctors who tended only to the Plain community set up their clinics to be a one-stop answer. Otherwise the multitude of uninsured Amish and Mennonites wouldn't go. So whether a patient needed a severed digit sewn back on or a cancer screening or an x-ray, Dr. Baxter took care of it at his office.

Beth crossed her arms, a slight pout on her lips. "We've been advertising tomorrow's specials since Memorial Day."

"And I'll see to it the store runs smoothly." He kissed her hand again.

"Lizzy's off on another trip with Omar. You'll need me."

Beth's aunt had married the bishop, so the two of them traveled regularly to visit the other church districts where Bishop Omar would be the guest preacher. It was all part of being a bishop. But since the wedding, Lizzy traveled more weeks than she was home.

Jonah squeezed her hand. "I'm sure I'll miss you being at the store, but I'll be fine, and most of the hired girls will be there to help too."

"It's the Fourth. The doctor's office isn't likely to be open."

"Dr. Baxter takes off about five weekdays a year, and the Fourth isn't one of them."

"Wonderful." Her playful frustration rang clear. "Are all doctors whose practice is limited to Amish and Mennonite communities that steadfast?"

"I don't know, but I'd appreciate if you'd stop trying to change the subject as well as my mind." He paused. "Please."

She sighed. "Husbands."

She whispered the word in mock disgust whenever he annoyed her. But her response let him know he'd won. This time.

Usually winning brought him a sense of amusement or playful victory, but the fact she'd given in as easily as she did only added to his concern.

Five

With the old Bible in her lap, Sadie prayed. But the more she did, the more she felt an overwhelming desire to ride Bay. How could she crave going against her father's wishes while praying for wisdom? That made no sense at all.

She closed the Bible. Was she so rebellious that she couldn't do as her Daed wanted for one evening?

She ran her fingertips across the worn leather of the Bible. *God, what is wrong with me?*

The desire to saddle Bay tugged at her even stronger. Apparently she *was* too rebellious to do as her Daed wanted. She sighed and took the lantern into her bedroom. She lifted her overnight bag onto the bed and pulled out her riding clothes. Once dressed, she removed her prayer *Kapp* and untwined her hair. After running her fingers through the waves, she created a long but loosely woven french braid. If she was going to ride Bay over unfamiliar terrain, especially at night, she had to wear pants. And she couldn't wear a prayer Kapp or have her hair pinned up. Her head would look Amish while the rest of her looked *Englisch*. If anyone saw someone riding who looked Amish, it could be traced back to her, and the news would bring shame to her father and trouble to herself. But if people spotted a girl riding who they thought was Englisch, no one would think anything about it.

She carried the lantern with her and left the house. A muggy breeze stirred the lush trees, and fireworks popped in the distance. The clear sky above carried a few white, shining jewels despite the summer haze.

Sadie opened the barn door, and the old mare raised her head. Bay wasn't particularly fast, but Sadie believed the horse loved their rare long nights of riding as much as she did.

When Sadie had Bay ready to leave her stall, she blew out the lantern and mounted the mare. The *clip-clop* of hoofs against the ground made Sadie's heart pick up its pace. She went slowly at first, giving Bay time to warm up. Once they were on the path that led to a stranger's pasture, Sadie loosened the reins, allowing Bay to pick up speed. The mare gave it her all, and Sadie intertwined her fingers through the mane to hold on over the rough landscape.

The sights and smells of summer in Apple Ridge revived her weary soul. Living in Stone Creek, a town of considerable size, had a very different feel to it. An occasional firework went off around her, but the loudest of them had ended before she began her ride.

The moon sparkled off the water in the brook as Bay trotted across the shallow creek bed. Sadie patted the mare's neck. "Good girl. We rode with the wind, ya?"

Bay continued onward, but an odd sound arose from the ground. Sadie tensed. She clicked her tongue, ready to nudge her heels into Bay's side and move back toward home, but then... Which direction *was* home? She tugged on the reins, slowing Bay while she searched their surroundings for a familiar landmark. How far was she from Mammi Lee's? Ten miles? Maybe fifteen?

Another groan made her skin crawl, and she studied the ground. Bay's hoofs shifted and trod the thick grass, leaving clear imprints.

The moon's glow revealed other horse tracks, and Sadie feared it was time to bolt from the area. But she directed Bay to follow the beaten path. The tracks continued for a short distance, then made a circle and went back in the same direction.

On the horizon she saw a shadowy figure. Was that an animal? Yes, it might even be a bridled horse standing at the edge of the field near a patch of woods. Although her curiosity was piqued, she wasn't about to go near that area to check it out. With fear rising, she nudged Bay into a gallop toward the creek.

Once there, Sadie risked a glance behind her. She didn't consider herself a coward. How many women went out by themselves at night for the sheer joy of it? Yet here she was, running home simply because she'd heard a groan in the darkness and seen something that looked like a bridled horse in silhouette.

Unable to shake free of her fear and yet chiding herself for being so skittish, she clicked her tongue and tugged on the right rein until Bay headed back toward the sound.

"Hello?" She peered into the woods, watching for any sign of life. Other than the animal she'd seen earlier—whether cow, deer, or horse— she saw no movement.

As she neared the creature, it whinnied and backed up. Definitely a horse. Reins dangled from the bit to the ground, but it wasn't tethered to anything.

She dismounted. *"Begreiflich." Easy.*

She made several attempts to get closer, but the horse kept backing away. *"Gut Gaul.* Kumm." The horse calmed a bit, ears perked to listen to Sadie's low voice. When Sadie drew close, she took hold of a dangling rein to keep the animal from running off.

"Begreiflich," she repeated softly as she ran her hand down the horse's leg. She didn't feel any broken bones. "Where's your rider?"

Peering into the woods, she looked for any sign of another person, a moving shadow or something. When she saw nothing out of the ordinary, she looked across the field. The grass stood at least a foot tall, high and thick enough to conceal a body. She didn't like the idea of hunting for someone, but even so, she tethered the stray horse to a low-hanging branch, mounted Bay, and followed the tracks in the grass.

She moved slowly, searching the area. Just beyond where the tracks ended, she saw a shadowy lump in the grass. She nudged the horse forward, one step at a time. The desire to flee overwhelmed her, but she paused a few feet from the mass, studying it through the darkness.

A man.

She got off her horse and crouched, realizing the man wore Amish clothing.

"Hello?" She patted his face, but he remained motionless. "Hello? Can you hear me?" She spoke in clear English, hoping not to reveal her Amish accent. If word of how she was dressed leaked back to Mammi Lee's community, her Daed's patience with her would go from thin to nonexistent.

How can you think about yourself right now?

She had to get help. Where had she seen the last house—two, maybe three miles back? Looking across the land, she realized afresh how turned around she was.

"Can you hear me?" When he didn't budge, she pressed two fingers against his neck. His pulse met her fingertips, and relief exploded in her, feeling much like fireworks themselves. "Please wake up."

Regardless of his being Amish, she patted his pants pockets, hoping he had a phone. He didn't, and she again checked his pulse.

His face turned toward her, and he lowered his jaw as if responding to her touch. He moaned, startling her.

Excitement suddenly soared in her, and she was tempted to double her fists and jab them into the air. Instead, she placed a hand on his cheek and rubbed her thumb across it.

"Stay calm and try not to move. I need to get help."

She studied her surroundings. A silhouette of massive trees was in the distance, a dirt road lay a few hundred feet away, and a fence line stood to the west. But where was the closest house?

He raised a hand toward her. "Please…"

He said something more, but she couldn't hear him. She lowered her ear to his mouth.

"If you can help me get up…"

She started to put her hand in his, but something about it didn't feel right, and she lowered her hand. "Not yet."

"Please."

"Stay still." She took his hand in hers, and he clutched it firmly as she lowered it to his side, allowing him to hold it. "We're doing this my way."

His eyes opened, staring at her with disbelief. Then his eyes closed, and his hand released its grip on hers.

She patted his face. "Hello?" Nothing. Now what? While trying to think what to do, she saw his fingers moving. "Hello?" She slapped his face a little harder.

"My…" The whispered word trailed off.

"Do you know where we are?" She lowered her ear to his mouth again.

"Phone."

"You have a phone?"

He didn't respond to her, and she got on her hands and knees, patting the ground around him.

Nothing.

A lot of unmarried Amish men and women carried cell phones. They weren't forbidden from doing so until they joined the church, but even then more and more of the younger generation kept them close.

She fumbled through the tall grass. "God, my most trusted friend, please, You know where his phone is. Help me, please." With the darkness of the night and the height and thickness of the grass, she could be within a hair of putting her hand on it and never see it.

Then a buzzing sound came from nowhere, and she focused all her senses on it. She followed the noise, going one direction and then another. She panicked. What if it stopped before she could find it? She listened intently. *Please, God...*

There! That's where the sound was coming from! She hurried, thrilled as the buzz grew louder. She spotted a blue glow in the grass and ran toward it. After snatching the phone from the thick growth, she dialed 911 and then ran back to the man.

After a few rings a female voice said something she couldn't make out.

"There's a man down in a field." Sadie knelt and nudged the man, hoping for another response, but he didn't budge. "I think he was thrown from a horse."

"Is he conscious?"

"He was for a few moments but not now."

"Is he breathing?"

She knelt beside him and pressed her fingers on his neck again. "He has a pulse."

"Is he bleeding?"

Sadie checked the ground around him. "I don't think so."

"What's your location?"

"I...I don't know. I'm somewhere in Apple Ridge, Pennsylvania."

"Is there a street sign near you?"

"I'm in the middle of a field. There's a road a few hundred feet away, but there's no intersection with a street sign for miles. I'd have to ride my horse to find out." She started to get up, but the man moaned.

Sadie's heart pounded. "When he woke, he asked me to help him get up. If he would wake up again, I could get him on a horse and get him to his family, a place with a known add—"

"Ma'am, *do not move him!* Don't move any part of him. If he begins to stir, you need to keep him still. Do you understand?"

"I understand." But what if he awoke and wanted to get up? How was Sadie supposed to make this man obey her?

"If he wakes, try to keep him conscious, and do what you can to keep him warm. But he must remain lying exactly where he is. Can you check his pockets for identification without moving him?"

What difference does it make who he is? Cupping the phone between her chin and her shoulder, she did as the woman asked, but there was no sign of a wallet. She hovered over his face. "Hello?"

His breathing altered, and the fingers on one hand moved.

"Do you know where we are?"

He seemed to reach for something. She put her hand in his, and he tightened his fingers as if needing reassurance that someone was here. She used her free hand to touch his face, hoping to coax him to respond. "It's okay. I've got help on the line. Do you know where we are?"

He stirred, even opened his mouth, but she could hear no words.

She moved her ear closer to his face again.

"Zook…Road. Three miles…north of…Cherry Hill…intersection."

Tears welled in Sadie's eyes. "Excellent!" She caressed his face as she reported this to the operator. The woman on the other end of the line repeated it back to her.

"Yes. That's right."

The woman didn't respond.

"Hello?"

Nothing.

"Hello?"

Sadie looked at the phone. No lights were on. She punched several buttons but heard no sound of any kind.

The man raised a hand.

She clutched it and lowered it to his side. "Stay still, please."

He shivered, and she frowned. It was hot and muggy, but he breathed and trembled as if he were freezing. Sadie went to her horse, removed Bay's saddle, and plunked it to the ground. She grabbed the blanket and unfolded it while walking back to him. After covering him with it and tucking it around him as best she could, she sat beside him.

"Help's on the way." Since his arms were under the blanket and he responded well to touch, she stroked his cheek. Thank heaven, his shaking had eased.

Under the glow of the moon, she saw him close his eyes. His body went limp. She jabbed her fingers into his neck, feeling a faint rhythm. "Hey! Wake up!" She screamed in his face. "Can you hear me?"

But he didn't budge, and his pulse seemed to fade.

Six

A female voice commanded Levi to wake up. He pried his eyes open.

The outline of a woman hovered over him. She held a cell phone in one hand. Did angels wear jeans and boots and carry a phone?

She seemed perturbed with the phone as she kept pressing numbers. He tried to speak but only managed a moan.

She crouched beside him. "Stay still. Completely still. Okay?"

He wanted to get his hand free of the blanket, but when he tried, she lowered the cover and firmly intertwined her fingers with his. "It's okay. Help is on the way."

"You're no angel."

She laughed. "I'm afraid my father would agree with you completely, especially if he arrives at my grandmother's place to discover I'm not there."

"He'll be worried."

"No. He'll know I've gone riding. He'll just be angry." She released his hand and eased his arm to his side. "What's your name?"

His head pounded. He had to concentrate to answer her. "Levi."

"I'm Sadie." She sat down next to him.

"Amigo...my horse... Is he hurt?"

"He's spooked but appears fine. I think he needs a name change, however, because that horse is no friend of yours."

Her sense of playfulness brought him some much-needed relief. He mustered his strength to talk. "I can't. I have no idea what the Spanish word is for 'enemy.'"

"Believe it or not, it's *enemigo*."

"You're making that up."

"One might think that, but I promise it's true." She shifted. "Do you live around here?"

"On Hertzler Drive."

"Is that near Hertzlers' Dry Goods?"

His head throbbed, and he closed his eyes.

"Levi, look at me."

He tried but couldn't find the strength. Her hands cradled his face.

"Levi," she sang his name. "Open your eyes." She paused. "Levi, *now!*"

A sensation of being pulled from the bottom of a pond tugged him awake. "It's not nice to yell at people you just met."

"If you don't open those eyes, I'm going to slap someone I just met."

It wasn't easy, but he made himself look at her.

"Good." She smiled. "I was asking where you live."

"A mile or so from the dry goods store."

"I've been to that store with Mammi."

His head spun. He'd never been so befuddled, but did she use the word *Mammi*? "You have Amish family?"

She hesitated. "Sort of." She stood. "I need to get something. Stay very still."

"You're leaving me?"

"I may hurt you if you close your eyes, but I'm not leaving." Then she disappeared.

She *sort of* had Amish family? Did that mean some of her family was once Amish but no longer?

She returned with a saddle, which she put near his shoulder. When she sat, she propped her elbow on it and leaned her head on her hand. "I'm just getting comfortable. I imagine, with the holiday, ambulance services are very busy. One might not show up for a while."

Pain shot through him, and he moaned despite his resolve. His breath came in short, catching spurts. "Sorry. My left leg hurts."

"Try not to think about it."

He glanced up at her, studying her features. "Great plan."

She chuckled. "Got a better one?"

"No."

"Since we're strangers, how about if we play twenty questions?"

He took short breaths. "I already asked one. You didn't answer."

She propped her knuckles over her mouth, watching him. "The question game is a good one—short, back and forth, only discussing things each of us is interested in. But before I began my ride tonight, I was careful so no one could connect me to my relatives in Apple Ridge, and if I answer you, I would place in your hands the power to change my life. I won't give that to anyone."

That was a telling statement. Did she mean it? "Not anyone? Ever? Not even the man you love?"

"Especially not him."

Despite his pain, an eerie sensation swept over him. "I'm not really awake, am I?"

She leaned close, peering into his eyes. "Levi?"

The warmth of her hand against his cheek seemed real, but he had to be dreaming. Catching a glimpse of her heart was like seeing into his own—filled with distrust and determination to steer life onto the safest path possible. Maybe this was God's way of talking to him. He was convinced the world was too big for this kind of coincidence. For him to be thrown from his horse, land on his back in the middle of nowhere, then be found by a woman whose thinking was so close to his own?

This was no coincidence.

Well, real or dream, he needed her to tell him more. "After what you're doing for me, do you think I'd betray your confidence?"

"Probably not, unless it profited you in some way, through money, pleasure, or maybe just ego."

He closed his eyes, trying to block out the pain. "I think you've got me beat."

"How so?"

"I thought *I* was distrusting of the opposite gender. You're way beyond distrust and square in the middle of intolerance. Why?"

She started to pull her hand away. He reached for it and then howled in pain from the movement. "If we wrestle, I'll lose."

She held his hand and eased it to his chest. "Then let's not. I'd hate to have to live with the guilt of having beat up someone I was trying to help."

"I appreciate that."

"Do you have someone special, Levi?"

"Do this often, do you? Find broken men sprawled in a dark field and ask them out? I'm in no mood for a date, but thanks."

She laughed, and the sound echoed against the night, easing his concern that she wasn't real.

He drummed his fingers on his chest, feeling more clearheaded.

Except for his leg, his pain was subsiding. "Much to my family's horror, I'm seeing no one."

"Boy, do I understand that. I didn't think parents were as hard on guys about that."

"You haven't met my brother. He's the worst."

"Okay, twenty questions, but past loves are off-limits."

She must have been in love at least once. He'd like to ask her about it, to understand what it felt like, what the big pull to find someone was really about.

He drew a sharp breath as pain throbbed through his leg and lower back.

She tucked the blanket around him and took his hand in hers again. "I'm Amish, and so is my family. But that's not how we're going to play this game. I'll ask a question, and I'll have twenty tries to get the right answer. You simply say yes or no. Whoever asks the fewest questions before coming up with the right answer wins. My turn. What color are your eyes?"

"That's hardly fair. There are only a few choices of eye color."

"Brown?"

"Someone give the lady a cigar."

"No thanks. I gave them up last week."

"My turn to guess yours. Brown?"

"Nope."

"Blue?"

"Nope."

"Green?"

"Nope."

"Okay, you're just lying to me."

"I'm not." Sadie giggled.

"I'm injured, and you're fibbing to win the game."

"They're hazel."

"Isn't that a shade of brown?"

"Technically I think it is. But if I wear green, my eyes look green. If I wear blue, they look gray."

"So what color do they look when you wear purple polka dots?"

"I told you, I'm as Amish as you are. There is no wearing of polka dots. Did you fall off your horse or something?"

He liked her spunk and how she said things dryly when teasing. "I hope we're here when the sun comes up, because I want to see your weird eyes."

"Do you want my entire family, including Mammi Lee, to turn my future inside out just so you can look into my eyes?"

"Well, since you put it that way…yes." He smiled as she chuckled. "I know a few Mammi Lees in the area."

"No shortage of Lees in this neck of the woods."

"You know someone Amish who has a unique name?"

She chuckled again. "You can choose any combination of names, and I bet you and I both know at least ten people with the same name."

"Which Mammi Lee is yours?"

"Verna Lee. Her husband was a woodworker who once made toys for Hertzlers'."

"I know Verna. We don't live in the same church district, so I haven't seen her in years. But my older brother apprenticed under your grandfather, and I went with him a time or two when I was around fifteen. One time she received a package from you. She loved her little Sadie, the girl who made soaps and candles and sent them to her."

"One of Verna Lee's grandchildren. Number four thousand five hundred and eighty-two, I think."

He chuckled.

Fireworks boomed in the distance, and Sadie jolted. "It's okay," he said. "I'll keep you safe."

"Uh-huh." Her playful tone mocked him.

Without moving his head, he could see multicolored flashes of light in the sky behind Sadie. "Look."

She turned. "Beautiful."

If the fireworks weren't exploding in the sky within his direct gaze, he wouldn't be able to see them. Of course, they could see only a portion of the light display. She moved to his other side so she could see them and face him. They watched in silence for a little while.

She patted the blanket, probably to make sure it was keeping him warm. "Does your brother make toys?"

"He did. I took over."

Her eyes grew large, and for once he didn't feel self-conscious for admitting he made toys. It wasn't his only business, but he enjoyed doing it. Their conversation kept a steady pace, and they stopped talking in English. It surprised him how much they could talk about and how interesting he found each topic. It'd come naturally to tell her he lived with his brother and nephew, but he'd stopped short of saying anything about his missing sister-in-law. Thankfully, either Sadie hadn't noticed, or she was too polite to ask. They even talked about where she lived and her need to earn money to return to the mission field. He was so caught up in their conversation, he didn't notice when the fireworks ended.

She tilted her head and sat up. "I hear a siren. It's probably the ambulance. I'd better move to the road so I can flag them down." She stood, brushing off her clothes. "I need to get back to Mammi's as soon as you're in the ambulance. Is there someone I can call for you?"

"You can find my brother's phone number in your Mammi's Amish directory. It's Andy Fisher on Hertzler Drive."

"You stay still. Okay?"

"*Denki,* Sadie."

She smiled. "You're most welcome, Levi."

She hurried toward the road, and Levi wondered if he'd ever see her again. As odd as it seemed, he hoped he would.

Seven

Beth fidgeted with her patient gown as she sat across from the doctor. Her heart was racing.

Pregnant?

She had missed a couple of cycles, but that wasn't unusual.

Pregnant? By the time she and Jonah had married, they were a decade older than most Amish newlyweds. They'd discussed children before they married, and their conclusion was to be grateful and content to have each other. Their well-meaning relatives on both sides of the family had said that because of their ages, it could take them longer to conceive than most Amish newlyweds. So she and Jonah had agreed not to put pressure on themselves about having babies.

Jonah had stronger opinions about conceiving than she did. He suggested they ignore the possibility, not think or talk about it for at least two years. After they were married, she'd found it very comforting to know he wasn't quietly pacing the floors, needing her to come up pregnant before he could feel satisfied or complete. Now, a mere seven months later, they were expecting.

"You're sure?" Beth tried to steady her voice.

He chuckled. "My practice is among the Amish, and whenever a married woman comes in with any flu-type symptoms, we run a blood test to check for pregnancy."

Beth ran her hand over her flat stomach. Jonah would be beyond thrilled. Excitement skittered through her.

The doctor stood. "Since you're unsure of your last cycle, I'd like to do a sonogram."

She nodded. He helped her lie back on the table. A nurse came in, and within a minute Beth saw a tiny, shadowy image on the monitor. Tears trailed down her face as the baby's heartbeat pulsed fast and loud. This tiny being had a heartbeat! Their child had been growing inside her, and she hadn't even realized it.

The realization of life's many gifts lingered in front of her, and she couldn't help but admire them. How had she gone from being a lonely woman wearing all black to being married to someone as perfect for her as Jonah? And now they were expecting their first child!

The doctor angled the wand one way and then another. Each time, he tapped some keys on the keyboard, and then green lines showed up on the monitor. "According to the measurements, I'd say you're about eleven weeks along. Most women feel a surge of nausea at around eight weeks."

"Food has tasted funny, and I haven't been very hungry. I remember feeling sleepy at the oddest times for a while, but I thought it was because the store's been busier than usual since we added larger-ticket items to our inventory."

He put the wand on the cart, and the nurse cleaned the gooey stuff off Beth's stomach.

"We'll let you get dressed, and then I'll be back to talk."

Both the nurse and the doctor left the room. She felt...invincible, as if the fear and death and sadness of the world couldn't erase the joys she and Jonah would have raising this child. Tears welled again. Once dressed, she sat in a chair and poured out thanks to God for this gift.

There was a knock on the door, and the doctor came in. He asked questions, answered the ones she could think up at the moment, gave her papers and pamphlets and loads of instructions and a prescription for vitamins. She couldn't wait to tell Jonah.

As hard as it was to keep secrets from her driver, Beth didn't say anything to her about being pregnant. Gloria had been her driver since Beth was eighteen, but Jonah had to be the first to hear Beth's news. When Gloria parked in front of the store, Beth hurried inside.

She made sure her expression was normal. Numerous employees said hello when she entered. She spoke to each while looking around the store for her husband. Finally she spotted him stocking candles.

As soon as he saw her, he asked, "How are you feeling?"

"Better."

He smiled, a sense of calm radiating from him. "Gut."

"But I didn't need a doctor because of a virus. By the time I arrived at his office, I was over it."

"It's still good you went."

"True." She took him by the hand, and without asking any questions, he followed her into the office and closed the door. They shared lunches here and talked about business, but most of all, this was where they went when they needed to talk...or steal a few kisses.

When they were courting, after their engagement but before he moved to Apple Ridge, she'd sit in the office and talk to him on the phone for hours.

Now she sat on the front edge of the desk. They were about to share the greatest gift yet with each other.

"What's on your mind, sweetheart?"

"I have news. Good news." She took his hand and put it over her stomach. "I heard our child's heartbeat today."

Jonah's brows tightened, as if he feared he'd heard her wrong. "You're pregnant?"

"Due the third week in January."

Jonah hollered and picked her up. She giggled. "Shh. Everyone must have heard you."

He set her down and jerked open the door. Several people were staring at the office.

"It's okay, folks. I just heard good news concerning the arrival of an important item." He closed the door. "They're fine now."

She laughed.

He hugged her tight. "I never imagined being so happy."

"Me either." Her lips met his, and she relished the moment.

The phone rang. She had to answer it. If she didn't, one of the girls would come into the office to get it. Beth picked up the receiver. "Hertzlers' Dry Goods."

A woman's voice said, "Beth, is that you?"

"Yes, it is. How may I help you?"

"It's Priscilla." Beth couldn't recall the last time Levi's mother had phoned the store. "Levi won't be able to keep his appointment with you today."

Beth flipped open her calendar, realizing Levi should have been at the store two hours ago. She wouldn't have been here, but Jonah would have made time for Levi. "That's fine, Priscilla. Does he want to reschedule for tomorrow?"

Priscilla explained what the last sixteen hours had been like for Levi. Beth's nausea returned, and when her eyes met Jonah's, he moved in closer.

"Levi has a mild concussion, a tiny fracture in his neck, and a broken leg."

While Beth's day had been one of exciting news, the Fishers' day had been one of turmoil. She let Priscilla tell her everything, and then they said their good-byes.

Jonah leaned against the desk. "Will he be okay?"

"Apparently so. His horse threw him. According to Priscilla, a doctor told him it's a good thing he didn't try to get up. Seems a lot of people ignore this kind of injury until it paralyzes them down the road. A woman found him and called for an ambulance. He's not even home yet. The hospital hasn't released him, but his family expects him in a few hours."

"One of us needs to go see him. I can't get away tonight. I have a shipment arriving after hours. Maybe Mattie could go with you."

"Ya, sure." Beth sighed. "Sometimes it seems there are too many accidents among our people."

"A lot of it is how we live—as rugged in some ways as our pioneer ancestors." Jonah put his finger under her chin. "Speaking of safety, I want you to make an appointment with the midwife. When she says it's time, you keep a cell phone with you so you can reach her. You don't balk. Okay?"

Beth grinned and moved into his arms. "Since you know exactly how you want this pregnancy to be handled, maybe you should be carrying the baby."

Jonah pursed his lips. "God knows what He's doing. You carry the baby, and I'll save my strength to carry or drag you as needed."

She chuckled. "Are you saying I'm stubborn?"

"No way I would say such a thing"—he kissed her—"out loud to my expectant wife."

Eight

With Levi and last night still fresh in her mind, Sadie put her bag into the car, said an awkward good-bye to her parents, and got into the vehicle.

Whitney put the car in reverse. "Did you have a nice visit?"

"It had some interesting moments."

Like meeting a stranger who saw life as she did. She'd like to know how Levi was doing. She'd used the phone in Mammi Lee's shanty last night to call Levi's brother. The phone had rung for a while before a groggy voice answered. At least it was summer, and the windows of the house were open, making a phone ringing in a shanty a couple hundred feet away easily heard.

"Whitney, would you mind taking me by a house about five miles from here and give me a few minutes to visit?" She pulled Levi's address out of her purse and handed it to her.

Whitney looked at the address. "Not at all."

Rumors had begun to swirl through the community about Levi's injury. Mammi had received three phone calls, and an Amish neighbor stopped by to tell her about it. The reports said "a woman" called an ambulance for him. That meant Levi had kept his word. He hadn't revealed who'd helped him, or at least it appeared that way.

Neither Mammi nor Sadie's parents had been home when she'd

returned last night, so they didn't know she'd gone out. This morning Sadie tended to the animals in the barn before Mammi Lee or Daed could. When her Daed wanted to go to the barn to hitch Bay to a rig, she volunteered to do that too. Anything to avoid answering questions about the strange thoroughbred in Mammi's barn. She didn't mind avoiding telling the truth. Adults had few people they told everything to. Even Jesus didn't tell everything to everyone. And she didn't have a problem trying to get her way when she felt God had given her the right to do so. But answering dishonestly wasn't something she could justify.

When Daed, Mamm, and Mammi had left today to visit Mammi's sister for the afternoon, Sadie had ridden Bay to Levi's and led Amigo home. But no one was there, so she put Amigo out to pasture and left.

As they continued toward Levi's, Sadie pondered all that had taken place last night. When the car braked, it pulled her from her thoughts.

"If you're going to be a few minutes, I have an errand I'd like to run."

"Sure. I'll be ready when you return."

Sadie went to the front door and knocked. Through the screen door she saw a young boy running toward her. He had silky blond hair and was wearing dark blue pants, a bright green shirt, red suspenders, and white socks with no shoes. For an Amish boy, he was wearing quite a mix of colors.

"Are you here to see Uncle Levi?" He skidded to a stop at the door. "Did he meet you at last night's singing? He didn't want to go, and I'm not sure he likes girls." The boy crossed his arms. "You look okay to me."

"Denki."

"Tobias." A thin man with curly brown hair and a beard walked up behind him. "That's not what you say to someone at the door, Son."

Tobias unfolded his arms. "What, that she looks okay or that Uncle Levi ain't fond of girls?"

"Both." The man opened the door. "*Kumm rei.* I'm Andy, and this is my son, Tobias."

"I'm Sadie, and I wanted—"

"You ain't from around here, are you?"

"Tobias." Andy put an index finger over his son's mouth before looking at Sadie with an apology. "He's very observant and feels the need to voice all his thoughts, however off-center they are."

"I like that." She grinned at Tobias. "I would like to see your uncle Levi."

Tobias frowned. "Are you the woman who helped him, the one who called last night and woke us up?"

"Of course not." Andy laughed. "Your uncle would have said if the person was Amish." Andy studied Sadie for a moment, and she tried to make her expression neutral. But when she saw realization dawn on his face, she knew she hadn't been fast enough. He grinned, a welcoming thankfulness radiating from him. "We owe you a great deal of thanks."

She shook her head, unsure whether she should admit she was the mystery woman. But dishonesty was not among her many faults. "I didn't know where I was when I stumbled upon him, and I certainly wouldn't have been riding through someone's hayfield had I realized what it was."

"Then I'm glad God used you. Old Man Hostetler told us a few weeks back he wouldn't be cutting that field again this year. I'm sure that's why Levi was there too."

He looked down and wiped sweat from his brow. "I got to the hospital before sunrise and spoke with a doctor not long after. Since that conversation I've been haunted by how things could have turned out." His brow furrowed. "When I returned home, I saw Amigo in the pasture."

"I tethered Amigo and rode my horse here earlier today, but no one was home." She glanced out the screen door. "My driver will return in a few minutes, and I would like to see Levi before I leave Apple Ridge."

"He's pretty groggy and not himself. He's a little more…bold and outspoken about what he's thinking and feeling."

"I can deal with that."

Tobias planted his feet and put his hands on his hips. "Uncle Levi's sleeping, and he said not to wake him up."

"You should listen to your uncle." Sadie touched the end of his nose, half expecting him to take a step back or complain. He didn't. "But I'm going to wake him." She looked at Andy. "Which way?"

Tobias looked at his Daed, and Andy nodded.

"Follow me." The little boy took off running and skidded to a stop several feet from a bed set up in the living room. "Don't touch the bed. Uncle Levi said to stay three feet away." Tobias held his hands apart, looking as if he were telling a fish story. "That's about this far. And he meant what he said."

"I'm sure he did." She couldn't believe how pale and stiff Levi looked. His left leg was in a full cast. A neck brace was fitted tight against his jawline. The base of the brace—a three-to-four-inch flat, circular piece—covered his chest and shoulders.

She turned to Andy. "I didn't expect this."

"It's an odd injury. He has a tiny neck fracture, and the doctor said it's the kind that can worsen until a person feels his arms and legs go numb. He could have done permanent damage. The kind that might have left him paralyzed from the neck down. As it is, Levi should be in a wheelchair in a week and on crutches later. He'll have to wear the neck brace for three to six months. The leg cast should be off in six weeks."

Sadie remembered Levi's pleas to help him up. God's mercy had surely extended to both of them last night.

Last night she'd seen that Levi was long and lanky with big shoulders. Now she could see his thick, curly hair, light brown with streaks of golden blond. It needed cutting—probably two months ago—but she liked his rugged, unkempt look. It meant that he, much like herself, wasn't interested in keeping every Amish rule of thumb.

His bed was midway between two double windows on opposite walls, inviting a cross breeze to cover him. But July afternoons weren't much for stirring air. A sheet lay over his uninjured leg and covered his hips and chest, but he looked uncomfortably warm, even without a shirt.

Levi shifted and groaned.

Sadie leaned over the bed, staring into his face. "Every time I see you, you're lying around and moaning."

His eyes remained closed, but a faint smile crossed his face. "Sadie." His gravelly voice was barely above a whisper and told of his exhaustion and, no doubt, of whatever pain medicine he was administered. "You *are* real."

"Ya, but I'm no angel."

The lines of pleasure deepened on his face. "And for that I'm very grateful."

If she'd been as angelic as her Daed wished, she wouldn't have been out last night or found Levi. Was he the reason she'd felt so moved during her prayers to saddle Bay and ride? Or had her own will been at work and stumbling across Levi was an odd coincidence?

"Tobias." Andy motioned to his son to leave the room with him. "Sadie, it was good meeting you."

"Denki." Where was the man's wife? In fact, now that she thought about it, it seemed odd Levi never mentioned his sister-in-law when they talked last night.

Andy started to leave, then turned back to her. "We're going to tend to the horses, but I'd rather Levi not be alone for too long. Just let me know when you're leaving by having your driver toot the horn."

"Be glad to."

"Andy." Levi's hoarse whisper brought his brother to a stop. Levi scrunched his face and opened his eyes for a moment. "A woman helped me last night, not Sadie." In the Amish community, one referred to people as Amish when they were such. The lack of that title would do exactly what Levi knew it would: indicate an Englisch woman had helped him.

Sadie appreciated Levi's sense of honor and his attempt to protect her.

Andy nodded, but questions filled his eyes.

Sadie shrugged. "I was grounded for the evening."

Andy's eyes narrowed, possibly thinking the same thing she did—she was too old for a parent to ground her. "It's not right for me to say it,"—Andy put his hands on Tobias's shoulders—"but I'm with Levi on this. I'm grateful you're no angel." He and Tobias left the room. A few moments later the screen door slammed.

His eyes still closed, Levi made a weak pat on the edge of his bed. She hesitated, but it seemed harmless with him injured and unable to speak much or keep his eyes open. They only had a few minutes to talk and were not likely to see each other again, so she sat.

He drew a heavy breath. "I was sure you'd already left Apple Ridge and I'd have no way to thank you."

She realized he was right. As determined as he was to keep her secret, he wouldn't have gone to her grandmother's to find out where she lived or how to reach her.

He tried to sit upright, and she helped by putting pillows behind him.

"Now." He eased back and waited for her to sit again. "Let's see those eyes."

She opened them wide.

"Hmm. You have big eyes."

"All the better to see you with." She waggled her eyebrows.

He laughed, then moaned. "No, not like a wolf. I meant they're large and pretty, somewhere between pale green and golden brown."

Sadie knew they weren't pretty, but she didn't believe he was trying to flatter her. He was just grateful to her, and gratitude changed people's views of everything they looked at. When she spent time in the Andes, soaking in the beauty of God's creation and fully aware of how poor and yet content the villagers were, her heart overflowed with gratitude. She learned then that the Daniels of the world—the ones she'd thought were better than her—were really no better or worse. The only thing that mattered was the honor and joy of walking with God.

Levi stretched his hand toward her face and ran his index finger across the bridge of her nose. "You have freckles."

Sadie found his observation a little amusing and intimidating. Her looks weren't a favorite subject. But she had no doubt his boldness to touch her was due to the medication he was taking.

He smiled, pinching her chin between his thumb and index finger. "You're very cute in a 'sunshine after the rain' sort of way."

She didn't know what he meant by that, but feelings fluttered through her, each tugging in a different direction. She'd grown out of being homely and horribly skinny. But she was no Aquilla. That was for sure. Still, she no longer felt she was less than other people.

"If you keep up this inspection, I'm going to demand you close your eyes and go to sleep."

"I can't help it." His dark brown eyes spoke of approval and friendship. "I've spent most of my waking minutes and half of my sleeping ones trying to imagine what you looked like and hoping you weren't an apparition."

She fidgeted, not sure she liked where this conversation was heading. Thankfully, she had to go soon. "It wouldn't be such a bad thing for me not to have been human. It'd mean you received help from God."

"I did receive help from God. He sent you to me."

Her muscles tensed, and she moved, ready to stand and say good-bye.

"Relax, Sadie." He put his hand on her arm. "You're gonna have to trust me when I say I'll be just as single when I die as I am today. We're alike in our determination to avoid marrying, so don't get your hackles up."

She took a deep breath. "Gut. You scared me for a minute."

He grimaced, looking hot and uncomfortable. Damp curls clung to his forehead.

Sadie fidgeted with the blanket. "Someone called Mammi's place today and said you had a concussion along with your other injuries."

"Ya, between that and the medicines, nothing feels real. But I want to get your address."

"Levi." She brushed his hair back, hoping it made him feel a little cooler. "We're saying all that needs to be said right now. I want to let it go at that."

"Knock, knock."

At the sound of a female voice behind them, Sadie pulled back her hand from Levi's face and stood.

Two young and attractive women stood at the open entryway of the living room, one holding a glass cake stand that encased a beautifully decorated cake.

Sadie turned to Levi, determined to speak softly so the others couldn't hear her. "Now that you're too injured to run away or ride off, you may be engaged in time for the wedding season."

Levi chuckled and slowly motioned for the women to enter, a movement that indicated how drugged he was. "These are my cousins Beth and Mattie. And this is Sadie. She returned my horse."

Sadie shook hands with the women. Levi's words were true enough. She *had* returned his horse. The odds were good that people who knew Levi had seen her on her trek to return Amigo. Levi had just given all the explanation anyone would need.

He scratched his jaw where the neck brace rubbed it. "Beth is a Hertzler of Hertzlers' Dry Goods."

Had they seen her sitting on Levi's bed and brushing the hair from his face? She hoped not. "When I was younger, I came to your store a couple of times with Mammi Lee."

"Verna Lee? The toymaker's wife?"

"Ya."

"We used to carry your *Grossdaadi's* goods."

"I remember."

Beth touched Mattie's arm. "Mattie is working at the store now. She owned a cake shop in Ohio, so she's running her own bakery section here. Our husbands built a small café for her inside the store."

"A dry goods store with fresh cakes?"

"And sticky buns, scones, muffins, and lots of coffee." Mattie walked to a side table and set the cake on it. "It's about the size of a small bedroom, and I only have those other items as refreshments for the customers. The true heart of my business is using that space to showcase and take orders for decorative cakes. You know, for birthdays and weddings and such."

"Sounds as if Hertzlers' has changed a good bit since I was there more than ten years ago."

"Definitely," Beth said. "You should come by."

"Sadie knows a thing or two about stores, don't you?"

If Sadie could, she'd give him a glare for putting her on the spot. "A little, I guess. I help manage a five-and-dime run by a Mennonite couple. Aside from a few nonperishable items my two girlfriends and I make, the store carries the same things they did sixty years ago—including hayseed and shovels and such."

Beth moved to the foot of the bed. "What kinds of things do you make, Sadie?"

"When time and money allow, I make an assortment of things. I dabble in wreaths, but my favorites are candles and soaps, and when I can collect enough scraps of material from the Amish community where I live, I make cloth dolls."

Beth pulled a business card from her hidden apron pocket. "If you ever have a surplus and are looking for a place to sell them, come see me."

"Denki." Sadie took the card and touched the bed. "Levi, I need to go."

"Not without leaving your address and phone number."

Beth and Mattie looked at each other, a definite glimmer of interest passing between them.

Mattie fetched pen and paper from an end table and passed it to Sadie.

What could it hurt for him to have her address and phone number?

Nine

*L*evi stood in the round pen. He held a thirty-foot line in one hand and a lightweight longe whip in the other. Despite the neck brace he wore, he turned in circles with the horse on the other end of the line, training the animal to understand and follow his commands. *"Geh."*

The horse picked up its pace.

Even though Blaze hadn't been training long, the colt moved more fluidly and even paced than Levi could. Still, it was far easier for Levi to get around now that the cast on his leg had been removed a mere two days ago. He moved like an old man in winter while he sweated under the grueling August sun.

Levi needed to make up for lost training time. *"Langsam."* Blaze didn't slow a tad. "Langsam," Levi repeated in the same even tone. The horse raised its head and altered its pace a little. "Gut... Langsam."

"Uncle Levi." Tobias sat on the split-rail fence and pointed at the whip. "You gotta at least let him see that out of the corner of his eye."

"Who's doing the training? Me or you?"

Tobias clutched a hand to the top of his head. "But you're *not* listening to me."

"You're being impatient again." When Levi had been on crutches, he'd had to enlist Tobias's help to tend and train the horses. The boy had a knack for handling the stout and sometimes difficult creatures, but he lacked patience with the tedious process.

"So who got throwed by a horse? Me or you?"

"I have a better question, peanut. Who's going to be sent inside if he doesn't stop telling me what to do?" Levi knew that threat would carry some weight. Tobias liked being in his or Andy's shadow at all times. Since Andy was in the barn tending to the other horses, if Tobias had to go inside, he'd be by himself.

Tobias made monkey gestures in the air, touching the top of his head and flailing his arms, huffing and making mocking gestures—but in all his silliness, he didn't say anything. For almost a minute. "Not everybody thinks you need to go as slow as you do with training horses, Uncle Levi."

"What's their motivation for feeling that way? Because it's what's best for the horse and the buyer or because it's what's easiest and most profitable for the trainer?"

Tobias frowned but seemed to mull over the question.

Amigo had been five years old when Daniel bought him last spring from an auction. Levi didn't know why the horse reacted so violently to the fireworks last month, but he'd learned some valuable lessons, ones that caused him and Andy to start training their horses differently. One brother fed the animal and soothed him while the other made an awful racket just outside the barn—beating a horseshoe against a ten-gallon tub, yelling and clapping, or sounding an old car horn. The technique seemed to be desensitizing the animals to loud noises, but it was too early to tell if that would translate to a calmer horse on a road.

"Look." Tobias pointed at the mailman pulling onto the gravel driveway. He hopped down. "Whatcha want to guess he's got another package from your girlfriend?"

Levi continued working with Blaze, but he hoped the man did have another package from Sadie. She needed money for her mission trip, and he wanted to do all he could to help her. He'd put some of the life-sized cloth dolls she sewed in his handcrafted cradles and highchairs. When the two items were combined, they sold like hotcakes at Hertzlers'.

He also enjoyed the short letters that accompanied her packages. When he first came up with the idea of her making dolls to go with some of his toy furniture, he called her. But she wasn't keen on the idea of partnering with him. It'd taken a few phone calls before he could sufficiently assure her that he was only interested in being a friend and repaying his debt to her.

Dealing with her was like working with a spooked horse. At first he thought she'd been in a relationship that had gone bad. But after coming to know her a little better, he understood that her heart belonged to the people in a remote Peruvian village, and she was determined to stay the course.

Tobias took the package from the man and held it up. "Ya, it's from her."

"Gut." He'd never known anyone like Sadie.

Just as the mailman pulled out of the driveway, he saw another vehicle coming in. Daniel rolled down the passenger window and waved.

Levi returned the wave. "Tobias, go put that on my bed before anything happens to it." The dolls' faces, arms, and legs were made of white cotton, and if they were smudged, they didn't sell as easily.

Tobias tore out running.

Levi didn't expect Daniel this week. Then again, Daniel may not have known himself until the mood struck him to head this way.

The truck came to a halt, and Daniel got out. "A man without a cast on his leg." Daniel shook Levi's hand and patted his shoulder at the same time. "Still got that noose around your neck, I see. How you feeling?"

"Lighter now." Levi ran two fingers around the top collar of the brace. "And ready to be free of this yoke around my neck."

"Sure you are. You're gettin' there. It's been a hot summer to have to wear that thing while working."

The screen door flung open, and Tobias ran outside.

Daniel didn't seem to notice the boy. He motioned to his driver, Tip. "I heard there are some good horses going on the block tonight at Toppers. I'd sure like it if you could join me."

"Your eye for buying horses at auction is much better than mine."

"Ya, but you're better at knowing which one should go to which trainer."

Andy emerged from the barn. "Daniel, I didn't know you were here...or even coming."

"I'm not staying. We'll talk horse-trading another time. But I'm hoping to borrow Levi for a bit."

Daniel called it horse-trading, but what he meant was buying the animals at auction, bringing them to Levi to train, selling them to people throughout the region, and settling up with the Fisher brothers what was owed. Nobody worried about a timetable for the payments. Daniel's word was good enough, and he was more than fair when it came to paying people for their services, but he did things in his own way and time.

Tobias bounced up and down. "Can I go?"

"Not this time, champ." Daniel pushed down on the top of Tobias's straw hat. "We might not be home until the wee hours of the morning, and if we arrive that late, your uncle will need some sleep, and your Daed will need your help tending to the horses the next morning." Daniel pulled a five-dollar bill from his billfold. "You'll agree to work for me, ya?"

"Wow." Tobias took the money, staring at it with wide eyes. "I'm available anytime."

"Gut. I'm glad to hear it."

It dawned on Levi that by going to Toppers, he'd be fifteen to twenty minutes from Sadie's place in Stone Creek. "What time does the horse auction begin?"

"Around eight, most likely. Of course, as usual, you and Tip will stay at Toppers while I find some lonely girl to take to dinner."

Daniel's dating habits were questionable at best, but at least he seemed to be trying to find someone. Still, it seemed odd how quickly Daniel could connect with a woman only to lose interest within the same evening.

Daniel's plans aside, it was around one now, and it'd take two hours to get there. If Sadie were home, that meant he could visit with her for a couple of hours before the horses were on the block. Daniel didn't need him to help buy the horses, only to pair each animal with a trainer.

"Levi?"

He looked at Daniel. "Sure. Just let me jump in the shower. I'll be ready in ten minutes." He headed for the house.

"The horses don't care what you smell like," Daniel hollered.

"Ten minutes." Levi hurried into the house, hoping he would see Sadie tonight.

Ten

The wooden floors of the old store creaked as Sadie carried a large sign to the window. She taped it to the glass: For Sale.

It seemed as if her hopes of having enough money to go back to Peru hung in the balance more than ever, teetering under the weight of yet another unexpected change in her world.

She turned, taking a long look around her, enjoying the sights and smells of the old-fashioned place. In her mind's eye she could see Loyd and Edna the day she'd wandered in here. She'd said she was looking for work, but she needed so much more than that. She'd been broken and mortified by Daniel. Although she hadn't told Loyd or Edna about her former fiancé, they seemed to understand what she needed and took her under their wing. At the same time, they taught her how to earn a living while her heart mended.

Now, as unexpectedly as a summer storm, Loyd had fallen ill, and Edna insisted on getting out from under the pressure of running the store.

"Sadie." Blanche, her coworker and a roommate, held up a large cardboard box. "Do you need another one?"

Edna had told them to get all their crafts off the shelves and to return what they could to the manufacturers. After some advertising, they would put everything else into a one-day-only, going-out-of-business sale.

"Ya. Denki." She took the box and moved to the candle aisle.

Edna insisted on rearranging her life so she didn't have to focus on anything but Loyd. The elderly woman had been ready to be free of the store for a long time, but Loyd enjoyed the work too much to let it go. Edna hadn't set foot inside Farmers' Five-and-Dime since Loyd's stroke two weeks ago, because she hadn't left his side for a moment.

Sadie pulled jars of her homemade candles off the shelves. Seeing Edna and Loyd like this made her ache all over, confirming her suspicion: life was easier if one never let in anyone else. If two hearts grow to become one, what happens when one stops beating? Sure, Loyd and Edna had good fruit to show for their years together, but today's heartache seemed to weigh heavier than all the harvests of yesteryear.

Maybe she was wrong. She hoped so, for the sake of all who'd ever married.

Someone tapped at the front door.

"I'll get it." Blanche headed that way.

They had a huge sign on the door that said Closed, but people knocked on the door anyway. This old place had been open six days a week since the early fifties.

Old habits died hard.

"Sadie," Blanche called, "there's a man here to see you. I didn't recognize him, so I told him to wait outside."

Sadie went toward the glass door. Her eyes widened as she reached for the handle. The man was facing the other way, with his hat in his hand, but there was no mistaking those loose curls of golden-brown hair. Of course, if his hair wasn't a dead giveaway, there was the neck brace too. A smile tugged at her mouth for the first time in quite a while. She opened the heavy door, and the bells suspended over the entryway clanged as she stepped outside.

He turned awkwardly, having to move his whole body because of the neck brace. There was a smile on his tan face, but what she noticed most of all was the spark in his eyes.

Sadie put her hands on her hips. "Well, look at you, standing on your own two feet."

"Hard to believe, isn't it?"

"It is indeed." She'd heard energy in his voice when they spoke on the phone, but this was the first time she could see vitality in his expression.

They moved away from the door, going a little farther onto the sidewalk as if they wanted some privacy. "What are you doing here?"

"There's a horse auction nearby."

"Decided to sell Amigo and get a new friend, did you?"

He chuckled. "No, nothing like that. Just helping a friend make some decisions. He doesn't need me for a while, so I had the driver drop me off at your place. I walked here from there."

"Good thing I was findable, or you'd be calling that driver to come back. You do have your phone, right?"

"Still there." He tapped his pocket. "I took a chance, figuring if you could find me in a dark field without trying, I could find you in a small town if I were willing to do a little searching."

"Gotta appreciate a man with confidence."

"I was right, wasn't I?"

"It's my understanding that you did indeed find me…I think."

Faint dimples appeared when he grinned. Heat radiated from the white concrete, and she considered asking him to step inside.

His expression became thoughtful, and his smile faded. He pointed at the For Sale sign in the window. "What's going on?"

"Loyd, the owner, had a stroke a couple of weeks back."

"I'm sorry to hear that. Why didn't you say something about that?" He sounded concerned, perhaps for how this would affect her.

"Truth is, until a few days ago, I couldn't make myself talk about it, not on the phone or in a letter. I finally wrote you about it. You'll get a package soon with a letter explaining what's going on."

"Oh, ya. I received one today, but I didn't get a chance to open it."

"Now you don't have to. Although you may wish you'd read it rather than hear me whine about how this stinks for Loyd and Edna, the town folk, my roommates, and..."

"You."

"Sorry, I can be really selfish at times."

"I know you're hurting for the Farmers, but this has to put pressure on you too. I can't see where it's selfish to admit to feeling the strain." He shifted. "I saw that there's a rodeo demonstration and fair at the park. I think a lot of people are starting to leave now. Would you care to see what we can?"

"It's Stone Creek Day at Stone Creek Lake. They have booths of crafts and a petting zoo with farm animals, some blow-up bounce castles for the children, and other family stuff."

"Stone Creek Lake?" He tugged lightly at the neck brace. "What's next, Stone Creek River?"

"Ya. We have that too."

"Of course you do." His grin made the tan lines around his eyes disappear.

"Stone Creek River starts about five miles south of here. If you named horses like they named places around here, you could have an Amigo Friend." She raised an eyebrow, trying to keep a silly smile off her face.

"Or an Enemy Enemigo."

"A river by any name would flow just as deep and swift and surely sparkle just as much under the August sun." Her goal to keep a straight face while teasing him was impossible.

"Did you just twist Shakespeare?"

"Are you an Amish man who knows Shakespeare?"

"I know all there is to know, which boils down to maybe three lines. That was one of them."

She giggled. "That's all there is to know?"

"That's more than I'll need in this lifetime."

"True, and your knowledge about equals mine." She broke into a grin. How fun to be able to talk with him whether he was injured in a field, in the living room of his home, on the phone, or here. "But Shakespeare must've been quite a writer for people like us to quote his work some four hundred years later."

"Never thought about it. But I can tell you something I have thought about"—he wiped sweat from his forehead—"getting under some shade trees."

It was hard to believe, but she liked the idea of spending a little time with Levi. "I'll be right back." She went inside the store and told her roommates she'd meet them at the house later. Edna had given each of them an area of the store to pack up, and as long as she got hers done before Monday, it didn't matter when she did it. She hurried out the door, grateful for the distraction.

Levi pulled his attention from the random items displayed in the store's window. "Ready?"

"Ya."

They walked down the sidewalks of the historic downtown. After a while they stepped into a café and ordered a couple of cold drinks to go. The conversation stayed light as they discussed the weather, Tobias, how well their handiwork was selling, and how Levi was progressing with the training of a yearling. It seemed as if Levi knew she couldn't talk about what really weighed on her. Not yet.

She had tough decisions to make now that the store was closing, and talking about them with someone who had nothing to gain, no reason to try to steer her one way or the other, was like a godsend.

But was he as he appeared, or was she so desperate for answers she was seeing what she wanted to? She prayed, asking for guidance on whether to turn to Levi for advice.

They meandered across the thick grass of the park, watching as some people were dismantling their booths. Children milled about with leashed dogs. Across the way, men led horses to trailers while other workmen dismantled the arena that had been set up so riders could demonstrate some of the stunts they would perform at next month's rodeo.

Levi took a sip of his orange soda. "Looks as if maybe you shoulda set up a booth here to sell your goods."

"The city doesn't allow the town shops to set up booths for Stone Creek Day. Since I work for Farmers' and they sell my stuff there, I fall under the can't-have-a-booth category." She played with the straw in her cup, poking at some ice chips. "I was boxing up the last of my craft items when you showed up."

"I could take them back with me. Beth would be happy to put them on consignment in her store."

Sadie paused, staring at him. That was a great offer—if she could snatch it up and not analyze it to death.

Levi lowered his drink. "You have a look on your face like the one I get when I'm baffled by a horse's behavior and unsure what to do to get him to do what I want him to do."

If he was this intuitive with his horses, he was no doubt a remarkable trainer. "I'm sort of baffled by all of life right now."

"Been there a dozen times. Want to tell me about it?"

She did, but the idea of actually sharing her thoughts made her squirm. What if his opinion affected her final decision and he was wrong? "Maybe later."

They remained there, a few yards from the lake, taking in the sights. A cooling breeze played with the strings to her prayer Kapp. A baby cooed nearby, and she searched for it.

A few feet away a woman sat on a blanket with a little one dressed in pink and wearing a silky headband. The baby girl was about six months old. She sat on her mother's lap. The woman smiled at her child. "Is that right?" She waited for the baby to respond. "You tell Mommy all about it."

The baby seemed mesmerized by her mother, cooing as if her tender sounds actually formed words. A toddler in a beige dress was asleep on the blanket next to the woman and her baby. The mom brushed black hair off the sleeping child's neck, her face glowing, as if this moment made up for all the nights of walking the floors while her little ones wailed.

Sadie and Levi headed toward the lake. Behind them a huge ruckus broke out. Men and women shrieked, yelling words Sadie couldn't make out. Some were grabbing their children and scattering. A man's voice rose above the clamor. "Stop him! Somebody grab a rein!"

A black horse appeared out of nowhere and thundered toward them. Sadie slung her drink to the ground.

Levi grabbed her hand, and in one fell swoop, he tugged her forward and forced her arms straight out, as if she were a scarecrow. "Stay." Despite his neck brace and not being able to turn his head, he took off running, pointing to people as he went. "Get behind a tree!"

People scattered, obeying his command. The path cleared—all except for Sadie, who stood like a target.

Everything was happening fast. Maybe six or eight seconds had passed since the chaos began. Sadie's head whirled the way it had when she was a child and her Daed spun her by her arms around and around, her little legs gliding through the air.

Levi disappeared behind a tree—and she was standing in the horse's path! Was he *crazy*?

The massive creature charged straight at her. Earth flew from its rumbling hoofs, but she couldn't budge.

A moment later Levi lunged forward, grabbing the horse's rein before throwing himself onto its neck. In a flash he was atop the animal. "Whoa!" Levi's voice carried calm firmness while she wanted to scream like a banshee—if only she could find her voice.

"Whoa!" He pulled on the reins, and the horse slowed, prancing as it did, finally coming to a halt twenty feet from her.

When Sadie could take her eyes off the horse, she looked behind her. Levi had put her ten feet in front of the blanket with the mother and two children. If the horse had gotten past him, he'd intended for her to scare it away from that spot. The mom had gotten to her feet, terror on her face, with the baby clutched in her arms. If the horse had kept coming, Sadie doubted the mother and child could have gotten to safety. What if she'd tried to grab her toddler first?

Impossible.

Sadie's heart pounded. "Are you okay?"

The woman sank to her knees, rocking her little one. "Yeah." The toddler awoke, unaware of what had happened. She brushed sweat-matted hair from her face and crawled into her mother's arms, next to the baby.

"Thank you!" another voice said. It was the same one that had begged for someone to stop the horse.

Sadie searched for the speaker.

A large man was struggling to breathe as he made his way toward them. He waved toward Levi, not that Levi saw him. "I'll be there as soon as…" His voice faded while he gasped for air.

Levi eased off the horse, moving much slower than when he'd gotten on. Had he hurt himself? He held the reins, stroking the horse and talking to it in a low, soothing voice. When Levi came toward Sadie, he led the horse. Levi put his free hand on his chest before moving it to her shoulder. "That was scary. Much more so than me landing in a hayfield."

He'd thought so clearly, covering possibilities that were just now dawning on her. If he'd simply scared the horse away from the woman on the blanket with her two little ones, the rampaging animal could have trampled other children or even adults. By hiding behind the tree, he avoided scaring the horse and sending him off in a different direction.

Sadie's legs shook, and she looked for a place to sit. She needed a few moments to absorb what had just happened. Her first thought when he moved into action was outrage that he'd dared to put her in harm's way while protecting himself. She couldn't have been more wrong.

"I think I hate horses."

"Don't do that." He patted the horse's neck. "They're like people— good hearts, occasional bad judgment, and sometimes volatile reactions when scared." Levi tilted his head, studying her eyes before he smiled. "You'll be fine in a bit. I can see it."

She drew a deep breath, surprised to find that she believed him despite how she felt.

"Excuse me."

They turned at the man's voice to find the woman from the blanket standing next to a man who now held the sleepy toddler. "I can't thank you enough." The man's voice cracked. "You did that for us, and you've got a neck injury." The man shook Levi's hand.

For the next few minutes, people gushed over Levi, thanking him and asking if he was okay. The owner retrieved his horse, also grateful for what Levi had done. When the man learned what Levi did for a living, he asked for a business card, and Levi gave him one.

Sadie and Levi moved to a bench that faced the lake, neither one talking. He had to be more drained than she was. The dad of the two little ones brought them cold drinks and a bag of popcorn.

Sadie opened the can of Sprite. "Did you hurt your neck?"

Levi set his drink on the bench between them. "I don't think so." He opened the popcorn and held it for her. "This collar is like wearing a cast. It protects against another break while allowing the healing to continue."

"That's good."

They grew still, staring at the lake for a long time. Her thoughts drifted. Surely a man who reacted in the best interests of innocent bystanders could be trusted with her puny problems.

Ducks waddled over to them, and she tossed bits of popcorn and watched sunlight sparkle on the water.

She ate a few pieces of popcorn. "When Daed finds out about the store closing, he'll insist I come home." She tossed a few more pieces onto the ground.

"Would moving in with Mammi Lee be any easier for you?"

"It's possible. She doesn't seem as bent out of shape about my not being married, but Daed won't tolerate it. It'd be an insult for me to be unemployed and homeless and still not return home. I can't afford for him to feel like I'm totally rebelling against him."

"I can understand how he'd feel that way."

"Me too, but I don't want to move back home." She sighed. "I have no job. Loyd and Edna paid a portion of our rent each month, but now Blanche is moving back home. That'll make our rent even higher. If I stay, I might be able to get another job, but I'll plow through everything that I've saved so far for my mission trip."

"I can't offer much advice, but I can tell you how I'd think this through."

"Please."

"I'd keep my focus on the goal. Yours is Peru. Avoiding living with your parents is a perk, not your ambition. Stay true to what's most important. Seems to me that since you're no longer working at the five-and-dime, you can reduce your bills by living at home and using your time to make crafts."

"You think if I made that many more crafts, I could actually sell them?"

"Seems likely. You just need to get them into every store possible. Beth can help you with that. She keeps several stores, both Amish and Englisch, supplied with Amish goods."

Sadie took another sip of her drink. The idea of moving home wasn't her favorite, but she had to admit, looking at the big picture as Levi suggested, it made sense. Of course, while she was there, her parents and the community would do all they could to spark a relationship between her and one of the single Amish men.

Too bad Levi didn't have an answer for that.

Eleven

Using tiny wooden pegs, Levi attached another brace to the bottom of a cradle. He needed to take a load of goods to Hertzlers' soon. He had a meeting set up for one o'clock. Later this afternoon, around three, Daniel was supposed to drop off some horses for training and pick up others that were ready to be sold. The process would take the rest of the day, perhaps until midnight.

The door to the shop creaked, and he raised his head. The neck brace made his workday harder because it was hot and unforgiving, but he tried not to let it grate on his nerves. He was healing, and that was all that really mattered.

Andy had a box in his hand. "This came for you."

"Denki. Just set it on the counter." He tapped the last peg into place and turned the cradle upright. "The stuff lined up against the wall is ready to go. Could you hitch up the wagon and pull it around?" Grabbing a sheet of fine sandpaper, he noticed that Andy lingered by the door. "Is there a problem?" Levi scrubbed the headboard, causing wood particles to swirl in the air.

He hoped nothing was wrong. He had neither the time nor the patience for any issues today.

"Mamm came by earlier to see if you'd heard from Sadie."

"And now I have." Levi removed a cotton rag from his pants pocket and used it to wipe off the headboard. He inspected the finished product, smoothing a few rough spots with sandpaper.

Despite Levi's request that Andy pitch in, he continued to wait by the door. Andy opened his mouth twice and drew a quick breath as if on the verge of saying something. Levi turned the cradle upside down again, ready to attach the two rockers.

"If you've got something on your mind, say it. We have fifteen hours of work to do during the next five hours."

Andy picked up one of the finished toy highchairs and propped it on his shoulder. "You know Mamm and Daed think you and Sadie have something going on."

Levi threw the rag onto the table, studying his brother. "And?"

Andy tucked another chair under his arm and picked up a cradle. "Do you?"

Levi turned his back on Andy and grabbed a hand drill. "I don't know who's worse, you or them." After putting a seat for a toy highchair on the bench, he pulled out a measuring tape. "All I want is a little peace on this topic. Could you get the horse hitched up and everything loaded, please?"

The screen door slammed, leaving the silence to heap guilt on Levi.

Three weeks ago, after his visit with Sadie in Stone Creek, he'd ended up staying in a hotel with Daniel and the driver. The auction and subsequent sorting and hauling of horses had lasted until nearly dawn. When he'd arrived at Andy's around noon the next day and stepped out of the car with a couple of boxes of Sadie's crafts, his folks were there.

Their parents lived across the back pasture, so it wasn't unusual for them to pop in, often with food for the bachelors. They were good people, and Levi loved them and enjoyed their company—when they weren't matchmaking. But since he had Sadie's boxes in tow, they had questions. He couldn't figure out how to avoid admitting he'd gone by to see the woman who'd returned his horse. So he told them the truth—he'd gone to see her, discovered the five-and-dime was closing, and planned to give her crafts to Beth for the store.

Neither Mamm nor Daed had asked any more questions. They simply nodded, but Levi recognized the look in his mother's eyes, and he couldn't douse it. She was a good woman whose heart had broken when Andy's wife had left. She believed if Levi didn't marry, he'd be worse off than Andy, because he'd die without ever having loved someone or having children or grandchildren.

Her ache for Andy and Levi was like a hole in her gentle heart.

Then Sadie sent another package of dolls, but also inside the box was a gift for him. It was a simple gesture, a candle shaped like a horse and made to smell of leather, but Tobias saw it and ran across the field to tell his grandparents that Levi's girlfriend was sending him presents.

The sound of horse hoofs and the creaking wagon let Levi know his brother was back. The screen door opened again. "Hey, Levi."

"Ya?"

Andy didn't say anything, and Levi turned to face him.

"You're annoyed with me, and I get that, but I carry this awful fear that my life has redirected yours in a negative way."

"Oh, all right. I'll load the stuff myself." Levi grabbed numerous pieces from along the wall. With a couple of cradles and a rocking horse in hand, he went out the door and to the nearby wagon.

"We're having a conversation here!" Andy followed him, carrying several more items.

The way Levi saw it, Andy's and Daniel's experiences had opened his eyes. That was a positive thing, not something Andy needed to feel bad about. But Levi knew his brother wouldn't see it that way. "You need to stop. Stop fretting. Just…stop!"

"Okay," Andy growled, setting the stuff in the wagon. "All I want to know is if you're courting Sadie. Just tell me straight up."

Levi stared at his brother, tempted to climb onto the wagon seat and drive off. "Look, I know what Mamm and Daed think, and maybe there's some whispering about Sadie and me in the community. But do you have any idea how nice it's been these last few weeks with no one prodding me about attending singings or making wisecracks about how I *can't* find a girl who'll have me? I'm sick of being needled about it." He removed his tool belt and threw it onto the porch of the workshop. "And you've joined them."

"Okay." Andy sighed and leaned his forearms against the wagon. "But it's been four years since you moved in with us to help me juggle work and raise Tobias, to help us cope with the hole Eva left, to make the house feel less lonely. You'll never know how much I appreciate that, but—"

"So?" Levi interrupted. "You want me to move out? Is that it?"

"Don't be ridiculous! For my sake, for Tobias's, being completely selfish, I'd side with you about avoiding singings and staying single. I'd have you live here forever." Andy shook his head. "But I want what's best for you. Not what's best for me or even Tobias."

Levi climbed into the wagon and took the reins. "Then be my brother, my friend, and my business partner. But stop trying to be my trainer."

Twelve

*B*eth picked up a large stack of empty handwoven shopping baskets from the counter near the register. She went through the main part of the store, heading for the front to return them to their rightful spot. Zigzagging between small groups of shoppers, she enjoyed the breeze that flowed through the aisles, caressing her skin. It was the second week in September, and today was the first hint that summer was fading and autumn was on its way.

Jonah was descending a ladder, holding a large clock he'd removed from the wall display. He stepped off the last rung and passed the clock to an employee, giving instructions. He then grabbed his cane off the ladder's hinge. As Beth skirted around the customers, someone put a hand on her arm, and for a moment she thought a patron had a question. But then she recognized Jonah's tender touch. His golden-brown eyes stared into her soul, melting her right there in front of everyone—if the others hadn't been too busy to notice.

"I'll take those." He lifted the baskets from her arms and repositioned his cane, all without moving his gaze from hers. His lopsided grin tempted her to kiss him.

Jonah moved in closer. "How about if you and I take a break?" He brushed his lips near her ear. "I'll make us lunch and bring it to your office."

"I'd planned to grab a few bites of a sandwich while working. I'm backlogged on the inventory. I haven't logged or shelved the items that came in this morning, and Levi will be here soon with his goods."

"Please. Take just a few minutes to get off your feet and rest."

She slid her hand over her slightly protruding stomach. The bump was hardly noticeable to onlookers. Five months pregnant and each day she'd witnessed the joy of their news in her husband's eyes, a pleasure that seemed to know no bounds.

"I'm going to be spoiled before this child is born."

"I don't think sitting at lunchtime qualifies as being pampered."

"How about if we sit at one of the outdoor tables of Mattie Cakes café?"

"Is the shade of the white oak calling you again?"

She grinned. He knew her well. "It is."

"Beth," Lillian said.

"It's not the only voice calling to you." Jonah brushed his hand against hers, smiling as they turned to the girl behind the register.

Lillian held up jars of Amish candles. "When will we get some more of these?"

Jonah squeezed Beth's shoulder. "Lunch will be served in twenty minutes."

"I'll meet you there."

She went toward the customer who was buying the last of Sadie's candles. "I don't know." Beth had left several messages for Sadie on her parents' answering machine, but that was in a phone shanty. And as of yet Sadie hadn't returned any of her calls. She made a mental note to ask Levi about it when he came in later. Surely Sadie returned his calls. "But I'll do what I can to get some more."

Beth took notes on what the woman wanted, chatted with her for a bit, and then headed toward the café.

The chimes of several clocks bonged, letting her know it was half past noon, and then one of them played music. Beth continued through the craft supplies aisle, but she always savored the only source of music allowed in an Amish store or household. She and Jonah had one of these timepieces in their bedroom.

As Beth went through the little section of the store that was Mattie Cakes café, Mattie glanced up. "Need anything?"

Beth pointed toward the door several feet behind Mattie. "I'm having lunch on your patio as soon as Jonah arrives with it."

Mattie smiled. "It's a beautiful day, even if we haven't had a change of seasons yet." Mattie turned to a customer and opened her portfolio of celebration cakes. She pointed one out to the woman. "This is probably similar to what you described."

"Yes. It's perfect. You can make this?"

Beth smiled as she stepped outside. She paused near the doorway, letting her eyes adjust to the sunlight.

The patio was as new as the area they called Mattie Cakes café. There were three wrought-iron tables with a couple of chairs each and a short picket fence that connected to the store. Since the patio abutted the gravel parking lot, Jonah and Mattie's husband, Gideon, had put in the fence mostly to keep little ones from escaping and wandering into a driver's path.

It was so nice to have Mattie back. She had lived three years in Berlin, Ohio, with her brother. Unfortunately, the transition from Ohio back to Apple Ridge hadn't been easy for Mattie. She returned only because her cake shop there had burned down just before Thanksgiving last year, and her parents had insisted she come home for a while. Mattie had moved away because of a rift between Gideon and her, but once she was back home, she slowly learned of the great sacrifices he'd made to protect her from the trials he was going through. Once the truth was laid out, Mattie made it known that nothing short of death could ever keep her from Gideon again. They had married in March, and Beth had the pleasure of witnessing their love and joy make up for the time they'd been apart.

Jonah crossed the parking lot toward her, his cane in one hand and a tray in the other. It was convenient having a home only a stone's throw from the store.

She opened the gate and let him in. He'd made two sandwiches and put several types of fruit in a bowl.

"I'll get some water from Mattie." Jonah set the items on a table and pulled out a chair for her to prop up her feet. They were pretty good at snatching downtime together during the workday.

Before he could turn to enter the store, Mattie brought out two glasses. "Water, anyone?"

"Perfect." Jonah took them from her.

She went back inside as he sat down across from Beth. "So what's on your mind for Sunday afternoon?"

She shared her thoughts about having a picnic by the creek, and the conversation rolled along as if they hadn't seen each other in months. They both looked up when Levi pulled into the lot.

Beth stood. "This was nice."

Jonah got up and threw away the trash. "But work calls us back."

Levi toted an armload toward the service door. All three headed for the stockroom to check in the items.

"Hey, Levi. How are you today?" Jonah asked.

"Gut, and you?" Levi knew the routine well, so he lined up several pieces for check-in. He set a red barn trimmed in white on the floor.

"You've outdone yourself." Beth inspected the two-story building.

He'd created wooden fences and farm animals to boot. The tiny sheep were covered in real sheepskin, and the cows had strips of rawhide glued to their wooden bodies.

"Glad you like it." Levi nodded, and Beth could tell he was in no mood to talk. "I have some more pieces in the wagon."

"Let's bring them in." Jonah clasped his hand on Levi's shoulder.

Beth grabbed the inventory clipboard and a pen and began logging the new items.

Levi walked in carrying another cradle. "This isn't the full order we discussed last May. I'm working on another two-story dollhouse, but it and plenty of other stuff aren't done yet."

Beth couldn't stop her smile. "I may want to keep the dollhouse you're working on for our little one instead of selling it."

Jonah chuckled. "Our *son* won't appreciate a dollhouse."

No matter how she referred to their child, as a boy or a girl, he'd pick the opposite gender to make a remark. But he never favored one or the other, because it didn't matter to either of them. They wanted the child she was carrying. Period.

"Levi,"—Beth scribbled a few notes in the margin of the papers— "I've been trying to reach Sadie and haven't heard back from her. Next time you talk to her, would you ask her to call me?"

"I...don't know when that'll be." Levi separated the rungs of a rocking horse from the base of a highchair.

Beth's eyes met Jonah's. That's all Levi had to say? He was as guarded as they came. Consistently nice. Always polite. Quite humorous at times. But discovering what he really thought? Impossible.

A salesclerk called for Jonah, and he headed back into the store.

Beth returned her attention to the invoice. "Is this everything?"

Levi counted the objects. "I think there must be two more items in the wagon…or still at the house."

While he ran another quick count, Beth stepped to the doorway, thinking she might spot any items in the back of his rig. Bright sunshine greeted her, and she blinked to adjust her eyes. An Amish woman in a horse-drawn wagon was pulling into the store parking lot. That was fairly common. The Amish brought their wares to Hertzlers' regularly. But… She squinted, trying to see clearly.

"Levi." She turned back toward the stockroom. "I think you might be talking to Sadie today."

Levi joined Beth at the doorway. A broad smile changed his countenance, but she was pretty sure something else reflected in his eyes—almost as if he felt hesitant.

Thirteen

*A*s Sadie brought the wagon to a stop at the hitching post, she saw Levi coming toward her, and she couldn't help but smile.

He grinned. "What are you doing here?"

"I could ask you the same thing."

He tethered Bay to the post and patted her neck. "I was making a delivery."

She motioned to the boxes in the back of her wagon before climbing down.

Levi moved to the back of the wagon and unhitched the tailgate. "How long will you be in Apple Ridge?"

"Only for the weekend." She helped remove the tailgate and slid it into the wagon. "I've been home in Brim for only three weeks, and my parents are already on my last nerve. Since Beth left messages saying she needed these items right away, and it was about as cheap to hire a driver as it was to ship them here, I couldn't pass up the chance to get away for a bit and for as long as possible."

"Looks like you've been busy." He pulled several boxes toward him and began stacking them.

"I just hope I can make enough money to be on my way come December, because my parents are parading me around like a horse at auction." She reached farther back into the wagon and pulled a heavy box toward her.

Two Amish girls emerged from the same door Levi had come through a few minutes earlier.

Levi picked up a stack of boxes. "Are these marked with what's in them?"

"Ya. I wrote a code on the box tops." She pointed to the markings. "See, 'CLG16' means candles, large, in glass containers. There are sixteen in each box." She pulled another box toward her. " 'SS36' means small soaps, thirty-six bars."

He gestured toward the women heading their way. "I'm sure Beth sent them to help unload. Why don't you stay at the wagon and tell them what's in each box. I'll clear out a spot in the stockroom so they can be grouped by kind. It'll make checking them in easier."

"Sure. Denki."

Levi smiled and gave a nod before disappearing with his stack of boxes.

Sadie climbed into the wagon and pushed more boxes toward the tailgate.

"Hi." A young woman waved. "Beth said you probably have some things we need to put on the shelves right away."

"Candles, soaps, wreaths, and dolls." Sadie got down and stacked several lightweight boxes. "These are wreaths."

The woman picked up the stack. "I'm Lillian. This is Katie."

"Nice to meet you. I'm Sadie."

Lillian's eyes grew wide, and she set the boxes back in the wagon. "Levi's Sadie?" She held out her hand. "It's nice to finally meet you."

"Denki." Sadie shook her hand, inwardly shooing away the thought of being called Levi's Sadie. There were so many Amish who shared the same name that they often referred to one another by nicknames. "I'm thrilled to have a place to sell my crafts."

"We are so glad you found Levi's horse." She giggled. "And found each other in the process."

Ready for Lillian to stop making her feel awkward about her friendship with Levi, Sadie edged in front of her and picked up the stack of boxes. She put them in Katie's hands. "These are wreaths," she repeated.

Katie grinned. "I'm with Lillian. It's great to meet you. All of Apple Ridge has been abuzz, and so few of us have ever met you." Katie turned and hurried into the store.

Concern and doubts over exactly what Levi was saying about her nagged at Sadie. She created a new stack of boxes and passed them to Lillian. "These are dolls, smaller than the ones Levi uses for the highchairs and cradles."

"Excellent." Lillian started to walk off.

"Lillian?"

The young woman turned.

"What's being said about me?"

"Not much. Just that you and Levi have been seeing each other since July." She shrugged a shoulder. "Levi's quite a catch, and everybody thinks it's wonderful he finally has a girlfriend."

Girlfriend? Sadie's heart knotted. Levi returned with Katie right behind him.

Lillian glanced at him and back to Sadie. "You don't mind that being said, do you?"

Levi clapped his hands once. "What do you have, Lillian?"

"Dolls, small ones."

"Put them on the far right of the stockroom counter."

Lillian left, and Levi gathered several boxes and gave them to Katie.

"CSNG24." He looked at Sadie. "Candles, small, no glass, and there are twenty-four of them, right?"

Sadie nodded. He was certainly smart enough to figure out her coding very quickly. What else had he figured out about her?

Levi slid another lightweight box onto Katie's stack. "Set these on the floor just inside the doorway to your left."

"Sure thing." Katie left.

Sadie's eyes met Levi's. "What have you been telling people?"

The muscles in his face went from relaxed to strained, but he didn't look at her.

"Nothing." He remained calm and steady as he sorted the boxes in stacks according to code.

Was he lying to her? Did Levi find it as easy to tell lies as Daniel had? That thought was disappointing at best and infuriating at worst.

The phone in his pocket buzzed. Short, loud, annoying rings. He pulled it out and glanced at the caller ID before sliding it back into his pocket.

Lillian and Katie returned, and he gave them each a stack with instructions and followed them into the store, carrying all but the last two boxes.

Sadie stood there, trying to make sense of who she'd thought Levi was compared to the man Lillian had just shoved in front of her face.

Lillian returned to the wagon. "Beth is writing up an invoice for you."

Sadie wasn't going to go inside the store right now. It was too much to pretend she was calm when she wanted to confront Levi. She put the last two boxes in Lillian's arms. "Tell her I need to go. We can settle up later. Okay?"

"You're sure?"

Right now, all she knew was that she needed to leave before she started an argument in front of everyone. "I'm sure. Denki."

Sadie climbed onto the bench of the wagon.

Levi strode back. "You're leaving already?"

"I'll ask you again. What have you been telling people?"

"Nothing." He shifted. "I mean, really, you know how people are."

This man right here, evading her questions and looking guilty, wasn't anything like the Levi she thought she knew.

"I think I'm beginning to understand how *you* are." With the reins in hand, she then realized she hadn't untied Bay from the post. "Do you mind untying my horse?"

His phone rang again. He ignored it this time and did as she asked. "What did Lillian and Katie say?"

"Oh, something about my being your girlfriend!"

A myriad of emotions crossed his face, beginning with surprise and ending with resignation. "Ya, about that... It's just people talking."

He had no idea how much she detested men who hid behind false behavior. It now tainted everything she'd thought or felt about Levi.

"Maybe you're new to how a woman would feel about what's happening here, so I'll clue you in. Honesty and an apology would be really wise moves about now. Anything less is just disappointing." She'd hoped to see a reflection of the true Levi in his countenance, but instead he seemed annoyed.

His jaw clenched. "I can admit I was wrong but not as bad as you're making it out to be. You're just doing the typical female thing. I saw Eva do that to my brother hundreds of times—make a mountain out of a molehill."

Once she'd asked about Andy's wife, and he'd said she was gone. What sort of man bad-mouthed someone who'd died? Did Sadie not know Levi any better than she'd known Daniel?

His phone buzzed again, and he simply stood there, staring at her as if they were strangers. Maybe they were.

"Would you answer that thing already?"

Levi pulled it from his pocket and pressed a button. "What?" He snapped the word out, and she startled. She'd never seen this side of him before. "He's here with the horses already?" Levi frowned and listened. "Okay, I'll be there soon." He said nothing for a moment. "I said *okay*." Levi disconnected the call and shoved the phone back into his pocket. "I need to go."

"Fine. Go." She tugged the right rein, steering Bay away from the hitching post. "Geh." Bay started toward the exit of the parking lot.

A few moments later Levi strode toward the horse's head and grabbed the leather cheeks of Bay's bridle, stopping her. His hand moved down the horse's neck, probably subconsciously assuring the animal she was safe. Animals he understood, but he studied Sadie as if disappointed in her.

Sadie's heart pounded. She'd thought they were friends, had been absolutely sure she liked who he was. Sometimes her ability to see what she wanted to see in someone astounded her. "So you have nothing to say to me?"

He shook his head. "I guess not."

"Geh!" She steered Bay out of the parking lot. Why had she ever come to Apple Ridge?

Fourteen

*L*evi could not believe himself. He watched as Sadie drove the rig from the parking lot and down the long road. Was he like an unreliable and high-strung horse that Sadie hated dealing with?

She'd been really good to him and was probably the sole reason his rescue included thorough medical help, the kind that ensured he took proper care of his injured neck. And he actually liked her. He respected who she was and admired her strength to politely stand against what their people expected of her.

He didn't know much else right now, but it was obvious he shouldn't have balked at what she'd demanded from him: an apology and honesty.

Jonah came up beside him with a clipboard filled with papers. "She left without stepping inside."

"Ya."

Levi had told himself to apologize to her. When he'd stopped her horse, he intended to tell her the truth. He'd wanted to say he was sorry. Instead, he'd just stood there. Whatever possessed him to use Sadie to make his life easier?

"Okay, here are the records for everything you brought in today." Jonah pulled copies of the receipts from the clipboard. "Should I give you Sadie's invoices too?"

"Probably not. If I tried to pass them on to her, she'd likely tear them up without looking to see what they are." Levi rolled up the receipts and swatted them against his leg. "I guess I messed up the meeting Sadie should've had with Beth."

"Businesswise, we can sort out everything with Sadie another day."

"Businesswise," Levi mumbled, watching Sadie's carriage disappear over a hill. "I don't think that'll help me at all."

Jonah stared at the horizon. "I don't know what happened, but I believe you are right about that."

Levi shoved the rolled-up papers into his pocket. "Apologizing to a woman doesn't come easy, does it?"

Jonah scratched the side of his face. "No, but it gets easier—for you and her."

Levi had never needed to apologize to a woman before, not really, certainly not like this. Oh, he'd apologized for some thoughtless incident at a church meeting or family gathering or such, for spilling a drink on a clean floor or nonsense like that. Those apologies came easy. The words flowed out of his mouth without his needing to think about them.

Apologizing to Sadie, though. That would've required him to make himself vulnerable. When he'd looked into her fiery eyes, it'd felt as if a team of wild horses couldn't have dragged the words out of him.

Levi debated whether to go home where work waited for him or to rush after Sadie. "This was my first argument with a girl. Not that I said much. But she sure said plenty."

Jonah chuckled. "Beth and I had our first argument the day she realized who I was. Long story, but I have to say you've nailed exactly how it went and how it felt. I think it's a female thing. They're usually more emotional than we are, and they've spent a lifetime trying to understand how they feel. They can think fast and argue with the past, present, and future in mind." He dug the bottom of his cane into the gravel. "If a couple cares for each other, though, you'll both learn to fight fair, and then you'll come away with a better understanding of her and yourself."

Levi stared at the storm clouds on the horizon. He wasn't interested in all that, but he did want to keep Sadie as a friend. He wanted letters from her when she was in the mission field. He wanted visits with her when she returned home. Twenty years from now, when they were both turning gray and their families had finally accepted who they were, he wanted to be on her to-visit list whenever she returned to the States.

"Jonah, I need to go. Tell Beth that I need to reschedule our meeting."

"Will do."

Levi untied his horse and climbed into his wagon. He soon pulled onto the main road, encouraging the horse to pick up speed. Even with his decision made, his chest had a weird heavy feeling to it. A kind of unfamiliar sadness.

But he wasn't sure why.

Maybe it was because of how he'd treated Sadie compared to what she deserved. Or maybe the sadness was because he knew he'd damaged her, and some part of him understood that they'd never get back the easy-flowing friendship they'd had.

<hr/>

Sadie ran wet towels through the wringer and dropped them into the clothesbasket. Why had her grandmother started a huge load of unsorted laundry while Sadie was at the store? on a Friday afternoon? Mondays were washdays, and Sadie didn't wash her dresses and undergarments with towels and black aprons.

She should never have come to Apple Ridge. The only reason she was here was to take a break from her parents. Well, that and she'd also needed to do some business with Beth.

And she'd wanted to see Levi.

What a mistake on every count. Clearly she'd put Levi on a pedestal. He'd seemed so nice, like a salt-of-the-earth person. How many times in life could she be fooled? How many times was she to feel this way...like an injured animal with nowhere to hide? December and the flight to South America could not come soon enough for her.

Mammi Lee pulled wet clothes out of the washer and put them into the clear water of the mud sink. "How you live isn't normal. You need to settle down, move back home permanently."

"I'm hoping that one day you'll accept that I'm not normal." She moved to the mud sink and plunged her hands on top of the soapy clothes, swishing them around. She pulled them out and plunged them again, not caring how wet she got. Her goal was to get this done and hang out the clothes by herself.

Mammi reached into the sink and pulled out a black apron. "You know the saying about bad apples? If Daniel was one, he doesn't ruin the whole barrel of them."

A knife plunged into Sadie's heart. "If?" She grabbed two handfuls of wet clothes from the sink and slung them into the basket. Forget running them through the wringer. She wanted out of this room. "So you're like everyone else and still stuck on *if* Daniel did what I said he did?"

Without saying a word, Mammi ran the black apron through the wringer.

Sadie picked up the basket and headed for the door. With her back against the door, about to push it open, she realized that Mammi was going to follow her. "I can do this by myself."

"I shouldn't have said 'if.'"

"But it's still what you think, isn't it?"

Mammi Lee pursed her lips, looking unsure. "I've never heard of an Amish man behaving like that. Not ever. But if you think that's what happened even all these years later, I tend to believe you saw it as you said."

That wasn't good enough, but Sadie wouldn't challenge her or anyone else on that topic. One couldn't make another believe. It was just that simple.

She drew a breath and stepped onto the front porch. Levi was at the hitching post, tying an unfamiliar horse. Of all the things she did *not* want to do, talking to him was at the top of her list.

Mammi stopped cold at the top of the steps, but Sadie descended, intending to ignore him.

"Afternoon, Verna," Levi called out. "I'd like to speak to your granddaughter for a few minutes if you don't mind."

"*I* mind," Sadie mumbled as she passed him on her way to the clothesline.

"It's mighty gut to see you again, Levi," Mammi spoke loudly. "You go right ahead, but she's testier than a yellow jacket in fall."

Levi fell into step with Sadie and leaned his head close to whisper to her. "That's the mood I've been in today. Maybe it's contagious."

"Go home, Levi."

"Come on, Sadie. Don't be like that. I know nothing about getting along with women. So cut me some slack."

She dropped the basket onto the ground and grabbed a dress out of it. It dripped, and she slung it, spraying water freely before pinning it to the line.

He glanced toward the house. "Could we maybe go for a walk or something?"

"No thank you, but please, by all means, go for a walk."

"So this is how you're going to be?"

"Pretty much."

He sighed and walked off. She didn't want him to go, yet she couldn't make herself do anything about it.

"Whoa!… Whoa!"

At Levi's holler, Sadie turned, then gasped. He was almost at her feet, flat on his back. Had he slipped on the wet grass? She knelt beside him. "Levi?"

He smiled. "You're nicer to me when I'm on my back and you think I'm injured."

"You faked that!" She got up, grabbed the basket of wet clothes, and dumped them on his face.

"Sadie!" Mammi yelled. "What has gotten into you?"

But he lay there, unmoving. "Denki."

She scoffed, trying to sound perturbed, but laughter stirred within her, and she cleared just enough wet clothing from around his eyes so he could see. "What is wrong with you?"

"I have a confession to make." His voice was muffled by the clothing.

She picked up most of the clothes and dumped them into the basket. "Doubt you can come up with one I haven't already figured out."

"Sadie!" Mammi sounded anxious.

Levi sat upright, picking a few more items of wet clothing off his chest and stomach. "It's my fault, Verna. Could you give me a few minutes to get it straight?"

Mammi pointed her finger at Sadie, giving a silent warning before going into the house.

Levi remained on the ground while he held the wet clothes out to

Sadie. When she took them, he hesitated about letting go. "I want to make things right between us."

"Ya, why?" She pulled the items free from him. "So you can start some other rumor of convenience behind my back when I leave?"

"Do you have to be ridiculous about this?" He stood, catching a last article or two of clothing that fell into his hands. "I came here to make it right. Isn't that enough?"

"*I'm* ridiculous? You're the one letting people think we're dating when you couldn't be bribed to ask me out."

"That's the stupidest thing I've ever heard. If you thought I wanted a date, you'd bar the door and hide under the bed." He held out the last item to her, and they both noticed it was a pair of her sky-blue lace underwear.

She jerked the underwear away from him. "You can't use the word *stupidest* when talking about how I feel."

"Okay, I promise not to use that word again. How about *dumbest,* most *blockheaded,* or *dimwitted*? Will those work for you?"

"Golly, you really *don't* know anything about getting along with women, do you?" She threw a wet towel in his face.

"No." He peeled it off. "But I know when I'm making progress, and you just hit me with one item instead of the whole basket."

Their eyes met, and she saw the same man who'd recognized her voice when she came to see him and had smiled before he opened his eyes. The same man who'd planted her feet in the path of an oncoming horse because he trusted she'd know what to do if need be.

She bent, picking some black stockings off the grass. "You shouldn't say disrespectful things about someone who's passed. We all make mistakes, and unlike us, they can't defend themselves or have one more day to try to make it right."

"I said something about a dead guy?"

"Eva! Remember?"

His eyes grew large. "*Ach,* ya, I do, but I didn't realize I'd said that. Look." He took the basket from her and set it to the side. "The subject of Eva is one I try not to think or talk about. I told you she's gone, and she is, but she packed her bags and left four years ago. That's when I moved in with Andy."

Eva wasn't dead? She'd abandoned her husband and son? That explained a lot. "And that's when you decided you'd never marry."

"It's a little more drawn out than that."

"It always is."

"If it helps, I never lied to anyone about you or us."

"Ya, it helps a lot." But that was it? He wasn't going to apologize?

She pinned a washrag to the clothesline, not at all sure she understood him, but the nice thing about being only friends was that she didn't have to. She could benefit from the enjoyable parts of their knowing each other and ignore the rest. That's what she'd done with her two roommates. "Katie said we're the buzz of the community. How'd that happen?"

"My guess is Mamm has been doing some hopeful whispering, and that with all the other connections Beth and Mattie know about—my getting your address and visiting you and our combining items to sell at the store—it just grew in people's minds."

"Why would your Mamm say anything?"

He explained about his parents being at his brother's house when he came back from her place with the boxes of crafts. The timing made it such that he couldn't hide where he'd been.

She secured a dress onto the line. "And since then we've been writing to each other, and I send letters and packages."

"Ya, and Tobias told my folks about the horse candle you made for me. All of it had Mamm so hopeful that I was seeing someone, and I couldn't tell her the truth."

"There's no way to keep that up for long. When were you going to tell them?"

"I don't know. Soon. But I went a few weeks with no one griping at me about not going to singings or needing a girl. It was really nice, but it was also selfish."

Maybe he was onto something. As long as Levi and Sadie knew where each stood, what could be wrong with people thinking they were dating? "It's not that I care whether people think we're dating or not."

"Wait. I'm confused. So what'd you get angry about?"

"I thought you had lied to me and about me."

"Oh, ya, I can see where that'd be angering."

She paused from hanging laundry and studied him. Did he know that hurt masqueraded as anger easily and often in a woman's heart? "It hurt, Levi. A lot."

Regret filled his eyes. "I'm truly sorry that I did anything to make you think I'd lie to or about you. I'd never do that."

Finally she had the heartfelt apology she'd wanted. And more. She believed in him again. "Forgiven." Ready to walk and talk, she left the clothes and went toward the dirt lane that meandered across the back field. Levi went with her.

"I think you were more selfish than you know." She poked his shoulder with her index finger. "You benefited from this, uh, misunderstanding. Why not let me?"

"I'm confused again."

"Maybe you don't need to set this straight with everyone. My parents are insisting I return home after I get my business with Hertzlers' squared away. It's so hard to be back there after living on my own for years. But they'd let me stay in Apple Ridge if we were courting. And Mammi Lee likes you, so she'd leave me alone about hiding from men. I could put all my focus on earning what I need to go with my mission team again."

"Isn't this too deceptive? I mean, not correcting someone's misconception is one thing, but to plot it out like this?"

"So we'll date. Look at us. We're a mess of distrust and not wanting to get involved with anyone. So if we were really dating, what are the chances of our staying together?"

"After what I just saw of us, I'd say zilch. You'd get hurt over something I didn't understand, and I'd find it impossible to apologize when you deserved it."

She knew he was here now only because of their friendship. If they were seeing each other romantically, they'd both have walked away today.

"Exactly. Besides, my parents say they believe in keeping the Amish ways and that I need to abide by them too, but according to the Old Ways, they're supposed to leave the matter of finding a mate in God's trustworthy hands, not their pushy ones. Right?"

"Ya, but I'm beginning to doubt the purity of your motives about mission work. Maybe you just don't want to cope with your parents' expectations."

"And you do?"

He grinned, looking like himself again. "You know the answer to that. So for how long?"

"We could break up a few weeks before I go to Peru. That would probably buy you six months to a year after I'm gone before people start pushing you to date again."

He looped his thumbs around his suspenders. "But if we're still courting when you leave, it'll be as if I'm waiting for you to return. That'll buy me a lot more time. A year. Maybe two years."

She turned onto the lane, and he joined her. "If we stay together and I try to leave on a mission trip, my Daed will go to the church leaders to keep me home. If he thinks I'm heartbroken, he'll let me go."

"Is that why they let you go the first time?"

"Ya, but I wasn't faking then. And going to Peru helped me heal in a way nothing else could have."

Levi nodded. He seemed to understand what heartache did to someone. "Eva shattered my brother's heart, and she ruined his life."

She'd had a pretty negative effect on Levi's life too. Did he realize that? "We've got three months to plan the timing of our relationship's demise." She leaned in, bumping his shoulder with hers. "There's something that's really important to me, okay?"

"It's okay with me if something is important to you."

She laughed and pushed against his shoulder again. "I'm not your mama or your girlfriend, so as we move forward, can we agree to be totally up-front with each other?"

"I believe I can do that."

"That includes no misdirecting me like your oddly worded statement that 'she's gone' or the like."

"Okay. But I've got one of those important things too."

"Let's hear it."

"I've already imagined us being friends and visiting each other even when we're old. Earlier today I thought I'd blown all chance of that."

She put her arm around his waist. "That's the best hope for a relationship I think I've ever heard."

"I'm glad you like it." He looped his arm around her shoulders. "Can we do it?"

She couldn't stop her grin. "I believe we can."

Fifteen

*L*evi fitted another piece of wood into place on the gazebo railing. The birch and maple trees around him swayed. Sadie said they were strutting their deep yellows and brilliant reds of fall like a peacock did his tail feathers.

He sighed. Girly nonsense. That's what she had him thinking these days. When he saw her in a bit, he'd complain about it too. He peered across the backyard and into his shop to check the clock again, then he hammered another nail into the railing. There was more work to do than he had morning left to do it.

Andy came around the corner of the house, two-by-fours stacked on top of one shoulder. Tobias was on his heels, carrying a two-by-two. Andy dropped his on the ground, and Tobias did the same. The planks banged and bounced, reminding Levi of the way sounds echoed through an empty home. Noise he wouldn't have noticed until these last few weeks with Sadie.

They used most of their courting time to work together on projects for the dry goods store. But when they weren't doing that, she liked to take long buggy rides and discover empty homes to walk through. It was an interesting pastime. Some of the places were new, unfinished homes that the builders abandoned when the economy changed. One home they went into was off by itself, a Victorian place. She loved that one best of all. Sadie's grandmother used to clean that house for the owners, a huge mansion Sadie had been in as a child. But the owners had passed away, and the house had yet to sell. She had few qualms about entering it, and even though the front door was locked, she'd found a side door that wasn't. When he'd balked, she said she knew the owners wouldn't have minded. If they were alive, she'd knock and visit with them, and she didn't care if the police showed up. He could hear her now: *"Let them take me to jail. I dare them."*

Just the thought made him laugh inside—a kind of hilarity he hadn't known until recently, where his outward expression showed little while inside he enjoyed great merriment.

They had yet to be caught breaking into a home. Although, if an officer or two did arrive, Levi would let Sadie do all the talking. She was the one who didn't mind defying authority as long as she wasn't doing any actual harm.

She was an odd bird, willing to bend her knee to whatever she thought God wanted of her and yet unwilling to yield to man's rules any more than absolutely necessary to stay out of serious trouble.

Levi had yet to fit those two women into one person—carefully defiant with a heart of utter obedience. Weird. The good news was that since they weren't really involved, he didn't have to be concerned about her attitude or outlook.

"Hello?" Andy set one of the boards on the sawhorses.

Levi looked up. "Did you say something?"

Andy turned to Tobias, shaking his head. Tobias clasped both hands to his head and moaned. The two kept telling him that lately he lived in a world of his own.

"I guess I was talking to myself." Andy brushed his hands together, knocking off the dust. "So what's today's game plan?"

Tobias jumped into the gazebo. "Ya, so what's going on tonight?"

Levi took a step back, looking at the clock inside his shop again. Did it need a new battery? It sure was moving slowly. "It's the annual hayride at Lizzy's, so I have about two hours before I pick up Sadie."

"Just two hours?" Tobias stomped across the gazebo, never looking up as he counted boards in some game he played.

"Ya." Levi pulled a nail from a pocket in his tool belt. "It's called a hayride, but it's an event for singles that starts right after lunch and lasts until midnight."

Tobias eyed him. "What'll you do all day?"

"Well, let's see. I've been told there'll be a cookout, volleyball and softball games, a hayride that'll last for at least an hour, a singing, and a bonfire."

Tobias shoved his hands into his pockets. "Why can't I go?"

"It's for singles."

Tobias rubbed his face, indicating he didn't have a beard. "I ain't married."

"You can't go, Son. It's for people at least sixteen years old." Andy pulled out a tape measure and put it against the two-by-four, his smirk undeniable. "Are you and Sadie staying at the gathering the whole time or coming by here after a while?"

"Don't know yet." Levi took a step back, inspecting his work. He shook the railing—steady as could be.

Tobias looked up, his eyes wide. "I hear something." He ran across the backyard and took off toward the front of the house.

Andy marked the wood with a pencil. "I can't believe Lizzy is still having those gatherings each year. I went to three before marrying, so my first time would've been twelve years ago."

Levi ran his hands across each nail, tapping certain ones a little deeper. "I've never been."

"Somebody your age and single shoulda been six or seven times by now. You do know Lizzy invites Amish from as far away as Illinois."

"Are you griping at me about girls again?"

"Sorry. Old habits die hard, I guess."

Tobias came around the corner of the shop. "Sadie's here."

"She is?" Levi left the gazebo, a smile tugging at his lips.

Tobias hurried back along with him.

Sadie had some craft items spread out in his shop, so maybe she needed something from her stash. Sometimes she worked here when there was no more shelf space at Mammi Lee's. It took quite a bit of room when juggling wreaths, candles, soaps, and dolls during the same workweek.

She came into view, wearing a purple dress and carrying a large basket lined with red fabric. Tobias was in front of her, walking backward and jabbering.

Levi spun his hammer around a few times, making the head of it rotate similar to a helicopter. "Is it soup yet?"

She'd made a batch of soap a couple of days ago that came out the consistency of soup—and he hadn't stopped harassing her about it yet.

Her eyes moved from Tobias to him. "Leave me alone, Fisher."

The way she talked—those firm words spoken dryly—made him chuckle. It was her best effort to sound tough despite teasing, and he knew she'd dish out equal amounts of whatever pestering he came up with.

He shoved his hammer into its loop on his tool belt and took the basket from her. "Or what? You'll wash my mouth out with soup...I mean soap?"

She pursed her lips, looking peaceful and sweet as he harassed her, but he knew she wouldn't just leave it at a smile. There would be a price to pay.

"Excuse me?" Levi leaned in, cupping one hand behind his ear. "What was that you said, Sadie Yoder?"

Sadie flashed him a mocking look of anger before spotting his brother. "Hey, Andy, how are you?"

Andy nodded, giving a welcoming smile as he remained at the sawhorse. "Morning, Sadie."

She pointed at the gazebo. "It's looking good. I suppose that means you managed to make Levi use a straightedge and a level."

"Of course." Andy winked at Tobias. "It's standing straight, ain't it?"

"Hey." Levi waved an arm. "I'm right here as you insult me."

She eyed him from head to foot. "With a tool belt, a girly basket in your hands, and doing absolutely nothing."

"Sadie." Tobias looked up, eyes bright with questions. "Can we sit on the fence and watch Levi work with the horses again?"

She glanced at Levi before clearing her throat. "He needs us to give him some lip while he's training, doesn't he?"

Tobias grinned. "I think so."

"I don't agree." Levi shrugged, but he actually enjoyed their harassment while he worked.

"Tobias, give me a hand." Andy held out a pencil, probably aiming to keep him distracted so Sadie and Levi could talk.

Levi opened the screen door to the workshop, and Sadie went in ahead of him. She took the basket and unloaded dried flowers, wire, and half-made wreaths.

"Lizzy asked me to bring centerpieces for the tables at the cookout, and I've cleaned Mammi's small patch of woods for other projects." She picked up her now-empty basket. "You can go on working while I hunt for flowers."

"Me, do woodwork when I can pick flowers?" He opened the door again. "No way." He could make up next week for taking off early today. Besides, he'd worked long, hard hours six days a week for years. Sadie was here for only two more months, so he had no problem taking off when it suited him.

They headed for a trail that hadn't been all that familiar to him before he'd started helping Sadie gather items for her wreaths. Now that she lived closer to Hertzlers', she was able to fill orders quickly and get them to the store without cost or delay. She was making great money.

"Uncle Levi?"

Andy shushed his son, but Sadie bumped her shoulder into Levi's. "Let the boy come with us."

Levi turned, motioning for him.

Andy angled a look at them. "You sure?"

"We're sure."

Tobias thundered past them. "I bet I can find the best flowers again."

They went deeper in the woods, leaving the trail at will and quipping nonsense at each other as they found treasures for the wreaths.

"Tobias," Sadie called, "kumm." She pointed to a patch of Johnny-jump-ups. Tobias headed their way.

Basket in hand, Sadie straddled a log, aiming to get what was on the other side.

Levi leaned against a tree, keeping an eye on Tobias as he made his way to Sadie. When Tobias passed him, Levi bumped the hat off his head.

"Uncle Levi!" Tobias bent to grab it.

Sadie screamed an ear-piercing shrill.

Levi bolted upright, but he was sure he knew what the problem was.

"It's something furry!" She hopped and danced before jumping up on the log. She shook her arms before gasping. Apparently she'd seen the culprit afresh. And a blur of purple hurtled toward him.

Before Levi could react, she jumped into his arms. "Ew, yuck!" She shuddered against him.

He didn't know what to do or say. While seeing a critter out here wasn't new, and it always caused her to immediately panic, Sadie jumping into his arms was a first.

A mouse ran out from under the log, and Levi laughed so hard it was difficult not to fall over backward.

"It's not funny!" Sadie smacked him with the flat of her fist. "Geh." She shooed the creature away as if it could see her antics from deep in the brush.

"I fear I'd be dead if a mouse had scurried out at any point that night I was thrown from my horse."

She studied the ground. "Where'd it go?"

He winked at Tobias and began searching around while holding her. "I don't know...wait, it's on my shoe." He kicked one foot up.

Sadie fled from his arms and didn't stop until she was on the log. "Where?"

Levi couldn't stop laughing. He didn't know which was funnier: the color of Tobias's face as he chortled or the look of terror on Sadie's face as she searched for the tiny, furry creature.

She pointed at him. "I'll get you for that, Fisher."

"I doubt you can top that, Sadie."

But he couldn't deny he looked forward to her trying. They had two months to go. Plenty of time for her to plot against him.

And for him to foil her plans each time.

Sixteen

Jonah stretched and reached across the bed for his wife. When he felt only air, he rubbed his hands across the sheets. Cold. Not only was she missing, she'd been gone for a while. He opened his eyes. Rays of golden light streamed through the windows.

He pushed back the thermal blanket and quilt and sat up. The room was unusually warm for late November. Had Beth been up toting wood and stoking fires while he slept? On a Sunday morning?

He slid into his pants and house shoes, pulled the suspenders over his shoulders, and grabbed his cane. His bad leg yelped in pain as he hurried down the hall without giving the muscles time to warm up. While passing the potbellied stove in the living room, he held out his hand. Heat radiated from it. That wasn't the only thing in this house that had an internal fire licking at it.

He and Beth had argued more than once about this. The last time occurred a couple of months ago when he'd walked into the store after hours and seen her at the top of a six-foot ladder getting something off a shelf. That explosion had been a real barnburner, but he'd won. Or so he'd thought.

Walking through the sitting room, he saw a roaring fire in the hearth.

"Beth!" Where was she? They had an agreement—no climbing ladders and no toting anything heavy. "Beth!"

Through the french doors a flash of patchwork caught his eye. She stood at the railing on the porch, a quilt wrapped around her as she studied the fields. He grabbed his coat from the rack and went outside.

She turned—steam rising from a mug of dark liquid in her hands. Her raven hair was in a long braid that draped down one shoulder. Her blue eyes were filled with peace and love. "Good morning."

Good morning? Was she kidding? "You should've woken me."

Her smile toyed with his emotions. She deserved his wrath.

"Look." She nodded toward the west. Low-hanging gray clouds hovered on the horizon. "I think we may see the first snow flurries of the year today." He knew she loved snow and all it symbolized, the things that had gone on between them. The fallen tree he'd dragged through the snow and up a ravine before he even knew her. He'd used it to carve a scene on a large base, one she'd stumbled upon in a store, and it'd called to her. It was the reason they'd eventually met. Snow reminded her of the storm he'd rescued her from in the sleigh he'd refurbished for her.

Despite the memories he held firm to his anger. "I'm not pleased right now."

She smiled. "Your little one is leaping for joy this morning. I think he or she senses the beauty of today." She opened one edge of her blanket, inviting him to place his hand on her round belly.

He sighed and set his cane aside before stepping up behind her. He wrapped his arms around her and placed one hand inside her quilt. The baby jolted numerous times, kicking or punching as if playing a game. "What am I going to do with you, Beth Hertzler Kinsinger?" The scent of lavender clung to her skin, and he kissed her neck.

"I don't know." She angled her head, inviting more kisses. "Love me? Create a family with me?"

"Attach bells to you."

She laughed. "Do what?"

"You've been good lately, well behaved as long as I'm on my feet, keeping an eye on you. Bells will give me a way to know when you get up."

"Ah. I see." She placed her hand on his as it pressed against her stomach. "Just make sure they're sleigh bells, and I won't mind too much."

He tugged her, and she faced him. He put his forehead against hers. "Please."

"Not even firewood to warm our home for you?"

"Not even."

"You do know you're being ridiculous and demanding—two things I did not expect from you when we married."

He cradled her face, still mesmerized by all God had done in bringing them together. "I'd gladly strike a match and burn down our home, the business, and every item we possess if it meant I could keep you even a little safer."

"That's a bit drastic, don't you think?"

"What I think is that you don't understand. You mean everything to me, and we're expecting something that cannot be replaced."

"It's a between Sunday, and I wanted to let you sleep."

"So your desire for me to get extra sleep matters more than following what your husband feels is important?"

Her eyes filled with tears. "Not when you put it that way."

It wasn't like her to be emotional, and he knew she struggled at times with the hormones coursing through her body.

She shrugged. "I don't believe it's necessary to be that pampered, but I'll not tote another thing."

"Gut." He moved his lips to hers, and their kiss lingered. He then stared into her eyes. "Extremely warm outside to be after Thanksgiving, ya?"

She giggled.

He opened the door for her to go inside. "So what has you up and moving like this on our off Sunday?"

"You know." She took off the quilt and laid it across the back of a kitchen chair. "The indoor picnic Mattie and I planned."

Jonah took the mug of coffee from her hands and took a sip. "But that's not until this afternoon."

"Life is too exciting right now to sleep." She put her hand on her round belly.

For a moment Jonah saw a tiny bit of what his wife was feeling. Their child's first steps, first day at school, and first time to ride a horse. It would all take place in the blink of an eye, and he understood her need to soak in the moments.

But for all the excitement that radiated from her, he couldn't shake the uneasy feeling nagging at him.

Nippy air and the familiar aromas of a barn—sweet feed, hay, and animals in wintry weather—surrounded Sadie as she removed the rigging that connected Bay to the carriage.

Mammi went to the bag of feed and scooped up the dry mixture. "We heard three good sermons today, ya?"

Church had been at the Ebersol place today, which was where she and Mammi Lee had been since morning. It'd be dark in an hour. Between the three-hour meeting, the after-church meal, and the long afternoon of fellowshipping, Sadie had been gone all day.

"I'm sure the preachers touched many a heart." But the truth was, Sadie hadn't heard much of what'd been said. Then as now, her mind lingered elsewhere. Thoughts of Levi drifted through her nonstop. Reflections of him—their many dates, hundreds of conversations, working side by side to make items for the dry goods store, visits with family and friends—all of it seemed to remain uncomfortably close.

Mammi's gait was slow and steady as she walked to the stall where Sadie would lead Bay in a few minutes. Mammi spread the feed into the trough. "Seems to me like you oughta attend a few Sunday meetings in Levi's district soon."

Sadie moved slower than her grandmother as she slid the bridle off Bay and attached a loose-fitting harness. Her muscles seemed as distracted as her heart. It was a between Sunday for Levi's district, and although they spent a lot of time together, they didn't attend meetings with each other. She wasn't sure why. "He hasn't asked me to."

Mammi shuffled across the hard-packed dirt, collecting pieces of straw on the wide rim of her flat black shoes as she went. "But you two are going to tonight's singing, right?"

She shook her head. "Not this time."

"Why?" Mammi jammed the scoop into the dry feed and dusted off her gloved hands.

Sadie wasn't sure about that either—except maybe she and Levi both knew they'd grown too close. "I don't know." They'd been dating and almost inseparable for twelve weeks. Their time together would be up in a month. Maybe he was laying the foundation for folks to believe they were having trouble.

But she wasn't ready.

She'd let her guard down with Levi, and she believed he'd done the same with her. He'd gotten under her skin, and she didn't know how to free herself of him. Or even if she wanted to.

Mammi rested her hand on Sadie's shoulder. "Everything okay between you two?"

Tears pricked Sadie's eyes. "Ya. I...I hope so." Weeks ago if Mammi had asked that, Sadie would have probably given the same answer, only then it would have been part of the show she and Levi were putting on.

The soft wrinkles around Mammi's eyes creased. Her smile held confidence in the situation. "I'm sure how he feels. I see it in his eyes."

Did Mammi really?

That was comforting.

And terrifying.

"You coming?" Mammi headed for the small door at the back of the barn. They'd already struggled through closing the double-wide door to keep out the cold.

"In a bit." Sadie stroked Bay's forehead and face, trying to sense what Levi sensed when training horses. It was as if he became one with the animal, seeing and feeling what the horse did, and then worked with the massive creature from its peculiarities and personality.

Closing her eyes, she let her fingertips caress Bay's neck. The mare's skin radiated warmth and quivered under Sadie's light touch. What must a saddle feel like to one that responded to such a feathery stroke?

In Sadie's mind, she could see Levi working a horse and hear his gentle commands. The features on his face altered ever so slightly, and she'd learned which tiny shift in expression meant he was perplexed or pleased or any of the other dozens of emotions that ran through him while training.

Someone cleared his throat, and she opened her eyes. Levi stood a few feet away, his black felt hat matching his winter coat as he studied her with quiet curiosity.

Her heart beat faster, but words failed her.

He moved in closer and placed his hands on the horse's neck. "If this was your first time getting to know the horse, you'd have to let go of your will." He drew a deep breath. "Relax, Sadie." He put his cold hand over hers. "It's not about what you want from the horse. Release your expectations. Your preconceived ideas."

The seconds ticked by.

"When I'm with a horse,"—Levi moved his fingertips across the back of her hand as if willing her to feel the horse's heart—"I have to set aside what the buyer has told me or what he hopes to gain. Let nothing get between you and simply accepting this creature for who she is."

Sadie inhaled and exhaled, trying to free her mind so she could sense what the horse felt. Levi's hand was warm now, his breathing less smooth than when he'd arrived. He wanted something, longed for—

She opened her eyes. "I think Bay is hungry and would like to go to bed for the night."

Levi shook his head. "Tobias could've come up with that at two years old. Clear your mind."

"I did."

"And?"

She eased away from him and grabbed a brush. "I thought we agreed that we weren't seeing each other today?" Running the brush down Bay's side, Sadie willed herself not to look up. But she did anyway.

Levi stared at her, seemingly wanting an answer to his question. "We received an invitation a few days ago from Beth and Jonah."

"Ya?" She placed the bristles on Bay's side. "Then you had the invitation when you suggested we not see each other. Didn't you?"

He shrugged. Did he miss her like she missed him?

He looked at the palm of his hand, the one that had been over hers moments ago. "They had an indoor picnic at their home earlier today.

With the exception of you, everyone is in the same church district, so they didn't have a service today. Gideon and Mattie, Lizzy and Omar, Annie and Aden."

"Who are Annie and Aden?"

"You met them once when we were making a delivery to Hertzlers'. He's Old Order Amish, and she was Old Order Mennonite, but she's in the process of joining our faith."

"I don't remember meeting them. Old Order Mennonites can have electricity. Why would she take a step into a harder life?"

"Because they fell in love, and she wants to be a part of his family, his church, and his business."

His words made her mouth and throat go dry. "Oh."

Levi drew a deep breath. "Omar, our bishop, has a lot of love for people, and as a bishop he can make it easy and appealing for people to return if they've left Apple Ridge or to join their loved ones here to build a life, like Jonah did with Beth."

She heard his words, but after he said "fell in love," she couldn't pay much attention. Running the brush down Bay's side again and again, she held her tongue, afraid her voice would betray her.

"We've missed most of it." Levi fidgeted with Bay's mane. "But if we go, the gathering will only include five couples. They had an indoor picnic earlier, but tonight they'll roast marshmallows inside, drink apple cider, and play board games."

She moved to the far side of Bay, staying focused on the short red hairs flying as she brushed the horse. What kind of people pretended to be a couple to those they cared about?

Or were she and Levi only pretending to each other?

"I guess." Emotions caught in her throat again, and she turned her back to him and walked to the weathered barn wall where she laid the brush on a chest-high beam. When she turned, Levi was directly in front of her.

There it was again—that feeling of him wanting something. Hadn't she sensed this same thing in him for weeks now? She could ask him about it, but as she looked into his eyes, she knew the answer.

And he wasn't the only one who'd like to stop their pretend courtship long enough to share a very real kiss.

Go around him, Sadie. But she stood there, feet planted, staring up at him like a schoolgirl. "What have we done, Levi?"

"I wish I knew." He sounded as confused as she felt, but he brought one hand to her face and caressed it. "Still, I think any courtship that's lasted three months should include one kiss."

Her heart turned a flip, wanting the same thing he did. From what he'd told her, it'd be his first kiss.

He looked at her face where his fingers barely touched her skin. "Seems like when I'm gray, this old bachelor should at least know what it's like to put his lips against yours."

His words were a mix of keeping up their pretense and letting it slip that he didn't want to experience just any kiss. He wanted to kiss her.

Is this who they were, only able to share their hearts when pretending they weren't?

"Seems like." She let her response continue their stupid charade, too afraid to let him know that somewhere along the way over the past three months, she'd crossed over from their faux nonsense into truly caring.

He lowered his mouth to hers. Stiffness greeted her lips, sort of like being kissed by a warm rock.

"Relax, Levi." She tugged on the collar of his coat. "Release your expectations and preconceived ideas. Let nothing get between us."

He moved his lips over hers again, and in one shared breath, her guard—and his—melted. His arms tightened around her, and as she let herself be lost in his embrace, she pushed away the question clamoring at her heart and mind…

How would she ever again convince herself that what they had was only make-believe?

Seventeen

*B*eth leaned over her desk and jotted down more notes for the morning meeting. In the distance a rooster crowed over and over, grating on her nerves. It'd begun its nonsense thirty minutes before sunrise, and it'd been daylight for about that long too. Wishing it'd stop, she opened a drawer and pulled out a file.

Her abdomen contracted again. Braxton Hicks contractions. That's what the midwife had called them. It was a sort of false labor the body used as it geared up for the real thing.

She glanced at the clock on her office wall, waiting for her muscles to relax. The night had been a long one because the tightness awakened her at least once an hour. Were the contractions getting harder?

Someone tapped on her office door, and before she had enough air to respond, Jonah opened it. "Everyone's here, and we've cleared enough space for a circle of twenty chairs. You ready?"

"Soon."

"Would you like a cinnamon roll?"

"No, denki." Another contraction made her heart rate go wild. It was just December 10. How many more weeks needed to pass before she'd be full term? Maybe she'd calculated wrong.

Holding that hope, she forced a smile and began gathering her papers. "I'll be right there."

He winked and closed the door, and she swiped the papers and folders off her desk calendar. Today was December 10. The doctor set her due date as January 21.

Maybe he was wrong. But what if he wasn't?

She pulled air into her lungs, wishing she could get a full breath.

"Beth?" Jonah called.

She grabbed a red pen and circled the date on her calendar, counting the days until she'd be full term. The midwife said there was a difference between premature and preterm—a vitally important difference. What had she explained? The pen squeaked as Beth marked each day. She'd be full term December 31. That was…nineteen, twenty, twenty-one days from now.

Could their child survive if born this early? She wiped perspiration from her forehead. *Look at what you're doing to yourself, Beth. They're Braxton Hicks, and you've got yourself all keyed up over it.*

"Beth." Jonah opened the door. His eyes moved to the papers in the floor, the pen in her hand, and the red marks on the calendar.

She smiled. "Sorry. I'm getting clumsier with each passing day."

"Not a problem." He picked up the mess, sorting out her meeting notes from the invoices.

She peered out the door.

With the exception of her and Jonah and Mattie and her husband, Gideon, everyone else attending was an employee.

Gideon stood next to Mattie, one hand on her back as they talked with Lillian. Gideon's eyes reflected such joy, and he looked vibrant and strong. He'd been given another clean bill of health a few weeks back. There was no trace of the rare cancer that had tried to destroy him. Mattie's return to Apple Ridge had allowed Gideon and her to face the truth that they loved each other enough to face an uncertain future together.

Beth thought about Levi. He wasn't here, but he'd been out of his neck brace for a few weeks now, another tale of woe turned into triumph. She could remember trials and triumphs in the life of almost everyone she knew.

Still, her heart beat faster and faster. Surely she and Jonah would have a triumph too. In fact, a beautiful little triumph to cherish for the rest of their days. But one common thread ran through each victory: no one had ignored their symptoms while hoping for the best.

She laid the pen on her desk. "Jonah, honey."

He looked up from the mess of papers on the floor, and the confidence in his eyes turned to concern. "Something wrong?"

She shrugged. "I'm not sure."

He moved toward her. "Do you need to be seen?"

"Probably not." She hated to cause the worry she saw in Jonah's eyes. "But maybe we—" Suddenly Beth felt a jolt, as if the baby was sideways. Another contraction tightened across her stomach, stealing her breath. She clutched Jonah's hand.

He grabbed the phone. "I'm calling the midwife."

<hr />

A gust of frigid air thrashed against Levi as he left the barn, leading the last horse toward Daniel's trailer.

Daniel had pen in hand and a forearm planted firmly on the papers piled on the hood of the truck. "She's number twenty-six fourteen, right?"

Tip sat inside the cab, talking on his cell phone.

"Technically,"—Levi patted the mare's strong cheek—"her name is Angel."

Like nearly everything in his life these days, she was a source of memories that connected Levi to Sadie. Tobias and Sadie had sat on a fence while Levi worked with Angel, and they'd each ridden her, helping him make sure the horse listened to women and children almost as easily as she listened to him.

He directed Angel up the ramp and into the trailer and closed the gate. One more task accomplished, and that meant he was one step closer to his date tonight with Sadie—an evening he hoped would change both of their futures.

After their kiss six days ago, he could no longer ignore the truth: he loved her. He couldn't let her leave without telling her how he felt. Sure, her plans were in place, but he could wait for her to return. Why not wait? It wasn't as if he was giving up anything—except time with her. He could wait.

That night, after the kiss, they'd gone to Beth and Jonah's. The evening of parlor games and fellowship had been a lot of fun, but he'd spent most of the time trying to figure out what to say to Sadie. On the way home, he'd told her to think about what she really wanted from their relationship and he'd do the same, and they'd talk about it next week.

Levi moved to the front of the truck. Daniel held up some papers and motioned to Tip, who was still on the phone behind the wheel.

Tip ended his phone conversation and got out. "I think we've got three of the four horses placed already. There's a man a hundred and fifty miles north of here who wants to see them. If he agrees they're all I told him they are, we'll get top dollar."

"Good." Daniel passed him the papers. "You know what to do."

Tip headed for the house. Andy handled the business end of Daniel's arrangements with the Fisher brothers.

Levi was headed inside to get warm and have some breakfast, but Daniel wanted to talk. He leaned against the truck cab and pulled a pack of gum from his coat pocket. "You're raking in a lot of dough off these horses lately, aren't you?"

Levi chuckled. "We aren't doing bad, me and you."

"Not bad? I'd say that's how we've been doing the past few years. But since being thrown from Amigo, you seem to have figured out the key to taming horses." He held out the pack to Levi.

Levi took a stick and put it in his pocket for later. He wasn't much for chewing gum, but Sadie liked it. He hoped that, after her week of thinking about their upcoming conversation, she'd accept how he felt. He'd certainly count that as a step in the right direction, but it'd be the night of his life if she actually had feelings for him too.

Daniel played with the foil wrapper, straightening it and flipping it. "It'll take me and Tip most of the day to make our deliveries, but we'll be back to pick you up if you want to go to the auction tonight."

"I have other plans."

"What?" Daniel's brows arched. "This seems to be a regular occurrence of late. Are you seriously seeing somebody?"

"I hope so… I mean, we haven't talked about how we feel or where we're going."

Daniel poked his shoulder, grinning. "I'll tell you how to feel—like your tail's on fire and you should run for the hills."

"I got plenty of that going on." Levi needed no encouragement when it came to wanting to run from relationships. But Sadie was different. "We met in July, so I think I'm getting to know her pretty well."

"Are you tellin' me this is the same girl you dumped me for in August?"

"I showed up at the auction."

"Ya, hours late and completely spent."

"Ya, it's the same girl."

"Really?" Daniel angled his head, apparently confused by Levi's change of heart. "You need a ride into Stone Creek again?"

Levi chuckled. "You're behind the times. She's living in Apple Ridge with her grandmother."

"You haven't talked about her much."

What could Levi say? He was pretending to court a girl and got caught in a very real snare?

Daniel crossed his arms, his breath a white vapor as he chewed his gum. "I guess it was bound to happen. You thinking about turning in your bachelor's license?"

"Thinking about it—if there is such a thing."

Daniel rolled his eyes. "You're playing a dangerous game, man. You'll be in love one minute and daydreaming of her demise the next. All the while she'll be stacking the deck against you, and you won't even know it."

"Sadie's not like that."

"I believe you. You've got a knack for seeing into horses. I'm sure that works on females too." Daniel chuckled. "Although you can clearly be wrong about horses, or you wouldn't have been riding one that overreacts to fireworks on the Fourth of July."

Daniel's aim was humor, but Levi didn't find anything humorous about what he'd said.

"It's sort of an odd coincidence." Daniel pulled his coat collar up high, shielding his neck from the wind. "That girl I was engaged to, she was a Sadie too." He sighed, shaking his head. "Messed up my life." He waggled a couple of fingers near the side of his forehead. "Did a real tap dance inside my brain." He stood upright.

Levi began to walk toward the house, ready to get out of the cold. Daniel followed him.

"Ya, I'm well aware that a woman can do that. I saw it happen to Andy, and I imagine Sadie could do it to me."

Daniel tossed the wrapper on the ground. "You say she's living near here?"

"Ya, her folks are from Brim, but she's living with her grandmother."

Daniel stopped, his eyes wide. "Tell me her grandmother isn't Verna Lee and her name isn't Sadie Yoder."

"How'd you—" Levi's worst fears swarmed like locusts and devoured every hope he'd imagined. His Sadie was the same girl who'd broken up with Daniel the day before their wedding? The thought of her courting Daniel, of her growing close to him the way she had with Levi sickened him. Worse, she'd run out on Daniel—just as Eva had done to Andy.

"It's your life, Levi. Maybe she's changed." He pulled the gum from his mouth and threw it into the bushes. "But years ago she was sweeter than candy and eventually showed me a side that was battier than bats. My concern is that, given time, she'll find some excuse and leave you like she did me." He went to the front door and paused. "Has she said anything about me?"

"Not a word."

He seemed relieved. "If you talk to her about this, she'll tell you I was to blame. But it was the day before our wedding, and I just happened to be in a room alone with one of her cousins. Sadie walked in. Maybe she actually thinks she saw something. I don't know. But I believe she was looking to bolt, and making up lies about what she saw was her way out."

Levi could easily imagine Sadie getting cold feet and wanting to run.

Even so, he loved her. Every goofy, funny, charming thing about her. How was it possible that he'd fallen for the same woman as Daniel? He hadn't been clear on who Daniel's fiancée was, but if he had, there were five Sadie Yoders that he knew of in the district. Since Daniel was a bit of a nomad, he'd lived in numerous Amish communities, and Levi imagined Daniel knew at least twenty Sadie Yoders.

Realization almost pounded him to the ground. He'd fallen for the same kind of woman as his brother had: a woman who hooked a man and then changed her mind about loving him.

God, why? He'd thought God was leading him *out* of the wilderness.

His thoughts came in disjointed fragments. All his senses seemed to heighten as his dream world shattered, causing him to see his reality for what it was.

Around him, the empty limbs of trees shook in the wind, and a few brown leaves tumbled across the dead grass—both evidence of the arrival of another long season of barrenness.

The horses he'd spent months training would be sold later today, becoming no more to him than a way to make money.

The woman he loved was incapable of building a life with anyone, banishing him to a life of isolation.

And Levi had to face yet another truth: he was a fool.

But he wouldn't stay that way.

He turned, seeing Daniel still standing at the back door, waiting in the cold for Levi to get a grip on himself.

Levi drew a heavy breath. The first of many, he imagined. "I've changed my mind. I will go with you tonight after all."

Eighteen

The horse's hoofs kept rhythm against the pavement, the familiar *clippity-clop* not moving swiftly enough for Sadie's liking. A muddled gray daylight had edged over the top of the mountain a little while ago. Snow flurries swirled, dancing on air, as the horse and carriage joggled its way down the road.

She shouldn't be on her way to Levi's on a Sunday morning. It seemed self-indulgent to *have* to talk to him first thing on the Sabbath. It was God's day, not hers. Still, she tugged on the left rein, turning the carriage onto Hertzler Drive.

What was going through Levi's mind? He'd made it very clear they needed to use the week to think about what they wanted. They were supposed to go out last night to talk, but then he left a message on the machine in Mammi's phone shanty. He said he wouldn't be coming by to pick her up and that he thought it best if they continued to follow their original plan.

What?

She'd been having second thoughts about meeting up with her mission team and leaving the country. How could she leave when she'd fallen in love with Levi Fisher? She had no doubt about that. So the only question was what God would have her do now: keep her plans to return to the mission field in Peru or stay here.

Levi had to be feeling the same things she felt. Both of them were terrified of making a commitment. But they were different together than she and Daniel had been. She imagined they were different than Andy and Eva had been.

She and Levi were strong enough to let go of their fears and love each other. She'd spent a week praying about it, after which she found that she had no reservations about Levi. But what would it take to convince him? Maybe he *needed* her to leave. Maybe they needed to spend a year writing to each other.

Sadie slowed the rig, preparing to enter Levi's driveway. It looked as if a lamp was lit in the kitchen. Gut. Maybe she wouldn't need to wake the house to get someone to the door. After tying the horse to the hitching post, she went to the front door and tapped on the glass.

Andy came into view, mug in hand. He smiled and opened the door. "Sadie. Kumm, get in out of the cold."

She stepped inside, and he closed the door behind her.

"You going to church with us this morning?"

"No." The aroma of coffee permeated the air, but there wasn't a sound anywhere else, as if even the house itself were still asleep. "Is Levi up?"

"Don't think so, but I can fix that for you." He set his mug on the table. "Take off your coat and make yourself at home. He was at the auction until late, so it may take me a bit to rouse him. Would you like a cup of coffee while I get him?"

"No, denki." She didn't know if she'd be here long enough to drink it, but she removed her coat and hung it on the back of a kitchen chair. "I'm fine."

Andy disappeared down the hall. She liked the way he treated her, as if he had a quiet hope of who she and Levi would become. He seemed to love his brother as much as he did his son. Despite his situation, Andy acted as if he believed in marriage. Why had his wife left him? He seemed pleasant and even-keeled—traits that could make a marriage work even if two people fell out of love.

Had he been unfaithful to her, so she just left? Sadie detested that she'd even thought such a horrid thing, but since she'd discovered Daniel with Aquilla…well, such thoughts came to her far more often than she liked to admit.

Andy returned, a smile on his face. "He jolted up the second I opened the door." He went to the stove and poured a little more black liquid into his half-full mug. "Any snow sticking to the roads yet?"

"Not yet." She wanted to ask him how Levi felt about her. If anyone knew, Andy would. But it wouldn't be right to do so. Levi had the right to insist he and Sadie stick to their original plan and break up regardless of any fondness he had for her.

He did care for her…didn't he?

"That's good, although I'm sure Tobias would love for enough snow so we could miss a church day. I imagine Levi and the two other guys who stayed over last night might be tempted to want the same. I don't think they crawled into bed until around four." Andy took a sip of his drink. "I was about to start breakfast. Will you stay and eat with us?"

"She won't be able to stay."

Levi's hard words sliced at her heart, and she turned.

He fastened the last button on his shirt and pointed at her coat. "Let's go outside."

"It's freezing out there." Andy set his cup on the table. "Everyone else is asleep. I'll go to my room."

Levi grabbed his coat off a peg. "It'll be warm enough in the barn."

She didn't move to get her coat, and a glance at Andy indicated she wasn't the only one baffled by Levi's attitude.

"It was good to see you, Sadie." Andy nodded and left the room.

Sadie put her hands on her coat, not quite ready to do as Levi had instructed.

"You broke our date rather last minute yesterday, and then you were out all night. Now I don't even get a hello, and you can't get me out of the house quickly enough. If I didn't know better, I'd say you had a girl you were hiding."

A look flashed through his eyes—disappointment in her, maybe. But why?

He reached over and picked up her coat. "We began our relationship as one thing, and it turned into another. We both know that's true. I think a clean break is best. Our breakup was supposed to be inevitable, so we'll let it begin today."

He held the coat out to her, waiting for her to slip into the sleeves.

Concern niggled at her, and she brushed hair away from his face. "Did you hit your head or something? You don't look or sound like the man I've come to know these last three months."

He didn't pull away, but the rigid look on his face said he wanted to. "Look, Sadie, you've been amazing from the start. And I know I owe you more than I can ever repay, but—"

"*Owe* me?" She backed up, staring at him. Had he mistaken gratitude for true caring? "All you feel for me is tied to my helping you that night?"

"Don't do this, Sadie."

"Do what? Try to understand?"

He said nothing.

She couldn't catch her breath, and her suddenly weak knees plunked her into a kitchen chair. "Maybe you're just spooked. Have we moved too fast? Because I could keep my missions plans. We could write to each other, and maybe by the time my work is finished, you'd feel ready to—"

"No." He hooked her coat on one finger and held it out. "I won't."

Tears stung her eyes, and she rose. "So this is it?"

He looked at the floor before meeting her eyes. "If it helps, I'm not happy about how things turned out either."

A door somewhere down the hall opened. It was probably Tobias.

Levi clutched the doorknob. "Kumm, I'll walk you to your carriage."

She put on her coat. "No, I'm fine." She paused in front of him. "When you asked me to spend a week thinking about where I wanted us to land, I thought…I mean, you sounded…"

His eyes locked on hers. "I know, and I'm sorry it has to be this way."

"Ya, me too." She choked back tears. "But it is what we agreed to."

He started to open the door, and she placed her hand in front of it. "Jonah was trying to reach you yesterday. He called Mammi Lee's looking for you. I didn't talk to him, only listened to the message, but he'd like for you to come by today when you can."

"I left my phone here last night."

"You, without your phone?" Her mind spun. People were seldom good at being direct, but their actions often told everything that needed to be said. "You called me to say you weren't coming, and then left your phone here…so you wouldn't be tempted to answer if I tried to call back."

In her peripheral vision, she saw a man walk to a cabinet. She glanced at him, expecting to tell Andy good-bye. Instantly her mind froze, struggling to accept what she saw.

Daniel?

He got a mug down and poured himself a cup of coffee. When he faced her, he gave her an undeniable smirk.

"Sadie." He nodded once as if her presence here was not the least bit surprising.

She looked at Levi for an explanation. As she stood there, feathery pieces of understanding fell from the clouds surrounding his call yesterday. "How long have you known Daniel?"

Daniel lifted his cup slightly, as if mimicking cheers to her. "A lot longer than he's known you."

Levi pointed toward Daniel. "You stay out of this!"

Sadie focused on Levi. "So this is who you really are, a friend to *him*? And you've chosen to believe whatever he's said, haven't you?" Tears welled. "I will not defend myself." Her heart pounded so hard she felt lightheaded. "But you know me, Levi, better than anyone ever has. Even if that wasn't true, how can you understand animals so very well, but you can't read what's happening here?"

Levi looked at Daniel and then to her. "I understand enough."

"You poor, stupid man."

Levi flinched as if she'd slapped him. "Good-bye, Sadie."

Nineteen

Jonah raised the blinds all the way to the top before taking a step back. "Can you see outside well enough now?"

Beth sat in bed, propped up by numerous fluffy pillows as she eyed his handiwork. "Almost."

Seeing her here, safe and smiling, brought a catch to his throat. He was so happy she was all right, he wouldn't care if she wanted him to re-arrange the bedroom ten more times. Twenty. However many.

The midwife, Mandy, said that Beth had only been having Braxton Hicks and that the baby's huge flop was the positioning of the head in the birthing position—all of which were normal and good things. Even so, Beth's blood pressure and heart rate remained high. So Beth was on bed rest for a few days, just to be safe.

Jonah went to her side, looking out the window from her angle. He shifted the bed a few inches. "How about this?"

"Perfect."

"Gut." He winked, taking the blood pressure cuff off the dresser and sitting on the edge of the bed.

She frowned. "Again?"

Jonah put his index finger over his lips before wrapping the band around her arm and pressing the bulb, watching the digital numbers that blinked her heart rate and blood pressure. The machine beeped time and again before it finally gave a long beep. He read the display, then grinned and removed the cuff. "It's normal."

He put the blood pressure machine on the bed beside her. Was she ready to hear his plan concerning the store and the rest of her pregnancy? He'd been waiting, not wanting to add any stress to the situation. "Listen, sweetheart." He fidgeted with the blankets. "The busyness of the store at Christmastime is enough to make anyone's blood pressure go up. It's only twelve more business days until Christmas. Maybe you should stay out of the store."

Her face clouded, and tears welled, but she nodded, confirming what he'd already suspected: yesterday's event had frightened her as much as it had him. "I don't know if it's necessary to be this careful, but I won't take any chances."

He kissed her forehead. "I love you."

She pursed her lips, wiping tears before she cleared her throat. "You'll need to hire some more workers."

"About a hundred to make up for you not being there." He winked. "Or a few well-trained ones who are familiar with how the store is run." He brushed a wisp of hair from her face. "I've been working on that. I left a message yesterday for Levi to see me today, and he came while you were sleeping. He's agreed to work as needed between now and when the baby is born." He lifted her hand to his lips and kissed it. "I've talked to Lizzy, and she'll work more and not leave town with Omar until after the baby is born. I think that'll get us through."

"I'd always heard it takes a village to raise a child, but I didn't know it took one to get a woman through a pregnancy."

From a love seat in Mammi Lee's sitting room, Sadie watched the snow fall outside the window. Night began to hinder her view as darkness crowded out the day. Her eyes burned from hours of crying, but she now had no more tears to shed.

At least she had all the funds for the mission trip. A trip that could not come soon enough.

Mammi's floor creaked as she entered the room. She had a cup in her hand and held it out to Sadie.

"Denki." Sadie took it, breathing in the aroma of hot apple cider.

"You've been in here for hours, child. Do you want to talk about it?"

Sadie wasn't sure, but she patted the cushion beside her.

Mammi sat beside her and took her hand. "What happened?"

Her throat constricted, and she took several sips of her drink. "I'm sorry, Mammi." She took a deep breath. "I've been lying to you and everyone. I guess I got what I deserved today. If I hadn't been willing to deceive everyone around me, Levi wouldn't be so quick to think me a liar."

"What have you lied about?"

Sadie explained about pretending to court Levi and how she'd fallen in love with him. "Last Sunday, on our way home from an evening with Beth and Jonah, Levi asked me to take this week to think about where I wanted our relationship to go. He said we should stop lying to ourselves, no more hiding from each other behind our walls of pretense." She took a sip of her cider before setting it on an end table. "We were supposed to talk about it last night. But after he didn't arrive when he should've, I went to the phone shanty and got the messages and learned he wasn't coming. That's why I went to see him this morning. For answers."

Mammi pursed her lips. "I told you not to go there this morning. A girl shouldn't be traipsing—"

Sadie jumped up, her hands balled into tight fists. "Why does it always have to be *me* who's wrong?"

Mammi stared at her, mouth slightly agape.

Sadie moved to the window. It'd stopped snowing, and a thin blanket of white covered the yard and fields. "I did everything you and Mamm and Daed and the church leaders asked of me, from the time I began courting Daniel to the day before we were to wed. You know that's true."

Mammi nodded. "I remember it as you've said."

"I put great effort into dotting every *i* and crossing every *t,* but when I saw him with Aquilla, it broke more than my faith in him and my heart. It shattered *me.*"

Now Levi had smashed her heart, and all she could do was long for the day she'd leave for Peru—but this time that thought caused an odd sensation inside her. She went to the end table and lifted her drink before sitting on the edge of the chair. The cider was now tepid, but she drank it, trying to examine her motives for taking—and enjoying—her mission trips.

What was it Levi said to her the day they began their pretend courtship? Oh, ya—*I'm beginning to doubt the purity of your motives about mission work. Maybe you just don't want to cope with your parents' expectations.*

Clearly she'd given him more cause to doubt her ability to be honest than she could admit to.

Was she going to Peru to minister to others or to hide from herself? She'd been a nineteen-year-old child when Daniel broke her heart. She'd believed his value as a person was far above hers. She'd thought that by marrying him she'd become more valuable. When he humiliated her, she'd found a way to hide.

Mission work was a worthy goal, and she had no right to use it to hide from disgrace. Truth was, she'd landed herself in an even more mortifying situation.

"There is no hiding, is there?" She asked herself the question, but then she looked to Mammi. "I mean, what are the chances that all these years later I'd have to face Daniel again?"

"Daniel's a part of your trouble with Levi?" Mammi went to the rocker and sat, staring at Sadie. "You've got to be mistaken, Sadie."

Her words were like a razor that opened an old wound. "Are you ever going to believe me about what I saw that day?"

"It was a confusing mess, and you were so young and impressionable." Mammi stared at the floor, her eyes filling with tears. "I believe you now."

Although her words had a little salve to them, Sadie had already weathered too much at the hands of Daniel's lies for Mammi's response to mean a lot.

"Daed never doubted me." For the first time in years, Sadie longed to talk to him, to soak in his wisdom, maybe even yield to it. "He was good to let me go when I needed to. It had to be hard to set me free as he did—a brokenhearted kid. I love him for it, but all we've done for years is battle each other."

"He's no more perfect in his ways than you or I. But this I do know: he tries so hard where you're concerned."

Sadie saw that now, and she knew what she had to do. She stood.

"I want to go home, Mammi. I need time to talk to Daed before I make any other decisions."

Twenty

For the second time in his life, Levi could not believe he'd treated Sadie so horribly. What kind of a man was he?

"Uncle Levi?"

Even if she were guilty of doing what Daniel had accused her of, she deserved so much more from Levi than he'd given. He should have offered her grace and compassion. He should have been her friend.

But, no, he'd judged her and let Daniel watch as she came undone. He didn't know why Daniel's being here ate at him so much. But it did.

If he went to Mammi Lee's, would she even speak to him?

Tobias slapped the kitchen table. "Uncle Levi!"

Levi glanced up. "What?"

"I've been talking, and you aren't listening." Tobias pointed at Levi's plate. "I thought me and Daed fixed 'em real good. You don't like scrambled eggs anymore?"

"Ya, I like them." He tousled Tobias's hair and forked some eggs. "Hmm, these are the best ever." Then he about choked trying to swallow them. The eggs were fine. They were exactly how he liked them. The same as how he liked life: easy and predictable. "I'm sorry. I'm just not hungry."

"Again?" Tobias scrunched his face and moved in close. "You sick?"

Levi looked to his brother. "Can you call off the dogs?"

"We don't have dogs, Uncle Levi. Only horses." Tobias sprinkled salt on Levi's eggs. "Just how sick are you feeling today?"

Andy removed the plate from in front of Levi. "Tobias, finish getting ready for school."

Tobias skipped out of the room and began singing about puppies.

"He's right about one thing." Andy swiped bits of egg off the table. "You gotta start eating."

It'd been three days since Levi had seen Sadie. Three days of not eating or sleeping. Three days without a minute of peace. He kept expecting his mind to stop going over things at some point and give him a break. But it hadn't happened yet.

Andy put the dishes in the sink. "You at the store today, your workshop, or training horses?"

Levi couldn't take it anymore. He had to talk about what ate at him before he lost his mind. "Why'd she leave?"

"Sadie?"

"Eva."

Andy scratched his head. "You know, seeing as it was me who lost a wife, you sure do carry a lot of scars."

"She was family. Like you and Tobias. But she just walked out. Who does that? And why?"

Andy poured coffee into a mug and sat across from Levi. "I know we should've talked about this a long time ago, but I couldn't." He swiped his hand across the table. "You and I are better suited for working and arguing, even for building a home worthy of raising Tobias. But we're not good at talking about the hard things."

"I can't deny that."

Andy rapped his fingers on the table. "But you needed me to talk, and I'm sorry I didn't. Eva was...a sinking ship. She didn't have the emotional strength to get through a day on her own. If you look back, you can see that. She stayed in bed most of the day, and when she got up, she needed help to do the simplest chores. Even at sixteen, I saw hints of that in her, but I didn't have to see it, because she told me about her struggles. She was completely overwhelmed by life, and despite knowing better, I chose to lie to myself, chose to believe that I had it in me to keep her afloat."

Levi remembered wondering why Eva had no zing to her, no desire to greet the day and enjoy it for what it was. He also struggled to understand why she'd make such a big deal out of the smallest things sometimes. But Levi had accepted Eva as she came. And now he couldn't accept any woman for who she was. He made himself sick.

Andy took a sip of his coffee. "I think Sadie is exactly who she told you she was from the start—no angel. But think about that night she helped you, and open your eyes—she's not Eva. She's strong and able to see a challenge through." He chuckled. "And she may always be in hot water with her Daed, but her joy for life is contagious."

Dozens of memories washed over Levi. "She's got this unreasonable fear of rodents, but that never stops her from doing what she sets out to do. It's one of my favorite things about her." Levi rubbed the back of his neck, grateful he no longer needed the neck brace. "None of what you've said helps me understand how Eva could've left Tobias."

Andy looked down the hall, checking for Tobias before he leaned in. "After he was born, she was more overwhelmed. Eva didn't believe she'd be a decent mother, and the idea of failing him—of having more babies—terrified her." Andy sighed. "Look, I know I sort of went crazy when she left, and I leaned on you too much. But this is a good life, and I have peace about the decisions I made that got me here. You've got to find some peace, Levi. You've got to learn to trust that if you ever have to face the unthinkable, God will be right there to give you strength. And so will I."

"Me too." Tobias walked into the room, smiling.

Levi glanced at Andy, and his eyes grew wide before he shrugged. Had Tobias heard much of what Andy had said or only the ending? But he knew by Andy's reaction that if Tobias had heard, he was okay with it.

"So who's taking me to school, because I don't want to walk. It's too cold out there!"

"I'll take you." Levi got up. "And then I'm going to apologize to Sadie. But that's all I can do."

Andy stared at him, looking as if he felt sorry for him. But Levi knew what he knew. Despite having strength and joy, she'd left Daniel the same as Eva had left Andy.

And he couldn't ignore that.

It didn't take long for Levi to hitch up the carriage and drop Tobias at school. Soon he stood on Mammi Lee's porch, as nervous as a mistreated horse. He lifted a hand and knocked on the door.

Someone moved the curtains back from the glass and peered out. A moment later Mammi Lee opened the door.

"Hi, Verna. I...need to speak to Sadie."

Mammi Lee stepped back from the door, and he came inside. "She's not here. Left a couple of days ago."

Levi knew it wasn't time for her to leave, not yet. Had she already gone ahead to be with some of her team? "But she's still in the States, right?"

She walked into the living room.

He followed her. "Do you know how I can reach her?"

Mammi pulled another towel from the pile. "Why do you want to talk to her?"

"I need to apologize. I...I wasn't much of a friend."

"So it's *friends* you want to be." She popped the towel in the air. "Is that the conclusion you came to during that week of thinking before you and she were supposed to talk—that you just want to be *friends*?"

"Mammi Lee...Verna, I—"

"That's a yes-or-no question, Levi."

He closed his eyes, seeing the only thing he'd seen for months: Sadie. "What do you want from me? You want the truth? I love her. How could any man get to know her like I have and not fall in love with her? But it's never going to work between us. We both knew that from the start. Still, I need to talk to her."

"Is that what you were going to tell her last Saturday night,—that it'd never work? Or did Daniel change your mind for you?" She set the folded towel on top of the others.

Her question didn't leave him anywhere to hide. And he finally saw. That's what he'd been doing, wasn't it? Hiding. Sadie had spent years pulling away from her family to hide—whether in Stone Creek or Peru. And he hid while living right here among his family and looking them in the eye every day.

Mammi Lee walked toward the door. "It's time you leave now."

"But—"

"You can rest your worry. Sadie will be fine. She'll grieve for a while, and then she'll be stronger and happier without you, just like she's been without Daniel. You're making the same mistake I did—you believe Daniel's lies. And just like me, you'll see the truth one day. And you'll be sorry for trusting the wrong person, but it won't matter to her by then."

Did he really believe Daniel, or did he simply *want* to believe him?

Verna opened the door. "We've been praying for her night and day for years, hoping she'd land right where she is."

There was only one place her family had been praying for her to be. "She's in Brim."

"I'll be sure she knows you came by, and I'll say that you'd like to remain friends and you're sorry, but I think it'd be best if you leave it at that. Please."

He stepped onto the porch, and she closed the door. Verna had freed him, had made it clear Sadie would be fine. Her reasoning deserved his respect. He should do as she asked and not try to reach Sadie.

So if he was free, why did he hurt worse now than before?

He drove his rig toward home. Dozens of emotions gnawed at him. It didn't matter what had taken place between Daniel and Sadie, did it? The problem was *him*.

His inability to let himself really care, to trust his heart to someone other than himself.

Still…

Levi's back teeth clenched. What *had* happened with Sadie and Daniel? He wanted to know the truth. He pulled his phone out of his pocket and called Daniel.

"Levi, where are you? I'm at your place, arguing with Andy about taking a horse. You know how he gets."

When Levi topped the hill near his home, he spotted the horse trailer. He hung up and drove onto his driveway.

Andy had Lightning, a white filly, by the harness, standing at the back of the open trailer. He and Daniel had talked about this. No horse would be sold until Levi said it was ready.

Levi got out of his rig and strode toward the trailer. Tip sat in the truck as usual.

Daniel spat a wad of gum onto the ground. "We've got a buyer willing to pay top price for this filly so she can be a Christmas present."

"She's not ready."

"Well, she may not be perfectly trained, but you've been working with her."

"She goes nowhere." Levi turned to Andy. "Take her back to the barn."

Andy patted Lightning and hurried the animal toward the barn.

"Why?" Daniel's voice echoed off the barn. "Buyers know the risks of owning an animal like this. Our goal has always been to make the horses reasonably obedient and move on to the next sale."

Levi could hardly absorb seeing Daniel in this light. He was wound tighter than Levi had ever seen him. Maybe it bothered him that Sadie had learned to care for someone else. But did his business partner realize he'd just lied? Their goal was never as Daniel just said. But everyone tends to get rather gray about things as time passes.

"Our agreement was never casual or careless when it came to selling horses. And I've made my sentiments about training them clear."

Daniel sighed. "Okay." He put up both hands. "I didn't come here for a fight. I assumed you'd be ready to let her go and make some good money. What about Amigo? Any chance he's ready? I'm sure you've done your magic by now. He's bound to be as rehabilitated as he'll ever get."

"None of the horses are ready. You took the last of the trained ones just four days ago."

"Well, sometimes you get a lot done in a few days. I bet you got one that'll work to fill this order."

That was nothing but flattery. Levi couldn't get to know any horse well within a few days, even if the horse already had some training. Levi needed repeat performances to ensure a behavior was ingrained.

"You're just a smooth talker, aren't you, Daniel?"

Daniel kicked at the gravel, moving his foot back and forth while clearing a spot. "This argument isn't about the filly or Amigo, is it? It's about Sadie, right? You came here ready to fight."

Daniel had some good points. Levi had climbed out of his rig thinking about Sadie and suspecting Daniel. But Daniel's earlier use of the word *rehabilitate* had caught Levi's attention. They didn't refer to horses in that manner unless something had happened to the animal that it needed to recover from—mistreatment, an accident, illness.

Levi's mind churned, burning through dozens of past conversations. Andy returned, and Levi looked to him. "Daniel just said something about Amigo needing to be rehabilitated. Do you recall anything about that in any discussion or seeing it in the paperwork when he unloaded Amigo here last spring?"

"No. I'd have remembered if it'd been said or listed anywhere."

Levi didn't doubt that Andy would've paid heed to it. His brother pored over the information that came in, often calling previous owners and taking careful notes on each horse. He shared that information with Levi at great length before Levi began working with them.

"Oh, come on!" Daniel's face turned red. "There is no way I'd do anything on purpose that would get you hurt. You've got to know that much. We're friends. Besides, what would be the point? I need you to be whole if I'm going to make the kind of money we do when working as a team."

"So you messed up and didn't provide that information to me. Is that what you're saying?"

"Ya, absolutely. It was a mistake. I don't know how I could forget that Amigo had been traumatized by some boys playing with firecrackers. He got tangled up in some wire fencing running away from them. You needed to know that. But I didn't recall it until after you were hurt. What good would it have done after you were injured to tell you I had messed up?"

Levi stared at him. He believed Daniel's account of overlooking crucial information where Amigo was concerned. But he was beginning to realize that this man was very good at covering up his mistakes.

In that moment Levi saw the truth. He didn't know why, but he could clearly see that Sadie had good cause to call off the wedding, just as she'd had good cause to go riding the night she'd found Levi in that field: God had directed her steps.

That revelation, however, brought him no relief or peace. Daniel had lied to him—more than once. And Levi had swallowed it. And Sadie had been hurt.

Levi had given up his chance with her because he'd believed a lie, not just the one Daniel told, but the one he'd told himself: that he had insight into how much of a gamble it was to get involved with a woman. But that wasn't insight. That was fear, and he'd chosen to believe it because he'd thought it would keep him safe and far away from a deceitful heart. And yet here he stood.

Daniel shoved his hands into his coat pockets, his shoulders stooped. "I'm sorry, Levi. You've got to believe me. It was a stupid mistake not to tell you about Amigo. Please give me a chance to make it up to you."

"I believe you. It's not like you to do something deceitful on purpose, any more than it was when you cheated on Sadie. Right?"

"Sadie?" Daniel rolled his eyes. "Is every conversation from here on going to circle back to her?"

"I'm in love with her. Can you understand that?"

"Far more than you'll ever give me credit for." Daniel sighed. "Okay."

Daniel's last word seemed to lodge in his throat, and an unfamiliar expression eased across his face. Was he going to be honest?

"I'm not like you, Levi. Never was. I've spent most of my life being so restless I can't stand myself. I've given into temptation more times than

I'm willing to admit. But when I got to know Sadie, I knew she was my best chance of finding peace and happiness. I'd hoped to be a good husband. But her cousin was *so* beautiful. And we were both smitten. I wanted to resist. I just…couldn't."

"You've lied about what happened since the day she caught you. When I told you I loved her, you lied to me. That's very deliberate."

"I had to lie. If the church leaders had known what happened, I would've been shunned. My family would've…"

"What, seen you for who you are?"

"I was so angry that she wouldn't give me another chance. But I never meant for any of this to happen. I'll make it up to you…and Sadie."

"No. We're done." He gestured toward the truck. "Just go."

"But we make great money with our horse-trading. We need to work through this. I told you the truth. That's gotta count for something."

Levi stepped forward, his hands balling into fists. "You and I are done. I'm not doing any more business with you, and if you think that's unfair,"—he met Daniel's stunned gaze—"feel free to take it up with God. He knows *exactly* how to handle someone who isn't just."

Twenty-One

*A*n icy wind rattled the windows and howled as Sadie set the dinner table. Each move she made inside her childhood homestead was as familiar as a Pennsylvania winter and yet as foreign as if she'd never lived here. A fire crackled in the hearth.

She'd come home. She'd yielded to her Daed's authority, and he'd embraced her with tears flowing. He didn't want her to leave the country again, and she'd called the head of the mission team and told him she wouldn't be going. The mission director understood that these things happen, and they had a young man who wanted to go. He could take her place, but he lacked the necessary funds. She became his sponsor and sent all her money to the board. It hadn't been easy, but she'd done as she thought God wanted—and she had peace.

Still, her heart ached, and she missed things about Levi she hadn't been consciously aware of, like the steady calmness of his movements as he worked with a piece of wood or his quiet tone when they talked. He had a zeal for life, and even his cynicism drew her in, as he never used it meanly. How many times had she startled awake because she saw him in her dreams, saw his smile from across the room when they went to singings, felt his sorrow, heard him calling to her?

Tomorrow was Christmas Eve, and she kept telling herself that the ache would pass after the holidays.

If only she could believe that.

The back door opened, and a rush of cold air came in with her father. "Sadie?"

"I'm right here."

He glanced at the kitchen table. "Yes, you are." He pulled off his coat. "I just got off the phone with Mammi Lee. I think we should talk."

Emotions flooded through her, and tears pricked her eyes. "Is it about Levi?"

"It is." He went to his chair beside the fireplace. Sadie went to the ladder back that faced the hearth. Her mother sat in the love seat across from her husband. Daed smiled, but his eyes looked sad. "It's not the first time since you arrived home last week that I've spoken with her. We thought it best not to be hasty. Levi came to her place more than a week ago, looking for you, and Mammi Lee asked him not to contact you."

Sadie waited, hardly able to keep her poise.

"A few days after Levi's visit, his brother came to see her. He didn't want to interfere, but he wanted her to know something that'd happened—in case she wanted to share it with you."

"Daed!" Sadie reached over and swatted his knee. "You're dragging this out too long. Tell me."

"It didn't take your Levi very long to come to his senses. He broke off all ties with Daniel."

Her heart jolted, and she wasn't sure how to feel about that piece of news. Did it mean Levi finally saw Daniel's true character and would no longer associate with him, or was it something more? Did he care for her so much that he had to do something drastic to heal some of the rift between them? "Why?"

"Well, I have it on good authority that he's a fine man who's reluctantly fallen in love with my daughter."

Her heart soared. Was it possible? She prayed it was.

The flames in the fireplace swooshed as a log shifted. And a memory caught her. Years ago she had sat in this same spot, broken beyond words and staring at a cold hearth.

A smile rose from within, and she looked at her mother. "Can we spend Christmas in Apple Ridge?"

Daed rocked back in his chair. "I see no reason why not, as long as we can find a driver on such short notice."

Mamm stood. "I've spent many a year doing favors for Englisch friends—baby-sitting, catering meals, and such. I know people who'll want to help. Maybe one of them will be able to do so, even on Christmas Eve."

⌘

Energy surged through Beth's body as she basted a ham. With so much time lately to devote to everyday chores—washing clothes and hanging them out, sewing new outfits for herself and Jonah and the baby, quilting, baking, making Christmas cards—she'd thought she had liveliness to spare. Today a stronger wave of desire to cook and clean and organize flooded her.

Of course, her good-natured husband remained by her side, making sure she didn't overdo anything. Jonah mashed the sweet potatoes, shoving the utensil into the pot of orange pulp again and again. "This seems like a lot of food for two people."

"Look at the upside. We won't need to cook for days."

"I sort of thought the idea of a quiet celebration was for you to stay off your feet."

"And I will. As soon as we celebrate today with a feast."

Suddenly a wave of Braxton Hicks hit her as she pushed the rack into the oven. Her lower back stung, and her thighs ached as the contraction grew stronger.

"Well, whatever we do, it'll be easier and safer than going out in this weather tonight. I certainly don't want you doing all it'd take to have that monstrous crowd known as your family coming here for their festivities." Jonah knocked the potato masher against the rim of the pan. "Smooth enough?"

Beth evened her breathing, surprised by the force of the contraction. "Ya...it looks good to me."

But rather than fading like usual, the contraction grew stronger. She clutched the counter, waiting for it to subside. The midwife had said she'd already dilated to a three but that women often stayed that way until their due date. Right now, Beth didn't know what to think.

"Sweetheart?" Jonah moved to her side.

"If that was a Braxton Hicks, it carried some real force."

"When was the last one?"

"Ten minutes ago. Until an hour ago I hadn't had any in days." Beth fumbled with her apron, trying to reach inside the hidden pocket. It was time to use the cell phone her midwife gave her. "I think I'll give Mandy a call to see what she thinks."

She planned to sound calm, but the idea of going into labor four weeks early made her feel sick, and she prayed for God's protection over her child.

<hr />

Snow fell harder and harder as Levi ushered the last employees out the door at Hertzlers'. It was time they all went home. There was no sense in letting snow accumulate and risk someone's having a difficult time getting home on Christmas Eve. He could handle the rest of today by himself, even if customers might have to wait until he could get to them.

Mattie was still here, however. She had customers picking up Christmas cakes, and Levi couldn't run the register, fetch layaways, and run the counter for Mattie Cakes.

The next few hours at the store weren't too busy, and as the snow deepened, people stopped coming in.

He stepped onto the porch and watched the white flakes silently fall from the black sky. The air smelled of Christmas, and everyone he'd come into contact with lately seemed to be in a festive mood, especially Tobias. But it didn't feel like a joyous holiday to Levi. What was Sadie doing today? Did she miss him? Would she miss him when she was in Peru?

As hard as he'd tried, he couldn't stop thinking about her. But he'd finally accepted the truth: it was his lot from now on to miss her. He went back into the store.

With the store empty, he went to the Mattie Cakes nook to see what was happening in her little area of the store. Mattie sat at a small table, talking to her husband.

Levi smiled. "Hey, Gideon. I didn't see you come in."

Gideon stood and said, "Merry Christmas, Levi."

"Denki. Same to you."

Gideon took a seat. "We're waiting on one more customer to pick up a cake, and then I'm taking Mattie home, where she can open the birthday presents her family has been dropping off throughout the day."

"Oh, that's right. I forgot. Happy birthday, Mattie."

"Denki, Levi."

"Gideon, take her and get out. When that customer shows up, I'll be here."

Gideon leaned in and kissed his wife. "What do you say, Mattie Lane? May I take you home?"

"Absolutely. We've got some singing to do along the way."

Gideon laughed. "We married folks can't go to any more Christmas singings. We need to have a private session, and it just happens to be the perfect weather for a sleigh ride."

Mattie grinned. "We're borrowing Beth and Jonah's sleigh?"

Gideon helped her get on her coat. "I worked it out with him before coming in today. Beth and Jonah send their birthday and Christmas wishes too."

Mattie kissed his cheek. "This sleigh ride isn't all you have planned, is it?"

"I'm not telling—not yet." Gideon winked at Levi.

Mattie put on her black winter bonnet. "The cake should've been picked up an hour ago. If June Smith doesn't arrive in another hour, she isn't coming."

"Okay."

Mattie waved at him as she left. "Merry Christmas, Levi."

"Merry Christmas." He closed the door behind them. The ticking of the clocks that lined the walls echoed through the quiet store.

He grabbed a push broom and began going down the aisles. He straightened shelves and returned items from the register area to their spot. No one else came in, and he finally put the Closed sign in the window.

"Welcome to your future, Levi," he mumbled. He'd wanted to live out his days as a bachelor, and he'd managed to give himself exactly that. *What a great gift idea. You should be proud.*

Before Sadie, he hadn't felt lonely, let alone miserable. What had she done to him—stretched his tiny heart until it could hold the vastness of his love for her? Now he had a huge heart and nothing to fill it.

He went through the store turning off the gas lamps. Since he'd ridden here bareback, he'd take the cake the customer never picked up to Beth and Jonah, wish them a Merry Christmas, and head home.

He emptied the register and took the cash to the safe in Beth's office. The bells on the door rang, and he went in that direction. It had to be Jonah.

Standing just inside the doorway, he saw the shadowy figure of an Amish woman in a winter coat and hat.

"You're just in time, Mrs. Smith. The cake is right over here."

She turned.

"Sadie!" His heart beat faster, and he nearly ran to her.

She shivered all over, and he grabbed a quilt from the display rack and wrapped it around her. He rubbed her arms through the layers of thickness, trying to warm her.

"What are you doing here?"

She shook. "I've been in Apple Ridge for hours, even spent some time with Andy and Tobias, waiting for you to get home. Then it struck me to come here so we could talk privately. Andy wasn't a fan of the idea, but I wouldn't listen to him." She drew a shaky breath. "Horses and buggies are better at getting around in the snow than cars and trucks, right?"

"Ya. I've used a horse and carriage to pull more than one four-wheeler out of a ditch."

She rubbed her gloved hands together. "Then why'd I have such a hard time getting here?"

"The roads must be bad, and you shouldn't have been on them."

"Like I shouldn't have been out riding the night I found you on the ground?"

"This is different, Sadie." He tugged at the fingertips of her gloves until he slid the half-frozen knit things right off. "You were in no danger that night." He sandwiched her cold hands between his, warming them.

"Actually." She shivered. "As things turned out, that's arguable."

"I suppose it is." If he could undo any of his rash behavior, he would. He kissed her hands before covering them again with his own. Would she think that too forward? Was she here to let him know they could remain friends like they'd agreed to be when they began their pretend courtship? He didn't want to do any more damage to their relationship—it was Christmas Eve, and she was here. That was far more than he'd dared to hope for. Still, he couldn't throttle his foolish heart.

He led her to Mattie Cakes and held a chair for her.

Although he didn't want to leave her side, he went to put a kettle of water on the stove and struck a match to light the burner. He could fix either tea or hot chocolate faster than he could fix a pot of coffee, and she needed something hot as soon as he could get it ready. "Tea?" He held up a box of peppermint tea bags. "Or hot chocolate?"

"Hot chocolate, please." She folded her hands on the table.

As he opened a pouch of powdery chocolate mix and dumped it into a mug, she said, "Levi, I think I know what happened the Saturday night we were supposed to talk. I'd like to know if it's accurate."

A shudder ran through him. *Please, God.* "Okay."

"The feelings you have for me are like a skittish and unfamiliar horse. Daniel was like the booming fireworks. And 'the horse' threw you. You landed hard and were too addled to think clearly."

He liked her analogy. It was very Sadie-like—honest but kind. He poured hot water into the mug and stirred. "I'm sorry." He set the mug in front of her and took a seat.

She wrapped her hands around it. "So Mammi Lee said." She took a sip. "The thing is, we have unfinished business. And while we're here where we can talk openly and freely, I want to know what you had planned to say that Saturday night before Daniel showed up."

He went to the display case and took out the cake the customer hadn't picked up. He removed it from its box and set it on the table between them. "It'll take a while to explain it all."

She peered at the many colors of the frosting. "It's beautiful."

He passed her a fork, kept one for himself, and sat down. "Mattie's cakes taste even better than they look. Dive in."

They ate several bites and shared the cup of cocoa.

Sadie peeled out of the blanket and her coat. "I about froze to death to get here to talk to you. You can't keep stalling."

He forked a bite of cake. "Try me."

She raised an eyebrow. "You want to eat the cake or wear it?"

He chuckled. "Okay. What I wanted to say was—"

Bells jangled. "Levi?"

At Jonah's yell, Levi stood. "Over here."

Jonah motioned for him as he made his way to the office. "We need to reach the midwife. We've called her twice, and each time she gave us some instructions. Now it seems her phone's not working." Jonah picked up the phone, punched several numbers, and waited. "Same as what's happening with the cell she gave Beth. We can't get through. It goes straight to voice mail, but it won't let me leave a message."

Sadie came up behind Levi. "Is she in labor?"

"The midwife didn't think so, but Beth's water broke ten minutes ago. I can't take her out in this weather. An ambulance can't get through, either—at least, not until morning. The baby will be premature, not by a lot, but we have to get Mandy here. She's been delivering babies for forever. She'll know what to do with a preemie."

"Where does she live?"

"Barton's Ridge."

Levi let out a whistle. "Even if you reach her, chances are she can't get here on her own."

Jonah pressed his fingers into his forehead and closed his eyes. "I know nothing about these things. Lizzy would at least know something about delivering a baby, and I've tried to reach her, but she and Omar are at his children's place for the evening. Obviously no one can hear the phone ringing in the shanty."

Sadie moved closer to the desk. "I'm not your best bet, but I have helped with several births. One was premature, and I watched a midwife tend to her."

"That helps, Sadie. Thanks. If you two will stay with Beth, I'll go on horseback."

Levi stepped forward. "I'll go. Beth needs you."

Jonah studied him. "It's bad out there. And Barton's Ridge is dangerous any time of year."

"I'll get through."

Twenty-Two

*S*adie paced the floors, stopping every few minutes to look out the window in the dark of night. No sign of anyone. It'd been hours, and they'd heard nothing. At least a dozen times she'd checked the cell phone the midwife gave Beth, but was it even getting a signal? She and Jonah were taking turns sitting with Beth.

Jonah came to the doorway, looking as if he were the one in pain. One look told him all he needed to know. No one had arrived. He left the bedroom door ajar. "She's dozing."

Sadie poured him a cup of coffee. "She'll be fine, and so will the little one."

Jonah nodded before taking a sip, but he didn't look convinced. "I haven't told you that it's nice to see you back in Apple Ridge. Will you be staying long?"

"I hope so."

"Has anyone told you the story of Beth and me?"

"No."

They heard Beth moan long and loud. Coffee spilled from Jonah's cup as he set it down. They both hurried to the bedroom.

Beth clutched each side of the pillow behind her head and panted. When the contraction eased, Jonah held her hand. "Sadie doesn't know our story."

Beth smiled. "I'd like to hear it too."

"One hot summer day I was minding my own business. I was in Pete's Antiques in Ohio, and this beautiful young woman about ran over me in her all-business-all-the-time way." Jonah told of the many months of letter writing and getting to know each other and the inevitable discovery of secrets that threatened to end their friendship. He stopped talking each time Beth had a contraction.

"Then, on a Christmas Eve night much like this one, Beth tried to get from Pennsylvania to Ohio to let me know she loved me and would marry me."

"Really?" Sadie sat on the edge of her chair. "That's what I'm doing here...sort of. Only I'm not sure how Levi feels."

Beth and Jonah gave each other a look. Beth smiled. "Be bold, Sadie." She groaned the words before she gasped and gripped Jonah's hands as another contraction took command of her body.

An odd rumbling sound vibrated the room. Jonah glanced at Sadie, and she left the bedroom to hurry down the hallway and onto the front porch. Lights shone in her eyes from an odd-looking vehicle coming straight toward her. A minute later the vehicle turned, and she saw a huge green tractor with an enclosed cab. An Amish woman with a medical bag climbed down. "Has she delivered?"

"Not yet." Sadie peered into the cab, desperate to see Levi. But all she saw was an Englisch man.

"Help him get the incubator and the car battery into the house."

"Where's Levi?"

She paused. "I don't know. On his way to find me, he saw a couple stranded in a ditch. He went back to help them while I finished delivering another baby. It was a long labor, but Levi never showed."

She placed her hand on Sadie's shoulder. "I'm sure he's fine."

But Sadie had heard Jonah's description. She imagined sheer drop-offs that couldn't be easily spotted on a clear day, let alone at night. In weather like this, a treacherous ridge could swallow lives whole.

Mandy grasped her arm. "Go on. Help Parker. He'll be wantin' to get back home as soon as he can."

Sadie stayed busy doing everything Mandy asked, but she'd never prayed so fervently in her life—for safety for Beth, her baby, and Levi. When Mandy no longer needed her for a bit, she hurried across the parking lot to the store and used the office phone to call Levi's cell. It went to voice mail. His phone apparently wasn't charged—again. She battled thoughts of his lying somewhere in the freezing snow. The moment she stepped back into Beth and Jonah's home, she heard Mandy.

"Kumm, Beth, push," Mandy coaxed. "It won't be much longer. Push."

Beth moaned, long and hard, and then—

A baby wailed.

Joy rose within Sadie.

Then silence.

Sadie waited, her heart pounding. She moved down the hallway and listened outside the closed door. She heard soft voices talking and Beth crying.

Sadie's eyes filled with tears. *Dear God, please.*

Should she go in?

She leaned her head against the doorframe and prayed. The door creaked open, and Jonah stood there, his eyes filled with tears. He smiled. "I have a healthy son and a strong, beautiful wife." He laughed and wiped his cheeks. "Kumm."

She stepped into the room.

Mandy was grinning. "That little one weighs a good six and a half pounds. He's technically a preemie, so keep a watch on his breathing, but he's a healthy boy if I've ever seen one. Pink as anything."

Beth continued to cry. "Look." She shifted the bundle in her arms up just a bit for Sadie to see him better.

Sadie edged in closer. "Merry Christmas."

Another round of sobs broke from Beth, and she looked to Jonah. "Merry Christmas, sweetheart."

Jonah moved to her side and brushed some damp hair from Beth's face. "Merry Christmas, indeed."

Sadie and Mandy slipped out of the room.

It wasn't long before everyone except Sadie was dozing. She pulled an armchair in front of the window. The snow clouds were gone, and the stars shone bright, but she saw no evidence of a moon. *Dear God, please help Levi get home safely.*

She studied the dark, white landscape until the sky wasn't quite as dark as before. In the distance she saw something moving, maybe a deer. She studied it for a moment, then rose to her feet to get a closer look.

Levi?

She slid into her shoes and grabbed her coat. She hurried through the house on her tiptoes. Once on the porch, she saw a man in snowshoes taking one slow step at a time.

"Levi!"

She ran as fast as she could through the white blanket. He spotted her and removed his snowshoes. As soon as he stood, she careened into his arms, knocking him over. They both tumbled into the snow, but she didn't care.

"Are you okay?"

"Before or after this encounter?"

She laughed, caressing his face. "I was so worried."

"I know." He gazed into her eyes. "I've been doing everything I could to get here. I didn't want you to worry. How's Beth?"

"The midwife got here, and Beth and Jonah have a healthy baby boy."

"Gut. Now I've got something I want to say." He pulled a glove off and ran the backs of his fingers against her cheek. "I love you, Sadie. And I want to marry you if you'll have me. If you need to serve a year or two of missions first, I'll wait. But I don't want to live a lifetime without you."

His words burrowed deep into her soul. He loved her! Not only did he want to marry her. He trusted her enough to fearlessly do so. Her heart jumped and skipped, but she couldn't find her voice.

Thank You, God, for bringing Levi and me together, for being greater than all the trials that have damaged and molded us.

Her soul overflowed, but she was unable to respond. She stood, and then helped him up. She picked up the snowshoes and held them up to him, silently asking questions.

He shook his head. "I've had a night like I can't believe. The kind only God could get me through." He put his arm around her shoulders, and they began walking toward the house. "I'd say someone's been praying."

She looked up at him. "Lots of someones—including me. One of my prayers went like this: 'Dear God, please help Levi get home so I can tell him that I'm not leaving Apple Ridge and that I'll make an excellent wife—not perfect, mind you, but excellent.'"

Levi halted and studied her. "Well, I survived last night, and I'm right here with you. I mean...I'm not dreaming."

She smiled. "I could slap you to prove it."

He barked out a laugh. "The first memory I have of you is being slapped, and then you threatened to do it again if I didn't stay awake."

"And look at us now. If something proves successful, it bears repeating. But we've grown a bit since then. Maybe I should kick you instead."

He laughed and pulled her into his arms. Despite his exhaustion, she felt the magnitude of strength within him. As cold as the air around them was, all she could feel was the warmth of his love.

He held her close. "I look forward to a lifetime of being with you. How about a kiss instead?"

"Well...since it is Christmas."

His warm lips met hers and lingered. "Merry Christmas, Sadie."

"The first of many, Levi." And she looked forward to every day with him between each Christmas, to honor and cherish him and their marriage, to assure him there was nowhere she'd rather be than by his side.

She lowered her head to his chest as the beauty of dawn began to sparkle against the snow. The sky held clouds of lavender and pink and orange.

It was a dawn to remember—the first one they'd share—the dawn of their first Christmas.

Oatmeal and Honey Soap

9 ounces olive oil

4 ounces coconut oil

3 ounces palm oil

1 ounce castor oil

$\frac{1}{4}$ cup colloidal oatmeal

1 ounce honey

2.52 ounces lye

8 fluid ounces water

*optional: extra whole oats and honey

Directions:

1. Prepare the lye water. Set it aside to cool.
2. Melt the solid oils together. Set them aside to cool.
3. Mix the olive oil, castor oil, and oatmeal.
4. When the solid oils are approximately 120° Fahrenheit and the lye water has cooled to approximately 100° Fahrenheit, gently pour the lye water into the oils. (Never pour oils into lye.)
5. Stir until trace.*

---

*   Trace is the stage of soap making when the ingredients are fully mixed and ready for additives and pouring into molds. In the mixing process when the ingredients resemble vanilla pudding, when the mixture is thick enough that dripping some of it across the top of the mixture leaves a trail of drips that don't immediately sink back into the liquid, you have reached trace.

6. Add the oatmeal mixture and then the honey until well mixed.
7. Pour into prepared molds and cover with plastic wrap. (Optional: sprinkle whole oats and drizzle honey lightly over the top of the curing soap.)
8. Allow to stand covered for 48 hours.
9. Remove from molds and cut as desired.
10. Allow to age in open air for 2 to 3 weeks before using.

I'd like to thank a reader friend for sharing her soap recipe with us. Thank you, Kristin Lail! I connected with Kristin through Facebook and later discovered she's an avid reader and book reviewer who loves to make soaps. She's a wife and mom to five daughters. If you'd like to read Kristin's reviews or purchase some of her soaps, you'll find her website at www.ASimplyEnchantedLife.com. Or you can find her on Facebook at https://www.facebook.com/Senchanted.

About the Author

CINDY WOODSMALL is a *New York Times* best-selling author with ten works of fiction and one of nonfiction. Her connection with the Amish community has been featured widely in national media, including *ABC Nightline*, the front page of the *Wall Street Journal*, and *National Geographic*. She has three sons, two daughters-in-law, and one granddaughter and lives outside Atlanta with her husband of thirty-five years.